Irish author **Abby Green** en... career in film and TV—whi... a lot of standing in the rain o... ... trailers—to pursue her love of romance. After she'd bombarded Mills & Boon with manuscripts they kindly accepted one, and an author was born. She lives in Dublin, Ireland, and loves any excuse for distraction. Visit abby-green.com or email abbygreenauthor@gmail.com.

Canadian **Dani Collins** knew in high school that she wanted to write romance for a living. Twenty-five years later, after marrying her high school sweetheart, having two kids with him, working at several generic office jobs and submitting countless manuscripts, she got The Call. Her first Mills & Boon novel won the Reviewers' Choice Award for Best First in Series from *RT Book Reviews*. She now works in her own office, writing romance.

HIS HOUSEKEEPER'S TWIN BABY CONFESSION

ABBY GREEN

AWAKENED ON HER ROYAL WEDDING NIGHT

DANI COLLINS

MILLS & BOON

First published in Great Britain 2023
by Mills & Boon, an imprint of HarperCollins*Publishers* Ltd,
1 London Bridge Street, London, SE1 9GF

www.harpercollins.co.uk

HarperCollins*Publishers*, Macken House, 39/40 Mayor Street Upper, Dublin 1, D01 C9W8, Ireland

His Housekeeper's Twin Baby Confession © 2023 Abby Green

Awakened on Her Royal Wedding Night © 2023 Dani Collins

ISBN: 978-0-263-30686-6

07/23

This book is produced from independently certified FSC™ paper to ensure responsible forest management.
For more information visit: www.harpercollins.co.uk/green.

Printed and Bound in the UK using 100% Renewable Electricity at CPI Group (UK) Ltd, Croydon, CR0 4YY

HIS HOUSEKEEPER'S TWIN BABY CONFESSION

ABBY GREEN

MILLS & BOON

PROLOGUE

CARRIE TAYLOR WAS too numb to be nervous about her job interview for a very prestigious job as a live-in housekeeper in London. She wasn't even sure how she'd been deemed a suitable candidate, considering her hospitality experience didn't stretch beyond working in three-star hotels in Manchester.

Clearly, going by the fact that she was in a detached Georgian mansion in one of London's most exclusive neighbourhoods, this was very much on another level. But her desire to move to London and the fact that she could start straight away because she had no ties might have had something to do with it.

No ties.

Emotion threatened to break through the numb barrier she'd pulled around herself in the last six months. She forced it down again. Not here…not now.

She would have time to lick her wounds and heal if she could just settle somewhere far away from where she'd been. At least physically, if not emotionally.

She diverted her mind from her recent traumatic past and tried to focus again on the interview. There was no way she was going to get the job. And that assertion was somehow a little liberating. A stream of considerably more glamorous and undoubtedly more experienced women had gone in before her. And one man in a three-piece suit.

They weren't wearing cheap high street clothes. Carrie

plucked at her shirt, trying to straighten it. Her jacket and skirt didn't even match, but they were the same colour so that would have to do. There was a hole in her nylons, but she was hoping it wasn't visible. She'd lost almost a stone in weight in the last six months, and she really should have bought a new outfit, but she'd literally had no time to waste before coming to this interview.

The recruiter had said, 'I won't lie, it's a long shot, but nothing ventured nothing gained, eh?' And then he'd asked curiously, 'Are you sure you've never heard of Massimo Black, Lord Linden? He's the Earl of Linden.'

Carrie had shook her head, already mentally adding up how much the train ticket to London would cost. 'No, should I have?'

The recruiter had just said, 'No reason in particular, I guess…' But he'd looked at her as if she had two heads.

Carrie wondered about that now. The man was undoubtedly wealthy. And an earl, *and* a lord. Maybe he was in politics? She couldn't take her phone out here and look him up. She cursed herself for not doing it on the train when she'd had a chance. Wasn't that what people did ahead of big fancy job interviews? They swotted up on the employer?

She imagined him to be elderly and very posh. White hair? Booming voice? The other people up for the job had certainly walked out of his office looking a little shell-shocked. Maybe he was very formidable.

'Miss Taylor?'

Carrie stood up so fast her bag fell to the floor. Flustered, she answered, 'That's me,' as she bent down to pick it up.

The stern-looking assistant swept her up and down with an icy gaze and Carrie fought not to let it affect her.

'Lord Linden will see you now. This way, please.'

She followed the young man back through the jaw-dropping reception hall, with its classic black and white tiles and a marbled staircase leading up to the first floor. There was a huge round table, polished to a high gleam. In the middle was the biggest vase she'd ever seen, with a stunning display of exotic blooms.

She was so distracted by the grandeur that she nearly ran into the man's back when he stopped abruptly outside a door. She stepped backwards. She wanted to check her hair to make sure it was still pulled neatly into its bun, but she didn't dare under his exacting gaze.

The assistant knocked and a deep voice answered, 'Come in.'

For some reason a little tingle went down Carrie's spine. The door opened and the man stood back to let her by. Carrie walked in, and for a second the sun was in her eyes, so all she could make out was a very tall, broad shape by the window.

Then she took another step and she could see. She heard herself suck in a breath. The first thing that came into her head was: *Young, not old.* And the second thing was that she'd never seen anyone more beautiful in her life. He was like a Greek statue brought to life.

Thick dark blond hair, swept back from his face. Strong jaw. Firm mouth. Powerful physique. Every line of his face and body screamed power and privilege and something far more disturbing. An earthy sensuality—an innate sexiness that she'd never experienced before.

He was saying something, but Carrie couldn't actually hear it for a moment. She tried to pull herself together. But she was shaken. This was the first time anyone or anything had pierced through the numbness in her body. And heart.

'I'm sorry, what did you say?'

Massimo Black, Lord Linden, curbed his irritation. 'I said, please take a seat.'

The woman who had just entered was looking at him as if she'd never seen a man before. He was used to slightly less obvious reactions. Maybe his assistant had been wrong when he'd said, before he went to summon her, 'This is the last one, boss, and apparently she's never heard of you.'

That had made Massimo sit up. It was rare for him to meet anyone who didn't know him and his lurid life story: inheriting the vast Linden wealth and his father's title of Earl of Linden at only eighteen, after the premature scandalous deaths of his parents—his mother of a drugs overdose at their family country pile after a debauched party and his father only a few weeks later, while piloting a helicopter with his latest lover. And then the tragic death of his beloved younger brother, who had inherited the destructive gene from his parents, in spite of Massimo's best efforts to keep him on a straight path.

Massimo pushed all that aside.

So far none of the candidates for housekeeper had impressed him, in spite of their more than adequate CVs and references. So he didn't hold out much hope for this one, who came with none of that.

The woman—he checked her name… *Carrie Taylor*—sat down gingerly on the edge of a chair. Massimo wondered why she was sitting like that, and looked down and saw she was tugging at her skirt, as if to pull it over her knee. He saw a flash of pale skin. A hole in her tights.

Massimo felt something stir in his blood. *Awareness.* He immediately scoffed at himself. For this scrap of a thing? Because she *was* a scrap. Her clothes hung off her, and she looked as if she needed to be sent to the sun for a few months, to put some colour in her cheeks.

Her blonde hair was pulled back in a bun, but tendrils were trying to escape. Her face at first glance was plain enough, but as Massimo took a seat opposite her and watched her looking around the room he could see fine bone structure, a straight nose, and a surprisingly lush mouth. Her eyes were huge, and very green. *Unusual.*

She looked at him then, and Massimo had to use all of his control to stop himself reacting.

He looked down at her file. 'It says here that you're widowed?' He looked back up just in time to see her flinch slightly.

'Yes.'

His conscience pricked. He knew what it was to lose someone you loved. The pain of his brother's death nearly ten years ago was still vivid.

'I'm sorry. It was recent?'

She avoided his eye. 'Six months ago.'

'It also says here that you're available to start right away and are available to live in?'

'Yes.'

Massimo felt curious now, about this woman who had travelled all the way from Manchester to apply for a job that she really had very little hope of getting.

He asked, 'What makes you think you'd be qualified to take on a job as housekeeper of this house?'

He saw her draw in a breath and her breasts rose under her shirt, fuller than he would have expected. He diverted his gaze up, once again incensed to be caught like this.

Affected like this.

She looked at him now, her gaze direct. Her voice was soft but clear, with a surprising hint of steel. 'I know I don't have any fancy university qualifications, but I've been working since I was sixteen.'

'Is that when you left school?'

She lifted her chin. 'Yes.'

Massimo couldn't help but admire her defiance.

She said, 'I started working in a local hotel, making beds and cleaning bathrooms, and I made it all the way up to become manager by the age of twenty. I hired staff, managed them, and was responsible for ensuring the smooth running of …everything really.'

Massimo put down her file and sat back. He found that he could well believe it. The unmistakable pride in her voice impressed him. She didn't have an academic qualification to her name, but she had more experience in her little finger than any of the other candidates he'd just met. Who had all been as dull and boring as he might have expected.

He said, 'So my question now is, why leave all that to come and manage one house in London?'

She avoided his eye again. A shadow passed over her face. 'Because I have no ties and I would like a change. I want to gain experience in the private sector.'

Massimo had a sense that there was more to it than that, but he resisted pushing. Then he made a split-second decision—very unlike him.

He said, 'You're hired. One month's trial. My outgoing housekeeper will be on hand for a week, to show you the ropes and get you acquainted with how we run things here. How long do you need to pack up and move down?'

She looked at him, her eyes wide, dazed.

'You mean it?'

He nodded. He was fascinated by the colour coming into her cheeks. Pink. His blood grew warm. He doused it with ice. This woman would be his housekeeper. Out of bounds. If she accepted the job, from this moment on he would not allow her to affect him again.

'Um… I just need a day or two… I could be back here after the weekend?'

Massimo stood up and held out his hand. 'Perfect, my assistant will give you any help you need with packing and moving.'

* * *

Carrie couldn't quite believe what had just happened. She stood up and her legs felt shaky. She put out her hand to Lord Linden and he took it, engulfing her in heat. His touch was like an electric shock, zapping through her body and blood.

She told herself it was the shock of the job offer. And because he was so charismatic and impressive. *And young.* She'd have to be made of stone not to be affected by a man like this.

She pulled her hand back and somehow managed to get out, 'Thank you for giving me this opportunity. I'll make sure you don't regret it.'

A wave of relief went through her to think that she could move away from all the grim reminders of her life up to now. She could make a new start. In a new place. Heal herself. And maybe some day move on with her life again.

Lord Linden's gaze was hard to look away from. It was very dark. Hard to read.

Good, she told herself. She did not want to be reading this man's emotions. He was her boss, and there was too much at stake to be allowing him to affect her in any way. Emotionally or physically.

'Thank you,' she said again, and vowed to make sure that he would have no reason to regret giving her this chance.

CHAPTER ONE

Four years later

MASSIMO FELT SLIGHTLY GUILTY—but only slightly. He'd just walked out of an interview with a leading financial newspaper. The car phone rang. He looked at the display and scowled. It was one of his assistants, no doubt wondering what was going on.

He ignored it and hit the accelerator to move around some traffic, the powerful throttle of the engine doing little to lighten his mood. For that he'd need the open road and no limits on speed.

He smiled grimly. Maybe his destructive family gene was finally kicking in? The one that had taken the life of his baby brother. He'd died on a race track, chasing an impossible speed.

The journalist had irritated him from the off, asking him coquettishly how he felt about being named the richest man in the world—*again.* And then, 'Do you feel a responsibility to ensure that the next generation carries on your legacy of philanthropy?'

In other words, would he be settling down and having children? He was hardly going to confide in a journalist that he had no intention of siring another generation of Lindens.

Not after the sterling example his parents had provided with their destructive, chaotic parenting.

He and his brother had been farmed out to nannies and boarding schools. There had been little to no consistency in their lives. The effect on Massimo, as the eldest, had been to make him develop a strong sense of responsibility. A desire to have structure and create order from chaos.

His younger brother had gone the other way, taking after their parents. Massimo had often wondered if he'd been less careful, would his brother have felt the need to rebel? But that way lay madness.

In any case, Massimo had the reckless blood of his Italian countess mother and his feckless playboy father in his veins too, and no way was he going to risk passing it down to another generation. He'd watched his brother crash and burn—literally. He wouldn't do that to his own child.

He chose his lovers scrupulously and only spent one night with them, so there could never be a hint of anything more. After witnessing his father decimate what little self-confidence his mother had had, by taking lovers without even trying to hide it, Massimo had no desire to test his own ability to be faithful. He wouldn't risk doing that to a woman.

So far, one night had always been enough. Well, up until about six months ago. Since then… He hadn't had the appetite.

Massimo drove through the electronic gates of his London home. The prickliness of his exchange with the journalist faded as he stepped out of the car. The late summer city air was still. He walked to his front door and it opened as if operated by some kind of magical device.

But there was no magical device—just his housekeeper, Miss Taylor, on the threshold. She was dressed in her usual uniform of black short-sleeved shirt and black trousers. Flat shoes. Blonde hair pulled back neatly in a bun at the base of her neck. No overt make-up. No jewellery.

And there it was. That little beat in his blood. *Awareness*. No matter how much he tried to ignore it or push it down. And lately it had been harder to ignore.

She held the door open. 'Welcome back, sir.' She frowned a little. 'I wasn't expecting you back this early...is everything all right?'

The irritation prickled back to life. Was his life so regimented, so predictable, that he couldn't even come back to his own home ahead of time? And that was strange, because Miss Taylor was one of the few people who didn't irritate him.

No, she had a unique effect on him. It was a mix of that illicit awareness and something far more disturbing...like a balm. How could he be both aware of someone and feel calmed by them? It was ridiculous. He was losing it.

She'd worked for him for four years now, and he'd often congratulated himself on trusting his gut and hiring her. She'd become one of his most trusted employees. And, as such, he was about to request of her that she do him a massive favour.

He said, 'Actually, there's something I need to ask you. Can you come to my office?'

Carrie didn't know why she hesitated for a second, but when Lord Linden looked at her pointedly she said, 'Of course.'

She dutifully followed him to his study and tried not to notice the way he effortlessly filled out his three-piece suit. His hair was curling a little over his collar, and Carrie had the most bizarre urge to touch it and comment that it was getting long.

She could sense he was in a strange mood because she could always sense his moods—like some kind of unwelcome sixth sense. And, really, the man wasn't at all moody. He could be brooding, yes. But he never took it out on staff.

He went into his study and she followed, closing the door behind her. This was where she'd had her interview. Strange to think that had been four years ago. A surge of emotion surprised her. This job had provided her with everything she'd hoped for. A place to settle and start healing a little.

Her inconvenient awareness of her boss had been manageable up till now. She generally avoided eye contact if at all possible, and their conversations were always centred around the house and schedules. And he travelled for work. A lot. Sometimes he could be away for up to a month at a time.

But in the last few months he hadn't been travelling so much. He'd been in London more. And seeing him almost every day had begun to wear on Carrie's nerves a little. Her sense of control around him was starting to fray, as if mocking her for thinking she had anything under control.

'Please, sit down, Miss Taylor.'

Carrie sat down, not sure what Lord Linden wanted to talk to her about. He sat down behind his desk, somehow still dominating the space even though he was no longer standing.

He hadn't taken a lover in months.

That random and incendiary thought popped into Carrie's head. She blushed. What was going on with her today? What did she care if he'd taken a lover lately or not?

Because it bothers you to see them the morning after and send them on their way.

Carrie fought to regain her composure. Maybe he'd been taking his lovers to a hotel? Or sleeping over in their apartments?

'Is everything all right?' Lord Linden asked.

Carrie nodded and said, 'Fine…just fine. It's a bit warm, that's all.'

Lord Linden got up again and opened the window that looked out over a lush back garden. A total luxury in central London. Carrie wasn't looking at that, though. She was mesmerised by the play of muscles under his suit.

He looked at her. 'Better?'

She was definitely losing it. 'Yes, thank you.'

He sat down again. Carrie clasped her hands together, praying she wouldn't betray herself again.

He said, 'You know I'm due to go to New York tomorrow?'

She'd actually forgotten. A wave of relief went through her. 'Yes—for a week, isn't it?'

'Possibly longer, actually. But there's an issue. My regular housekeeper who looks after the Manhattan apartment has retired early, due to ill health. So far my team haven't found anyone suitable. I have to entertain while I'm there—a small drinks party—and I'd like to feel that things are being taken care of…properly.'

Carrie's relief drained away. She wasn't sure where this was going.

Lord Linden sat forward. 'I was hoping that you might consider coming with me.'

The relief drained away and Carrie felt panicky. 'Go to New York? With you?'

He nodded. 'To work in my apartment as housekeeper for the duration of my trip. Hopefully by the time I leave we'll have found a replacement.'

Carrie clasped her hands even tighter. 'I… I don't really know what to say. I've never been to America. I wouldn't know the first thing about how things work over there.'

She was beset by a million things. Disbelief, confusion, terror and, probably most disturbingly, excitement. This was exactly what she *didn't* need. More time in Lord Linden's company!

He looked at her, supremely at ease. 'Is your passport up to date?'

She nodded. 'I just had it renewed recently.'

An old habit that she hadn't let go of.

'That's all you need.'

He made it sound so simple. Not a big deal. He was just transplanting her from here to there.

But then you'll have no peace.

She would be in even closer proximity to him at a time when she felt as if she was losing her sense of control around him. It would be madness to go…and yet she didn't really have a choice.

Nevertheless, she resisted. 'But won't you need me here?'

Lord Linden responded easily. 'You've ensured this property runs like clockwork. I think it can do without you for a week or two. As I said, I have an important event to host at my apartment. I would appreciate having someone I trust there to oversee things. You don't need to worry about the minutiae—my assistant in New York will work to your orders.'

She absorbed this. And then, 'A week or two?'

He nodded. 'Until my commitments there are finished. I'm sure that by then my team will have sourced a new housekeeper.'

She said it out loud. 'I guess I don't really have a choice?'

He arched a brow. 'Would it really be so terrible to spend a couple of weeks in New York? You'll have time off to do whatever you wish.'

Carrie knew that if she said no it would be weird. She was

his London housekeeper. What he was asking of her was perfectly reasonable. And it was New York. She'd never travelled much beyond the UK at all.

'Okay, yes. I'll go with you.'

Lord Linden said crisply, 'Good. We'll be leaving before lunch tomorrow. I trust that'll be enough time to get your things together and ensure the house is left in good hands?'

'Of course,' Carrie answered smoothly.

Maybe this was all in her head and she was just being ridiculous.

'Very good. That'll be all, Miss Taylor.'

Carrie hurried out before she made a total fool of herself.

Four years working for this man without a ripple and suddenly it felt as if a storm was brewing.

Carrie had only ever been on a plane a couple of times before, and never on a private jet. She thought she'd become accustomed to luxurious living in Lord Linden's London house, but the sleek jet mocked her for being so complacent.

The interior was cream and gold. Plush soft carpets. The chair she sat in felt as if it had been contoured especially to fit her body. It was beyond decadent.

She sat towards the front of the jet and Lord Linden sat behind her at a desk with his laptop, working. Throughout the flight she'd been offered any beverage she would like, and a menu featuring the kind of food usually served at one of Lord Linden's dinner parties. She'd settled for sparkling water.

She was too keyed up to sleep, so she alternated between looking at the clouds out of the window and flicking through a magazine she wasn't reading. After a couple of hours she noticed that she hadn't heard the low rumble of Lord Linden's voice in a while.

Feeling like a voyeur, she sneaked a look behind her and saw that he was sitting—no, sprawling—with long legs stretched out across the aisle under his table, reading a document with a small frown between his eyes.

With his collar open and shirtsleeves rolled up, his hair messy as if he'd run a hand through it, and stubble on his jaw, he looked as if he should be swilling champagne with a beautiful woman on each arm—not reading a report. The man oozed sex appeal in a way that Carrie suspected he didn't even appreciate.

Oh, he knew he had it—that was obvious in every move he made—but there was something else…an air of jaded insouciance that gave his appeal another edge. He seemed so utterly arrogant and aloof all at once. It was an intoxicating combination, and doubtless one that drew women in droves.

Not her, though. She knew better.

As if sensing her intense focus on him, he looked up, and Carrie was too slow to escape that dark gaze. She gulped and could feel heat rising into her cheeks.

A small voice mocked her. *Sure you're so in control?*

His gaze narrowed on her. 'Everything okay?'

She nodded. 'Fine…just fine, thank you.' He put down his sheaf of papers and she said hurriedly, 'Sorry, I didn't mean to disturb you, Lord Linden.'

He looked at her steadily. 'You don't need to keep calling me Lord Linden.'

She'd been calling him that for four years.

Carrie contained her surprise. 'I… Okay.' She couldn't possibly call him by his name. It reminded her too much of the lovers she had to help dispatch the morning after…'

'Did Massimo leave me a message?'

He hasn't taken a lover in months, that sly voice reminded her.

Carrie pushed it down desperately. She asked, 'What should I call you?'

'Call me Massimo.'

Carrie blanched. 'Are you sure that's…appropriate?'

Her boss frowned at her. 'It is if I say it is. Lord Linden makes me feel old and stuffy, and I don't think I'm either of those things, do you?'

Looking at him in that elegant, sexy sprawl, Carrie couldn't help saying, 'No.'

His gaze slid to her table. 'No champagne?'

Carrie straightened. 'It's the middle of the day.'

A small smile played around the corner of his mouth. 'Well, it's actually evening now.'

She felt exposed. Gauche. Boundaries set in stone for four years seemed to be dissolving around her.

'You're not drinking,' she said.

The faint smile disappeared. 'I don't really drink all that much.'

No, he didn't. Carrie had often observed him at parties in his own home, where he would stand on the edge of the crowd holding a glass of sparkling wine, but not drinking it. There was a drinks cabinet in his study, full of some of the world's most expensive and exclusive whiskies, and it was hardly touched.

He always looked brooding at those parties. Unapproachable. But inevitably there would be a stream of women who *did* approach, not taking his air of impermeability as anything but encouragement.

Carrie was about to say, *I should let you get back to work*, but instead what came out of her mouth was, 'Would it be okay if you called me Carrie? Miss Taylor makes me feel like a schoolteacher.'

For a moment she thought she might have overstepped the mark, in spite of his request for her to use his first name. But then he said, 'That would be absolutely okay.'

'Thank you. I should let you get back to work.'

For a moment he said nothing, and then, 'You're probably right... Carrie.'

She turned around again before he could see the heat in her face. They'd exchanged more words in the past twenty-four hours than they had in the whole term of her employment. And now they were on a first-name basis. She felt giddy again.

But she needed to remember that she was just here because her boss needed her to *work* in New York.

Driving into Manhattan was sensory overload for Carrie. She couldn't get over the buildings towering over the wide streets. The chaos of the traffic, horns honking constantly. The sheer number of people.

She felt eyes on her and looked to her right, where Massimo sat on the other side of the SUV.

He was looking at her. 'Okay?' he said.

Carrie felt like shaking her head. Her heart-rate was about triple its usual speed. They'd just taken a helicopter from the airport to a rooftop in Manhattan, and had then been met by this chauffeur-driven car down at street level. She couldn't pretend she was au fait with what was happening.

She smiled ruefully. 'I wasn't expecting a helicopter ride into the most famous city in the world.'

Massimo shrugged. 'It's expedient when I have a lot to do in a short space of time.'

'Of course,' Carrie murmured.

She'd almost forgotten who she was dealing with here. It wasn't as if it was for her benefit.

'The driver is going to drop me at my offices and take you on to the apartment, if that's all right? The concierge has been instructed to let you in and show you around, and my assistant will come over later to give you a full briefing on the event I'm hosting and what's required.'

Butterflies erupted in Carrie's gut. She was used to dealing with high society in London, but Manhattan was a whole other level.

'Okay.' Impulsively she added, 'Look, I don't want to let you down—are you sure you want me to take care of this?'

'I trust you and your judgement. You'll be fine.'

He meant in a professional capacity, of course. Not personally. But Carrie couldn't stop the little glow in her chest. She knew how exacting her boss was.

The car was slowing now, and it came to a stop outside a vertiginous steel building. Even when Carrie craned her neck at the window she couldn't see all the way to the top.

Before he got out Massimo said, 'I'll be working late, so feel free to do whatever you like. We can discuss things tomorrow morning.'

Carrie felt like pointing out that he didn't have to tell her his movements, but instead she just nodded.

Massimo uncoiled his large body from the back of the car and immediately left a vacuum behind. Carrie watched him stride into the building in his three-piece suit, not one inch of him looking as if he'd just got off a transatlantic flight.

Carrie grimaced. When she'd dressed much earlier that morning in a dark trouser suit and short-sleeved light woollen top, flat brogues, hair coiled up into a chignon, she'd hoped to project a coolly professional image. Now she felt thoroughly wrinkled and badly in need of refreshing.

Even though it was late summer, almost tipping into autumn

season, she hadn't expected the heat in Manhattan to be so intense. She'd only been outside in between transferring into different vehicles, but in spite of the air-conditioned car she could still feel perspiration on her lower back and the back of her neck.

Not long after dropping Massimo at his office the car turned down a wide street that was immediately less frenetic. When they emerged at the other end Carrie could see a leafy green park ahead of them.

She leant forward to ask the driver, 'Is that Central Park?'

'Yes, ma'am.'

The car turned onto a street bordering the park and came to a stop outside another impossibly tall building—except where Massimo's office had been all sleek modernity, this building oozed old Manhattan grandeur. When she got out of the vehicle and looked across the road she noticed the iconic address: Fifth Avenue.

Of course.

A man in uniform hurried out from under the awning of the building and said, 'Miss Taylor?'

She nodded and smiled, feeling the heat quickly enveloping her.

'I'm Matt, the concierge. I've been instructed to show you around Mr Black's apartment.'

Carrie allowed him to lead her into a blessedly cool marbled reception area. There was a massive round table holding a vase of opulent blooms the size of a small tree. The air was subtly perfumed.

Matt led her into an elevator and as the doors closed said conspiratorially, 'This is Mr Black's private elevator. He owns the whole building, but he just uses the top floor for himself.'

'You don't have to call him Lord Linden, then?' Carrie observed.

The older man shrugged. 'He prefers not.'

Carrie absorbed that nugget. Maybe he appreciated the relative anonymity and more relaxed social protocols of America. The elevator doors opened into a reception hall that oozed classic sophistication. Tiled floors and panelled walls. Doors leading off in different directions.

The concierge led her over to one and opened it. It was only because Carrie was used to Massimo's London house that she didn't gasp out loud. She'd never seen ceilings so high nor windows so huge. She walked over to a window to see the green expanse of Central Park laid out before her. And there was a terrace beyond the windows, lined with flowering plants.

The furnishings were opulent, but understated. This was obviously a formal reception room, with different seating areas, chairs and couches around low coffee tables, upon which sat various massive hardback tomes featuring art, photography and architecture.

There were numerous antiques and a lot of art was hung on the walls. Carrie wouldn't have been able to name the artist, but she recognised one painting of a Parisian scene featuring a woman that must undoubtedly be an original.

'If you come this way I'll show you where the kitchen and utility rooms are, and also your private rooms.'

Carrie flushed. For a second there she had almost been imagining herself inhabiting this space as a visitor, not an employee.

She followed Matt out of the room and down another plush corridor. He led her up some stairs and opened a door into a kitchen that made Carrie gasp audibly. It was stunning—state of the art. A gleaming marble-topped central island was surrounded by acres of countertops. There was a Belfast sink. A cooker that looked as if it could launch a satellite. And a walk-in pantry, stocked to the gills—as was the massive fridge.

'I was told to let you know that the chef will work to your instructions when you have them.'

Mute with awe, Carrie reluctantly left the kitchen and followed Matt again. He deftly showed her an informal media room that looked more like a home cinema. A formal dining room. A gym with a lap pool. And then an elevator door which Matt pointed to and said, 'That brings you up to Mr Black's sleeping quarters, his office and the rooftop terrace.'

There was also an entertaining space the size of a small ballroom with French doors leading out onto a wide terrace and a wrought-iron staircase that led to the rooftop terrace on the upper level.

It was dizzying…the sheer scale of the apartment over three floors.

'And these are your rooms, Miss Taylor.'

The man opened a door with a flourish and Carrie walked inside, taking in a huge bedroom, en suite bathroom and walk-in closet. French doors led out to a balcony, with jaw-dropping views over the park.

'Please help yourself to anything in the kitchen. The phone in the reception hall will dial directly down to me if you need anything. I believe your luggage will be arriving soon.'

Carrie turned around, feeling overwhelmed and seriously doubtful that she'd ever find her way back to that reception hall. 'Thank you, Matt.'

The man ducked his head and was gone, leaving her alone in the vast space. She went over to the French doors and opened them, stepping out onto her own private balcony with sweeping views across Central Park.

Carrie shook her head and smiled wryly.

Not bad for a housekeeper.

Not bad for a girl who had grown up on a council estate with a single mother who had worked her fingers to the bone to provide for them both.

Carrie's mother had never hidden the truth of her birth, once she was old enough to understand. Her father had seduced her mother into an affair, but as soon as she'd fallen pregnant he'd revealed he was married and had dumped her. Carrie had never met him, but she knew he'd had a family of his own the whole time he'd been with her mother.

The stain of abandonment was something she could never fully wash away, no matter how much her mother had tried to make up for it, and it had left a weak spot in her self-esteem. A weak spot that had been exploited and manipulated when she'd been at her most vulnerable, after her mother had died.

That was when her husband had come along and made her believe he could heal the hurt places inside her…give her a life that she'd only imagined in her most private moments. A family. Unconditional love. Security.

But it had all been a toxic lie.

Carrie forced unwelcome thoughts of the past out of her head and rested her arms on the stone wall, taking in the view…the verdant green and the tall, elegant buildings on the other side of the park that mirrored the one she was in. The sounds from the street far below barely even permeated the rarefied air up here.

She wandered back through the apartment and stood at the doors of the elevator that went to the upper floor. Telling herself she was only doing her job by acquainting herself with everything, Carrie got inside, and the lift ascended silently, its doors opening again with a melodic *ping.*

She entered a corridor much like the one she'd just left, except up here there was only a couple of doors, one at the end. She walked to it and hesitated, before telling herself she was being ridiculous. She routinely had to go into her boss's bedroom in London, for various reasons.

She opened the door. His scent immediately hit her nostrils. Dark and woodsy and something like…leather. The room was vast and dressed in dark earthen tones. A massive bed dominated the space, but she avoided looking at that and investigated further to find an en suite bathroom and a walk-in closet.

There was also a lounge area, with a TV and floor-to-ceiling bookshelves. They contained mostly non-fiction books on economics and business, and some thrillers and light fiction. Carrie couldn't imagine Massimo sitting still for long enough to relax and read. The man had an electric energy about him.

She was turning to leave when she saw some photos on a table, framed. She walked over and picked one up. It showed a young man—gorgeous, but not Massimo—with a wide smile, dressed in a motor racing suit standing beside a car, holding up a trophy. Carrie knew that her boss had had a younger brother who'd died tragically on the racing track.

She put the picture back, feeling even more like a voyeur. She'd looked her boss up after she'd been offered the job, and knew about as much as any of the general public did about his infamously tragic family history. His brother's death had been only the tip of the iceberg…

His mother had been a stunningly beautiful Italian countess and his father the aristocratic heir to one of Europe's biggest estates. The Earl and Countess of Linden had lived a fast and glamorous life, rarely out of the papers with their tempestuous relationship, allegations of affairs, and more sordid rumours of drugs and gambling.

Massimo's mother had died of a suspected drug overdose on the family estate outside London, and then a year later his father had died in a helicopter crash en route to a casino in Monte Carlo. The fact that he'd been flying the helicopter, and had been responsible for the death of his young and beautiful lover—another European aristocrat—had only added to the reams of newsprint about the ill-fated family.

As far as Carrie had been able to make out Massimo would have only been eighteen and his younger brother sixteen at the time his father had died.

The current Earl of Linden certainly hadn't inherited his family's excesses. Quite the opposite. His lifestyle was positively monk-like in comparison.

Monk-like, and yet he didn't make Carrie think of chaste monks…

She felt warm all of a sudden, and spied more French doors leading out onto what had to be the rooftop terrace. She opened them and went outside to a vast, breathtaking space that gave even more spectacular views than the level below.

'Not bad, hmm?'

Carrie whirled around. Massimo was standing behind her, tie off, shirt open at his throat, hands in his pockets. She felt caught. Exposed. Hot.

'I'm sorry, I shouldn't be up here. I was just…exploring,' she finished lamely.

Being nosy, more like, said a little tart voice.

He walked towards where she stood by the wall. 'I've asked you here as my housekeeper—this is your domain.'

She turned around to face the view and gulped. The apartment might be her domain, but his private suite was *not* her domain and never would be.

'You need to know the layout.'

Carrie appreciated his diplomacy. 'Your concierge told me this floor was your private suite.'

'But it's also the roof terrace, where I will be hosting my function tomorrow night.'

She looked at him, her heart palpitating. 'Tomorrow night?'

He nodded. 'I've come back early to work from my office here—it's less distracting. One of my assistants is with me... he's in the lounge downstairs. He'll go through the week's events with you and give you all the information you need for the smooth running of the apartment.'

'I'll go straight down and meet him.'

She turned and left, eager for an excuse to get out of Massimo's orbit, and cursing herself for allowing her curiosity to get the better of her.

CHAPTER TWO

THE FOLLOWING EVENING Carrie's equilibrium was slightly restored. She was back in her comfort zone—directing operations for the drinks party Massimo was hosting.

His assistant had described it as a fairly low-key event, consisting of drinks and canapés, but the organisation involved to make it all look as effortless as possible resembled a minor military operation.

Carrie had seen the guest list and it was most definitely *not* low-key. Some of the names had made her gasp out loud. An ex-United States President... One of the world's best-loved actresses... She'd seen plenty of A-listers in her time at events in the house in London, but this was another level of intimidating.

Thankfully an events team were taking care of everything, so all she had to do was supervise and liaise between the events company and Massimo's own staff.

The party was taking place between the ballroom and the roof terrace, with guests moving back and forth. Now Carrie was making her way up to the terrace, moving unobtrusively through the crowd. She was wearing her habitual events uniform: a black sleeveless shift dress and black court shoes, a string of faux pearls around her neck. Her hair was up and pulled back into a low bun.

The dress code for the guests was cocktail wear and, surrounded by women in a glittering array of colourful slinky dresses, Carrie faded into the background exactly as she preferred to do. Or as she *had* always preferred to do.

For the first time in her life at an event like this, she was ashamed to admit that she felt slightly envious of the women in their sparkling dresses. Yet the thought of being front and centre in a crowd like this, with everyone looking at her, made her go clammy with horror.

She hovered on the edge of the crowd, her expert eye taking everything in and noting that all was running smoothly. She tried desperately not to let her gaze go to where Massimo stood, head and shoulders above almost everyone around him, but it was next to impossible.

He was magnificent in a dark suit, a lighter coloured silk tie and white shirt. The dim lights made his hair look darker. His arms were folded as he listened intently to what someone was saying to him and his muscles bunched under the expensive material. As if his suit couldn't contain him…

An electric pulse zinged through her blood. There was something so illicitly thrilling about how sexual he was underneath the civilised veneer.

Carrie went hot and then cold as that disturbing thought registered. She'd never considered herself a sexual person—her husband had certainly tried and failed to arouse her…she'd always found sex painful and somehow demeaning…and yet here she was, ogling her boss like a hormonal teenager.

Carrie impulsively took a tray full of canapés from one of the wait staff to help out with serving. She needed a reminder of why she was here.

'So, you see, without the funds you provided we absolutely wouldn't be where we are today, and it's thanks to the Linden Foundation that…'

Massimo tuned out the voice again.

Where was she?

Even though he was surrounded by some of the most charismatic, powerful, interesting and beautiful people in the world, he wasn't interested in them.

He looked over the heads of the guests around him and a flash of blonde hair caught his peripheral vision. He turned to look and his blood leapt in reaction. A reaction that no other woman here had elicited.

She had her back to him and was wearing the plainest dress imaginable. Perfectly appropriate, of course, but it irritated Massimo. She was offering canapés to his guests and handing them napkins.

Without thinking about what he was doing, he murmured something into the constant flow of his companion's words and moved away, instantly feeling a sense of relief. *And anticipation.*

He walked up behind Carrie and took her arm lightly in his hand. He could feel her muscles. She was strong. She looked at him, and he saw the way she flushed.

Awareness. Not just him.

Satisfaction rolled through him in a way he hadn't experienced in a long time.

He took the tray with his free hand and handed it to a passing waiter. Then he led Carrie to a quiet spot. She turned to face him. Reluctantly he let her arm go.

'What are you doing?' he asked.

He noticed that her mouth was very soft. Pink. No lipstick. It was a beautiful shape. Naturally pouting. Her eyes were huge and very green. He felt as if he'd been underestimating just how beautiful she was for a long time, and now he was being punished for it.

'I'm just helping out.'

'There are staff here for that.'

'I don't mind.'

I do.

Massimo just about stopped himself from saying those words. He had a very strong sense that he never wanted to see her in a role of subservience again.

This was unprecedented. He *never* got involved with staff. He trusted them to do their jobs—none more so than this woman. If she'd decided to lend a hand then he was sure she'd had good reason to. He was exposing himself.

He took a step back. Became aware of the crowd around them. Eyes on him. 'Of course. I trust your judgement.'

Carrie watched Massimo turn and walk back into the crowd, swallowed up in seconds by people clamouring for his attention. She was still trembling from the way he had put his hand on her and led her aside. Her skin burned as if from a brand.

It was crazy, but it was the closest proximity she'd had to a man in a long time. And it had brought up a multitude of emotions and sensations, none of which she had expected, considering the fact that her husband had been so abusive. Never physically, although the threat had always been there, but mentally and verbally.

For the first time in a long time excitement flowed through her veins—not fear or disgust.

For years she'd avoided physical contact with people, which was easy enough to do in a work environment and when you didn't have a partner. Usually if someone touched her she tensed, recoiled. But as soon as *he'd* touched her she'd known it was him.

She'd welcomed his touch.

The realisation made her feel light-headed. For the last four years she'd carried the fear that she would never be able to allow someone physically close again. Not to mention emotionally.

Absorbing this revelation distracted Carrie from thinking too much about why Massimo hadn't wanted to see her serving his guests in the first place. She would unpick that later.

The events manager caught her eye and came over. 'Sorry to disturb you, Miss Taylor, but the chef wants a word?'

Carrie welcomed the diversion and fled.

The rest of the evening was a blur as Carrie threw herself into activity, doing her best to avoid going back up to the terrace.

When people started to leave, the events manager found her and smiled. 'Thanks for all your help, Miss Taylor. We can take care of things from here.'

Carrie took her cue and went to her rooms. She didn't want to witness Massimo choosing a woman to spend the night with. She would find out in the morning when she checked the bedrooms, no doubt. He might not have taken a lover in London for some time now, but she was sure New York would provide him with fresh...*inspiration*.

Carrie scowled at herself in her bathroom mirror. She'd changed into her pyjamas—shorts and a short-sleeved shirt—and her hair was long and tangled around her shoulders. She looked about as far away as it was possible to get from one of Massimo's sultry lovers.

She couldn't hear a thing from the party in her rooms—the apartment was well sound-proofed. She got into bed, but felt too restless to sleep. She got up again, pulled on a short dressing gown and went out onto her balcony.

The music had stopped but she could still hear conversation and sporadic bursts of laughter. Was Massimo with a woman now? A woman he had chosen? Looking at her? Touching her? Surely he would smile when he seduced a woman?

Carrie was surprised at the jealousy that rose up inside her. She had no right to be jealous of any woman.

She took a deep breath and tried to calm her restlessness. She had to admit that in the space of the last few days she'd tipped over the edge of being acceptably aware of her boss in a way that hadn't affected her too much, into full-on crush territory.

It was as if a Pandora's box had opened inside her and four years of repressed emotions and longings were being brought back to life.

It had been a long time since she'd felt like this and it troubled her. Because the last time it had ended in a marriage that had reduced her to a shell of the person she'd been.

She'd had to work hard in the intervening years to try to forgive herself for letting her husband into her life. For trusting him and allowing him to wage upon her a slow and insidious campaign of abuse that had worn her down.

They'd met just after her mother had died, when Carrie had been at her most vulnerable and feeling very alone in the world. Her mother's death had made her even more acutely aware that her absent father had chosen his own family over her. Her mother had been her rock and her guide, and without her Carrie's strength had felt very shaky.

Her husband, a master manipulator, had sensed that and exploited it. Carrie knew this wasn't her fault, and she knew that women even stronger than her had been taken in in similar ways, but the reflex to blame herself for being weak was still strong. Strong enough to let her relish working as a housekeeper for a man whose house was like a fortress, and which had provided her with much needed space and time to heal.

And she *had* healed—on many levels. Perhaps this ridiculous growing desire for her boss should just be taken as a welcome sign that she was ready to open up a part of herself that she'd locked away for a long time.

She'd vowed never to marry again, because she knew she could never trust anyone that much, but she hadn't ruled out the possibility of a relationship. Companionship. Maybe this fascination with her boss was her body's way of telling her that she was ready for the next step in her healing. As terrifying as that thought was…

The morning after the party, Massimo answered a call in his home office with a disgruntled-sounding, 'Yes?'

It was his executive assistant, informing him that one of the guests from the party—a famous model—wanted to know if Massimo had a date for the charity ball at the end of the week, and if not could she offer herself?

Massimo would never cease to be shocked by the ways and means and audacity of women looking to get his attention. He couldn't even picture the woman in question.

'No,' he responded. 'I do not wish to accept her kind offer of a date.'

'So you'll be going solo?'

Massimo stood up and walked over to the window. He was feeling restless. He hadn't seen Carrie yet that morning. One of the other staff had served him at breakfast. He'd looked for her at the end of the party last night, but one of the events staff had informed him chirpily that she'd gone to bed.

There was no reason for that fact to have irked Massimo so much. Carrie would routinely slip away before the end of a party, once it was largely over and in the capable hands of the events manager. But it had irked him last night.

Impulsively he said, 'Actually, I already have a date.'

'You do?'

The incredulity in his assistant's tone made Massimo

scowl. He couldn't help but be acutely aware that his lack of interest in taking a lover lately had become a fevered source of speculation.

Hence why the plan he was now considering would be the perfect solution. A way to curb the gossips while also proving to himself that this sudden fascination for his housekeeper was an anomaly.

'Yes, I do,' he repeated, pushing aside the pricking of his conscience.

He cut off the connection and threw the phone back onto the table behind him. He stuck his hands in his pockets. He couldn't deny that he was behaving completely out of character, and that this plan would potentially blur the boundaries between him and his housekeeper, but for the first time in his life he chose not to think about the consequences.

'Would you join me for lunch?'

Carrie's mouth fell open.

She'd just shown Massimo out onto the terrace, where she'd laid a table for lunch. A light chicken salad and crusty bread. He was looking at her, perfectly composed, as if he hadn't just asked her a preposterous thing.

'I…' She was about to tell a white lie and say that she'd already eaten when something reckless moved through her. *Temptation.* 'Okay.'

'Good.' He went and sat down.

In a bit of a daze, Carrie got another place setting and went out to the table. There was more than enough food for two. Maybe Massimo was just being practical. He had always erred on the side of discretion and frugality over ostentation. Perhaps in reaction to the lurid and lavish ways of his parents and brother.

Massimo helped himself to a portion of salad and handed her the utensils.

'Thank you.'

Carrie still felt dazed. What was she doing, sitting at a table with her boss, dressed in her very plain uniform of white shirt and black trousers, flat shoes. Hair pulled back, as always. Minimal make-up.

He hadn't taken a lover last night. Or at least there had been no evidence of breakfast for two. Carrie hated how relieved she felt. This crush was becoming ridiculous.

'You prefer working here to the office?' she asked, aiming for polite interest.

'I would be inundated with requests and interruptions there. I'll spend some time there once I've got my actual work done.'

Carrie swallowed a mouthful of food, too self-conscious to meet Massimo's eye. 'I'd never realised the amount of work there is in philanthropy. Surely it's easier to give money away than to make it?'

'You would think…'

She glanced at him now, because he sounded so grim, and saw he was looking at her.

He said, 'It turns out that giving money away involves almost as much as trying to make it, and the responsibility for who to give it to and when is more complicated and delicate than negotiating a peace agreement between two warring countries.'

Curious now, Carrie asked, 'Do you actually…*enjoy* it?'

Massimo blinked and sat back, as if surprised by her question. 'No one has ever asked me that before. I like giving the money away… I don't much like all the bureaucracy and politics that comes with it.'

'At least you can have a clear conscience.'

His gaze narrowed on her then. 'Actually, I have an ulterior motive for inviting you to dine with me. I need a favour. Another favour.'

Carrie put down her fork. For no good reason her heart-rate had doubled. 'A favour?' What on earth could she possibly do for the man who literally had everything?

He nodded. 'There's an event at the end of the week—a charity ball. I need a date and I would appreciate it if you'd consider coming with me.'

I need a date.

Arguably the wealthiest man in the world, and inarguably one of the most gorgeous, wanted *her* to accompany him as his date?

Carrie shook her head, as if that might make sense of what he'd just said. 'Why on earth would you want *me* to come with you?'

'Because, quite frankly, I don't want to bring a date who might be under the impression that anything else is on offer.'

'You mean like...?' The word *sex* hovered on her tongue but then Massimo spoke.

'Like a relationship.'

Carrie could feel a hot flush rising.

Of course.

Maybe that was why he hadn't taken a lover in months— because his lovers inevitably wanted more.

His offer—*suggestion*—was causing a maelstrom inside her. A mixture of girlish excitement, which was entirely inappropriate, and terror and exhilaration. And yet more terror. Mainly terror. And confusion.

'Wouldn't it be a little...unorthodox?'

He gave a small shrug. 'It doesn't have to be. It would obviously be considered as out-of-hours work for you. You'll be well recompensed.'

Immediately the heat inside her cooled. Of course. He just wanted her to act as a buffer. She remembered the crowd around him the previous evening, clamouring for his attention.

The stark facts that she had grown up on a council estate and left school early made her no match for the kind of people he socialised with. She had to face reality: she would be a liability. Not to mention the thought of the scrutiny she would face being on his arm. Every flaw exposed!

She shook her head. 'I'm sorry, but I really don't think I can do that.'

Massimo took a bite of his salad, seemingly unconcerned. 'Why?'

'I've never been in that kind of situation before. I wouldn't have a clue how to behave. What if someone talks to me?'

'You talk back—they're just human beings.'

Carrie made a noise. 'To you, maybe… It's different for someone like me.'

'What do you mean?'

Carrie pushed her plate away. There was no way she could eat now. 'To those people someone like me is invisible. I'm just there to top up a drink or serve food or clean up after them.'

'You mean people like me?'

Carrie flushed. 'Well…yes, but you're different…'

Massimo acknowledged all his employees in a way that she knew most others didn't.

'You don't sound bitter about it,' he responded.

Carrie looked at him. 'I'm not. I've never expected anything else. I wouldn't want your life if you paid me.'

She realised what she'd said and put a hand to her mouth, a nervous giggle escaping. She took her hand down.

'That's literally what you're proposing to do. To pay me to be in your world.'

'What's so bad about my life, then?'

Massimo sat back and Carrie wanted to kick herself. How on earth had they got *here*?

'I guess in many ways it's not bad—you have everything you could ever want... But I think, if I'm not speaking too much out of turn, it's isolating. I don't see you having much... fun.'

'Do *you* have fun?' There was no sharpness to the question, as if she'd offended him, just curiosity.

Carrie felt self-conscious. 'I don't suppose I can claim to have much fun...no.'

'So maybe we're not that different after all.'

She'd never thought about it like that.

He continued, 'And maybe it might be considered fun to dress up and come with me to something you've never experienced before?'

Before she could even acknowledge how adroitly he was manoeuvring her Carrie thought of something far scarier. She thought of the women at the party the previous night, in cocktail dresses of every hue, with gems glittering from ears, necks and hands. She thought of how she'd envied them.

'In any case, I don't have anything remotely suitable to wear.'

Massimo waved a hand. 'That's easily taken care of.'

Carrie was rendered momentarily speechless. 'But... I'm your housekeeper.'

'Like I said, you'd be doing me a favour.'

He was saying all this in such a reasonable way that Carrie felt she would be overreacting if she kept protesting. Her boss wanted her to go to an event as his date—in a work capacity—in order to keep him from the hordes of women.

For a moment Carrie wondered if she might actually be dreaming. Or hallucinating. She wanted to pinch herself, and did so under the table. *Ouch.* Not a dream, then.

But previous experience had hardwired her to be wary of any kind of 'persuasion'.

She said, 'If I refuse what happens?'

Massimo took a drink of water and shook his head, 'Absolutely nothing. Things proceed as normal. You are under no obligation to agree to this. I realise that it's asking you to blur the boundaries of our work relationship. I don't want you to feel uncomfortable. You don't have to answer now, Carrie. Think about it and let me know later.'

Something in her eased. She was an expert in reading passive aggression and aggressive aggression, and she perceived nothing here. Massimo was telling the truth. He really was just looking for an easy option in something he considered irksome.

But nevertheless her urge to self-protect was stronger than her instinct that she could trust him.

'I'm sorry but I can't agree to do this. I don't need to think about it.'

Immediately a knot of regret clutched at her gut. She pushed it down.

His expression didn't falter. 'If that's your final decision then I accept it.'

His gaze was steady. Dark. All-encompassing. They were outside on the terrace but she felt she needed air.

She stood up, 'I think I'll take my break now, if that's all right, s—' She'd been about to say, *sir*, but stopped herself.

'Of course—take all the time you need. I have to go into the office for the rest of the day, and I'll be eating out this evening.'

Carrie left the lunch table with her half-eaten plate of food and went inside. There was a housemaid who came every day—a friendly young woman. She was in the kitchen now, and Carrie instructed her to clean up once Massimo had finished his lunch, and to make sure the chef knew that he was dining out this evening.

Then she made her way straight down to ground level and stepped outside, where she was met with a wall of still, humid air. Not the clear, refreshing oxygen she needed so she could try and wrap her brain around what Massimo had just asked of her. And her answer. Which had been met with equanimity.

She bought an iced tea from a nearby coffee shop and made her way over to Central Park, looking for even the smallest of breezes under the shade of the massive trees. She sat on a bench and watched people go by, sipping her drink.

A pair of young lovers, hand in hand, clearly besotted, caught her attention. Her heart spasmed. Growing up with her mother's stoicism after being dumped so comprehensively, Carrie had always prided herself on not having any illusions when it came to love and fairy tales of happy endings. But when she'd been vulnerable, and her husband had used all his manipulative charm to seduce her, she'd allowed herself to believe briefly that maybe it would be different for her.

But it hadn't been, and she should have known better. There was no such thing as romance. Only people who want to control and dominate others...take advantage of any vulnerability. There was no equality. Only power games. And she'd never be on the wrong side of that equation again.

She'd had to refuse Massimo, to see how he'd react. Like some kind of test. And because she'd sensed no passive aggression that might threaten to blow up at a later point she couldn't help but wonder if she'd overreacted.

As if to mock her for her cynicism, the young lovers had stopped to kiss now, and it was sweet yet passionate. They were oblivious to voyeurs. Before she could deny it, Carrie felt a sense of yearning. An ache for something she'd told herself didn't exist. Maybe it did for some people, who weren't damaged or driven to manipulate and dominate.

Then a mother passed her, with a baby in a stroller, and an even bigger ache gripped Carrie right in her womb. She put a hand there unconsciously, as if that might dim the pain. That was when she realised that it wasn't sharp, as it had used to be. It was softer. Still there, but not so acute.

Time really was a healer. Such a cliché. But she couldn't deny feeling a sense of peace after four long years of hiding and licking her wounds.

Maybe, whispered a little voice, *just maybe it's time to stop hiding yourself away? Maybe it's time to live a little again?*

A tiny bud of something light unfurled inside her. Along with a frisson of electricity at the thought of being brave enough to accept Massimo's invitation.

If there was a way to start embracing life again, then surely standing beside Massimo, Lord Linden, had to be a pretty audacious place to start?

CHAPTER THREE

MASSIMO WAS DISTRACTED, and he'd been distracted all after-noon and evening. It wasn't every day that a woman turned him down. That *anyone* turned him down. He felt irritated with himself at the fact that it bothered him. Carrie was his housekeeper—clearly she was being professional and he should commend her for it.

If he'd been trying to test her she'd passed with flying colours. What he had asked of her was beyond the realms of regular service and he knew well that his motives weren't as straightforward as he'd led her to believe. He'd hoped that if she said yes, then she would lose whatever fascination she held for him.

More than fascination.

He shifted in his seat in the back of his car as it made its way through the night-time Manhattan traffic.

He'd just endured an interminable dinner where, as his peers had grown drunker and drunker, he'd found his mind wandering back to Carrie. The look of shock on her face earlier when he'd suggested eating together. The way she'd sat there so primly. The way she'd spoken to him, asking him things no one else ever had.

She intrigued him.

But perhaps she'd sensed his interest and her low-key and humble demeanour was an act.

A part she'd been playing for four years just to engage his interest?

The voice mocked his cynicism, but at the same time, considering the lengths some women had gone to to get his attention, it was not entirely beyond the realm of possibility.

But he couldn't deny that she'd first intrigued him four years ago, when she'd come to be interviewed for the position as his housekeeper. So it had been brewing under the surface for a long time.

Massimo tried to be rational about this irritating growing desire for a woman who was plainly out of bounds—and for good reason. Apart from anything else, it went against all his tenets to pursue a woman like Carrie Taylor.

He only pursued women who knew how to play the game and who were like him—from a world that had calcified them into something hard and cynical.

He only pursued women who were happy with one night. Because he never wanted anything more. And he certainly had no desire for any kind of longevity.

He scowled at himself as the car pulled up outside his apartment building. How had he somehow meandered to *these* thoughts?

Carrie Taylor, his aggravating housekeeper. That was how. As he stepped out of the car and went inside he sent up silent thanks for her refusal to accede to his wishes. She had done them both a favour. Tomorrow he would instruct his assistant to set up that model as his date.

That intention lasted as he arrived in the apartment and loosened his tie. It lasted as he went into the kitchen, looking for something more substantial to eat than the risible air and leaves they'd been served at dinner. It lasted right up until a familiar voice came from behind him.

'There's some leftover steak. I could make you a sandwich if you like?'

Massimo stopped and turned around. And all his good intentions dissolved in a flash of heat. And lust.

Carrie was out of her uniform and wearing something soft and slouchy...a sweatshirt and leggings. But far more incendiary than that, her hair was down. He'd never seen her hair down. In four years.

It was far wilder than he would have expected. And longer. Flowing loose and wavy over her shoulders and down her back. He suspected some would say it was unfashionably long, and it certainly wasn't styled, but seeing it down like this made him feel like a voyeur from another era. It felt ridiculously intimate, and for the first time in a long time he was speechless.

She gestured to herself, looking embarrassed, 'Sorry, I'm off duty. I hope you don't mind. I know you don't normally see me like this.'

Massimo shook his head. 'No, not at all.'

Had she mentioned food? His head felt foggy. He struggled to remember. All he knew was that he didn't want her to leave.

He said, 'Did you say a sandwich? That would be amazing. Thank you.'

He slipped off his jacket and saw how her eyes followed his action. Her cheeks went pink. Massimo's blood was on fire.

She came into the kitchen, the lights glinting off her bright hair. She was wearing socks. Her legs were long and shapely. The soft clothes clung to her body, showcasing womanly curves. She'd put on weight since she'd started working for him and it suited her. She'd been so delicate in those earlier days...she'd looked as if a puff of wind would blow her over.

The sweatshirt slipped off one shoulder and Massimo had

an almost overwhelming urge to go over, pull her hair aside and press his mouth there. She pulled it back up and he gritted his jaw.

He moved around to the other side of the island, suddenly aware of his body's response.

She was efficient in her movements, brisk, and she said over her shoulder, without making eye contact, 'If you'd like, I can bring it to you. it shouldn't take me long.'

A perverse devil inside Massimo made him say, 'No, it's okay. I'll wait here.'

He draped his jacket over a chair and went over to the fridge and pulled out a bottle of sparkling water. He took a glass off the shelf. Sat down on the other side of the island.

There was silence as Carrie busied herself taking out the steak to warm it up, along with some bread. After a while she said, 'They didn't feed you at dinner?'

'Oh, they fed us. It just didn't remotely resemble any nutritious food group. Or consist of calories, for that matter.'

Massimo thought he heard a sound like a stifled laugh, but he couldn't be sure.

'Did you have dinner here?' he asked.

She could have gone out, for all he knew—perhaps even on a date. He'd never used a dating app in his life, but he'd heard of them. Maybe Carrie had one on her phone...

'Yes, I had steak and salad.'

Massimo really didn't like his sense of satisfaction at hearing she hadn't gone out.

She turned around and deftly put the sandwich together, then arranged it on a plate along with some side salad.

She reached across the island and placed it in front of him. Massimo had to admit it looked and smelled delicious.

Before he could taste it, Carrie cleared her throat and said,

'Actually, I was hoping to catch you when you came in…to say something.'

'Of course.'

She looked nervous, avoiding his eye. Fingers plucking at a tea-towel. Then she seemed to muster her courage and looked at him. Once again he marvelled at how green her eyes were. Unusual…

Beautiful.

'I…um… I know that I refused your request that I join you at the event this week…and you've probably already asked someone else…' She trailed off here, as if waiting for him to interject.

Surprise kept Massimo's mouth shut.

She went on, 'But if you haven't asked anyone else, and you'd still like me to accompany you, then I will.'

A steady thrum of satisfaction beat through Massimo's body. A short while before he'd been telling himself he was pleased that she'd said no. But now he was even more pleased.

He said, 'I haven't asked anyone else yet, so…yes, I would like you to accompany me.'

Her mouth compressed. 'Like I said, I don't have anything suitable to wear… I can have a look on my lunchbreak, or after work…'

Massimo shook his head. It was already filling with visions of how she might look draped in silk and satin. Jewels glittering against her pale skin.

'Leave that to me. My assistant will be in touch to ensure you have all that you need.'

'Oh, okay…goodnight, sir.'

She turned to go and Massimo said softly from behind her, 'The name is Massimo.'

She turned around again, her face pink. 'Sorry, I forgot. Goodnight, Massimo.'

A lick of pure lust went straight to his groin at hearing his name on her tongue. He wanted to hear it over and over again. Begging him.

'Goodnight, Carrie.'

She turned and left. Her scent lingered on the air. Nothing expensive, but no less compelling. It was delicate and floral with an earthy undertone.

He looked at the steak sandwich. His appetite had fled, to be replaced by something far more carnal.

Carrie had never much indulged in fantasy. Not even as a child with a single mother, living in a council flat. The life she'd seen around her had been bleak and hard and she'd accepted her place in it.

She shook her head at herself, trying to dislodge the painful memories. But it was hard, because the present moment felt dangerously close to a fantasy she'd never allowed herself to have before. A fantasy of transformation. Of becoming someone else. Of being someone else. Someone far... sleeker. Shinier. Someone almost beautiful.

Her mother had been beautiful. Carrie had always recognised that. But her beauty had been dimmed and hidden under years of disappointment, loneliness and back-breaking work.

For the first time, as Carrie looked in the mirror, she thought she could catch a glimpse of what her mother might have looked like with a different life.

You're not your mother, whispered a little voice.

No, she wasn't. She was herself. And she was looking disbelievingly at a vision.

A team of people had arrived at Massimo's apartment earlier—stylists with racks of clothes, hairdressers, make-up artists...beauticians. She still blushed when she thought of how they'd attended to parts of her body that hadn't seen daylight for a long time.

They'd trimmed her hair, taking out some of the heavy weight before pulling it up into a kind of chignon. They'd spent an hour on her face only to give her the effect of not wearing any make-up at all. Her eyes looked bigger, and very green. Cheeks dewy. Had her mouth always been so plump? Had they injected something into her lips without her even realising? She touched her mouth experimentally. It felt the same.

She was almost afraid to look at the dress. She barely even felt it on her, it was so light. Strapless. Black. Snug around her chest and waist and hips, before falling to the floor in soft folds, some of which were draped over her hip, giving an almost Grecian effect.

It was too low across her breasts. They looked…*provocative* to her eye. And yet she knew well that compared to the kind of thing some women wore at the events Massimo attended and hosted, this was positively discreet.

One part of her wanted to rip everything off, clean her face and jump into bed under the covers, but another part of her—a very fledgling part—felt excited at the thought of Massimo seeing her like this. Looking at her. Seeing her differently?

Her pulse throbbed. In her head a small voice was warning: *Danger! Danger!* But it was too late, because Massimo was coming to get her any minute now.

She tried to claw back some sense of reality before he came, telling herself that this was just a Cinderella moment. He would see how inferior she was next to all those other women tonight and he wouldn't ask her to accompany him again. Things would go back to normal and that was okay.

That was more than okay, she assured herself fiercely.

She took a deep breath. Tried to calm her pulse. This was a moment out of time. A moment to indulge in fantasy and then go back to the real world in approximately three hours. Massimo was ruthless about the time he spent at functions. In and out.

There was a knock on the door.

He was here.

Against Carrie's better efforts, all her attempts to keep her feet on the ground dissolved in a rush of nerves and heat. For a moment she felt light-headed. Tipping dangerously close to the edge of losing herself again…of allowing herself to dream of another life.

She took a deep breath. Calmed herself. She was not that girl any more. Any dreams she'd harboured had been well and truly shattered. She was a grown woman, and she knew exactly what was going on here.

Nothing much at all.

She called out, 'Come in,' but at the last moment couldn't turn around to face Massimo. Because she was too afraid to see the look on his face when he saw her and compared her to every other woman in his life.

When Massimo walked into the room Carrie had her back to him. The dress was strapless. The top of her back was bare, shoulders straight. Her skin was pale, almost pearlescent in the light. Her hair was swept up into a rough chignon and the line of her neck seemed to him to be incredibly delicate. Vulnerable.

For a heart-stopping moment Massimo didn't want her to turn around. He had a superstitious notion that once she did everything would change. That he'd embarked on something that was already leaving his control.

But it was too late. She was turning around, and he couldn't stop her, and she was…breathtaking. Literally. Like a gem revealed after layers of dust had been brushed away.

His first thought was, *Why has she hidden herself away?* His second thought was, *I want her.* It beat through him like a drum. Heavy and insistent.

The dress was black and form-fitting, a classic design. The bodice was cut low over her chest and clung lovingly to the fullness of her breasts, held up by some feat of engineering that Massimo could only guess at.

His gaze continued down to where the material defined her small waist and then gathered and draped over her hips and thighs before falling in long loose folds to her feet.

It was all at once classically elegant and indecently sexy.

Incredibly, he managed to drag his gaze back up and find his voice. 'You look…beautiful.'

'I feel a little exposed.'

He looked at her. High cheekbones. Delicate jaw, but strong. She was pink in the face. Her eyes looked very green, as if they too had been dulled until this moment. She wore minimal make-up because she evidently didn't need it. A slick of flesh-coloured lipstick. Slightly smoky eyes.

'Your dress is fine, believe me.'

'If you say so… I've never been to anything like this before.'

And they hadn't even left his apartment yet.

Massimo's conscience pricked. He ignored it. There was no way he could turn back now. A floodgate had been opened and for the first time in his life he felt like throwing caution to the wind.

He walked towards her and held out the box he was holding in his hands. He'd almost forgotten.

She looked from it to him, suddenly wary. 'What's this?'

'An embellishment.'

Not that she needed it.

She took a step towards him, and Massimo gritted his teeth as her scent tickled his nostrils. Light, but with those subtle undertones of something much more potent. Like her...with hidden depths.

He opened the box and she looked down. He could see the pink leach from her face. Not the reaction he would have expected when a woman laid eyes on an art deco diamond and emerald necklace from one of the world's most iconic jewellers.

'What is this?' She looked up at him.

Massimo lifted the necklace from the box and put the box down. He said, 'Turn around.'

She looked stricken. 'I can't wear that...it's too much.'

'I've been given strict instructions by the stylist that it's an integral piece of your ensemble. Plus, the jewellers who have loaned it to me will be at the event this evening.'

Some colour came back into her cheeks. 'It's on loan?'

'Yes. Now, turn around.'

Slowly, she did so, and Massimo reached over her head to place the necklace at her throat and close it behind her neck. His fingers brushed her skin and it felt warm and soft. Was it his imagination or did a little tremor go through her body?

He took his hands away. 'Okay, you can turn around again.'

She did so, her hands touching the necklace as if she was afraid it might fall off. She was avoiding his eye. His blood pulsed.

She was as aware of him as he was of her. She wanted him.

Except normally when he realised a woman wanted him he felt a sense of satisfaction. Now all he felt was intense hunger. The kind he hadn't felt in a long time. Raw and urgent.

'Carrie, look at me.'

Carrie really didn't want to look at Massimo. Her skin was still tingling from where his fingers had brushed against her.

Her eyeline was on his bow-tie. Even in heels the top of her head only grazed his jaw. The necklace felt cold and heavy around her neck. No plastic gems here. Real emeralds and diamonds.

She'd seen Massimo dressed in a tuxedo a million times before, but it had never impacted on her the way it did this evening. Even his scent seemed stronger. More potent.

Boundaries and lines felt very blurry right now, standing here in front of her boss, dressed like someone who was not her—plain old Carrie Taylor, a girl who hadn't even done her A-levels, nothing but a humble housekeeper...

'Carrie?'

She forced the cacophony out of her head, took a deep breath and looked up. Everything about him should be signalling danger to her—he was so much bigger and stronger physically than her husband had been—but she felt no danger. Only intense excitement and anticipation.

Her heart skipped a beat when she registered the intensity in his dark gaze. She instantly felt self-conscious. As if she'd been caught playing dress-up.

She took a step back. 'If you've changed your mind it's okay, honestly. I don't mind.'

Massimo frowned. 'Why would I change my mind? You look stunning.'

Self-consciousness turned to awareness. Even though she knew he was only being polite. 'I think the team you provided could make anyone look presentable.'

'You're more than presentable, Carrie. You're beautiful.'

Her heart hitched again. Warning bells rang in her head. Memories of her husband...

'Carrie, you're so special. I want to protect you.'

She forced her brain to cool down and slow down. 'Thank

you, but it's really not necessary to say things like that. It's not as if this is a real date.'

'I'll spare you the platitudes, then?' Massimo responded dryly.

Carrie just managed to stop herself from reminding him that she wasn't one of his usual lovers. *As if he needed reminding.*

He seemed to wait a moment for a response, and when she said nothing he said, 'My driver is waiting downstairs. We should go.'

Carrie welcomed the respite from his focus and let him lead her out of the apartment and down to the waiting car. They got into the back and it moved smoothly through the evening Manhattan traffic.

She looked out at the crowds of people. Some rushing home, some just strolling along, some lovers holding hands. And here she was, dressed in a gown she could never afford in her lifetime, sitting beside one of the world's most eligible bachelors, about to attend a glittering event. She was living out a fantasy she'd never even admitted to having.

'Don't worry, you'll be fine—just follow my lead.'

Carrie looked at Massimo, who glanced down at her hands in her lap, where she was gripping her clutch bag so tight her knuckles were white.

She realised how tense she was and took a breath, loosening her grip. 'I don't want to embarrass you.'

'You won't.'

She wasn't so sure about that. She felt certain that everyone would see her shortcomings and lack of credentials like a branded letter on her forehead.

As if he could hear her thoughts, Massimo said, 'You know, not everyone you'll meet will have been born with advantages. Some have made their livelihoods from nothing. Literally from living on the streets. Some of them had rough starts in life.'

Carrie's face flushed. She didn't want to come across as prejudiced. 'I know that…but if anything that makes people even more intimidating. To know the obstacles they've overcome to succeed…'

'Unlike someone like me?'

There was no edge to his tone, but Carrie thought of all the stories about his young life—unbelievably privileged, but also chaotic. Losing his parents so young. Then his brother. Did wealth and privilege make those things any easier to bear? She suspected not.

She smiled a small smile, 'I guess it's all relative. Everyone has obstacles.'

He looked at her for a long moment. She thought he was about to ask her something, but then the car was pulling to a stop outside the very grand entrance of a building. Flashing lights almost blinded Carrie before they'd even got out of the car. Her terror was instant. She went cold all over.

She didn't even notice Massimo taking her hand and tugging her from the car, standing up straight beside him. It was a barrage of lights. She was stunned.

'Just follow me. We don't need to stop.'

But as they walked along the red carpet all Carrie could hear was, 'Massimo! Over here!'

'Massimo who's your date?'

'Massimo!'

She tried to tug at his hand, to tell him he should stop and get his photo taken, but to her relief he didn't seem to be inclined to stop. And now they were through the doors and into the most opulent and beautiful foyer Carrie had ever seen.

Marbled floors…a domed and frescoed ceiling soaring far above their heads. Elaborate chandeliers with hundreds of tiny lights cast everything in a golden hue. Black-suited waiters moved among the gilded crowd, offering tall, delicate glasses of sparkling wine.

Massimo took two glasses and handed her one. She felt light-headed without even taking a sip. It was like the set of a Disney movie. Except it had come to life. There was a grand staircase in the middle of the space leading up to the next level, where more people mingled.

The acoustics were perfect, letting the strains of live classical music float through the chattering crowd without sounding discordant.

'Where are we?'

She hadn't realised she'd spoken out loud until Massimo said, 'One of Manhattan's oldest buildings. Newly renovated as an event space exclusively for charitable events.'

Carrie looked at Massimo as something occurred to her. 'You own this, don't you?'

'It's an acquisition I made, yes. It seemed prudent to have a space to host events.'

In spite of her lingering intimidation and terror Carrie's mouth twitched at the thought of simply acquiring what had to be one of New York's most expensive properties to make one's life easier. Massimo looked at her mouth, and then into her eyes. It sent all sorts of languid heat along her veins.

He asked, 'What is so funny?'

He had his hand on her elbow. A light touch, but it burned. The twitch left her mouth. She shook her head. 'Nothing. It's just a lot…to take in.' She took a sip of wine to try and quell her nerves.

Massimo guided her to the stairs and they walked up. He greeted people with a nod here and there. Carrie couldn't help noticing the intense interest he drew. And her. She felt all the eyes on her. Could almost hear the whispers.

Who is she?

What on earth is someone like her doing here?

Carrie had thought she'd be totally cowed but strangely, with Massimo by her side, she felt her spine straightening and her head coming up. She felt the protection of his very solid presence beside her like a forcefield.

When they reached the next level Carrie was glad they'd lingered in the reception foyer for a while, giving her time to prepare her for the grandeur that awaited: a ballroom bigger than any space she'd ever been in, in her life.

Massive French doors were open to terraces outside. The glittering crowd mingled under thousands of lights that seemed to be hung by invisible threads over their heads. Flowers and greenery bloomed all around them, giving the effect of a garden inside. A small orchestra played on a dais in one corner.

They weren't alone for long. People started to approach Massimo in a steady stream. Out of nowhere, one of Massimo's assistants that Carrie recognised materialised by his side, and she could hear him reminding Massimo of who people were before they got to him.

Massimo introduced her to everyone, and they were perfectly civil, but their eyes and their attention skated over her. She wasn't interesting to them. Certainly not recognisable. That suited her just fine.

She was fascinated with how Massimo expertly gave his full attention to everyone, getting what he wanted to know from them, or imparting some information, and then moved onto the next person. He had the effortless diplomacy of a statesman.

When they moved into the adjacent space a short time later, Carrie realised it was a dining room. Lots of circular tables with elaborate floral centrepieces. They were led to one near the front, where there was a small stage with a podium.

Food was served and it looked surprisingly hearty. Not what she would have expected at an event like this. She picked up her fork, suddenly realising she was starving, but when she looked around her she put it down again quickly, her face growing hot at her faux pas.

Massimo turned away from the man he'd been talking to on his other side. 'Something wrong?'

Carrie whispered, 'No one is eating.'

'And you're hungry?'

She looked at him. 'I haven't eaten since this morning.' It had taken most of the day to make her look presentable.

Massimo picked up his fork and speared a large morsel of food, putting it into his mouth. It was almost comical the way everyone else at the table suddenly followed suit.

He winked discreetly at Carrie.

She ate some food and instantly felt a little less light-headed. A woman near her leaned towards her. She was older, and she had a pleasant expression on her face—less frozen than most of the women she'd noticed.

'And what's your name, dear?'

Carrie's mouth went dry. Was she meant to make conversation with these people? With her less than refined accent?

But before she could answer Massimo was saying smoothly, 'My apologies, Dorothy, this is Carrie Taylor.'

The woman's eyes lit up. 'One of the Taylors from Long Island? Now which one are you, dear? One of John's daughters?'

Massimo put a discreet hand on Carrie's arm. He said, 'No, she's not related to those Taylors. She's from London— that's where we met.'

Where we met.

As if she really was with him. As if she wasn't just an employee doing him a favour that crossed several boundaries.

Carrie could feel an urge to give in to this fantasy that somehow she was a peer of Massimo's and they'd met at an event like this, but it was too much of a stretch for her. She'd had the life she'd had, and there was some comfort in knowing that she didn't regret it. It had made her who she was and she was proud of that.

The older woman's face immediately blanked, now that Carrie was no longer someone she could relate to. She turned away to the man on her right.

Massimo said, *sotto voce*, 'Don't mind Dorothy…she's old school. She only knows how to talk to people descended from the pilgrims on the *Mayflower*.'

Carrie stifled a giggle. Then Massimo's thigh touched hers under the table. It was fleeting, but it sent a shockwave of arousal through her body. The urge to giggle faded and her appetite fled. She left the rest of the food on her plate.

She *had* to control herself. She couldn't allow herself to believe that this was somehow real. She'd believed in a fantasy before, and the consequences had been tragic. She'd promised herself she'd never be so blind again.

The waiters discreetly cleared their plates. There was a tapping sound on a microphone and then a woman stood on the podium and spoke a few words, welcoming everyone, before she said, 'There's no point in my saying another word—I might as well hand it over to the man best qualified to tell us more about his vision for this space, Massimo Black, Lord Linden.'

There was thunderous applause and Massimo was striding onto the stage before Carrie had even registered that he was gone from her side.

He was mesmerising. He shushed the crowd with a self-deprecating expression and then not a sound could be heard except for his deep voice as he spoke with clear confidence. And Carrie wasn't even taking in half of what he was saying about wanting to create a space that would be solely available for charitable causes…wanting to give organisations no excuse not to raise funds.

'And to that end,' Massimo was saying now, 'I will cover the costs of every event held here for the first year…'

Applause broke out and Massimo put up a hand.

'But that's only if a certain threshold is met tonight with charitable donations. I like to ensure that people feel galvanised into raising as much money as possible.'

He smiled the smile of a shark, and it reminded Carrie for a moment of who he was.

The applause was mingled with wry chuckles and some good-natured heckles. Carrie heard someone from the table behind her saying, 'Typical Massimo Black—generous, but always with a ruthless edge.'

Massimo put his hands together. 'Thank you. Now, please enjoy the rest of the evening and start conceiving all the events you will host. I look forward to the invitations.'

He was a consummate diplomat. And he was the most intimidating and charismatic man in the room. And now he was stepping down from the stage and walking towards where Carrie sat, his eyes on her.

Along with everyone else. Wondering who on earth she was. Why on earth she was with him. But she didn't have time to worry about what everyone was thinking because she was so consumed by that dark gaze.

Massimo stopped beside her and held out his hand. 'Shall we?'

Carrie wanted to ask, *Shall we what?* But, aware of people looking and listening, she stood up and put her hand in his.

Her skin broke into goosebumps as he led her away from the table and she noticed everyone else getting up. As if they'd been waiting for his signal.

They moved through the dining room to yet another glittering room. A ballroom. Soft lighting and lots of gilded mirrors made it seem as if it was shimmering.

Carrie couldn't help a little sigh of awe. If someone pinched her right now she was sure she'd wake up and not just be back in London, in her little suite of rooms in Massimo's house, but back on the council estate where she'd lived with her mother.

There was a different band in here, playing music that was smooth and slow. Rhythmic. Carrie only realised what was happening when Massimo stopped, drew her in front of him and pulled her close, putting one arm around her back and taking her other hand in his and moving it up close to his chest.

Dancing.

She stiffened. And then, when he started to move and she had no choice but to follow him, she darted a look at everyone else milling about the room around them.

'I can't dance,' she hissed.

A toxic memory inserted itself into her head—her husband smiling at her indulgently, but with an edge, saying, *'Bless you, Carrie, you just don't have any natural grace.'*

'Neither can I—I've been faking it for years,' Massimo said, pulling her out of the past and back to the terrifying present. 'Just follow my lead.'

Carrie had no choice but to do as he said, and she found that once the panic started to dissolve her feet were moving of their own volition, in some approximation of dancing.

His arms felt very secure.

She felt safe.

It was a rogue thought, flashing through her mind and going again before she could refute it.

Other people were dancing too. Laughing. Chatting. Carrie relaxed a little more into Massimo's embrace. She let the music wash over her...through her. She had to stop herself from moving even closer. She wanted to press her body against his. It made her tremble.

'You're doing great, Carrie.'

She looked up at him and couldn't look away.

Massimo nearly stopped dancing. Carrie's eyes were huge, and full of more expression than he could remember seeing in any woman's face. Usually what he saw was fawning. Guile. Calculation. Hard cynicism.

What he saw in Carrie's eyes was totally unguarded. Awe. Fear. *Desire.* His body thrummed with need. She felt like steel and silk in his arms. Incredibly strong but also vulnerable.

He couldn't take his gaze off her mouth. He wanted to cover it with his own. Brand her lips with a kiss so deep and carnal that she would be left in no doubt that he wanted her.

'I want you.' It came out of his mouth on a raw breath. He only realised he'd spoken out loud when Carrie stopped moving.

Her eyes widened with shock and her cheeks went pink. 'You...what?'

But she didn't wait for him to say anything. She pulled free of his embrace and pushed through the crowd.

Massimo cursed. What the hell was wrong with him?

He followed her.

CHAPTER FOUR

CARRIE BLINDLY MADE her way through the crowd and off the dance floor to the closest escape route she could see. Open French doors leading out to a terrace. She needed air. Blood was thundering in her head.

The terrace was mercifully quiet. For once she didn't notice the city laid out before her, buildings soaring tall on either side.

Massimo's words reverberated in her head: *I want you... I want you...* Away from him now, though, she wondered if she'd misheard him. A different kind of heat crept into her face. Shame.

Did he overwhelm her so much that she'd conjured up the words that she wanted to hear?

'Carrie.'

He was behind her. Her skin prickled. She composed herself and turned around, forcing a breezy smile. 'Sorry, the heat got to me.'

I thought I heard you say you wanted me.

'I needed some air.'

She was avoiding his eye, fixing her gaze somewhere around his jaw. It was tight. A muscle popped.

He said, 'Look, I'm sorry about that.'

Reluctantly she looked at him. His face was in shadow. All angles and edges. 'Sorry about...?'

Sorry about wanting her, of course!

He grimaced. 'I was thinking it. I didn't realise I'd spoken out loud.'

Carrie's heart thumped. 'Thinking that…?'

'I want you.'

He'd said it again. She hadn't been dreaming or hallucinating. She felt trembly. She was glad the wall of the terrace was behind her, giving her some sense of support.

'I don't know what to say.'

Massimo came and stood next to her, facing out towards the city. Hands on the wall. 'You don't have to say anything. I've overstepped the mark.' He looked at her. 'You're under no obligation, Carrie. You can leave now if you wish. My driver will take you back to the apartment. I won't put you in this position again.'

He turned around and went back into the ballroom. Impossible to miss. He was soon accosted by an eager crowd.

Carrie knew he was giving her an opportunity to restore the boundaries of their relationship. To go back to how it had been. But something seismic had just happened. He'd told her he wanted her. He desired her.

Massimo Black, an earl and a lord, one of the world's most charismatic and enigmatic men, wanted *her*. Carrie Taylor. A woman who had seen and experienced the rougher edges of life since birth. A woman who had been brought low by her own vulnerability and hollowed out by grief.

Sometimes Carrie felt much older than her twenty-six years. She'd never really indulged in anything frivolous and just for her. She'd never had the luxury of being so selfish. She'd gone from grieving for her mother to embarking on a relationship that would dominate her life until tragedy finally ended it.

She'd never felt the range of sensations that Massimo could

evoke with just a look or brief touch. Not even with her husband, a man she'd believed she loved.

Just now, in Massimo's arms… It was almost embarrassing how aware she'd been of every inch of her body. The way her breasts had felt heavy. Her gut tight with tension. And lower, between her legs, she'd felt achy with a longing she'd never experienced before.

Massimo was still standing in the crowd, towering above almost everyone else. He was surrounded by people. Women. Yet in that moment he cut a very lonely figure to Carrie. She felt no pity. What she did feel—shockingly—was a sense of possessiveness. Especially when one of the women put a hand on his arm to get his attention.

Acting on instinct, not thinking of what her actions might mean, Carrie walked through the crowd to Massimo. As if sensing her, he turned his head and saw her. She saw a flare in his eyes. A flare of heat. And…gratitude?

He put out a hand, dislodging the woman's fingers from his arm. Carrie took his hand, feeling ridiculously thrilled by the attention. He pulled her into his side, hand tight on her waist.

So this was what it felt like. To be chosen by Massimo. Like basking in the benevolent warmth of the sun, heat prickling along her veins.

He introduced Carrie to some more people but they all blurred into one at some point, and her cheeks hurt from smiling. Her feet were also killing her in the high heels.

Eventually he said, 'Ready?'

Carrie blinked and looked around. There was no one else waiting to talk to Massimo. The crowd had thinned out. Only a few people were left on the dance floor.

She thought of that word. *Ready.* Was she ready for whatever she'd tacitly put in motion by not leaving? Not in a million years. But she knew that she'd prefer to be here than back at the apartment feeling a sense of regret.

Carrie looked up at Massimo. She wanted to project cool confidence, but in that moment, under his penetrating gaze, her insides quivered.

'The truth is, I'm not sure.'

Massimo lifted her hand to his mouth and pressed his lips to her palm. A touch that felt shockingly intimate considering that up till now every physical interaction between them had been totally solicitous.

'Nothing will happen that you're not comfortable with, Carrie. I can promise you that.'

Something eased inside her. She hadn't expected Massimo to be so unapologetically direct. He wasn't trying to charm her, or flatter her, or guilt her into anything.

He led her from the room, saying goodbye to a few people en route. His car and driver were waiting outside. The evening was still and warm. It felt as if the world was holding its breath for something.

Carrie shook her head at herself. She was being ridiculous. The car was moving now. She tried to pretend she was absorbed with what was happening outside the windows, but she was attuned to every tiny move Massimo made. His scent. The fact that he'd undone his bow-tie and the top button of his shirt. The fact that he lounged beside her, long legs sprawled out.

In contrast she felt incredibly uptight. Tense. Suddenly wondering what on earth she was thinking. She couldn't possibly do this. What had she even agreed to do? Sleep with Massimo? Panic started to rise. If they slept together she'd lose her job! She really hadn't thought this through at all.

She turned to Massimo—and promptly forgot what she was going to say. They were pulling up outside his building now. He took her hand again and led her inside. To his private elevator. He and the concierge exchanged words. She didn't even take it in. His hand was tight on hers, as if he sensed her vacillating turmoil.

The elevator ascended. Doors opened. Carrie's breath was coming short and fast. If she wasn't careful she'd hyperventilate. She took a deep breath. She had nothing to fear here. Massimo wouldn't force her...

A sliver of cold went down her back. But how did she know that for sure? She'd witnessed how a man could turn into something else entirely.

Massimo let her hand go to enter the apartment and Carrie put some distance between them. She put her bag down on a table. The lights were low. She had her back to Massimo, but she sensed he wasn't coming closer.

She turned around. He was near the door. Jacket open. Face cast in shadow. But she could still see its hard angles. The sensual curve of his mouth.

'Carrie...?'

She bit her lip and then said, 'Look... I don't want to be a tease...but I'm not sure this is such a good idea.'

He shook his head. 'You're not being a tease. No woman is ever a tease, Carrie.'

Another knot inside her eased. 'We haven't really spoken about what this is...'

He stepped forward, out of the shadows. She could see his face now. It held a stark expression she'd never noticed before.

He said, 'It's desire. Mutual desire.'

'But how...? Why now?'

'I think it was always inevitable...we just didn't acknowledge it till now. The first day I met you I noticed you, Carrie. But I managed to push it away...ignore it. Until I couldn't any more.'

To know that he had felt a similar sense of awareness from day one made something shift inside Carrie. Gave her a sense of confidence. Nevertheless, she felt compelled to be the voice of reason when it felt as if everything she knew was going up in flames around her.

She shook her head faintly. 'I don't know if this is really a good idea...'

Massimo took another step closer. Now he looked serious. 'You're probably right.'

Carrie's stomach dropped. And that told her all she needed to know about how she really felt about the potential consequences.

'But...' she said, and stopped, not wanting to sound too desperate. She forced a light tone into her voice, 'We're both adults, it's not as if I'm under any illusions about what this would be...'

Massimo frowned. 'What do you mean?'

Now Carrie felt self-conscious. 'I know that it would be one night only. You don't ever do more than one night...with a woman.'

Massimo's face had turned to stone. Completely expressionless. Then he said, 'You're right. I don't.'

'So this would be no different.'

After a beat he said, 'No, it wouldn't.'

Carrie didn't like the little twist near her heart when she heard that, but it was important to let him know that she wasn't some starry-eyed fool who didn't know the score.

'Okay, then.'

Massimo's expression relaxed. 'Okay, then?'

Carrie's heart thumped. She felt gauche. Embarrassed by the fact that she didn't know how to be sultry. Seductive.

Massimo seemed to take pity on her. He said, 'Turn around.'

She did so, relieved to escape that gaze. She could see Massimo's tall figure reflected in the window across the room. She could feel him come closer behind her and shivered a little.

'Cold?' he asked.

She shook her head.

He knew that she wasn't shivering from the cold. He was probably enjoying watching her less than sophisticated reaction. She would have scowled, but he moved even closer, and now she could feel the heat from his body licking around her.

She quivered with anticipation. She had no idea what he was going to do, where he was going to touch her. But then she felt him touch her hair, starting to take the pins out. Gently.

Bit by bit, the mass of her hair came undone and tumbled around her shoulders. Then Massimo put his hands in her hair and massaged her scalp. Carrie's eyes closed. She didn't know what she'd been expecting but it hadn't been this, and it felt good enough to turn her bones to rubber.

'Your hair...' Massimo said from behind her. 'I never expected your hair to be like this. You never leave it down.'

Carrie struggled to wrap her tongue around words. 'Not at work, no.'

He put his hands on her shoulders and slowly turned her around. She felt light-headed. Dreamy, but wide awake at the same time. Languorous, but energised.

'Do you mind if I take off my shoes?' she asked.

'Let me.'

Before she could stop him Massimo was down at her feet, reaching under the silken folds of her dress. She lifted her foot and he slipped off one shoe, then the other. It dropped her a few inches, but he was still at her feet. His hand was around her ankle. He looked up at her and her throat went dry at the sight of this beautiful man, kneeling at her feet.

Never taking his eyes off hers, he moved his hand up from her ankle, around her calf and to her knee. She had to put a hand on his shoulder to stay steady.

His hand moved up the back of her thigh.

Her skin tightened all over and a sharp arrowing of need went straight between her legs.

His fingers brushed against the lace of her underwear.

To her dismay and relief, Massimo took his hand away and stood up, letting her dress fall. He didn't touch her.

For a split-second Carrie wondered if he'd just realised he was making a terrible mistake. But then he said, 'Carrie, if you want to stop, just say the word and I'll stop. It doesn't matter at what point.'

Carrie had a very unwelcome flashback to her husband, saying nastily, *'At some point men can't stop. It's physically impossible. So don't put me in that position again. It's your fault.'*

She went cold.

Massimo put a hand on her arm. 'Carrie? What is it?'

She shook her head. She did not want those memories here. This was not the place for them. This was the present and her new future opening up. She wouldn't go back to that dark place.

She looked up at Massimo, lifted her chin. 'I'm not an innocent. I was married…but it's been a while.'

Massimo frowned slightly. 'Your husband…was he…?'

'I don't want to talk about him.' Carrie cut him off sharply.

He seemed to accept that. 'We'll take it slow…okay?'

Carrie nodded. Glad that she'd at least warned him not to expect fireworks. He put a finger under her chin and his head dipped towards hers. A burst of nerves suddenly assailed her.

She blurted out, 'You know, I'm really not very good at… this.'

Massimo paused inches from her mouth. His mouth quirked. 'Let me be the judge of that.'

Carrie was about to say, *That's what I'm afraid of*, but her words were swallowed by Massimo's mouth settling over hers, stealing her breath and every conscious thought in her head.

It wasn't a kiss. It was a claiming. It was elemental. Carrie opened her mouth unconsciously, allowing Massimo access. Allowing him to delve deep and find all her secrets, feel her reticence. Her inexperience.

But she couldn't worry about any of that now. She was acting on instinct. An instinct as old as time. An ancient dance. She was freed of all concerns. There was only here and now and the hot intensity entwining her with this man.

His hands were in her hair, holding her so that he could explore even deeper, and then he was tipping her face up so that he could trail his lips along her jaw and down along her neck to her shoulder.

The dress felt too tight around her breasts. She couldn't breathe. She wanted to break free of every constriction. Without even commanding her hands to do it, she was pushing Massimo's jacket off his shoulders and down his arms, pulling away his tie and throwing it aside, opening his shirt to reveal his chest, broad and magnificent. Mouth-wateringly masculine and hard-muscled.

She'd never experienced such a carnal feeling before. This man was hers and she wanted him. Any insecurities were burned to ash by the strength of her desire.

For a moment Massimo pulled back, and Carrie looked up at him, breathing harshly. Her hands were on his chest. She was marvelling at his heat and perfection. Her mouth felt swollen. Her heart was pumping so hard she could almost hear it.

Massimo looked down at her, his shirt half on, half off, hair mussed. Eyes burning.

He reached out and cupped her jaw and said, almost as if to himself, 'Who *are* you?'

Massimo was fairly certain he'd never met this woman before. Her hair was a wild tangle around her bare shoulders. Cheeks slashed with colour. Eyes huge and glowing like two jewels. Mouth a lush, plump invitation to keep kissing her and never stop.

Carrie swallowed. 'I'm just me…no one special.'

Everything in Massimo rejected that. She was temptation incarnate. She was fascinating. And he wanted her with a hunger he couldn't ever remember experiencing before.

He caught one of her hands and led her out of the reception area and through the apartment to the elevator. Inside, he put her apart from him and watched her as it ascended the short distance. He knew that if he so much as touched her now he wouldn't stop and they'd make love right there.

He thought for a second of what she'd said—that she wasn't innocent, she'd been married, and how she'd cut off his attempt to ask her about her husband.

It occurred to him that she'd cut him off because she couldn't bear to talk about him—because it pained her to talk about him. Because she'd loved him.

That thought shouldn't affect Massimo, but it did. Like a little sharp burr under his skin. He knew the awful pain of losing someone you loved, and the thought that she'd loved someone that much sent something dark and incomprehensible through him.

Before he could try and figure it out, the doors of the elevator opened. He welcomed the distraction, took Carrie's hand and led her, barefoot, into his bedroom.

She stalled. He looked at her.

She said, 'You don't usually…you know…in your own bedroom.'

No. He didn't. He usually avoided bringing his lovers into his personal space. But nothing was usual about this situation. He found he didn't really care that Carrie was in his bedroom. She already inhabited his personal space, so maybe that was what made it different? He certainly wasn't prepared to analyse it right now. He just wanted her.

'We can go to your bedroom if that's what you'd prefer?'

She shook her head and her hair slipped down over her shoulders, resting close to the swells of her breasts. 'No, it's fine…it doesn't matter. I don't know why I even said that.'

Carrie was kicking herself.

Just stop talking!

As if she needed to *remind* Massimo that this was not his usual modus operandi!

Her hand was still in his. He led her over to the bed. The room was cast in shadows and she was grateful. She felt far too exposed.

He said, 'Turn around.'

She obeyed, with a little shiver. What was it about him telling her to turn around? The fact that she didn't know what he was going to do? The fact that she was prepared to trust him to such an extent was seismic, but she did. It was instinctual and bone-deep. Perhaps four years of living alongside this man and observing him had given her more of an insight into him than she'd realised.

His fingers touched the top of her back as he moved her hair to one side, over one shoulder. Deftly he undid the necklace and lifted it from her neck, putting it down on the bed-side table. Then his fingers trailed down the centre of her back to where the dress's zip started.

He started to pull it down and Carrie's breath grew shorter and sharper. She wasn't wearing a bra because the dress had enough support. It loosened around her chest and fell away as Massimo pulled the zip all the way down to just above her buttocks. With a little tug he pulled it over her hips, and it fell to the ground around her feet in a pool of satin. Now she was naked except for her very flimsy underwear.

'Carrie...'

She slowly turned around, her arms over her breasts in a self-conscious gesture. Massimo gently pulled them down and she heard his harsh intake of breath. She was too afraid to look at him. Not sure what she might see.

He reached out and traced the curve of one breast. Her nipples puckered into hard nubs. She had to bite her lip.

He said, 'You are...more than anything I could have imagined...'

Carrie couldn't quite fathom that he'd actually said that to her. But before she could let herself be overwhelmed by everything that was happening she reached for his shirt and pulled it all the way off and down.

He was now bare-chested, and he was beautiful. Power-ful. Awesome. She reached out and put her hands on him again, spreading her fingers wide as if she could try and en-compass every gleaming inch of flesh. He felt like steel un-derneath her palms.

She moved her hands down, emboldened by the way he was just letting her explore him. Trailed her fingers over the ridges of his abdominals. And then down to his lean waist. Not an ounce of excess flesh.

But then her attention snagged on his trousers. Belt buckle.

She looked up and almost lost her nerve. She'd never seen such a stark expression on his face. All expression had leached away to be replaced with what she could only recognise as what she was feeling herself.

Need.

She couldn't move. She was transfixed. She heard rather than saw Massimo undo his belt, and then the sound of a button popping, the zip being lowered. Trousers dropping to the floor.

Mouth dry, Carrie looked down—and her mind blanked at the sight of Massimo's aroused body. He wrapped a hand around himself, as if he had to try and contain it.

'Get on the bed, Carrie.'

She half fell, half climbed onto the bed. Landing on her back, she looked up at Massimo, who seemed to have assumed the proportions of a mythic god. It was as if the world outside had fallen away completely and now they were in some parallel world, where nothing mattered except this man, this room and this moment.

Massimo came and rested over Carrie on both arms, muscles bunching. He bent his head and kissed her. This time it was slow and thorough. An exploration. When his tongue thrust deep it was a promise of what was to come. Between her legs she grew hot and damp…her body readying for its mate.

Massimo pulled back, as if she'd spoken that incendiary thought out loud. She looked up at him. But all he said was, 'Touch me, Carrie.'

She put her hands on him, running her palms down over his narrow hips and around to his buttocks, full and firm. One of his knees was between her legs, and with his hands he gently parted her thighs so they fell apart, opening her up to him.

Her avid gaze went to his erection. She'd never thought of that part of a man's body as particularly beautiful before. But Massimo's was. Long and thick and hard. Veins along the shaft. A thicket of dark hair at the base. Unashamedly masculine. Vital.

Unable to stop herself, she reached out and encircled him, shocked at how vulnerable he felt in her hand, yet strong. Silk over steel. He pulsed against her. A bead of moisture appeared at the tip.

She heard a small groan and wondered if it had been her or him. But then she did groan, as she felt his hand cup her between her legs. The flimsy lace was no barrier to the heat of his hand. His fingers tugged it to one side and he explored her, seeking and finding the heart of her that hadn't been touched in so long. That hadn't ever ached to be touched like this.

Sex had always felt cold to her. Tight. Uncomfortable. This was the direct opposite. She was on fire, pliable. Melting. Expanding. Opening.

Her back arched when Massimo thrust two fingers inside her. Her body was already clasping them, wanting more.

He said something guttural, and then, 'You're so responsive...'

Faint echoes of the past rang bells, reminding Carrie that once she'd been told the exact opposite. A voice sneering at her, *'You just lie there like a dead fish.'*

But the past melted away and she pushed it even further back, as Massimo's fingers moved in and out of her. Her hand tightened on him in a reflex response. He muttered a curse and took her hand away. She looked at him, feeling feverish, her hips circling in response to his hand between her legs. She barely recognised herself. Wanton. Fluid.

He took his hand away and left her for a moment. She

heard him say something about protection and put an arm across her face. She hadn't even thought of it—that was how intoxicated she was.

He came back, rolling a sheath onto his body, totally unselfconscious. He moved between her legs, pushing them even wider, and with a quick economical movement ripped her underwear and threw it aside.

'I'll buy you new ones.'

Carrie couldn't care less. She was ravenous. She welcomed Massimo between her legs. Revelled in the way he took himself in his hand again and held the tip of his body against her hot, weeping flesh before pushing in, just a little. Just the swollen head. She sucked in a breath—not at the invasion but because it felt so *right*. As if something had been missing and was now slotting home.

'Okay?' he asked.

She couldn't speak. She could only nod and put her hands on his hips.

He sank deeper, and the stretch bordered on being painful, but then it bloomed into pleasure. He started to move in and out in slow, leisurely movements, letting her get used to the sensation, letting her body adapt to his.

Carrie bit her lip as the tension grew at her core, stoked and heightened by the way Massimo's body moved in a remorseless rhythm. She could feel perspiration on her own skin and see the sheen of moisture on Massimo's.

It was so earthy. So raw. She'd never known it could be so base. Instinctively seeking relief, Carrie wrapped her legs around Massimo's waist and he slid even deeper. He came down on top of her, chest crushing her breasts, powerful buttocks moving faster now, one of his hands on her thigh, holding it against him.

She was trembling. Searching for something just of out of reach.

'That's it…come apart for me, Carrie.'

He put his mouth to her neck and bit her gently. She wanted him to bite harder. He palmed her breast and brought it to his mouth, sucking her nipple deep. She cried out, every atom of her being begging for release.

Massimo took his mouth from her breast and put a hand between them, where their bodies were joined. He touched her there and it sent shockwaves through her entire body. Shockwaves followed by an explosion of pleasure so exquisite that it bordered on being painful.

She was barely aware of Massimo's big body going still before jerking against her as he found his own release. She was undone. Torn apart and unable to piece together the sequence of events that had led to this seismic moment of pure and unadulterated bliss.

All she knew was that she'd never felt so at peace or so replete. So safe.

Silence settled over them. They were both breathing heavily. Their bodies were still joined and Carrie didn't want to let go of Massimo. She relished the sense of his heavy body on hers…in hers. Such a carnal thing. She'd be shocked at herself if she could drum up an ounce of sanity.

But slowly he moved, extricating himself.

Carrie felt a sense of loss and regret.

That was it. They'd never do this again.

But with the aftershocks of pleasure still moving through her body Carrie thought that maybe it was greedy to want to experience such transcendence again.

Emotion gripped her before she could stop it. Massimo had just restored something massive to her. The revelation that she was not cold, nor incapable of pleasure. Ever since her marriage, and in spite of knowing better, she'd always harboured a secret fear that she wouldn't ever feel sexually desirable or experience the kind of pleasure people talked about.

What she'd just experienced had exploded those fears apart. For ever.

Massimo lay still beside her. She was afraid to look at him, suddenly shy. A delicious lethargy was taking over her blood and bones, but she couldn't stop herself from saying, in a slightly hoarse voice, 'I never knew it could be so…'

Carrie's voice trailed off. But there was an answering thought in Massimo's head.

Neither did I.

He'd been having sex for years. Since well before he should have. And in all that time his first experience still stood out as being the moment that had blown his mind. Thanks to a very experienced older lover who had promptly dumped him once she'd taken the innocence of the legendary Linden heir. One of Massimo's first lessons in reality.

Since that first time sex had been pleasurable, yes, but never transcendent.

What had happened just now…*had* been transcendent. And he couldn't understand it.

From the moment he'd started to undress Carrie his brain had fused with white heat, and it was only returning to some semblance of normality now.

He felt drunk. Drunk on an overload of pleasure.

He turned his head and looked at her. She was asleep, curled on one side, facing him. Hair spread in a tangle around her head and on the pillow. Hands up under her chin in a curiously childlike gesture.

But the shape of her mouth, still swollen from his kisses,

mitigated any childish gesture and was a reminder of how adult she was.

Massimo didn't have transcendent sex. He didn't *need* transcendent sex. He didn't need to transcend anything. That was why the Linden family fortune was still intact. Growing. Thriving. Precisely because, unlike his parents and his brother, he kept his feet firmly on the ground.

He'd never had the luxury of that kind of self-indulgence. From an early age he'd always known that he had to be the one to keep a clear head.

A memory came back out of nowhere. The housekeeper from Linden Hall—one of the few people in Massimo's life who had been a consistent benevolent presence. During one particularly chaotic party weekend at the hall he and his brother had been in the kitchen. She'd taken him aside and said, 'You don't have to live like this, Massimo. One day this will all pass to you and it'll be yours to keep. You can do things differently.'

Massimo could remember looking at his brother, who'd only been about ten, playing with toy cars on the other side of the kitchen while loud music still thumped upstairs. He'd seen his brother stop playing and look up with a yearning expression on his face, and he could remember vowing in that moment never to disrespect his legacy. To protect his brother from the excesses of their parents.

He'd managed to keep one promise at least.

A familiar hollow ache made his chest tight.

He pushed the memories aside.

Not now.

He looked at the woman beside him. For the first time in his life he wanted more than just a transitory meaningless encounter that left him momentarily satisfied but dissatisfied again within hours. He knew that he wouldn't feel dissatisfied after this. He would feel even hungrier. It was already building inside him—the clawing urge to join his body with hers again and seek oblivion.

He'd never wanted that with another woman. He'd always been happy to walk away.

Maybe this was what his parents and his brother had chased? This pull of pure pleasure? Maybe now it was his turn to indulge?

Carrie stirred on the bed. She opened her eyes a crack. Then a little more. She looked deliciously tousled. Sleepy. *Sexy*. Massimo sat back against the pillow. His body was already stirring. Again.

She came up on one elbow. She looked shy. 'We're still in your room...'

'You're very fixated on where we are.'

This was new territory for Massimo. Lingering in bed with a lover. But he found that his desire for Carrie was drowning out any concerns he should be heeding.

She pulled the sheet up over her body. He wanted to pull it back down. Put her on her back. Slide between her legs again. He gritted his jaw.

'I can go to my own room...' she said.

'Do you want to go to your own room?'

'Maybe I...should?'

'That's not answering my question.'

A flare of something made her eyes glow bright green. A flash of the personality that she usually hid. Massimo found it mesmerising.

She sat up, pulling the sheet over her chest. 'You don't do this.'

'As you keep telling me.'

'Are you saying you want me to stay?'

Massimo's gut clenched.

You really don't do this, prompted a little voice.

But he ignored it. 'I want you again.'

'I—' She stopped. Her cheeks flushed.

A sound like a giggle came out of her mouth and she put her hand up, embarrassed. Then she took it down. She was serious. And shy. An intoxicating combination.

She said, 'I want you too.'

Desire surged. Massimo reached out and lazily flicked the sheet away from her body. 'Then we won't be needing this, will we?'

CHAPTER FIVE

WHEN CARRIE WOKE up she was totally disorientated and still drowsy. It was bright outside. She wasn't in her own room. Her body had never felt so heavy. Or so tender. Especially between her legs...

She was fully awake in an instant. The bed beside her was empty. She sat up, holding the sheet to her chest. Someone had pulled it over her. *Massimo.*

Carrie had no idea what time it was, and she had that awful stomach-swooping sensation of having overslept. There was no sound at all. The en suite bathroom was empty but there was still a hint of steam in the air, as if it had been used not that long ago.

She spotted her dress, carefully laid over the back of a chair, and groaned when she recalled Massimo ripping off her underwear. She gingerly got out of the bed and found a robe hanging on the back of the bathroom door. It was still warm. Instant heat flooded Carrie's veins and she had to resist the urge to bury her nose in the fabric.

She saw the glittering necklace on the bedside table but couldn't see her underwear anywhere, so she gathered up the dress and shoes and crept out of the bedroom, using the stairs to go to her own room on the lower level.

Once in her room, she shucked off the robe and dived into the shower, turning the water to hot. She closed her eyes and lifted her face to the spray—but suddenly she was inundated with a slew of X-rated images from the previous night.

The second time they'd made love Massimo had almost forgotten to use protection and had thrust inside her before he'd remembered, with a curse. The thought that she could enflame such a man was seriously intoxicating. She had to put her hands on the wall of the shower, suddenly feeling unsteady at the memory of such passion.

The significance of what had happened hit her again. The fact that one night with Massimo had shown her in no uncertain terms that she was a woman capable of feeling intense pleasure and—she blushed—giving it. If Massimo's reaction had been anything to go by...

But it was over now. One night. Massimo never deviated in that practice.

She went cold in spite of the hot spray.

The thought of never again experiencing the sublime rapture of last night sent a skewer of pain through Carrie's gut. Then she felt disgusted with herself. She wasn't like the lovers she'd seen over the years with desperation in their eyes. She knew better.

She got out of the shower and briskly dried her hair, tied it back and put on her work clothes. She needed armour.

She went to the kitchen and the chef was there. Carrie felt as if she was branded with a scarlet letter on her forehead—H for Harlot—but he just said, 'Morning, Carrie, having some breakfast?'

She shook her head. She had no appetite. Not until she'd seen Massimo and got over that first hurdle. 'No thanks, is Lord—I mean, Mr Black, here?'

The chef indicated with his head. 'In the dining room.'

Carrie took a deep breath and straightened her shirt. She

was wearing trousers and flat shoes. Cool, clean, crisp. Professional.

When she went in, Massimo was hidden behind a newspaper. She cleared her throat. He lowered the paper and she felt a wash of heat go out to every extremity from her core. He looked…amazing. Clean-shaven. Hair still a little damp.

He put the paper down, his eyes flicking over her clothes. 'Good morning.'

Carrie was almost struck dumb. 'I… Good morning…can I get you anything?'

'What's going on?'

'What do you mean?'

His hand indicated her clothes. 'You're dressed for work.'

'Of course I am. How else would I be dressed?'

Massimo reached over and pulled out a chair. 'Sit down… have some breakfast.'

'But I don't ever eat breakfast with you.'

'You do now.'

Carrie sat down, bemused. She'd expected Massimo to be professional, business as usual. Brisk. But he was looking at her with a light in his eyes that didn't make her think of being brisk *or* professional.

'Coffee?'

Carrie blinked. Massimo was holding up a pot. Her boss was offering her coffee. 'Yes, please.'

He poured her a fragrant cup. Then he held up a plate of pastries. She took a croissant.

Suddenly she blurted out, 'This feels wrong. I shouldn't be here…like this.'

'Like what?'

Carrie felt a spurt of irritation at the way he was behaving so obtusely. 'Like a guest.'

The corner of Massimo's mouth twitched. 'I think we burned any such formalities to the ground last night.'

Mindful of the chef, not too far away, Carrie hissed, 'But you don't *do* this.'

Massimo rolled his eyes. 'This again...'

Carrie sat back. 'You don't have breakfast with them the morning after.'

Massimo took a sip of his own coffee, unconcerned. 'That's *them*. This is you—and now.'

Carrie's heart thumped. A little rogue inside her made her say, 'You're saying I'm different?'

His gaze sharpened on her. 'This whole situation is different. But I'm not offering anything more, Carrie. I made that decision a long time ago, and nothing and no one will convince me to change my mind. Let me be very clear: this lasts for as long as it lasts and then it will be over. I have no intention of making a long-term commitment to anyone.'

Why? The word hovered on Carrie's tongue, but anyone with an ounce of intelligence would be able to deduce from this man's well-documented history why he might be averse to making any long-term commitment. Not to mention whatever other personal reasons he had.

And in many ways—albeit for completely different reasons—she felt the same. She too had vowed never again to enter into a union that might destroy her.

Then she frowned when what he'd said fully sank in. *'This lasts for as long as it lasts.'*

Carefully, she asked, 'Are you saying that this...isn't it?'

Massimo sat back in his chair. 'I'm due to go to Brazil for the next few weeks. Rio de Janeiro. I have a conference to attend and then I was going to take a break.'

'I saw that on your schedule.'

She was due to go back to London when he was in South America.

'I want you to come with me.'

Carrie would have choked if there had been anything in her mouth

'You want me to come with you?' she repeated.

He nodded.

'As your housekeeper?'

He shook his head. 'No, as my lover.'

Carrie went very still. But inside she didn't feel still. She felt so many things she couldn't begin to decipher them. Confusion, excitement, trepidation. *Relief.* He still wanted her. She would experience the sublime again.

You'll lose yourself, pointed out a fearful voice.

'I don't think that's such a good idea.'

Carrie wasn't sure how she was managing to sound so cool and assured when she was still reeling and her insides were knotting and fizzing.

'If you agree to come with me it will be in a personal capacity. Not professional. But of course I will not stop your pay. When we leave Brazil you can decide how you want to proceed. You can continue to work for me or you can move on. I will give you excellent references. You will have no problem finding other work, if that's what you wish.'

Carrie felt prickly at the way he seemed to have it all worked out. 'You wouldn't have a problem with me resuming my role in a professional capacity after our affair?' Nor, apparently, with letting her go.

'Not unless you did.'

One of his lovers, upon being told that Massimo had already left the country by the time she'd woken, had said, *'Wow, he really is as cold as they say...'*

Carrie needed to remember that. She was dealing with a

consummate player—even if he didn't end up splashed across the tabloids. This knowledge would protect her.

She wanted Massimo. For as long as he wanted her. What he'd given her last night—shown her about herself—was too seductive for her not to want to experience again. She knew she was weak, but this time her weakness felt like a strength. This would be for *her*.

'If I did agree, I wouldn't want you to keep paying me for the duration. It would feel…wrong. If I come with you it will be of my own accord and it will have nothing to do with our professional relationship. As for what happens afterwards… I'll see how I feel.'

In the past, she hadn't had a voice. She'd let it be silenced under layers of grief, confusion, insecurity and fear. She wouldn't let that happen again.

Massimo inclined his head, 'As you wish—and of course it'll be your decision as to what happens, Carrie.'

She felt heady, going toe to toe with Massimo and holding her own. She felt strong for the first time in a long time. She'd known that she was stronger, but she hadn't really *felt* it like this before now.

Buoyed up by that surge of power and confidence, Carrie spoke before she had time to change her mind. 'Okay, then, I'll come with you.'

Massimo found himself mesmerised by Carrie's reaction to Rio de Janeiro.

They were driving along the famous seafront and the tang of sea salt and sensuality was in the air. Carrie turned to look at him. She was wearing knee-length shorts and a sleeveless white shirt under a jacket. Mint-green. Clothes of a lover. Not her uniform. Because she was no longer his employee.

Massimo waited for a feeling of regret to hit him, but it didn't.

Her hair was down, long and tousled over her shoulders, and she went pink in the cheeks when she registered him studying her.

'You must think I'm very gauche.'

Massimo shook his head, surprised at the strength of his reaction on hearing her putting herself down. 'Not at all. This city should take everyone's breath away each time they see it.'

'But not yours.'

Her mouth quirked and Massimo had to fight the urge to haul her over onto his lap. He took his eyes off her mouth and shook his head, a familiar feeling of pain gripping his chest.

'The last time I was here my brother was here too. He was...a distraction. He had a tendency to cause a little chaos wherever he went, so I spent most of my time cleaning up his messes.'

'He died very young.'

'Ricardo died *too* young,' Massimo said grimly.

When he'd gone to identify his brother's body at the morgue in Monte Carlo, after the crash, there hadn't been one blemish or mark on his beautiful face. He'd looked as if he was sleeping. Such a waste. Such a toxic legacy. Such a failure on his behalf to save his brother.

'How old were you?'

Massimo swallowed the ball in his chest. 'Twenty-two.'

'You were young too.'

'Old enough to know that my brother had a death wish.'

'It must have been hard to watch him self-destruct.'

Massimo's chest felt tight. 'The hardest. The worst thing is knowing I could have done more to stop it.'

Carrie shook her head. 'I doubt that. If someone is hellbent on destroying themselves then they're the only ones who can stop it. When they want to. No power on earth can stop them.'

'You sound like you talk from experience.'

Carrie shook her head again. 'Not personally. I just grew up in an area where I saw it all around me. Luckily my mother kept me away from malign influences as much as possible. I saw people self-destruct, but I also saw amazing examples of people pulling themselves free—and, believe me, they had a lot less to live for than your brother did. So it can be done… but it needs to come from the person themselves.'

'Your mother was strong?'

Carrie nodded. 'The strongest.'

'Your father…?'

She tensed visibly. 'He left her as soon as he knew she was pregnant. She found out that he was married with a family. She hadn't known. She'd hoped that…'

Carrie stopped talking. Massimo could fill in the blanks. Betrayal and dashed dreams. He was surprised at the anger he felt towards the man for leaving them both like that.

After a moment, Carrie observed, 'You never went down the same self-destructive road as your brother?'

'No. I knew I had to be responsible because no one else was. I had a legacy to protect for both of us—even if he seemed intent on destroying it.'

'You made a choice, Massimo. You could have easily decided the easier path was to lose yourself.'

He'd never thought about it like that before. And suddenly he realised that they had veered into very personal territory.

Normally Massimo shut down any attempt to talk about his family—especially his brother. But she hadn't asked. He'd brought it up. He realised he trusted her. A revelation that he chose to push aside for now.

The car pulled to a stop outside a building and he said, 'We're here.'

Massimo led Carrie up to his apartment—a penthouse with panoramic views of Ipanema Beach in front and Christ the Redeemer on Mount Corcovado behind them.

'Wow...'

Carrie's eyes were wide as she took in the sleek modern furnishings and the bright pop art on the walls. She let go of his hand and walked around. Massimo opened the sliding doors that led out to a terrace, where there was a seating area and a pool.

'Wow...' she breathed again, looking out at the view.

Massimo took her hand, saying, 'And if you come up here...'

He led her up to the very top, where there was a bar area. Ric's favourite place to party. But he knew she wouldn't be interested in that.

He pointed into the distance. 'Christ The Redeemer.'

'Oh, wow...' And then, as if she'd just realised what she'd said, 'Sorry, I sound so stupid... But this is just...'

'Wow. Yes, I know.'

She scrunched up her nose a little. 'Don't take this the wrong way, but I wouldn't have had you down as owning an apartment like this.'

'That's because it wasn't always mine. It was Ric's.'

'Ah...'

'Makes more sense now?' he said dryly.

'A little.'

Massimo said, 'He loved it here. It appealed to his party side.'

'Is that why you didn't sell it?'

'I was going to, and then I realised that this place reminded me of the best of him. The joyous, excited boy he was. Before the drugs and excess took over.'

In spite of his grief, this place made Massimo feel less jaded. His brother had loved it here. Maybe that was one of the reasons. And he felt close to his memory here. Strangely, for the first time in a long time, thoughts of Ricardo weren't weighing on him as heavily. He felt lighter.

Maybe it was this woman? Maybe it was the mind-blowing sex that only seemed to be getting better? He knew that should be freaking him out on some level, but here, now, with the breeze blowing through Carrie's hair beside him and her wonderment at their surroundings, and the lingering pleasure from last night that he could still feel in his blood and bones, he couldn't seem to drum up much concern.

He pulled Carrie into him so he could feel her very feminine curves. All woman... He pushed her jacket off her shoulders and started opening her shirt. She was already a little breathless.

She said, 'When does the conference start?'

'Not for a few days,' he said, as the lace of her bra was revealed under the open shirt.

He reached inside to cup her breast, relishing the weight in his palm. It fit perfectly, the tip already a hard nub. He rubbed his thumb back and forth and Carrie's eyes started to lose focus.

'What else do you have lined up?' she asked, sounding as if she was desperately trying to cling on to some semblance of sanity. Like him.

'A hectic schedule of rest and relaxation. Wall-to-wall pleasure.'

She looked at him, her eyes focused again. 'That sounds... very lazy.'

Massimo smiled and cupped Carrie's face, lifting it towards his. Just before he covered her mouth with his, he said, 'Very, *very* lazy.'

* * *

Carrie wasn't sure if she was still human. In an embarrassingly short space of time she'd become a sloth-like sybarite. Addicted to pleasure and to the relaxed, sensual pace of Rio de Janeiro.

Everything was easy and just flowed. Minutes and hours were melting into days that had melted into…a week? More? Carrie had stopped counting.

The day after their arrival a stylist had come to the apartment with her assistants and racks of clothes for her to wear in Rio—even though a stylist had already appeared in New York to help her with a travel outfit and a suitcase of clothes to bring with her.

It appeared the Rio stylist had been instructed to provide clothes of a far more frivolous variety—swimwear that left absolutely nothing to the imagination. Underwear so light it was like air. Sparkly long dresses. Floaty kaftans.

Massimo had been at his conference for the past few days, so Carrie had got used to sleeping late, then going across the road for a dip in the crashing surf before getting coffee and breakfast at one of the local cafés.

She loved the vibrancy of the culture here, and the way everyone smiled, and the unashamed ease they had with their bodies, no matter what size. She loved the lyrical language, and was even trying to teach it to herself via an app on her phone.

Her skin was turning golden without her even sunbathing, and a smattering of freckles she hadn't seen since she was a child were spreading across her nose.

Before Massimo had become busy with his conference he'd taken her sightseeing, up to the Redeemer statue, and he'd organised an overnight trip to see the breathtaking Iguazu Falls. Carrie still couldn't get over the natural phenomenon of the spectacular waterfalls that straddled the border be-tween Argentina and Brazil.

But his conference was finishing today, and he was taking her out to dinner later that evening. She stretched luxuriously on the bed, entirely naked, feeling so decadent that a little giggle escaped her mouth. The huge glass doors were open to the terrace outside and a warm breeze wafted over her skin.

'Don't move.'

The voice came from the doorway. Carrie might have freaked out, but it was too familiar. She lifted her head to see Massimo, already shedding his clothes.

The fact that she didn't try to pull the sheet up over her body was testimony to how this man had rewired her brain into accepting that she was a sexual creature.

'What about the conference?'

'Last day. I bailed early.'

Gloriously naked, he strolled to the bed. Feeling utterly bold, and yet still shy, Carrie said half-heartedly, 'I haven't showered yet.'

Massimo moved over her on his hands and arms, muscles rippling. The sounds of the sea and joyous laughter drifted all the way up from outside. It infused Carrie with a sense of lightness. And then, totally unexpectedly, emotion gripped her. She realised she was grateful to Massimo for giving her this amazing experience. For restoring her womanhood back to her.

She felt free of something heavy that had weighed her down for a long time. Grief and regret. Chiefly regret. Be-cause the grief would always be there, like a bruise that hurt sometimes more than others. But the regret she was willing to let go of. Regret for having made a bad choice in her hus-band…for having trusted him.

Massimo went still. He obviously saw something in her eyes. 'Hey, what is it?'

That undid her even more—that he'd noticed her emotion and stopped.

She shook her head, terrified he'd make her say it out loud. 'It's nothing... I just...'

She reached up and pulled his face down to hers and kissed him before she could make a complete fool of herself.

Thankfully, after a moment, Massimo curled one arm under her body and arched her into him as he seated himself between her legs. Then he thrust so deeply into her body that all talking and thinking became irrelevant for another few hours.

Later that evening, they had eaten dinner and were walking hand in hand through a vibrant nightlife area. An infectious samba beat spilled from countless different clubs and bars.

Carrie spotted something in a boutique window and stopped dead.

Massimo looked back. 'What is it?'

But Carrie couldn't look away. It was a dress. But not just any dress. It was the kind of dress that laid bare all the fantasies she'd kept in the deepest recesses of her imagination but would never have admitted to a living soul. It was a dress that screamed youth and fun and frivolity—things that she'd never really experienced. And it was only seeing it now, in a window in Rio de Janeiro, that made her acknowledge she'd ever even harboured such dreams.

It was pink and very short, with a deep V-neck. Pink sequins covered the material to the waist, and then pink ostrich feathers adorned the skirt which ended high on the thigh. An ostrich feather adorned its one strap.

It was ridiculous. It was audacious. And Carrie had never seen anything more beautiful.

Massimo saw what she was looking at. He said, 'It would look good on you.'

Carrie came out of her embarrassing trance. She looked away. 'No, it's ridiculous. Far too short and flashy for me.'

But Massimo was already tugging her towards the shop.

She tried to dig her heels in but it was no use. They were in the shop, and a perky attendant was coming over. Before she knew what was happening Carrie was in a dressing room, being helped out of her own clothes and into the dress. She couldn't wear a bra. Her breasts looked positively provocative, exposed by the deep vee.

'Muito bonita!'

Carrie blushed in the mirror. 'I'm sorry, I don't understand.'

'You look very good.' The attendant smiled. 'You should buy.'

'Oh, I don't know—

'We'll take it.' Massimo spoke from just outside the dressing room. And then, 'Keep it on and try these to go with it.'

A pair of shoes appeared through the curtain, perfectly matching the dress. High and sparkly. Pink. Carrie put them on and wobbled a bit, but then steadied herself.

The attendant picked up the clothes she'd been wearing— jeans and a silk top—and took them away before she could protest.

Carrie suddenly felt too shy to show herself to Massimo in the dress. As if it would just remind him of how unsophisticated she really was. She doubted any of his previous lovers would be seen dead in a dress so frilly, sparkly and short.

But then, in a fit of rebelliousness, she pulled the curtain aside and stepped out.

Massimo's eyes widened. Carrie held her breath.

But he didn't look horrified or disgusted. He looked...ravenous. Almost feral. Eyes dark and burning.

Her legs felt wobbly again.

She said, 'I can't wear this out of the shop...it's crazy.'

He shook his head and stalked towards her, putting his hands on her waist. 'We're going to go to the only place we *can* go with you in this dress.'

Carrie felt breathless. 'Where is that?'

'To a club. Not usually my style, but my brother was always moaning at me that I was too boring. I think it's time to live a little, don't you?'

Less than an hour later, Carrie and Massimo were in the most exclusive nightclub in Rio de Janeiro. A vast, high-ceilinged space with VIP booths on the first level with views of the dance floor, which was lit up with disco balls and coloured squares. It was retro, and yet effortlessly modern. Very cool.

A slick DJ was playing the glamorous crowd like a violin, choosing a series of well-known pop classics interspersed with samba beats. It was infectious. She and Massimo hadn't even drunk any alcohol, but she felt as if she'd had a bottle of champagne. Fizzing and bubbly.

He took her hand. 'Come on.'

'Where?'

He nodded towards the dance floor. 'Down there.'

Amongst the mass of heaving bodies, all moving far more sinuously than she knew how to, Carrie held back. 'I don't know, Massimo... I don't mind watching.'

But he pretended he couldn't hear her and tugged her along in his wake, all the way down the stairs and into the mass of people who moved aside to let them through.

Massimo pulled her close, hands on her hips. She gave up

protesting and put her arms around his neck, bringing their bodies flush. She could feel the hard press of his arousal against her belly and moved against him, mimicking the movements of the people around them. She knew she probably looked like a total amateur, but she didn't care.

Massimo caught some of her hair and tugged her head back, so she had to look at him. He still had that slightly feral expression on his face. It sent spirals of heat and desire through her whole body. When he bent his head to kiss her, the entire nightclub fell away. It was just them…getting lost in a vortex of climbing tension and beckoning pleasure.

Massimo broke the kiss. She could feel his chest moving with his breath. Her heart was pounding.

He said, 'I think we're done with the nightclub experiment.'

Carrie couldn't argue. She let Massimo lead her back through the crowd and out of the club onto the street. She felt young and free and buoyant.

Desired.

When Massimo had hailed a cab and they were both sitting in the back, Carrie turned to him impulsively and said, 'Thank you.'

'For what?'

She felt silly now. Exposed.

She shrugged minutely. 'I never got to experience anything like this before…'

She'd never got to revel in her youth, make mistakes and live without consequence.

He frowned. 'Do you want to go back to the club?'

She shook her head and closed the space between them. 'No, I saw enough.'

He put a hand around her waist and pulled her even closer.

'Good. Because if we'd stayed there, right now we'd be giving the entire crowd a very explicit floor-show.'

He kissed her deeply, passionately, and Carrie gave herself over to the oblivion that Massimo promised and delivered over and over again.

CHAPTER SIX

'OKAY, CAN I ask where we're going now?' Carrie said.

A couple of days later she was in the back of a chauffeur-driven car with Massimo. He'd told her to pack an overnight bag a short while before, but had been mysterious about why.

He was sitting on the other side of the car in faded jeans and a polo shirt. He looked more bronzed than usual. He looked younger. He looked ridiculously sexy.

'Yes, you can. We're going to Buenos Aires for the night—to the gala opening night of a tango show.'

Carrie's mouth opened. 'All the way to Argentina?'

'It's a three-hour flight—not too onerous. We'll have dinner and see the show.'

She was stunned. 'But I didn't bring anything with me except casual clothes.'

Massimo half smirked, half smiled. 'Don't worry, I've arranged all that.'

Carrie almost rolled her eyes. She was suddenly terrified of getting used to being spoiled like this. 'This is too much, Mass. You don't have to take me to Buenos Aires.' Even though she would *love* to see a tango show in the home of Argentine tango.

He reached for her. 'I like that.'

She went willingly. 'You like what?'

'What you just called me… *Mass*. My brother was the

only one who used to shorten my name—except he would usually say something like, *"Mass, you're so boring..."* Or, *"Mass, you're a stick-in-the-mud.""*

Carrie's heart clenched. She could hear both love and pain in his voice. 'I wish I could have met him. I think he sounds like an amazing guy.'

'He was—and he would have liked you because you bring out a side of me that he would have approved of.'

Carrie pulled back. 'Are you saying I'm a bad influence?'

Massimo reached for her again and pulled her hand to his lap, where she could feel his body hardening against the material of his jeans.

He growled, 'You're a very bad influence.'

Carrie's mind blanked when Massimo kissed her and she welcomed it. The moment was too full of something delicate and hopeful, and she knew if she wasn't careful she would lose herself in it. Massimo was just flirting and being charming. That was *all*.

Buenos Aires was breathtaking. Carrie loved the wide streets and elegant buildings. It had a much more European feel to it than Rio de Janeiro. It felt sophisticated.

'They call it the Paris of Latin America,' Massimo said as they walked into the most opulent hotel Carrie had ever seen—apparently it had once been a palace.

One very dramatic woman, with golden skin and long, flowing brown hair, was crossing the foyer wearing a royal blue strapless silk jumpsuit with eye-wateringly high heels, and leading a dachshund by a jewelled collar.

Carrie's eyes were almost falling out of her head.

She glanced at Carrie disdainfully. Carrie couldn't blame her. She was wearing a green silk shirtdress that had felt perfectly smart in Rio, but here it felt like beach attire. And her hair was down and she wore no make-up. She felt practically feral, compared to the clientele who all oozed effortless glamour and sophistication.

A manager rushed over to greet them, and Massimo conversed with him easily in fluent Spanish. They were led up to a corner suite at the very top of the hotel, with terraces that had views over the vast city.

She wandered out to one of the terraces while Massimo issued instructions to someone on his cell phone. A profusion of plants and flowers infused the air with glorious scents, and little iridescent birds darted from flower to flower.

When the manager had left, a personal butler appeared, to enquire if they wanted anything. Carrie heard Massimo tell him that a stylist would be arriving shortly and that they'd have a late lunch on the terrace.

When they were alone again, Carrie said, 'You really don't have to spend all this money on me.'

Massimo walked over and put his hands either side of her on the wall, caging her in deliciously.

'I want to.'

Carrie grimaced. 'Let's face it…you need to, to make me look presentable.'

Massimo shook his head. 'Insecurity doesn't suit you, Carrie.'

She went still. It was such a profound thing to say to her after she'd been made to feel so insecure by someone else.

She said, 'You don't have to say that, but thank you.'

Massimo cocked his head to the side. 'Who made you feel so insecure?'

Carrie cursed her expressive features. She hadn't built up a poker face like Massimo.

He said, 'It can't have been your mother. She loved you.'

Carrie felt claustrophobic. She ducked out from under Massimo's arm and moved away. She didn't want to go there—back to the past. Not when she was enjoying the present so much. But then she thought of how generous Massimo had been, and what he'd shared about his brother.

She looked out over the city, at the people moving far below. 'My husband… It wasn't a happy marriage. At first I thought it would be—obviously, or I wouldn't have married him. But it didn't take long for him to show the real reason he'd married me.'

Because she'd been weak. Vulnerable.

'Did he hurt you?'

Massimo's voice was harsh. Carrie glanced at him. His face was stark. It sent something dangerously warm to her heart.

'No—*no*. Well, not physically, at least.' *Except for the sex you never enjoyed*, reminded a little voice.

Carrie said, 'It was mainly verbal and moods and manipulation…'

That nearly made it more humiliating. She didn't even have a physical scar to show for it.

She faced Massimo. 'Do we have to talk about this now?'

He shook his head and came towards her. 'I'm sorry you experienced that, Carrie. You didn't deserve it.'

She felt sad. 'No one ever does, do they?'

She desperately wanted Massimo to touch her, to negate the cold chill blowing over her soul, but there was a knock on the door. Massimo didn't move for a long moment and then, as if sensing what she needed—*him*—he said, 'I can send them away?'

But Carrie felt as if she was falling…slipping and sliding down a steep hill. The fact that she needed Massimo in such a very visceral way terrified her.

She pasted a bright smile on her face. 'No, don't be daft. I'm starving.'

Massimo went to answer the door and Carrie turned to face the view blindly. She wasn't falling in love. *She wasn't.* But she was in serious danger of needing Massimo in a way that had too many echoes of the past. She had to be careful...

That evening Carrie felt like a princess. After lunch a team had arrived to get her ready for the gala event that evening. And now she was wearing a long flowing chiffon evening gown. In a very light blush shade, it was whimsical and romantic, the material gathered at her waist and over her breasts by a delicate rope. Her arms were bare. Her hair was pulled back into a loose chignon. She'd been given gold drop earrings and a gold armlet.

She saw herself in the mirror and felt a jolt. It was so strange to see herself transformed like this. It felt right...but it also felt wrong. More wrong than right.

Massimo walked into the room, resplendent in a black tuxedo, fixing his cuffs. He saw her and stopped in his tracks, dark eyes moving over her so thoroughly that it felt like a caress. But not even that could shake the uncomfortable sensation that she didn't really belong here.

His gaze narrowed. 'What is it? You look as if you've seen a ghost.'

She gestured to herself. 'This isn't me. I feel like I'm in the wrong place and it's only a matter of time before I'm asked to leave.'

He moved towards her. 'You know what they call that?'

She shook her head.

'Imposter syndrome.'

'Well, that's because I am an imposter.'

He shook his head. 'You have as much right as anyone else to be in this place.'

'I don't belong here.'

'And I do belong here just because of an accident of birth? That's not very fair, is it?'

Carrie shook her head.

Massimo reached out and cupped her neck, tugging her gently towards him. The dress whispered around her body, in a sensual reminder of the woman this man had awoken.

'You're here because I asked you and you said yes. You want to be here, don't you?'

She knew that she did. In spite of all her doubts and feeling that she didn't belong. Carrie nodded slowly. She did want to be here, and she'd chosen to be here.

'Good,' Massimo said, and he lowered his mouth to hers before whispering against her lips, 'Because you are beautiful, and there's no one else I'd want to be here with me right now.'

Carrie's chest swelled with an unnamed emotion, but she pulled away from his kiss even though it killed her. 'Please don't say things like that, Mass. I don't need to hear it.'

I want to hear it...too much.

Massimo looked at her for a long moment, his face unreadable. Eventually he said, 'Fine.'

They left the suite and Massimo only lightly touched her on her back as they walked out of the hotel to the car.

She felt as if she'd broken something, but it was better this way.

Sitting in a box seat at the theatre in Buenos Aires a short while later, Massimo was still feeling exposed. No woman had ever complained before when he'd issued a compliment.

Although he'd spent so little time with any of them that it wasn't usually necessary.

But what he'd said to Carrie earlier, he'd meant. He really didn't want to be here with anyone else. And it had spilled from his mouth as easily as breathing. *She'd* been the one to pull back. Say there was no need.

What the hell was wrong with him? Did he want her to fall for him? *No way.* And yet the way he was behaving anyone would be forgiven for thinking he was waging an all-out campaign. He'd never seduced a woman so comprehensively.

He looked at the stage. The hauntingly beautiful strains of the music of Astor Piazzolla, one of the world's most famous tango composers, mocked him now. Mocked him for being complacent. For losing his mind for a moment.

The couple onstage danced, their bodies moving in sync, twining erotically before coming apart again, then melding again so closely that it was hard to see where one ended and the other began.

Massimo glanced at Carrie and his gaze narrowed. There was moisture in her eyes. The melancholic music would affect the stoniest of hearts. Ricardo, his brother, had found it deadly boring but Massimo had always found it moving.

His brother had teased him once. 'Admit it, Mass, you're a secret romantic!'

Massimo had put Ricardo in a head-lock.

But it looked as if Carrie, for all her protests at being complimented, was a secret romantic too. Or maybe she was still lamenting her toxic relationship with her husband.

Massimo hadn't expected her to reveal that he'd been abusive. The white-hot surge of anger he'd felt when he'd believed he might have hurt her had surprised him. Still surprised him.

All through his parents' volatile marriage they hadn't ever

been physically violent with each other. Which was about the only saving grace of that marriage.

But the fact that it had been mental abuse rather than physical in Carrie's case didn't make it any better, of course. Mental scars left deeper wounds.

If anything, she'd done him a favour—reminding him of what this was. An affair. A deeper one than he would have expected, granted. But just an affair.

The couple on the stage moved into a classic Argentine tango pose as the last strains of the music faded away. Carrie felt hollowed out and wrung dry. She'd never expected a dance and its music to affect her so deeply.

She'd found herself desperately trying to suppress her emotions and, worse, her tears. But it had been almost impossible. The exquisitely beautiful dance, together with the most melancholic music, had touched every deep and hidden yearning she'd ever had. Regret, her loss and grief. And, the pain of confusing the need for security with love which had ended in tragedy.

She avoided looking at Massimo when he reached for her hand to lead her out.

Their car was waiting for them, and as it moved smoothly into the Buenos Aires traffic Carrie felt a little more composed.

From the other side of the car, Massimo said, 'You were moved by the performance?'

Carrie cursed him for noticing. He noticed too much.

She glanced at him. He was watching her. She'd noticed him watching her a few times during the evening and wondered if perhaps he was insulted that she'd rebuffed his compliment earlier.

She turned to face him. 'Look, about earlier, I didn't mean to sound—'

But Massimo cut her off. 'I think it's the music. It has that effect on people. You know the dance originated among the migrants and slaves in the poor areas of the city? Men danced it together because there were no women. Its roots are European and African. I'm not remotely romantic, but that music more than any other has the power to make me believe that romance exists.'

'I'm not remotely romantic.'

A clear message that he knew what she had been about to say.

So she said, 'I'm not remotely romantic either.'

She certainly wasn't. Not any more—if she ever had been. So why did that assertion cause a little pang in her chest? As if she was betraying some part of herself?

She ignored it.

She could see their hotel in the distance, and then Massimo surprised her by saying, 'We could go straight back to Rio now, if you like? Wake up there in the morning. Or we could stay here for the night?'

Carrie didn't want to leave Buenos Aires. But the truth was that this city seemed to evoke in her too many emotions and revelations for her liking.

She said, 'Would you mind if we went back to Rio?'

Massimo shook his head. 'Not at all. I can have the hotel pack our things and send them on. We can sleep on the plane.'

He took her hand and lifted it, pressing a kiss to the palm. It felt shockingly intimate.

And then he said, 'Or not sleep…it's your choice.'

The car turned around to head in the other direction and Carrie felt inordinately relieved—as if she was escaping her conscience and her emotions.

Coward, whispered a voice.

She ignored it. 'I'm not that tired, actually.'

Massimo put his hands on her waist and pulled her close. 'That's funny, I'm not either...'

As soon as the plane hit a certain altitude Massimo undid his belt buckle and stood up, holding out a hand to Carrie. He'd taken off his jacket and bow-tie. His shirt was undone. Stubble lined his jaw. He looked uncharacteristically roguish.

She put her hand in his and let him pull her up. She should have felt ridiculous on a plane in full evening dress, but she didn't. It seemed that nothing fazed her any more. It was as if something had just happened between them. A clarification.

This is just an affair. We're not romantics. We know what's happening. We're in control.

Massimo led her into the bedroom suite, where there was a massive walk-in shower. He let her hand go and went and turned it on. Steam quickly filled the space.

Carrie realised the audacity of what they were about to do. 'The cabin crew won't disturb us?'

'They know not to.'

Ouch.

An even clearer reminder that she wasn't the first woman Massimo had done this with and wouldn't be the last.

In a bid to hide how that made her feel, she started to take down her hair. Massimo watched her as her hair fell down around her shoulders. She shook it out. Then she found the zip at the side of her dress and pulled it down. The dress fell to her feet in a soft swish of expensive fabric.

She stepped out of the shoes. Now all she wore was a strapless bra and matching briefs. Mere wisps of material.

Feeling bold under Massimo's hungry gaze, and aware of

how finite all this was, Carrie turned and walked straight into the shower.

She turned around and Massimo looked almost feral as he took in the water sluicing down over her body, turning her underwear completely translucent. She might as well have been naked.

He didn't wait. He ripped off his clothes and they scattered around him. Gloriously naked and aroused, he stepped into the shower with Carrie. Dispensing with her underwear with a mere flick of his wrist, he caught her under her arms and lifted her up.

'Lean back against the wall.'

She did. Her legs were shaking now. She wrapped them around his waist. Water flattened his hair to his head. His cheeks were slashed with colour.

For her.

He bent his head and took the hard tip of one breast into his mouth, rolling and sucking the peak until Carrie's mind was blissfully blank of anything but this devastating pleasure.

Her hips were moving against Massimo, seeking for him to assuage the spiralling tension at her core. He put his hand there, against her body, feeling how ready she was for him. Sliding his fingers deep, making her moan.

And then he took himself in his hand and fed himself into her, inch by inch, until she couldn't breathe. She was impaled, and it was delicious.

Slowly he moved in and out, bearing her weight with an arm around her waist. It didn't take long. She could feel the swell approaching, gathering force, and she had to bite down on his shoulder to stop herself from screaming out loud as the waves pounded over her and through her.

Massimo's body moved against her powerfully as he sought his own climax, and then he pulled free abruptly, making Carrie gasp, and let the powerful jet spray wash away his climax.

It hadn't even occurred to her to think of protection—the feel of his body within hers had been too exquisite. And now she was too spent to dwell on it. She would have slid down the wall of the shower if Massimo hadn't caught her and lifted her into his arms.

He sat her down and took a towel, drying her and then scooping her hair up into another towel. He carried her from the bathroom to the bed and placed her down, and for a fleeting moment before Carrie lost consciousness she thought to herself that it was the kindest thing she could remember anyone doing for her for a long time...

'I need to go back to New York for some meetings.'

Carrie's insides sank.

She'd known this was coming. They'd been back in Rio for over a week now. She'd been wondering how long Massimo could duck out of his life.

She'd worked it out that morning: they'd actually been away for a month. She'd been on holiday for one month. More time off than she'd ever had in her life. But they couldn't exist in this sensual tropical idyll for ever.

She affected a look of polite uninterest, as if his pronouncement wasn't sounding the death knell on their relationship. 'Okay...when?'

'Today, actually.'

Her insides lurched even more. Not even another day or night?

The sound of the crashing surf from Ipanema mocked her from the background.

'You'll come with me,' Massimo pronounced.

Carrie felt prickly. 'Will I? It's about time I thought about what I'm going to do next.'

'This doesn't have to end yet. Come back to New York with me. You'll have plenty of time to think about the future.'

Her treacherous heart squeezed.

Maybe it wouldn't be over yet, but it would be soon.

She could feel it like the inevitability of a rising tide. And she was in way too deep. Any control she might have exerted over this whole situation was well and truly gone.

Buenos Aires and then these last few days in Rio with Massimo had dismantled all her very careful defences, leaving her nowhere to hide. And, as much as she knew it would be wiser to take the initiative here and be the one to leave first, she knew she wasn't ready to walk away from Massimo and the way he made her feel.

He'd opened up her eyes to a whole world of experience—and not just sexually. She'd changed. Relaxed. Found a measure of peace she'd never expected. Selfishly, she wasn't ready to let that go, because she knew that whatever happened to her after this, and wherever she went, she would never experience that again.

Still trying to affect a cool level of nonchalance, even though she knew what she was about to do spelled certain pain and humiliation in the future, she said, 'Okay, why not?'

'Good.'

Massimo's satisfied, knowing smile, as if he'd known exactly what she'd been thinking, made her want to wipe it off his face. So she did.

She got up from her chair and let her robe fall open enough so that he could see her bare breasts. She sat on his lap and said throatily, 'Exactly how long do we have before we leave?'

Massimo's eyes were burning and his arms were snaking around her waist, holding her tight. 'Long enough.'

He picked her up into his arms and took her back to the bedroom, and Carrie exulted in this very minor measure of control she wielded.

Even though it had only been a few weeks since they'd been in New York, the seasons were changing. The humid heat was gone and the air was much milder. Fresher. Carrie felt as if she'd been abroad for ever. Her old life and her work as Massimo's housekeeper felt very far away.

This was reinforced when they went into the apartment and the new male housekeeper met them, treating Carrie with deference, as if she was Massimo's mistress.

Which you are, pointed out a snarky voice.

'Miss Taylor, if you'll give me your dietary preferences, I'll pass them on to Chef.'

Carrie blushed when she thought of what Chef would make of her new status. She said quickly, 'That's really not necessary. I eat everything and anything.'

'No allergies?'

'No.'

He looked almost comically disappointed. Carrie might have laughed if she hadn't been feeling a little nauseous after the journey. She'd asked exactly the same questions of Massimo's guests, countless times.

When the housekeeper had left, Massimo said, 'I have to go straight to the office now, but we can eat out later if you like.'

To Carrie's surprise, she felt a surge of queasiness at the thought of eating out. She shook her head, 'That's really not necessary. I'm happy to eat in.'

She realised she was feeling quite tired too, all of a sudden. A very faint warning bell went off in her head, but she couldn't put a finger on what it meant.

'I'm happy just to potter here.'

Massimo frowned. 'Potter? You are making pottery?'

Carrie laughed. 'No, silly. *Potter*—as in mooch about, doing things with no real aim.' She saw the confusion on his face and took pity. 'Don't worry about it. The concept doesn't really exist in your world.'

He grinned, and the sight of it took Carrie's breath away for a moment.

He tugged her close. 'That's a pity…maybe you can teach me more about this *pottering* later. Does it apply to bed?'

Carrie giggled. 'Not really.'

She realised they were both grinning at each other. A swell of emotion gripped her before she could stop it.

She took a step back, rearranged her face. 'You should probably get going…'

To her surprise, Massimo reached out and traced a finger down over her cheek to her jaw, leaving her skin tingling.

'Later, then.'

She felt breathless, and wondered how he could still have this effect on her when she now knew his body as intimately as her own. 'Okay, then, later…'

His hand dropped and he walked out.

Carrie lifted her hand to her face and touched where he'd touched. It had been a tender gesture. Not even sexual. Like when her mother had used to tuck hair behind her ear. It made her feel—dangerously—a kernel of hope.

But for what? asked a questioning voice.

She sat down on a chair, suddenly deflated.

Massimo had made it very clear he didn't want a relationship, and even though she might want to try again at some stage, he was way out of her league. He didn't have relationships. He had lovers. Yet, no matter what he'd told Carrie, he would marry a woman from among his peers eventually.

At some point he would realise that he had a responsibility to carry on the Linden title.

Massimo might be happy to keep her on as his mistress indefinitely, while he wanted her, but it would come to an end. And Carrie knew now that she would have to be the one to take the initiative. To walk away. Because if Massimo kept touching her like that she would be right back at square one. Believing in things that didn't exist.

But maybe not today, she told herself weakly. Surely another few days couldn't hurt?

Telling herself that maybe a nap would help ease the queasiness, she went up to the room she'd used before. She dithered on the threshold when she couldn't see any of her bags or other things.

Curious, she went up to Massimo's room—and there they were. Already laid out by the unseen hands that did this kind of thing in his world. The unseen hands that had used to be hers.

All the beautiful clothes she'd been given were hanging up in his dressing room…laid out in drawers. Her toiletries were lined up in his bathroom beside the other sink.

Overcome with another wave of fatigue, Carrie put it down to the whirlwind of the last few weeks and took off her clothes to slip into a robe. She washed her face and climbed into one side of Massimo's massive bed. She was asleep before her head hit the pillow.

When Massimo returned to the apartment later that evening it was quiet. Very quiet. He moved through the downstairs rooms and they were empty. The chef had left, having been instructed that they would be fending for themselves.

The new housekeeper had also left.

The apartment was exactly as it had always been after he'd been away on trips before.

He'd never invited a woman into this space unless it was just for the night, but he couldn't see any traces of Carrie anywhere and that was disconcerting. She'd left more traces of herself when she'd been his housekeeper. Shoes by the front door. Flowers on the table. A throw over a chair in the kitchen.

But he realised now that she'd been tidied away by the staff—just as his things were tidied away all the time. So that wherever he went it was always pristine.

For the first time in his life he resented that. He wanted to walk into a room and see a book left open on a table. Or cushions out of place. Signs of life.

Massimo smiled a mirthless smile when he thought of his little brother, who would undoubtedly have welcomed this desire for a little messiness.

He took off his jacket and draped it over the back of a chair. Then he undid his top button, pulled off his tie and left that hanging over another chair. He had a sudden urge to find Carrie and bring her here, into the living room, so they could really mess it up by making love on every couch and chaise longue. Ricardo would approve.

But when he stuck his head into the kitchen it too was silent and empty, except for the hum of the appliances. Massimo had never really noticed that before...

A thought occurred to him. Maybe she'd gone out? To do this...*pottering*. Her independence was something that he liked about her, but an uneasy sensation moved through him as he went to her bedroom and found it untouched.

For a second he imagined that she'd changed her mind and just left...and the lurch in his gut was not welcome. It shouldn't bother him if Carrie had decided to end their relationship. It had transgressed so many boundaries that he had no right to expect her to stay.

But he wasn't ready to let her go.

Not by a long shot.

He went up to his bedroom. He hesitated at the door for a moment, before telling himself he was being ridiculous and opening it.

The first thing he saw was a shape in the bed. *Carrie*. She was here. Just asleep.

He walked over and looked down. She was on her back, one arm flung up by her head, her hair spread out around her head in a halo of gold waves. Her face was clean of make-up. He could see the spatter of freckles across her nose. The sun-kissed glow.

He ignored the sense of relief. *Not* relief. Desire.

He sat down on the side of the bed and she stirred, eyes flickering and then opening. She saw him and it took a second for her to come wide awake.

She sat up, slightly groggy. 'I fell asleep...what time is it?'

Massimo noticed that actually, underneath the sun-kissed glow, she was a little pale. 'Are you okay?'

She frowned. 'I think so... I was just really tired all of a sudden, so I lay down.'

'Are you hungry?'

She absorbed this—and then, with almost comical speed, she went green and leapt out of the bed and into the bathroom, slamming the door behind her.

Massimo winced at the sounds that ensued. He would have gone in, but he had a feeling Carrie wouldn't appreciate it.

She emerged a few minutes later with her hair pulled back, looking very pale.

Massimo jumped up. 'You're not well. I'll call a doctor.'

She put out a hand. 'No, it's nothing serious. It's just food poisoning or a bug.'

'But I'm okay and we've eaten all the same things.'

'I'm sure it's nothing...'

She looked as if she was about to collapse.

Massimo reached out and grabbed her, leading her back to the bed and letting her lie down.

But she struggled to sit up again. 'I should go to my own room.'

Massimo pushed her back down, gently. 'No way. This is your room. What can I get you?'

Carrie said, 'Maybe just a little water and a dry biscuit, if there's anything like that?'

Massimo pulled the robe over Carrie's chest, where it was gaping open, showing the curves of her breasts. *Not now.* He went and pulled a pair of silk pyjamas from a drawer and came back, helping her to sit on the side of the bed.

'You'll be more comfortable in these.'

With superhuman strength, he managed to help her out of the robe and into the pyjamas without turning into a caveman. He left her in bed and went to the kitchen to get the water and a biscuit—which, of course, took him an age, because he couldn't find the pantry where the dry goods were kept.

When he got back upstairs, though, Carrie was asleep again, so he left the water on the table, with a couple of biscuits on a plate, and went to his study.

He'd never been in this situation before...

During the night Carrie woke and had a little water and some of the biscuits. She said to Massimo, 'I'm sure by the morning I'll be feeling much better...'

CHAPTER SEVEN

BUT WHEN CARRIE woke at dawn she wasn't feeling better at all. She managed to get to the bathroom just in time.

When she'd finished being sick she stood up and looked at her wan features in the mirror. She could only remember feeling this sick once before, and her whole body went cold as she realised it.

She put her hand on her belly. *No.* The universe wouldn't be so cruel, would it?

She went back out into the bedroom and saw Massimo standing there, bare-chested, wearing sleep pants that hung low on his hips. For the first time Carrie didn't feel a sizzle. She felt even queasier.

She only realised Massimo was talking into a mobile phone when he said, 'Okay, Doctor, thank you.'

Carrie went cold. 'Who was that?'

'My doctor is coming to see you.'

'But it's really nothing,' protested Carrie, while silently saying a prayer that it wasn't the potentially huge thing she feared it could be.

She climbed back into bed, feeling too weak to stand and face a brooding Massimo.

'I'm really sorry about this.'

It wasn't exactly lover/mistress behaviour.

Massimo frowned. 'Don't be silly. I'm going to take a shower and then wait for the doctor.'

Carrie lay back on the bed and tried not to let her mind go to scary places. She felt numb. Which was a bit of a relief after the constant queasiness. But if this was what she feared it was, this stage would pass soon enough…

Carrie looked at herself in the bathroom mirror again. She'd had a shower and was dressed in faded jeans and a shirt. Hair still damp and loose around her shoulders. She looked marginally better. She felt marginally better. At least physically.

Emotionally was another story.

She'd just had her fears confirmed by the doctor and the doctor's handy little pregnancy test, which had very definitively spelled out *PREGNANT* on its digital display.

The wonders of modern technology…able to diagnose a pregnancy even at this early stage…

He'd said he thought she was about a month in, so Carrie had dated conception back to when they'd first slept together in New York. The moment when Massimo had thrust inside her before remembering to put on protection.

She hadn't even realised she'd missed a period.

There was a knock on the door. 'Carrie?'

Her belly lurched—but not with nausea this time. With fear and trepidation.

She called out, 'I'm fine. I'll see you downstairs.'

Hesitation outside. Then, 'I'll have Chef prepare some tea and toast.'

Carrie put a hand to her mouth to contain a semi-hysterical giggle at the thought of how things had veered so off-course. But then she sobered again when she thought about telling Massimo. She had no choice. His doctor knew, and even though he wouldn't have told Massimo she couldn't sit on this. It was too huge.

She went downstairs and found Massimo in the private media room. He was dressed in jeans and a long-sleeved top, his hair mussed as if he'd been running a hand through it. He was watching a news channel, but switched it off when she came in. He stood up.

Carrie opened her mouth, but at that moment the chef appeared with a tray of tea and toast. He put it down on the coffee table by the couch.

Carrie smiled at him weakly, not sure what he must be thinking about this reversal of her status. He was discreet, though, as were all of Massimo's staff. As she had once been.

When he'd left, Massimo said, 'Sit down…have something.'

Carrie felt like just blurting it out there and then, but Massimo looked concerned, and she knew she needed to fortify herself for whatever reaction she was going to get. So she dutifully sat down and had some tea and buttered toast. It tasted like cardboard in her mouth.

After she'd had a few mouthfuls, Massimo said, 'So… what is it?'

Carrie wiped her mouth with a napkin. She looked at Massimo. Only about a foot separated them on the couch. He was too close.

She stood up and walked over to stand behind an armchair. Massimo stood too. 'Carrie…?'

'It's nothing serious.' She thought about that, 'Well…that's not exactly true.'

Massimo frowned. 'Carrie, what the…?

'I'm pregnant.'

Her words hung between them. Massimo looked confused. 'What did you say?'

Carrie's hands gripped the back of the seat. 'I'm pregnant.'

Massimo shook his head. 'But…how? I used protection every time.'

Carrie thought again of that moment—the second time they'd made love.

Massimo's face darkened. 'There was only *one* instance, and I made sure to put on protection as soon as I remembered.'

But that was all it took. A moment.

Weakly, she said, 'No form of protection is one hundred per cent reliable.'

He looked at her. His face stark. 'You don't seem surprised.'

Carrie took stock of what she was feeling. Shocked? She shook her head. 'It's not something I considered even a remote possibility.'

Massimo didn't say anything for a long moment, and then, 'Are you sure about that?'

'What's that supposed to mean?'

Massimo's expression was stone. 'Did you set out to trap me?'

Carrie was flabbergasted, and hurt that his cynicism would take him to that conclusion.

She found her voice eventually. 'Why on earth would I want to trap you?'

'To be set for life? To never have to worry about anything ever again?'

Carrie came out from behind the chair, incensed. 'Why, you arrogant bastard! You think wealth can stop anything bad from happening? That wealth magically insulates you from ill-health or loss?' She pointed at him. 'You know better than most how that's not true. All wealth does is insulate you from doing your own dirty washing! Or having to use public transport. Or talking to normal people and realising that maybe not everything is about you!'

Massimo folded his arms across his chest. Her words seemed to have made no impact.

'Like I said…you don't seem surprised.'

Because on some level she wasn't. Because she'd known it even before she'd allowed herself to think it. Because it was exactly what had happened before.

Considering where they were now, she knew she would have to tell Massimo everything.

Massimo wasn't sure how he was still standing when he felt as if a million rugs had just been pulled from under his feet. The last time he'd felt this blindsided had been when they'd told him that Ric had died—and even that hadn't come as such a huge shock.

Which somehow made this level of shock feel like a betrayal.

He also felt exposed. *Again.* He'd been so careful never to let anyone too close. When he'd realised he hadn't been able to trust his own parents, he'd learnt a very early lesson in depending on himself. Ric was the only person who had breached Massimo's defences, and he'd vowed never to endure the pain of that kind of loss again.

Yet he'd been letting Carrie sneak right under those defences for weeks now.

Her words mocked him, *'You think wealth can stop anything bad from happening? That wealth magically insulates you from ill-health or loss?'*

Of course he knew it didn't. But he also knew that wealth could make those things a lot easier to bear. And right now it seemed crystal-clear to him that he'd vastly underestimated the sweet and innocent Carrie Taylor.

She was just like everyone else who'd circled like vultures as soon as his father's death had been announced. Women looking for a rich lover, or better yet a husband. Men looking for a deal. Charities looking for handouts. He'd decided to focus on charities because at least that was transparent…

'Well?' he prompted.

He could see the emotion on Carrie's face. Anger. Because he could see right through her. He pushed away the pricking of his conscience that he was letting his own anger skew his judgement.

She closed her mouth. Swallowed. Turned away.

He wanted to go over to her and demand she look him in the eye and spout her lies.

She turned around again, but still avoided his eye. She said quietly, 'I was pregnant before and the symptoms were the same.'

That took a second to sink in. And then the thought of her being pregnant with another man's child sent a series of conflicting emotions through Massimo.

'With your husband?' he asked.

She nodded. 'Four years ago.'

'You came to work for *me* four years ago.'

'Six months before I came to be interviewed for the job.'

'What happened?'

Carrie looked at him. Her eyes looked bruised.

She said, 'I was three months pregnant. My husband and I were involved in a car crash. That's how he died. And I miscarried. We were arguing. I had just told him I wanted to leave him, even though I was pregnant.'

She'd blamed herself for what had happened for a long time, but now she knew it hadn't been her fault. It had just been a tragic accident.

Massimo's anger drained away, leaving just shock. He

could remember what she'd been like four years ago. Painfully thin. Pale. Delicate.

'I'm sorry he died like that…and that you lost your baby.'

She said, 'If my ambition all along had been to seduce you and trap you, I'd like to think I would have done it before now and not waited four years.'

Massimo didn't like the logic of that. He had to concede that he'd overreacted. He said, 'I'm sorry for accusing you of premeditating this. I know you better than that.'

She swallowed. 'I know it's a shock. It's a shock for me too, no matter what it might look like. I hadn't ever thought I'd be pregnant again.'

Pregnant.

The concept of such a thing was too huge for Massimo to contemplate right now.

'Why? You'd make a great mother.'

Carrie shrugged minutely. 'After…what happened, I vowed never to marry again. I won't trust anyone that much again. I almost lost myself in the process before, and as it was I lost too much.'

'Do you want to keep it?'

He heard the words come out of his mouth but couldn't recall having the thought.

She flinched and looked at him accusingly. 'Of course. I lost one baby. I won't lose another if I can help it. And it's not an *it*. She or he is a baby. Your son or daughter.'

His baby.

Massimo's head throbbed. He needed to push her away. Push this whole thing away.

He said abruptly, 'I have to go to a meeting this morning. We'll continue our conversation later.'

He walked out of the room and left the apartment.

It was only when he reached his office and he noticed people looking at him that he realised he was still wearing jeans and a light jumper. He never appeared at the office in anything less formal than a suit. He'd vowed never to give anyone the opportunity to question his dedication or his professionalism after his father had decimated the family's reputation.

He felt exposed.

When Massimo got to his floor he bit out instructions to his assistant. 'Hold all my meetings and do not disturb me.'

He went into his office and straight to the drinks cabinet. He poured himself a generous mouthful of whisky and downed it in one. Then another. As the fiery liquid burned its way down his throat and into his chest he poured another and went over and looked out of the window, not seeing anything.

His brain felt like a solid rock in his head. His chest was tight. Every muscle tense.

The very thing he'd told himself he would never, *ever* pursue—a family—was now a very unwelcome possibility. And Massimo knew he had no choice but to accept this new reality and protect his legacy.

Carrie heard Massimo's arrival back to the apartment. She was sitting in the formal reception room, waiting. She felt calm. She knew that it was most likely still shock. But she would take it. Just so she could deal with this next bit.

She stood up.

One thing was certain: whatever had been between them, still electric and alive only yesterday, was well and truly dead now.

Massimo came into the room and saw her. He stopped. He looked more dishevelled than he had earlier. A little wild. Carrie couldn't stop a sizzle of awareness. It was back, in spite of the acute morning sickness and everything else that had happened.

Massimo looked her over and she stood tall. She was dressed in the same clothes she'd worn to come to New York. Work clothes. Smart. Hair tied back.

He said, 'Where are you going?'

Carrie looked down at her compact suitcase. And then up to him. 'I'm going back to London.'

'And what's your plan when you get there?'

Fear and not a little panic gripped Carrie. 'To find a place to live and a job.'

Massimo shook his head. 'That's not how this is going to play out.'

'It isn't?'

'No.' He looked at her, eyes narrowed. 'We are going to get married.'

Carrie might have fallen backwards if the couch hadn't been behind her legs. She saw something in his eyes—determination.

She shook her head and moved away from the couch. 'No way. That is not the solution.'

'Do I need to remind you of who I am? Once this gets out it'll make headlines.'

Carrie's level of panic rose by several notches. 'Well, it's not going to get out unless you tell anyone. There is no way I would agree to marry you, because you've made it quite clear that you never want to marry, and also, as I told you, I vowed never to marry again. I will never allow myself to be made vulnerable again—and marriage makes you vulnerable.'

'I can't dispute that,' Massimo said grudgingly.

'Good, then you agree.'

'No, I don't agree. It just means we're both on the same page. We'll know that we're only doing this for the sake of our child.'

'A marriage based on duty is no place for a child to be brought up. Children need love and security. Happy parents.'

'We survived in less than ideal circumstances.'

'I wouldn't be so sure about that,' Carrie commented.

Massimo couldn't seem to answer that. He said, 'And where would I be in this non-marriage scenario?'

'You would be part of our child's life. I would never deny you that—especially not after my own father rejected me.'

'So how will this work, exactly, with me in the child's life but not really part of it? Do we live near one another? How does access work?'

Carrie's head started to hurt. 'We can work all that out.'

'And how are you going to cope with your pregnancy? How will you survive when you become too pregnant to work?'

Carrie lifted her chin. 'I will manage. My mother coped just fine with a lot less. I won't expect anything from you until the baby is born. Anything could happen—as I know.'

'That is not a viable plan, Carrie. Marrying me would give us control of the situation in case the news leaks out, and also give you security and protection while you're pregnant.'

The thought of being wedded to this man who clearly despised her now sent bile through Carrie's guts. She already knew what it was like to be rejected by one man—her father—and then used as a thing to dominate by another man—her husband.

She lifted her chin. 'You couldn't pay me to marry you.'

Massimo's face darkened. 'Not even...?'

He named an astronomical amount of money. A life-changing amount of money.

Carrie felt sick. 'You know, up until this moment I actually believed you had integrity, but you're really not so different to your family, are you?'

Massimo's face was like stone. 'If you're saying you can't be bought, then you might as well admit to being a mythical unicorn. Everyone has a price.'

Carrie felt sad. She shook her head. 'Not me. My price is my baby being born healthy and having enough to live on and get by.'

'Without me.'

'I'm not saying that. I would want you to be part of his or her life.'

Massimo paced back and forth. He stopped and looked at Carrie. 'I might never have planned on having a family, because I don't want to pass down whatever destructive genes I might carry, but I will not shirk my responsibility.'

Carrie's heart lurched. 'You don't carry any destructive genes.'

Massimo dismissed her comment with a wave of his hand. 'I need to know that you are both safe and well. I need to be able to control the PR in case something is leaked to the press. Do you have any idea of what a child of mine stands to inherit? This isn't just about you any more, Carrie.'

She balked at that. She really hadn't got her head around the fact that her baby would be heir to a vast legacy.

She put her hand over her belly instinctively, as if to shield the child within from its own future. And a reluctant father.

And then something came to her—a compromise. She said carefully, 'It's clear now that whatever was between us is...over?'

'Yes.'

The speed with which he agreed sent a little knife into her gut, but she ignored it. It was better this way. What if he actually tried to charm her into marrying him? She wouldn't have a hope. At least he was being honest.

'I have a solution...if you're willing to agree to it.'

Six weeks later

Massimo pulled his car into the forecourt of his London home. He was tense. He'd been tense for weeks now. Tense and something else he didn't quite want to admit to. But he knew what it was: sexual frustration. A sexual frustration that only one woman could alleviate.

He got out of the car. A distinct chill in the air and the leaves on the ground foretold of winter settling in, but he noticed none of that. He approached the immaculately glossy black front door and it opened as if operated by some kind of magical device. But there was no magic—just his house-keeper, Carrie, on the threshold. She was dressed in her uniform of black shirt and black trousers. Flat shoes. Blonde hair pulled back neatly in a bun at the base of her neck. No overt make-up. No jewellery.

She had no discernible expression on her face. 'Welcome back, sir.'

The sense of déjà-vu was strong enough to almost knock him backwards. Had he in fact imagined the last couple of months? Had he imagined the best sex he'd ever had?

No. His blood was humming to see her again. The one woman he wanted and the one woman he couldn't have.

He looked at her midriff. Was it thicker? With his child?

An unsettling feeling of pride took him unawares.

He'd spent the last six weeks mired in crisis after crisis that had kept him from coming back to London.

He'd spent the last six weeks trying not to think about the fact that he was going to be a father, whether he liked it or not.

On the one hand he had to admit he'd welcomed the distraction, but on the other hand he'd felt rudderless. And for the first time in his life *lonely*. A new concept.

But every time he'd spoken to Carrie on the phone she'd been breezy, as if there was nothing strange about the fact that they'd agreed to her continuing to work as his house-keeper. He'd only accepted her proposal because it was that or she was going to leave entirely and make her own way.

He walked into the house. Her scent caught him. The same scent. Uncomplicated. But nothing about this situation was uncomplicated. Her calmness made him feel volatile.

He said, 'Can we talk? In my office?'

'Of course,' she said smoothly. 'Shall I bring you a coffee?'

Massimo felt like snapping, *No, get someone else to bring it*, but he forced himself to be civil. 'Yes, sure, a coffee would be lovely. Thank you.'

Carrie went towards the kitchen and Massimo undid and ripped off his tie as he went to his office. He took off his jacket and paced back and forth, full of restless energy in spite of a transatlantic flight.

A light knock on the door and Carrie came in with a tray. She put it down on the table and stood back.

'Please, sit down.'

Clearly reluctant to do so, she finally did. On the edge of a seat on the other side of the table.

Massimo sat down too and took a sip of coffee. He studied Carrie, which was easy to do when she was looking anywhere but at him. She looked…well. Really well. Pink in her cheeks. Eyes bright.

His gaze moved down. Her breasts looked bigger. Did that happen in pregnancy? The thought of her body growing ripe with his child sent another unsettling wave of a mixture of pride and possession through him. But underlying it all was desire.

He still wanted her.

He'd wanted her even when she'd dropped the bombshell of her pregnancy.

'How are you?' he asked.

She looked at him, a little startled, as if she'd forgotten he was in the room. Massimo clenched his jaw. Her eyes looked greener.

'I'm… I'm okay, thanks.'

'Have you been sick again?'

She shook her head. 'No, thankfully it was just that twenty-four hours. It was the same the last time. Luckily.'

'How is it being housekeeper again?'

'It's fine. Totally fine.'

'So this…arrangement is working for you?'

Carrie knotted her hands together in her lap. It had been working a lot better when Massimo wasn't here. She'd had space to come to terms with everything that had happened and to try and convince herself that any desire she'd felt had died along with their affair.

But that had been wishful thinking. The moment she'd seen him uncoil his tall frame from the car on his arrival it was as if she'd been plugged back into an electrical main-frame. It had taken all her composure to open the door and let him in and not tremble when his scent washed over her.

Even now she wanted to let her gaze rove over every inch of him. Was his hair longer? Did he look tired? Was there stubble on his jaw?

Had he been with another woman?

That question made her feel queasy. Maybe she did still have morning sickness…

She gathered her wits to answer him. 'It's working fine. But if you're not comfortable—'

'No,' he said abruptly, cutting her off. 'It's fine for now. The scan is this afternoon, right?'

She nodded. 'After lunch.'

She didn't like that ominous-sounding, *It's fine for now.*

Massimo said, 'I'll drive us there.'

'You don't have to come if you're too busy.'

He looked at her. 'I'm coming to my baby's first scan.'

My baby.

What had happened in six weeks? Had he decided to embrace fatherhood? And what did that mean for her? Was he going to ask her to marry him again?

Carrie stood up abruptly, in case any of those questions tumbled out of her mouth. 'If that's all? I should get back to work. You have that drinks event at the end of the week.'

'Very well.'

Carrie went to take the tray but Massimo said, 'Leave it. I'll bring it back.'

Before, Carrie would have argued, but now she just left. She closed the door behind her and stood against it for a moment. She looked down at her hand. It was trembling. Her whole body was tingling. She felt sensitive.

Already there were changes happening. Her waist thickening and her breasts feeling fuller. Had Massimo noticed? Did she want him to notice?

No. That side of their relationship was well and truly over.

It was time to move on and make the best of their new situation.

A few hours later Carrie was lying back on a clinic bed in a very plush private practice. They were briefly alone while the radiographer went to get something. Massimo had changed into a fresh suit. He looked clean-shaven. Carrie's head was suddenly filled with lurid images of Massimo in the shower, naked, with water sluicing over his hard muscles...one in particular.

She wanted to scowl at him for automatically turning her into a hormonal mess on his return. She felt frumpy and lumpen. She *was* a lot thicker in the waist now. More than she remembered being at this stage the first time around.

The worst thing, though, was that she had to admit that the last six weeks had felt very hollow without him. The world had gone from Technicolor to a sort of grey. At night it had been the worst, when she'd wake sweating after a particularly vivid dream, her whole body aching for satisfaction.

She missed him. She missed sex with him.

The radiographer came back in and bustled around Carrie, lifting up her top to spread gel on her belly.

Before Carrie was fully prepared, a loud, rhythmic *thump-thump* filled the room. She went very still as the woman moved the wand over her belly.

'That's a nice strong heartbeat and— Oh, my word...'

Carrie tensed. 'What is it?' She couldn't make out what she was seeing on the screen.

Massimo stepped forward, 'Is everything okay?'

The radiographer looked at Massimo and then at Carrie and smiled beatifically. 'Everything is absolutely fine, but I need to tell you that you're not having just one baby—you're having twins.'

Carrie didn't remember much of what had happened after that—only that the shock she'd felt had been mirrored on Massimo's face. He'd looked as if he'd been punched in the gut.

He was driving them back to the house now, and she might have feared he was in too much shock to drive, but they weren't moving fast in the traffic.

Carrie looked blindly out of the window. She didn't take in the twinkling colourful lights everywhere that indicated Christmas was just around the corner.

She held a print from the scan in her hands. It clearly showed two fig-sized shapes.

Massimo broke the heavy silence. 'There are no twins in my family that I know of.'

Carrie looked at him. His face was in shadow. She didn't want to see his expression.

She felt defensive. 'Mine either. Except,' she had to concede reluctantly, 'there could be, because I don't know my father's side at all really.'

Massimo said nothing for a long moment, and Carrie could imagine that he must be thinking how distasteful it was that the mother of his children should come from such a sordid background.

Eventually he said, 'I can understand your aversion to marriage. You haven't had the best examples.'

Feeling even more defensive now, Carrie said, 'I could say the same of you.'

'It wasn't a criticism. It was an observation. I'm not a snob, Carrie. My brother and I grew up with silver spoons in our mouths but that didn't protect us from the dysfunction of our family.'

Carrie rubbed at her head. 'Sorry... I'm still in shock.'

Mercifully Massimo was pulling into the forecourt of the house now. Carrie got out. He met her at the front door.

'We need to talk about this. It changes everything.'

Carrie's head thumped. 'Can we talk tomorrow? I'm quite tired.'

Under the light of the porch Massimo looked forbidding, and as if he might refuse, but then he said, 'Fine—tomorrow morning. You're taking the day off tomorrow.'

'But I—'

'No arguments.'

Feeling like a petulant teenager, Carrie went into the house and escaped to her private suite of rooms. She paced back and forth, her arms around her midriff, as if that could contain the lingering shock at what they'd just discovered.

Not one baby. Two babies. Twins.

For a moment Carrie felt absurdly emotional when she thought of losing her first baby and the awful grief she'd felt. Maybe now she was being given another chance.

She felt absurdly protective of these tiny beings that were only just forming. She thought of what Massimo had said: *'This changes everything.'* No. He was wrong. It changed nothing. If anything, knowing there was more at stake now only made it even more important for her to make sure she wasn't railroaded into anything. Massimo, in spite of his family history, was undoubtedly thinking of marriage again.

But she wasn't weak and she wasn't vulnerable—not any more. She was strong and she could stand on her own two feet.

In his office, Massimo couldn't get Carrie's face out of his head—the way she'd looked just now under the porch light. Her eyes had been huge pools of sage-green. Shadows underneath. And she was so pale. The sun-kissed glow from their trip to South America was long gone.

When they'd returned to New York from Brazil Massimo had known he wasn't ready to let her go. He'd actually been considering setting her up in London in her own place. Extending their relationship.

That was one of the reasons he'd felt so exposed when she'd announced her pregnancy. It was as if she'd known and had the trump card to secure her future. But he had to concede now that he hadn't been thinking clearly. Her insistence since then on maintaining her independence was not just for show.

In any case she would have his protection for life now. She was the mother of his child...*children*. He felt slightly light-headed at that thought as it sank in again.

Twins. Two babies. Not one. Two. A ready-made family.

Except Carrie didn't want them to be a family.

And what did he want?

He wanted something he wasn't even ready to name. Was it out of that well-ingrained sense of responsibility? Or was it more?

Something very fragile was unfurling inside him. The possibility of something he'd never considered before because he'd ruled it out so long ago after losing Ricardo. *Love.*

He couldn't keep pretending that what he felt for Carrie was a fleeting thing, or just physical. It was more...and it was deeper.

A sense of resolve filled Massimo's chest. It was happening whether he liked it or not. A family. And even though it terrified him he wanted it. He wanted the chance to live a different life. To have it all.

All he had to do was convince Carrie that there simply was no other option but for them to unite. In every sense of the word. He wouldn't settle for anything less.

CHAPTER EIGHT

'Merry Christmas!'

'Merry Christmas.'

Carrie smiled at the departing guest who was weaving a little unsteadily to a car on the forecourt. As soon as she closed the door, the smile slid from her face.

She put a hand to the small of her back to soothe the slight ache there. She'd been on her feet all day, helping to prepare for Massimo's legendary Christmas party. Always a fixture on the London social scene, it was the last hurrah for everyone before Christmas Eve the next day.

She felt constricted in her black shirt and trousers. Soon she would have to stop just buying bigger sizes and invest in some actual maternity wear. Maybe even start wearing dresses.

She was still keeping her pregnancy from the rest of the staff, but she'd noticed a few looks lately. With twins, she was definitely bigger than she would be in a regular pregnancy, and she was approaching four months—almost halfway.

She was exhausted from avoiding Massimo for the last couple of weeks.

The morning after the scan he'd been called away on urgent business—something to do with a charitable fund accused of corruption in Bangkok. Ominously, before he'd left, he'd told her that they'd talk when he got back.

Since he'd come home she'd gone to bed early every night, had volunteered to run all the errands that meant going into town, and had made sure she was otherwise generally occupied.

But the way he'd been looking at her tonight at the party told her the jig was up. Everywhere she'd looked, he'd been there. At one point during the evening she'd taken a full tray from one of the waiters and within seconds Massimo had been there, taking it from her and handing it to someone else.

He'd said in a low voice, 'This is ridiculous, Carrie. You do not serve. You supervise. And I've changed my mind. *This*—' here he'd gestured to her and then the room in general '—is not working for me.'

The intensity of his gaze had stopped her from saying anything and he'd melted back into the crowd—well, as much as someone like him *could* melt, when he stood head and shoulders above almost everyone else.

She went and stood at one of the doors, looking into the party. It was winding down now. She didn't know how he did it, but Massimo had some magical way of letting everyone know that it was time to go home. There were never the scenes of debauchery here that she imagined he must have witnessed as a child.

The butler came and stood beside her. 'You were up earlier than me today, Carrie,' he said. 'You take off. I can look after things from here.'

She looked at Dave. 'Are you sure? The events manager is standing by, to make sure the last guests get away without delay and the initial clean-up has started.'

He nodded. 'It's all sorted. You head off.'

The thought of escaping Massimo's brooding gaze and their inevitable conversation was too much to resist. Carrie slipped away, and when she got to her room she ran a bath, stripping off and sliding into it with a groan of thanks.

She put her hands on her burgeoning belly. It felt hard. Her breasts were definitely bigger too, the areolae changing colour. She felt…ripe. Full of something she couldn't quite understand. An edgy sense of restlessness.

Whenever she'd caught Massimo looking at her this evening she'd felt a very unwelcome jolt of awareness, as if he could see right through her clothes to the naked flesh underneath.

One hand drifted to her breast, cupping its weight. She let her fingers graze the nipple and gasped out loud at the immediate sensation. She'd been feeling sensitive, but had had no idea just how close to the surface it was.

The edginess she'd been feeling dissipated for the first time in weeks. Trapping her nipple between two fingers was inducing a delicious feeling of tension. Acting on pure instinct, she put her other hand between her legs, where she could feel the slippery evidence of her very obvious desire.

Had it been brought on just from watching Massimo from across the room? Or had it been building since the last time she'd slept with him?

The thought of never sleeping with him again made something reckless move through Carrie, and she pressed her hand against herself—hard. It wasn't enough. She slipped two fingers inside herself and her back arched at the sensation. She started to move, desperately chasing the coiling tension deep inside, as her other hand squeezed her breast. She imagined it was Massimo's big hand between her legs, his fingers filling her as he urged her to *Come for me, Carrie… That's it… come on…let go…*

She did—in a helpless rush of undulating pleasure.

It took her a moment to realise she could hear knocking, and a voice.

'Carrie?'

Massimo.

Carrie panicked in a wave of hot mortification. Had she literally conjured him up out of her fervid imagination?

She called out, 'I'm in the bath…give me a minute.'

She cursed him as she got out and dried herself roughly, before pulling on a voluminous robe. Her body was still pulsating. She was red in the face. She put her hair up in a rough knot. She cursed him again, and went to open the door.

He was standing on the other side, bow-tie undone, top button open. She would have thought him every inch the disreputable rake, if she didn't know that he was actually quite serious and conscientious.

That only made her heart squeeze. *Weak heart.*

She pulled the lapels of her robe together like a virgin maiden. 'I was having a bath. Is everything all right? Dave said he'd look after the last of the party…'

Massimo waved a hand. 'It's fine…they're all gone now.'

Carrie was glad he couldn't see through to her skin, where her blood was still pulsing. Seeing him here like this in a tuxedo so soon after she'd just been—

'What can I help you with?' she blurted out, trying not to remember what she'd just been doing.

He said, 'It's Christmas Eve tomorrow.'

Carrie blinked. 'Yes, it is.'

She usually spent Christmas alone in her suite. A couple of times other staff had invited her for dinner, but she'd made up an excuse. Christmas wasn't an especially significant time of the year for her. It had always just been her and her mother, and she'd learnt very early that she shouldn't ask for things that made her mother feel she had to work harder to provide.

Her husband hadn't particularly enjoyed it either, and so Carrie had channelled any childish Christmas fantasies into her love of Christmas movies. Since his death, and losing her baby, she'd seen spending Christmas by herself as a sort of penance.

'What are you doing on Christmas Day?' asked Massimo.

'I have the day off.'

'I know you do. What are you doing?'

'Taking it easy.'

'I've given all the staff the day off.'

'You usually do,' Carrie pointed out.

Massimo was rarely here for Christmas himself—he'd usually be abroad. Christmas and New Year were high season for parties and philanthropy.

'Well, it looks like it'll just be the two of us here, then.'

Carrie was suspicious. 'I won't disturb you.'

'It would be very sad if we were both alone in the house on Christmas Day and didn't even share dinner together.'

'There's no one to cook it.'

She could cook it. She wouldn't mind cooking it. But cooking an intimate Christmas dinner for Massimo would be both far too seductive and terrifying.

'Chef is going to leave an idiot-proof Christmas dinner. All I have to do is heat it up for us.'

'Us.'

'Yes, *us*. I'm not taking no for an answer.'

He'd turned and walked away before Carrie could formulate a response.

After all her successful efforts to avoid Massimo, how had it happened that she was now going to be spending Christmas with him?

Feeling ridiculously nervous, Carrie made her way to meet Massimo on Christmas Day, late afternoon. Sounds emerged from the kitchen. The loud clatter of metal on tiles and a voluble curse.

Carrie couldn't help a smile and bit her lip as she stood in the doorway and surveyed the scene. Massimo had his back to her. He was wearing a white shirt and black trousers, and he was holding up a saucepan and looking at it as if he'd never seen one before. Which he might well not have, up close.

As if sensing her presence, he turned around with a rueful expression on his face. His gaze swept her up and down, and to Carrie's mortification she felt the heat of it, when she knew there was no heat intended. As soon as she'd told him of her pregnancy, any desire he'd had for her had died a death.

She regretted picking out the soft jersey dress in dark green. Pairing it with tights and high heels. She felt too conspicuously dressed up, and the material of the dress felt too clingy. Especially around her burgeoning midriff, which seemed to be going through a growth spurt.

She regretted leaving her hair down too—had she done that subconsciously? Was her own brain trying to betray her? It was too late in any case to do anything about it.

'Are you having some trouble?' she asked, walking into the kitchen.

Sounding a little defensive, he said, 'I'm not sure which pan to use to heat the gravy.'

Carrie walked over and opened a drawer and pulled out a small one. 'This one should do.'

There was a piece of paper on the counter-top with a list of things to do in sequential order to prepare the meal.

Carrie took pity on Massimo and put on an apron after handing him one. 'Let me help.'

They worked in a surprisingly companionable silence as they moved back and forth, taking the food Chef had prepared out of its packaging and putting it into the oven to heat.

Once everything was heating, Massimo said, 'You can go upstairs. I'll bring the food once it's ready.'

Carrie thought of the dining room and imagined them sitting there at the table, with low lighting, while a fire burned in the fireplace and the skies darkened outside. Far too intimate.

'I don't mind eating here. It'd be a lot easier.'

Massimo said, 'It's no trouble at all. I've laid the fire upstairs. All it needs is to be lit.'

The tone of his voice brooked no argument. So Carrie took off the apron and said, 'Whatever you prefer. I'll light the fire, then.'

She escaped upstairs and found the informal dining room table already laid and prepared for dinner with plates and cutlery and condiments. A bottle of wine sat open on the table, and a choice of non-alcoholic drinks. Thoughtful. An impeccably decorated Christmas tree twinkled in the corner of the room.

She found matches and lit the fire. As if to mock her, it blazed immediately and cheerfully in the hearth, sending out delicious heat. She stood before it, feeling a little dazed at all that had happened in the last few months and by the fact that she was pregnant. With twins.

She put a hand on her belly. She couldn't feel any movement yet, apart from the odd, very light fluttering sensation.

She sat down in a chair beside the fire, kicking off her shoes, and curled her legs up, mesmerised by the flames and not even noticing her eyelids getting heavy.

Massimo came up to the dining room with the first tray laden with their Christmas dinner. He stopped on the threshold when he saw Carrie asleep in a chair by the fire.

He put down the tray silently and looked at her. Her hair

was tumbling over her shoulders. He'd like to think she'd left it down on purpose, but the way she looked at him these days—so warily—made it not likely.

He let his gaze rove over her body, greedy to see it revealed under the soft material of the dress. He couldn't stop his own body's helpless and wanton reaction to seeing the evidence of her body growing riper and fuller with his child. With his *children*.

Once again he was taken aback that the dominant force of emotions moving through him wasn't negative. It was wonder, trepidation and an urge to protect, mixed with a sense of possessiveness. And a feeling that his fears of destructive genes being passed down was just that—a fear.

He'd allowed himself to hope that perhaps, with a new generation, he could make things right. Create a healthy and functional family. But for that he'd need Carrie. Body, heart and soul. He knew he wouldn't settle for less.

Her insistence that she had to keep working here as a means to stay close and let Massimo be involved in the pregnancy couldn't go on for much longer—if at all.

If he had to wage all-out war to get Carrie to see sense then he would. And he would play as dirty as he needed to.

At that moment, as if she sensed Massimo's intense focus on her, her eyes fluttered open. He noticed she was unguarded for a moment, and that something flared in her eyes when she saw him, but then it was gone. As if she'd brought down shutters.

She still wanted him.

His blood leapt. If she still wanted him they were halfway there.

She sat up, looking flustered, cheeks pink. 'How long was I asleep?'

'Not long.'

Carrie stood up and came over to him, helping take the plates off the tray. 'It smells good.'

'Alas, I can take no credit at all.'

'Heating food isn't without its challenges.'

'I'll take that as a compliment,' Massimo said dryly.

Carrie watched Massimo walk out to go and get the rest of the food. She still felt a little fuzzy. She put the plates on the table and tried not to think about how it had felt to wake up and find Massimo watching her so intently.

She'd thought she was dreaming...until she'd realised she wasn't.

Massimo returned with the rest of the food.

Carrie was finding it hard to shake the slightly dreamy feeling brought on by her nap. With the fire lit and darkness falling outside, the intimacy of the scenario was exactly as she'd feared. But she couldn't seem to drum up the energy to care too much.

She sat down and Massimo served up a delicious traditional roast with all the trimmings.

After a few mouthfuls, Carrie put down her knife and fork. 'I wouldn't have thought you were a big fan of Christmas—you're not usually here.'

Massimo made a face and took a sip of wine. He put down the glass. 'I can take it or leave it. Christmas when I was growing up was chaotic, so I've never really had the traditional experience.' Almost as an afterthought, he said, 'Except for once.'

'Oh?' Carrie had to admit she was intrigued by any glimpse into Massimo's early life.

'Well, Christmas with my parents was all or nothing. They either lavished us with gifts when they were organised and had remembered, or we were left with the nanny while they went on holiday. But one year the nanny couldn't stay with us, so we went to a schoolfriend's house to spend it with his family.'

'What was that like?'

'A revelation. For the first time in our lives Ric and I witnessed a functional family. A loving family. Who celebrated Christmas the same way every year. Very simple, nothing fancy—the boy was at our school on a scholarship—and yet when it came to it his parents were the ones who offered to take us in for the Christmas holidays.'

'Did you enjoy it?'

'It was a little unsettling—like being an alien beamed down from another planet and learning how to behave like normal people. Playing games. Watching movies. There was none of the high-octane glamour and chaos that we usually witnessed. I think Ric discovered drugs for the first time at one of our parents' parties.'

Carrie couldn't help feeling a pang at the thought of two young boys feeling so lost in a normal situation that most people took for granted.

She said, 'Christmas when I was growing up was just me and my mother. We didn't have enough money for this kind of feast, but she always tried her best so that we'd have some kind of treat. And we'd watch movies. She loved all the old classics, like *It's A Wonderful Life* and *Miracle on 34th Street*.'

'You miss her?'

Carrie nodded, avoiding Massimo's eye. 'She was all I had. She was wonderful.'

'You were lucky to know a mother's love. Our mother was a kind person, but she didn't have the ability to be responsible. She'd been totally pampered as a child, and yet her own parents had farmed her out to nannies and boarding schools.

She literally didn't know what to do with us. And her fragile emotional state meant she was very susceptible to alcohol and drugs. Our father's philandering only made things worse.'

Carrie looked at Massimo. He was staring into his wine glass.

She said, 'That must have been tough.'

He shrugged. 'It was all we knew.'

He looked at her and Carrie was caught by his dark gaze, turning golden in the low lights and the fire in the background.

He said, 'You must have been young when you married.'

'I was eighteen.'

Massimo made a faint whistling sound. 'That's *young*.'

'My mother had recently died. I was feeling a little...lost. Vulnerable. I was an easy target for someone who recognised weakness and wanted to exploit it and exert control.'

'You weren't weak. You were grieving.'

Carrie let his words fall into that place inside her where she'd punished herself for so long. They didn't sting. They were like a balm.

'I let him in and he took advantage. That's why I won't marry again. I don't trust myself not to let it happen again. The thought is...terrifying.'

'So you'd prefer our children to grow up with separate parents?'

Carrie tensed. 'You'd have access. Separate parents has to be healthier than a marriage made for the sake of the children. I could keep—'

Massimo cut her off. 'Do not say you could keep working here. It's not feasible Carrie. Not any more. You're already showing a little.'

Carrie was feeling claustrophobic. 'The staff don't have to find out the babies are yours.'

The sudden tension in the room crackled.

Massimo stood up. 'These babies are the heirs to the Linden fortune and a legacy that stretches back to the Middle Ages. You'd deny them that?'

Instinctively Carrie put her hand on her belly, as if to shield the babies from Massimo's terrifying words. 'I… I hadn't thought about it like that, to be honest.'

She really hadn't. She'd known it was there in the ether, like some existential thing she would have to deal with eventually. And she'd also known deep down that she couldn't keep going as she was. Massimo wouldn't stand for it. He was a proud man.

He started to pace back and forth, the delicious Christmas dinner forgotten. '*This* is why we need to talk—but you've turned avoiding me into an Olympic sport.'

Carrie said, a little weakly, 'We're talking now.'

'Because we are literally the only two people in the house.'

When he said that a different kind of tension filled the air. Something that was more charged.

Carrie put it down to her imagination. Since that other evening in the bath she'd felt ridiculously aware of everything.

'Look,' he said, running a hand through his hair, 'we do need to discuss this properly. Our children deserve security and stability.'

And two parents who love each other, thought Carrie, surprised as that assertion slid into her consciousness.

Obviously two parents who loved each other would be the ideal. But, having not experienced that herself—and nor had Massimo—it would have to be good enough that they loved their children.

Massimo sat down again. 'Why did you stay with your husband?' he asked bluntly.

Carrie balked a little. But then, 'At first it was because

he charmed me and flattered me. He made me feel safe and secure. Cared for.'

Loved.

But that had been her mistake. It hadn't been love. It had been an obsessive need to coerce and control someone.

'And then…?'

'When I realised it was destructive and potentially physically dangerous for me, I told him I wanted to leave him. But then I discovered I was pregnant. I felt conflicted. On the one hand I knew I had to leave, for my own safety and sanity, but on the other hand I had grown up without a father, and I didn't want that for my own child. That's why we were having a row in the car…he'd sensed my turmoil over what to do.'

'That was a terrible price to pay and it wasn't your fault.'

Carrie looked at Massimo. 'I know… It took a long time to forgive myself, though. I think you can understand that.'

Massimo's jaw clenched. 'I don't know if I can ever forgive myself for not being stricter with Ric.'

Carrie reached out. 'Mass—'

But he'd stood up again. 'Let me clear this and I'll bring up dessert.'

Carrie stood up too. 'I can do it.'

But he was already stacking the plates and taking them out.

Carrie wandered back over to the fire and threw a couple of logs on, making the flames jump and hiss. She knew Massimo was right. They did need to talk about the future and how it would look. She knew that under no circumstances did she want marriage. Not after her last experience. Even though she had to concede that Massimo had proved over and over again that he was not like her husband.

She trusted him.

She cared about Massimo—she couldn't deny it. Cared deeply. He'd not only been her lover, he'd been a friend.

But something was holding her back from investigating just how deep those feelings went.

Fear.

She'd believed herself in love before, and she'd been so wrong that she didn't trust herself to know what love was. If she named what she was feeling as love, then Massimo would use it as an excuse to make her agree to marriage. And if she agreed to the marriage and she was the only one in love it would destroy her all over again.

You're a coward, whispered a little voice.

There was a sound as Massimo reappeared with dessert. A choice of traditional Christmas pudding or crumble. Tea and coffee.

Carrie sat down again and chose some crumble, focusing on it very intently so that she could avoid looking at Massimo.

'You've turned avoiding me into an Olympic sport.'

She couldn't imagine any of his previous lovers avoiding him as she'd been doing.

Thinking of them made her feel spiky. She hadn't even thought about what would happen if he did marry. Someone else. The prospect made her feel a little breathless.

Almost accusingly, she said, 'For someone who never wanted to marry or have a family you seem pretty sanguine about it.'

Massimo took a sip of coffee. Carrie couldn't help but notice his big hands. It had been so long since she'd felt his hands on her. She ached to be touched...

She scowled inwardly. Pregnancy hormones. Apparently in the second trimester it was common to feel...aroused.

'It's one thing to take a position on a hypothetical situation,' he said. 'But when that situation is no longer hypothetical and becomes a reality, it's a very different thing.'

'What are you saying?'

'I'm saying that I might not have wanted this, but now that it's happening I find that I'm not as averse to it as I thought. I want to do things differently. Our children deserve a better life than I experienced or you experienced. We can give that to them.'

We.

Carrie's head was starting to throb a little. She said, 'Can we agree to talk about this again in the New Year?'

Massimo looked as if he wanted to disagree, but eventually he said, 'Fine.' And then, 'I have something for you.'

Carrie watched as Massimo went to the Christmas tree in the corner of the room and picked up a small box. Her heart thumped. Surely he wouldn't…? Flashbacks of her husband giving her a small velvet box made her feel queasy.

Massimo handed it to her. She took it reluctantly. She was afraid to open it.

'You look terrified. It's not horrible, I promise.'

Carrie glanced at Massimo and then back down at the box. She took a deep breath and opened it. And was immediately filled with a mixture of relief and—more worryingly—disappointment. It was a stunning pair of diamond drop earrings, glinting in the light.

She looked at Massimo. 'They're beautiful but they're too much.'

When he spoke his tone was dry. 'I've never given jewellery to a woman before. But you're going to be the mother of my children.'

Relief flooded her to know she was the first woman he'd given anything like this to. 'Well, thank you, but you really didn't need to.'

'Try them on.'

The air became charged again. Carrie cursed her hormones, telling herself it was only natural that he would want

to see them on her. She took them out of the box carefully
and slipped them into her ears.

Massimo's gaze narrowed on her. Carrie felt heat rising.
'They suit you.'

'Thank you.' And then, before she could make a fool of
herself, Carrie said, 'I have something for you too.'

She got up and went over to the tree, where she'd put his
gift the previous day. She'd panicked, realising she had to
give him something.

She picked it up, suddenly feeling incredibly nervous. At
the time it hadn't felt like a particularly intimate thing, but
now, in this cocoon-like room, it felt like an unexploded
bomb.

She handed it to Massimo before she lost her nerve, saying, 'I didn't know what to get you... I mean, what do you
get the man who has everything?'

He looked up at her. 'You really think I have everything?'

Carrie was taken aback at the bleak tone in his voice.

She sat down again. 'Well, I guess...materially, yes...'

He was taking off the pretty golden bow and pulling back
the paper.

She babbled nervously. 'I just had an idea...maybe I'm
totally off the mark...'

Oh, God. He was going to hate it.

But Massimo had taken off the paper now, and was looking down at the simple silver picture frame. His voice when
he spoke was a little hoarse, and he didn't look at her. 'Where
did you find this picture?'

'I found it on the internet. I remembered seeing it a long
time ago, when I'd just started working here and wanted
to find out more about you...my boss. It always struck me
as such a happy picture, and I realised I hadn't seen it anywhere here.'

'That's because it was taken by a paparazzo.'

The picture had been taken after a motor race that Ricardo had won. He had his arm around Massimo and they were looking at each other, both smiling. Massimo had an affectionately exasperated expression on his face and Ricardo looked as if he'd just said something cheeky.

It seemed to encapsulate everything Massimo had told her about how he felt about his brother and the great love and bond between them.

Massimo touched the glass with one finger.

Carrie said nervously, 'Look, if I've intruded…'

Massimo glanced at her and said dryly, 'I think that horse has bolted now, don't you?'

She blushed. She was sitting here with the evidence of that statement in her belly.

As if hearing her thoughts, Massimo's gaze travelled down to her midriff.

'Can you feel anything yet?'

Carrie shook her head. 'Another couple of weeks.'

He looked back up at her face and put the picture down. He said, 'Thank you for that…it's very special.'

'You're welcome.'

Carrie didn't seem to be able to break eye contact with Massimo… Afraid he'd see her desire laid bare in her eyes, on her face, she stood up and said, 'Thank you for going to all this effort to make Christmas special. It was nice. But I think I'll head for bed.'

Massimo stood too. Surprising her, he said, 'Look at your earrings in the mirror.'

The air was charged again. Carrie's blood felt heavy in her veins. 'I can do that in my room.'

'Humour me?'

He took her hand—their first real physical contact since

she'd told him she was pregnant. Her legs turned to jelly. He led her over to where there was a mirror on the wall above a small table.

He placed her in front of him. She looked so small with Massimo towering behind her. She couldn't look at herself.

He said, 'May I?'

She didn't even know what he was asking until she felt him draw her hair back. He let his fingers linger, lightly massaging her scalp. It was the most decadent, blissful thing Carrie had ever felt. She wanted to melt like liquid back into Massimo's strong frame and—

She stiffened and looked at herself in the mirror. Hair down and tousled. Cheeks pink. Eyes too bright. She could see her nipples, hard and thrusting against the material of her dress. The diamonds in her ears glittered.

And Massimo was watching her. Reading all those glaring signs. He was playing with her.

She pulled away and Massimo's hands dropped. She tried to smooth her hair into some semblance of tidiness.

'What are you doing?' she asked.

'I still want you, Carrie.'

She took a step back, as if he'd physically pushed her. 'No, you don't.'

He made a face. 'Oh, I can assure you I do. I've never stopped wanting you.'

'But when I told you I was pregnant you agreed that whatever we'd had was over.'

'I was in shock. Angry. After a lifetime of maintaining a healthy distrust of everyone around me I felt like I'd been the biggest fool, falling for the oldest trick in the book.'

That still stung. 'And now?'

'I know you're not like that, Carrie. I knew it then. I just couldn't undo a lifetime's teaching in twenty-four hours.'

'So you trust me?'

Massimo nodded. 'Yes, but even now it's not easy for me to admit it.'

Carrie appreciated his honesty.

He said, 'But you don't trust me.'

She balked at that. 'I… I do.'

And she knew she did…but deep down there was a place where doubt and fear lingered.

Massimo shook his head. He took a step towards her. She could feel his heat.

'No, there's something holding you back,' he said, 'And after your experiences I can't blame you. But I do still want you, Carrie. These last couple of months have been the longest of my life…wanting you. I think that if you can come to trust me, and knowing that we want each other, we have as good a chance as anyone in making a marriage work.'

She opened her mouth but he put up a hand, stopping her from talking.

'We certainly have a better chance than our parents had. I'm just asking that you give this…*us*…a chance.'

Carrie had been about to refute his claim that they wanted each other, but she was glad now that she hadn't spoken that lie, because he would have laughed in her face.

But how on earth was she going to cope now that she knew he did still want her?

CHAPTER NINE

Two weeks later

CARRIE GROANED AND stretched her back. It was getting harder and harder to hide her growing bump. She'd noticed staff looking at her and whispering behind her back. And whenever she had dealings with Massimo their last conversation hung in the air between them, as pregnant as her belly.

Her whole body ached to be touched. The air crackled with live electricity whenever they were close.

It was embarrassing.

He was growing more brooding, matching the inclement January weather outside. Lowering grey skies and a bitter chill. Winter had come and it was here in Massimo's townhouse.

Carrie knew she was running out of time. Massimo was right. She couldn't keep working here as if nothing had changed. She had to face up to her future and decide what was best for her and the babies.

But not today. It was Sunday morning and she had the day off. She planned on spending it hiding from the world, from Massimo, and all of the things she should be thinking about.

She planned on paying homage to her mother and binge-watching all the old movies they'd loved.

She was dressed in leisurewear—joggers and a sweatshirt. She stopped in front of a mirror and pulled her sweatshirt up to reveal the very distinct bump of her belly. Without her uniform and trying to suck herself in, it was very noticeable now. In another month she would have a scan that would reveal the sex of the babies—all being well. Making this even more of a reality.

The back of her neck prickled and she tensed. In the mirror she saw a reflection of Massimo in the doorway. She was caught for a moment, wondering if she was imagining him there, like she imagined him far too much in her dreams, and also when she was awake.

But he didn't disappear.

She whirled around, dropping the sweatshirt again to cover her belly. 'Excuse me?'

Massimo looked unrepentant. 'I did knock. You didn't hear me.'

That was very possible. Carrie felt exposed. And shabby. And then she noticed that Massimo was wearing faded jeans and a woollen sweater. He hardly ever dressed down.

'Was there something you wanted?'

He looked at her and she felt the zing of his silent response. Her cheeks grew hot. Then he said, 'Yes, I want to show you something, but it's out of the city. It's a drive. Will you come with me?'

Carrie automatically wanted to say no, but she felt as if she'd been running for a long time, and she just wanted to give in and let someone else take over.

'Okay.'

Massimo looked shocked. 'You'll come?'

'Yes.'

'You might want to change into something warmer—it's cold out.'

She'd heard snow being forecast on the radio earlier. 'When do you want to go?' she asked.

'As soon as you're ready.'

'Give me fifteen minutes.'

He left, and Carrie slipped out of her casual clothes and picked out a pair of maternity jeans, which she paired with thick socks and an undershirt and a fleece top. She pulled her hair back, and then at the last moment a rogue part of her made her leave it down.

Because Massimo liked it down.

She made a face at herself. But she left it down.

She went downstairs to meet Massimo and took a sheepskin jacket out of the closet. She was effectively swaddled. No chance of anyone noticing the bump.

But Massimo had just seen it.

He appeared then, as if conjured from her thoughts. He pulled on a warm jacket too, and said, 'Ready?'

She nodded and followed him out to his SUV. He was driving. He opened the passenger door and she got in. She watched him walk around the front and sighed a little at the way he moved with such effortless athletic grace.

They were silent as Massimo drove through the relatively quiet streets and then took one of London's main arteries out of the city. Carrie saw signs for Surrey.

Massimo asked, 'Aren't you curious about where we're going?'

No, because that would mean initiating conversation.

Carrie said, 'I like surprises.'

'Fair enough.'

The skies were even lower now, and that particular leaden colour that signalled snow. But Carrie wasn't unduly worried. Even if it did snow, it most likely wouldn't settle.

After about an hour, Massimo drove through a picturesque village and then slowed down on the other side as they drove alongside an old wall. After a few minutes he turned into a wide gateway. The iron gates opened automatically and he drove up a long and winding drive, surrounded by nothing as far as the eye could see except rolling hills and bare trees, lush fields even in winter.

Carrie sat up straight when a very imposing and frankly intimidatingly large house—no, surely a castle?—came into view ahead of them, between two long lines of manicured bushes.

'Where are we?'

Massimo's voice was tight when he answered. 'The family seat, Linden Hall.'

Ah. Understanding dawned. He wanted to show her exactly what their children were going to inherit.

At first glance the building was almost pretty, but Carrie shivered slightly. All the windows and the two imposing wings on either end of the building gave it a slightly less pretty edge.

Massimo drove the car right up to the front door. But 'door' was too ineffectual a word for what this massive entrance really was. He got out and the door opened to reveal a relatively normal-looking older couple, who were smiling at Massimo.

Carrie was surprised to see him greet them warmly, with kisses. She got out, curious.

He turned to her and said, 'Carrie, I'd like you to meet Sheila and Tom Fields. They live here and caretake the estate for me.'

Of course. Carrie had heard their names over the years, but she'd never met them.

She moved forward and shook their hands, smiling shyly. 'I can imagine that's some undertaking.'

Tom chuckled. 'Oh, yes! We have four hundred acres here, not to mention the house, but we have a dedicated team to help us.'

Sheila smiled warmly. 'Please, come in out of the cold. We've prepared a light lunch.'

Carrie's stomach rumbled embarrassingly. She saw Sheila's shrewd eyes drop to her midriff and widen slightly. Carrie looked down to see her coat hanging open and the unmistakable bulge of her growing bump on view. She smiled weakly.

They were ushered in and taken straight down to a massive state-of-the-art kitchen that still managed to be warm and homely. While Tom was talking estate business to Massimo, Carrie went to help Sheila with the lunch.

The older woman said, 'So you're Massimo's London housekeeper. We never really go up to town, but we have heard of you.'

Carrie went still at the thought of what Massimo might have said. The woman seemed to take pity on her.

'Don't worry, he hasn't said a thing. I'm putting two and two together and probably coming up with six. But all I know is that Massimo has never brought anyone here, and unless you're coming to take over our jobs...'

Carrie smiled weakly again. 'No, your jobs are safe.'

'Well, then,' Sheila said, with a twinkle in her eye.

But she didn't elaborate on that, and Carrie was grateful as she helped her to set out soup and bread and some salad.

After lunch, and a very genial chat, Carrie knew she liked the couple. They were down to earth and straightforward.

Massimo stood up. 'I'm going to show Carrie around.'

Tom stood up too. 'Okay, but maybe not outside for now. I don't like the look of that sky.'

Neither did Carrie when Massimo led her back into the entrance hall and she saw the vast mass of slate-grey outside. She shivered again.

'Cold? Do you want me to get your coat?'

Carrie shook her head. 'No, I'm fine.'

'Come on—let me give you the tour.'

Carrie dutifully followed Massimo through vast reception rooms, ballrooms, dining rooms, and then upstairs to more bedrooms than she could count. It was dizzying.

When he took her up to the top level, where the servants' quarters used to be, Carrie stopped in the middle of a corridor. He stopped too, and looked at her.

She put her hands out. 'Okay, I get it, Massimo. Consider your point made. Our children stand to inherit one of the country's finest estates.'

Massimo leant against a wall and folded his arms. 'I've always hated this place. I had actually intended donating it to the National Trust, ensuring that all profits made would go to charity.'

'Oh.'

'But in light of our current situation I've decided to hold off. I will open it to the public, though, to help Sheila and Tom with the upkeep. And again any profits can go to charity. But I'll leave it up to our children to decide what they want to do with it.'

Our children.

Those words sent far too many conflicting emotions through her.

Carrie saw something out of the corner of her eye and looked out of the window. She gasped.

Massimo looked too, and cursed softly. He said, 'Come on, we need to get back to Tom and Sheila.'

Carrie was still mesmerised by the fact that in the space of time it had taken them to walk through the house—admittedly it was vast—the world had turned white outside. A thick blanket of snow now covered everything and it was still falling heavily.

She hurried after Massimo and found him in the hall with Sheila and Tom, their coats on. They looked worried.

Tom was saying, 'The forecast isn't good. They're already saying the small roads are blocked. If you don't have to go back, I'd advise staying the night. They're saying it'll clear tomorrow.'

Carrie immediately wanted to protest, but she bit her lip.

Sheila came over. 'I'm sorry we have to leave you here, but the kitchen is well stocked and Massimo will light some fires. The water is hot—you'll be fine.'

'Where are you going?' asked Carrie. 'Will you be all right?'

'Yes, fine. We live in a cottage on the estate, not far from the house—if we leave now we'll get there safely. Tom can clear the road from there in the morning.'

Carrie didn't want to worry this woman, so she said, 'We'll be fine here. I think a night in a listed mansion can't exactly be considered a hardship.'

The woman smiled, and her eyes shone with genuine warmth as she said conspiratorially, 'I'm so glad Massimo has found someone like *you*, dear. He deserves to be happy.'

The woman was gone with her husband before Carrie could fully absorb that nugget.

When they were gone, driving off in their own sturdy SUV, Massimo put on his coat, saying, 'I need to go and get some supplies for the fires.'

'Do you need help?'

'Not for this. Maybe see what's in the kitchen that we can have for dinner later?'

Carrie watched as he left and got into the car and drove off. The snow was already a few inches high against the tyres. She felt a moment of fear, watching him go out of sight, and the house suddenly seemed huge and ominous around her... as if ghostly eyes were watching her.

She shook it off, telling herself she was being ridiculous, and made her way down to the comforting kitchen.

She was poring over a cookbook when Massimo returned. She tried not to let it show how relieved she was. He was carrying an armload of logs and he was covered in snowflakes.

He put the logs down by the fireplace and started to light it. He did this with an ease that spoke of his doing it many times before.

Carrie said, 'I wouldn't have thought you were used to doing the manual labour around here—weren't you the cossetted heir?'

Massimo made a huffing sound. 'That's what my mother would have preferred, but there was usually so much chaos going on upstairs at any given time that Ric and I used to come down here and do our homework or hang out with the staff.' He stood up and looked around. 'This was always my favourite part of the house. Sheila and Tom weren't living on the estate then, but they were a consistent presence and provided some security—more than the revolving door of nannies.'

Carrie marvelled again at the dark reality of Massimo's supposedly gilded life.

Massimo took off his coat and hung it on the back of the door. 'Do you mind staying here tonight?'

She shrugged. 'Looks like we have no choice. And I can think of worse places to stay.'

As if he couldn't help himself, he came over and reached out, touching her cheek with a finger. 'You're one a million, you know that?'

His touch was like an electric shock, zinging right into her blood.

Warmth bloomed near her heart.

Around her heart.

In her heart.

She froze inside. *No.* She wasn't ready to allow that thought in.

She pulled down Massimo's hand and stepped back. 'I'm really not.'

Stubble was lining Massimo's jaw. His hair was damp and dishevelled from the snow. Carrie ached for his touch again. To touch him. Wanting him and needing to keep her distance was making her dizzy.

She took another step back and babbled, 'There's the makings of a stew in the pantry and fridge… I've found a nice recipe… I can make that later.'

'Keep resisting, Carrie, for as long as you can. I'm not going anywhere.'

Massimo sauntered back out of the kitchen and Carrie called after him. 'You planned this, didn't you?'

He came back to the doorway and opened his hands out wide. 'I can do a lot of things, Carrie, but even I can't influence the weather.'

He disappeared again and Carrie cursed him.

To take her mind off Massimo and their situation, she put on an apron and started preparing dinner. It was best to keep herself busy.

Carrie looked up at one point and realised that the fire was dying down and it was growing dark outside. She threw some more logs on the fire and put the stew in the oven.

Wondering where Massimo was, but also reluctant to find him, she wandered upstairs. Massive portraits of the people who must be Massimo's ancestors glared down at her.

She shouldn't be here.

She shouldn't be carrying his child.

Worse, his children.

On an impulse Carrie stuck her tongue out at one particularly glowering dour-looking man.

'I used to do that too.'

Carrie jumped about three feet in the air, her hand over her heart. Massimo was standing in a doorway nearby.

'Sorry, I didn't mean to scare you.'

Carrie looked back at the picture and admitted, 'I can't help but feel they're judging me.'

'You're not the only one. Remember, we were the children of an Italian woman who might have been a countess but was still considered not exactly the best choice of society wife at the time.'

Carrie looked at him. He'd obviously inherited his looks from his mother's side. 'You really did stick out your tongue at them?'

'Yes, just like this.'

And he stuck out his tongue—which immediately made Carrie think of how it had felt on her mouth, in her mouth, on her skin…between her legs.

She blurted out, 'I just came to tell you that the stew should be ready in an hour or so.'

'Lovely, thank you. I'll come down shortly.'

Carrie fled back to the kitchen.

'This is delicious,' Massimo declared when he'd swallowed some of the stew.

'I can't really take any credit. Sheila had the ingredients ready to go—all I did was throw them together.'

The kitchen, in spite of its size, was cosy. The fire crackled in the huge fireplace, sending out comforting warmth.

After they'd eaten in companionable silence for a few minutes, Carrie said, 'I was thinking about some things…'

Massimo put down his cutlery. 'Oh?'

Carrie could see the gleam in his eyes. She said quickly, 'Not that.'

Massimo took a sip of water. 'What, then?'

'About the children. They'll have this huge legacy, of course, but I don't want them to go to a boarding school in the middle of nowhere with posh kids.

'Sorry,' she said then, in case she might have offended him.

'I agree.' Massimo wiped his mouth with a napkin.

Carrie was shocked. 'You do?'

'Boarding school did nothing for me and Ric except teach us how to stand up to bullies who thought we were inferior because we were half-Italian. I'd be happy for the children to go to a day school.'

'Near us?'

Massimo's gaze narrowed on Carrie. '*Us?* So you'll be living with me?'

She cursed herself—she hadn't been thinking. 'Not necessarily, but I would be nearby.'

Massimo looked exasperated. 'Carrie, look—'

Suddenly the lights went out.

Massimo cursed. 'That's the power gone. I guess it was inevitable.'

'What do we do now?'

It was pitch-black except for the firelight.

'Find some torches and candles...they're in a cupboard here.'

He got up and turned on his phone light, found some torches and thick candles.

Carrie took a torch. Its powerful beam lit up the kitchen enough for her to gather the plates and put them in a pile by the sink.

Massimo said, 'If the power is still off in the morning we have a generator we can power up.'

Carrie felt panicky. 'Tom said it was only going to snow tonight.'

'It's just a back-up,' he said. 'There's nothing for it now but to go to bed—it'll soon get cold. I'll go up and light fires in the bedrooms. You wait here.'

Carrie immediately thought of herself, sitting there in the dark, and said, 'No, I'll come with you and help. I don't mind.'

Massimo shrugged. He led her upstairs, his torch lighting their way.

Carrie asked, 'Does this happen a lot?'

'Regularly enough, which is why we have the generator. These days, though, they usually have the power restored within hours. I'm sure it'll be on again by morning.' Then he asked, 'Are you scared of the dark?'

'I'm not overly keen on it...put it that way.'

Her husband had known she hated the dark, and had insisted on turning off every light at night. It had increased Carrie's sense of fear even though he'd never lifted a hand to her.

Massimo took her hand and another one of Carrie's defences wobbled precariously.

They reached the first floor and Massimo opened the door to a massive bedroom. 'You can have this room.'

Carrie knew immediately it must be his. 'I don't mind a smaller one...really.'

He ignored her. 'I'll take the adjoining one. I'll just light the fires.'

Carrie could see he must have set them earlier, and within minutes they were both burning brightly, instantly reducing her sense of fear and bringing warmth to the rooms.

Massimo pulled something out of a set of drawers and handed it to her. 'They'll drown you, but they're all I have.'

It was a pair of pyjamas. His.

He said, 'There's some clean unused underwear in the drawers too. Again, far too big, but they'll do just until we get back to town.'

The thought of wearing Massimo's briefs, even if unused, sent an erotic thrill through Carrie. 'I'll be fine.'

'Here's another torch.'

Carrie misjudged the distance and the torch fell to the ground between them. She bent down to get it, and when she stood up again found Massimo was much closer. Suddenly it was hard to breathe.

The lines of his face looked much harsher in the flickering light of the fire. His eyes were totally dark and unreadable. He looked huge, too—a massive broad shape. With every cell in her body Carrie wanted nothing more than to step close and wind her arms around him, let him silence all the voices in her head with his mouth and his tongue and his body.

Carrie could almost feel him compelling her to do it. She just needed to take a step forward and he would catch her. It would be so easy...but it would make her forget why it was so important to resist his pull.

She took a step back. Massimo's jaw clenched.

She said, 'Goodnight, Massimo.'

'If you need anything during the night, I'm just through that door.'

'I won't...but thank you.'

Why did her voice sound so thready and unsure?

Disgusted with herself, Carrie watched Massimo disappear and shut the door behind him. She felt wide awake, keyed up. She found the en-suite bathroom and ran herself a bath. As promised by Sheila, the water was hot.

Carrie sank down into the water, relishing the feeling of weightlessness. She put a hand on her bump, but quickly diverted her thoughts when images of Massimo intruded. She was *not* going to humiliate herself again when he was mere feet away.

She quickly washed and stepped out, drying herself and

pulling on Massimo's pyjamas. She didn't bother with the trousers as the top came halfway down her thighs.

She turned off the torch, climbed into the bed and fell into a fitful sleep that was dominated by dreams. Dreams of running through this house looking for something…or someone. In the dream she eventually she stopped outside a door and pushed it open. Massimo was in bed with his back to her. A woman's manicured hand was on his shoulder. He turned to look at Carrie and his expression was remote, cold.

'You are not welcome here. Get out.'

It was like a knife sliding through her ribs. White-hot pain and then red-hot jealousy. Carrie ran around the bed and pulled at the other woman, crying and saying, 'But I'm different…you told me I was!'

Carrie woke up and sat bolt upright, heart pounding.

Massimo's rejection of her was so vivid, the pain real.

She knew where she was, even though it was dark and the fire was low. She was breathing heavily. Her skin was hot and she was perspiring. She could still feel the strength of emotions running through her. The pain and the jealousy. The aching for Massimo to be in bed with *her*. No one else.

She didn't think.

She acted on an instinct too strong to deny.

She turned on the torch and got out of bed, went to the door. Hesitating for only the briefest of moments, she opened it and went into the next room.

Massimo was sprawled across the bed. Torso bare. Sheets tangled around his waist. He looked as if he was in the throes of some dream too.

Carrie almost turned back, but at that moment Massimo woke up.

He came up on one elbow. 'Carrie?'

'Yes.'

'Are you okay?'

'I had a bad dream…but that's not it. I'm saying yes.'

'Yes, to what?' He sat up, threw the sheet back. He was naked.

'I want you.'

'Come here… I'm not sure if I'm dreaming or not.'

She walked over, dropping the torch as she did so. It sent its beam of light over the wall, illuminating faded wallpaper, but she didn't see that. She just saw Massimo, looking like a god, sitting on the bed.

She walked right up to him. There wasn't a moment of doubt in her head or body. This felt *right*. She couldn't even recall why she'd been so determined to deny herself now.

Massimo reached for her, taking her by the waist. Her much thicker waist. She wore nothing under the pyjama top. He started to undo the buttons and it fell open. Massimo sucked in a breath and Carrie's blood surged. She felt powerful under his burning gaze.

He cupped her fuller breasts, his thumbs moving over her nipples. She was so sensitive she trembled. Massimo pushed the pyjama top off completely and tugged her until she fell on the bed.

His hands roved over her whole body, learning the changes, rousing her to a fever-pitch of need. His mouth found her nipple, tugging it into his mouth, laving it with his tongue.

Carrie grabbed his head, her fingers tunnelling through his hair. Holding him. But then he moved down. His hand was on her belly now. Fingers spread wide. There was a reverence in his gaze that undid something inside her. Another defence that she knew she would have to rebuild tomorrow. But for now…

'Mass… *Please*… I need you.'

He moved down between her legs, spreading them so he

could see her. Carrie's hips twitched. She had dreamt of this so much… And then he was there, his hot breath on her, fingers pushing her even wider as he bent his head and placed his mouth right on the core of her body, his wicked tongue pushing her over the edge of pleasure.

The waves were still ebbing when he moved over her, his erection in his hand, moisture beading the tip. For a moment he hesitated, and Carrie almost begged him again, but then he said, 'Is this okay…? Will I harm the babies?'

Carrie reached for him, greedy. 'It's fine…the doctor said it's fine.'

She might have been embarrassed if she hadn't been feeling so desperate.

Massimo was careful to keep his full weight off her even as he sank deep inside, and Carrie let out an almost feral sound. Slowly he moved, taking their bodies on a dance that was unique to them. Slow at first, and then fast and hard. Carrie wasn't ready for the next rush of pleasure. It caught her by surprise and she couldn't breathe for a long moment, aware of Massimo's body jerking against her and his own guttural sounds as he climaxed inside her.

Carrie woke as dawn was breaking outside, tucked into Massimo's embrace, her back to his front. She knew instinctively that he was awake too and without a word they made love again, without even changing position. He cupped her breast and put a hand between her legs, opening her up, and she gasped when he thrust deep and hard. When she came in a rush of pleasure Massimo tumbled just behind her, and as she fell asleep again she felt completely at peace and wondered faintly if she was still dreaming.

CHAPTER TEN

BUT IT HADN'T been a dream. When Carrie woke again the sun was high and Massimo was standing at the window. Dressed in his jeans again and a jumper. She felt thoroughly dishevelled, and deliciously sore between her legs.

He turned around and Carrie pulled the sheet up. It was a bit late for modesty, but she was hurtling into full-on regret and recrimination.

What had she done?

'Don't do that,' Massimo said.

'Do what?'

'Regret what happened.'

Carrie's face grew hot.

Massimo muttered, 'I knew it…'

Carrie sat up. 'Can you pass me a robe or something, please?'

Massimo plucked a robe off the end of the bed and handed it to her. He didn't look away as she got into it, and she hated it that her body responded to his unabashed gaze with such eagerness, her blood thrumming as if she hadn't just spent the night in his bed.

She got out of bed and tied the robe tightly around her. 'Do we have to have this conversation now?'

'It's as good a time as any.'

'Look, what happened last night… It's pregnancy hormones. It's common for women to feel more—'

'Horny?' Massimo supplied crudely.

'Something like that.'

'You're saying that's all it is?'

'Well, how would I know? I've been pregnant since the last time we slept together.'

Liar, whispered a voice.

She knew well it had nothing to do with being pregnant. And she knew she couldn't not be honest.

'No,' she admitted. 'Of course it's not just that. I've wanted you too.'

'There's something I need to tell you,' he said.

Instinctively Carrie sensed it was something she really didn't want to hear, but she said nothing.

He said, 'I've realised something over the past few months. I think I always knew, but I told myself that I just wanted marriage in order to provide security and stability…to offer our children a better life. But it's more than that. Carrie, I know what a bad marriage looks like. How much damage it can inflict on children. That's why I never wanted one. I felt sure I'd pass something on…the same destructive streak Ric and my parents had… But I know that's not rational. They reacted the way they did due to whatever dysfunction it was they experienced. But since meeting you…since being with you… I've seen how two people can communicate and be together. I want more, Carrie. I want it all. The chance to build a happy life together and for our children. But I won't settle for anything less than *all* of you.'

Carrie instinctively took a step back.

Massimo saw the movement and wouldn't let her escape his dark gaze.

'Carrie, I love you. Those six weeks without you after New

York were torture. I missed you so much it was like a physical pain. And it wasn't just about the sex. You crept under my skin and into my heart. There's only one other person I have loved this much...'

Carrie was hearing his words but it was as if they were very far away. As if there was a glass shield between her and Massimo. She felt numb. Encased in ice.

Flashbacks were filling her head. Her husband saying, *'But I love you so much, Carrie. Marry me and I'll look after you always. You need me.'*

Past and present were tangled, and all Carrie could think was that she had to protect herself from being manipulated all over again.

Before Massimo could speak again, she said, 'You don't need to lie to get me to marry you, Massimo. If I decide to marry you it'll be for all the reasons you've already outlined.'

His jaw clenched at her rejection of what he'd said. 'So you're agreeing to marriage, then?'

'No,' Carrie said quickly, feeling claustrophobic. 'I mean, I haven't really thought it through...'

'Because you're scared. You're scared of losing yourself again—of handing over your agency to someone who will take advantage. But you're not that woman any more, Carrie. And I am not that man. You *know* this.'

It was as if he was reaching inside her and rooting through all her deepest insecurities, plucking them out to expose them to the bright daylight. She felt unbelievably threatened.

'Last night was a mistake,' she said.

'No, it wasn't. It was inevitable,' he said. And then, 'I'm not lying, Carrie. I'm not denying that people can use love to be manipulative and cruel, but what I feel for you isn't that. I told myself I'd never love again after losing Ricardo, and I was so careful. I never allowed any woman a chance to get close, and that worked fine—until you. The minute I touched you I knew it was different.'

Carrie wanted to put her hands over her ears. She wanted to block out Massimo's smooth words. The way they were winding around her like silken threads beckoning her to believe him. Trust him.

But her past loomed like a large, malevolent spectre behind her. Reminding her not to be so weak.

She looked at Massimo. 'I want to go back to London now.'

Tension crackled between them. When he spoke, Massimo's voice was as cold as she felt.

'Luckily, Tom has cleared the drive and most of the snow has already melted. We'll leave as soon as you're ready.'

Carrie fled the room on shaky legs. She closed the door between them and with a numb brain had a shower, avoiding looking at the faint marks of Massimo's hands on her body.

She dressed in her own clothes again and roughly dried her hair, pulling it back.

Downstairs, Massimo was waiting, grim. Sheila and Tom were there, and Carrie said goodbye to them. The older couple seemed to sense the tension and weren't overly chatty. Carrie was glad. Her emotions bubbled too close to the surface, raw and volatile.

The journey back into town was silent. But the tension was mounting to an unbearable pitch.

When they were driving through central London, not far from Massimo's house, Carrie acted on impulse. 'You can let me out here,' she told him.

'What? Here?'

There was an art gallery nearby—Carrie had recognised it. 'Please, Massimo, I just need some time on my own.'

With evident reluctance he pulled in at a safe spot and Carrie put her hand on the door.

He said, 'Wait, do you have your mobile with you?'

She nodded.

'Call me and I'll come and get you, okay?'

Carrie nodded and got out.

Massimo drove away. She could see him looking in the rear-view mirror and then he was gone.

She let out a shaky breath.

She headed for the art gallery, just wanting to lose herself in a crowd. Inside it was warm, and not that busy. There was an exhibition featuring Mexican artist Frida Kahlo, and on a whim Carrie bought a ticket.

She went in and within minutes, in spite of her own turmoil, was transported into this fascinating woman's life.

Her early polio illness. The shattering bus accident when she was a teenager that left her with lifelong injuries and chronic pain. The passionate love affair with Diego Rivera that lasted until she died, in spite of many infidelities on either side.

She, too, had poignantly lost more than one pregnancy. And yet through it all she'd lived, loved and created. Her life force had been strong in spite of her many struggles. She hadn't cowered pitifully from the world, nor from the man who loved her—*really* loved her. She'd trusted. And she'd loved.

Love.

As if she had just needed to see it from another perspective, Carrie felt her heart crack open. She couldn't stop it. The walls of fear and defence she'd been clinging on to so desperately dissolved.

She'd never known love before—not like this. She'd had a toxic example of love. She'd known intellectually that she hadn't really loved her husband, or he her, but it had taken until this moment to really understand what real love looked like.

And that was why she'd been so scared. Because it was terrifying. And magnificent. And transformational. From the moment Massimo had first looked at her, four years ago, he'd unlocked something inside her.

She didn't even realise she was crying until a woman handed her a tissue and said, 'She's an inspiration, isn't she?'

Carrie could only nod.

Somehow, she stumbled out of the art gallery. She was undone. She was in pieces. But it felt okay. These were pieces she could use to put herself back together. She had no choice now but to trust, and she knew that no matter what happened she would be okay—because she was strong enough to withstand anything. Even Massimo telling her he loved her just to get her where he wanted her.

Because she loved him with every fibre of her being.

Massimo paced back and forth in the reception hall. He'd tried calling Carrie, but her phone was off.

He shouldn't have left her alone on the street.

He shouldn't have told her he loved her.

He'd spooked her.

It had been hours now. She could be anywhere.

The thought that he'd spooked her so much that she'd run away sent a chill down his spine. The thought of never seeing her again was terrifying.

It was getting dark outside.

Massimo was almost in full panic mode. He'd only been like this once before, when he'd seen his brother spin off that race track in Monte Carlo.

He was about to find his keys and get into his car to go and look for her when the gate intercom rang.

The butler appeared and Massimo snapped at him. 'I have it.'

He answered.

'Hi, it's me. I forgot my keys.'

Carrie.

Relief made Massimo feel shaky.

He pressed the buzzer and saw her slip through the gate. He could see her on the security monitor by the door. When she approached the front door he opened it—as she had done countless times for him.

The irony wasn't lost on him.

He tried to curb his panic when she came through the door. 'Where were you?'

She looked at him, and she had an expression on her face he couldn't decipher.

'Can we talk?' she asked.

Massimo nodded and closed the door and led her to his study. His relief was tempered now with the frustration he'd felt earlier, and anger at himself for saying what he had.

It was too soon.

She came in behind him and slipped off her coat, draping it over a chair. She looked wind-tousled. She looked beautiful.

The memory of her reaction earlier made him say, 'Look, Carrie, I don't want to pressure you into anything. I just—'

'Did you mean it?'

He looked at her. She was standing behind a chair and her hands were gripping the back of it. Knuckles white.

He went still inside. 'Did I mean what?'

'That you love me.'

Massimo knew that this moment counted for everything. If he couldn't convince Carrie of this, they didn't have a chance.

'Yes,' he said simply. 'I did. I would not use that word to manipulate anyone. I have avoided using that word my whole life. I didn't even tell my brother I loved him, and I've always regretted that.'

Carrie's eyes looked suspiciously bright. 'I'm sure he knew.'

'Do *you* know? That's what's important here.'

'I'm no one special. I'm just your housekeeper.'

Massimo shook his head. 'You are the woman who has humbled me. No one else ever managed that because no one else ever interested me enough. I never wanted another woman beyond one night, and that made me arrogant...complacent. I thought I was in control. Then you came along and I realised I'd been fooling myself. I just hadn't met you.'

Carrie came out from behind the chair and took a small box out of her jeans pocket. She came over to stand in front of him. Her hands were trembling.

She opened the box to reveal a thick gold band. She looked up at him and said, in a voice full of emotion, 'Massimo Black... Linden... Earl, Lord, all that you are, will you please marry me?'

Massimo was in shock. Emotions were rushing through him, filling him and breaking him wide open. He shook his head faintly, 'None of that matters, and yes, I'll marry you but on one condition.'

'What's that?'

'That you love me too. I want everything, Carrie. Your heart and soul and body and mind. And our babies.'

Carrie's eyes filled with tears. She smiled, and it was wobbly. 'You have me—heart, soul, body and mind. I love you, Massimo, and I've known it for so long. I was too afraid to admit it, because I knew that once I did I'd have no control over what happened... I was terrified to think that I'd repeat the mistakes of the past. I was afraid I'd be handing you power over me... It was all tangled up... I didn't want to be weak again.'

Massimo cupped her cheek with his hand. 'You were abused by a master manipulator, Carrie, and you paid the highest price. You were never weak and you are *not* weak. You're the strongest person I know.'

Massimo bent his head and kissed Carrie so softly and with such reverence that her heart cracked open all over again. The pain of the past dissolved completely, and the hope she'd been holding back expanded and filled every inch of her being.

When he pulled back she felt dizzy. She was still holding the box. She smiled at Massimo and took the ring out of the box, took his hand in hers. 'It's only a placeholder until you can choose your own ring,' she said.

'Shouldn't I be saying that to you?'

Carrie put the ring on his finger. It fitted perfectly. She wound her arms around his neck and pressed close. She lifted her face to his and said, 'We have time to say all the things... but first, make love to me, Mass.'

'Always, my love,' he breathed—and did exactly as she asked.

Massimo never did choose another ring. A month later they were married in a discreet civil ceremony in London, with Sheila and Tom from Linden Hall as their witnesses.

EPILOGUE

Two years and three months later, Rio de Janeiro

THE TWO SMALL bodies were sprawled side by side on the sun-bed under the shade. They had just turned two the day before. They were sturdy and mischievous and demons and angels all at once. They both had dark hair, but Ricardo's eyes took after Carrie's, greenish hazel, and Frida's were dark, like her father's. And for a short time, blessedly, they were asleep.

Sheila and Tom had come with them to help look after the babies and to have a holiday. They'd become much beloved adoptive grandparents to the twins, and were now off on a tour for a couple of days.

Massimo and Carrie had kept Ricardo's penthouse apart-ment down on the beach for themselves, as a secret bolthole, but they'd bought a more practical villa-style house in a leafy suburb of Rio for the family.

Carrie sighed contentedly and settled back into Massi-mo's embrace on their own lounger. His arms were wrapped around her, their legs entwined.

She could feel the rumble of his chest against her back when he said, 'You never did tell me why you wanted to call our daughter Frida.'

Carrie turned so that she was looking up at him. She traced the lines of his face with a finger. Love for this man filled her entire being. For everything he'd shown her about what love really was. Empowering and unselfish and amazing.

She'd grown into herself in a way that still made her emotional, fully stepping into her power and her confidence. There were no dark corners any more, and if there were they worked through them together.

'I love you,' she said simply, the words flowing out easily.

Massimo took her hand and lifted it, kissing her palm. 'I love you too… Now tell me why you wanted to call our daughter Frida.'

Carrie smiled. It was one of the last secrets she'd kept from him… 'Well, do you remember the day I proposed?'

Massimo smiled too. 'The best day of my life? Of course.'

Carrie told him about the exhibition, and how it had opened her up and allowed her to be brave.

Massimo dropped her hand. 'You mean that if it wasn't for Frida Kahlo I'd still be chasing you and trying to get you to agree you love me too?'

Carrie chuckled. 'I was already caving by then…she just helped.'

Massimo put his fingers to his mouth and kissed them, sending the kiss to the sky. 'Thank you, Frida Kahlo.'

Carrie took Massimo's hand then, and brought it to her belly. She saw his eyes widen.

She nodded, feeling emotional. 'We'll have to start thinking of a new name soon.'

The pure joy on his face rippled through her too. But she was apprehensive. They'd been in such a little bubble since they'd married, and with the twins…

'What is it?' Massimo asked, of course seeing everything.

'Are we moving too fast?' she asked.

Massimo grinned and lay down, pulling Carrie over him. Her hair fell around them like a wild golden curtain.

Massimo twined some strands around his fingers.

'Not fast enough,' he said. 'Didn't I mention I want at least six children?'

Carrie groaned. 'Can I have the commitment-phobic man back, please?'

Massimo shook his head. 'That man is gone for ever. You ruined him.'

Carrie could feel his body responding under hers. After all, they were wearing minimal clothing. She in a bikini and him in swim-shorts.

She squirmed against him deliciously.

He groaned softly and kissed her, saying, 'You'll pay for that.'

Then Massimo sobered for a moment. 'I can't wait for our family to expand. The joy that you and Frida and Ric have brought me... I think what we're afraid of is that we can't take any more joy...'

Carrie felt emotional. 'Maybe that's it.'

He shook his head and smiled. 'There's no one else I'd want to be on this adventure with. You are the centre of my being, and as long as you're with me we can do anything.'

Carrie mock-growled at him. 'You'll never get rid of me.'

'Good.'

At that moment there was movement, and a small sleepy voice from nearby. 'Mama? Dada?'

Carrie and Massimo looked at one another, and then he said, 'Later, Lady Linden.'

She put on a look of mock outrage. 'I do believe that as you're an earl, I'm actually a countess.'

'I knew it—you only married me for my titles.'

Carrie laughed. 'Well, that and...'

She moved against him, and after one more indulgent kiss she got up to tend to the twins, who were both awake now.

Later, once the twins were asleep for the night, in the soft darkness under a tropical moon, they celebrated their news again, in a very private and intimate way.

Afterwards, deliciously sated and drowsy, Carrie pressed a kiss to the place between Massimo's neck and shoulder. 'I love you, Mass. For ever.'

He kissed her mouth and then put a hand on her belly. 'I love you. I love *us*. It's not too fast—it's perfect.'

And it *was* perfect.

* * * * *

AWAKENED
ON HER ROYAL
WEDDING NIGHT

DANI COLLINS

MILLS & BOON

CHAPTER ONE

"You'll die out there!" the Prince shouted from his speed-boat. "I'm not coming after you!"

Good, Claudine Bergqvist thought, even though the sea was cold enough that her muscles were already cramping. The water was dark and pulled at the maxi-dress she wore. The jersey silk tangled against her legs as she tried to frog-kick. Waves dipped and rolled, making it hard to catch her breath without taking in a mouthful of water.

She was swimming a breaststroke so she could keep her vision fixated on the island ahead of her, but even though she was a strong swimmer, that black rise of land with only a few twinkling lights upon it was still terrifyingly far away. Barbed hooks of panic were trying to take hold in her while her imagination ran away with her. What else lurked in these waters besides her and that horrible man who had lured her onto his boat?

She heard the engine start up and stopped to tread water, swiveling to see if he was coming after her.

No. The running lights turned away from her. The aero-dynamic speedboat shot away in a burst of its engine, spew-ing froth behind it.

She couldn't see the yacht that had birthed it, or the super yacht where she had started her evening. This whole night had been a nesting doll of ever more perilous situations, not that she had seen it at the time.

"Come to a big party on a big boat. Why don't some of you come to a smaller party on my smaller yacht? Actually, let's take my runabout for a spin, just you and me."

Now it was just him, the Prince, heading back to Stella Vista, the biggest island in the chain that made up the Kingdom of Nazarine. And her, Claudine. Alone in the sea.

Her heart thumped erratically. Her abdomen tightened with so much anxiety her lungs could barely draw a breath. The wake from the departing speedboat rippled toward her, picking her up and dropping her into the trough so she lost sight of the boat.

When she spun in the water, the small island she'd seen a moment ago was gone.

She turned and turned.

Do not panic.

There it was. She kept her gaze pinned to it while she fought the clinging material of her dress. She pulled her arms from its straps before she pushed the sheath off her waist and hips, freeing herself of the encumbrance.

I can do this.

She had done many things that were difficult, including becoming the Swedish contestant in the Miss Pangea pageant despite living in America for the last fifteen years.

She had also once won a bronze medal for her breaststroke. She'd been eleven and it had been a medley relay. Her portion had only been one hundred meters, but her team had made it to the podium.

Mom needs me alive, she reminded herself as she resumed her kick, stroke, breathe.

The thought of her mother only made her more anxious, though. Ann-Marie Bergqvist hadn't wanted Claudine to do this pageant. Not any pageant. They were archaic and sexist, she'd insisted.

They were, Claudine agreed, but she'd stumbled into the first one on a lark with friends, then kept winning. At first, she had competed for a scholarship and some trendy clothes. Then luggage and a vacation in the Caribbean. She had been flattered by the modest fame and the interviews with TV personalities, but when her mother's well-managed multiple sclerosis suddenly took a sharp turn into more serious symptoms, Claudine had sold the car she'd won along with the appliances.

The cash had bought her mother some time off work and a number of specialist appointments, but her disease was not one that could be cured, only managed. Each time Claudine leveled up and won a bigger pageant, she was able to afford better care for her mother.

The global Miss Pangea pageant was one of the most lucrative. It had brought her to Nazarine, near the ankle of Italy's boot, and if she was chosen to appear in their notoriously sexy swimsuit calendar, she would receive a very generous compensation. If she made the cover, she would earn even more. In fact, she was the favorite to win the whole contest.

If she made it to shore.

Was that why the Prince had targeted her? Because she was odds on to win?

She tried not to think of it. She was already tired. The exertion of swimming was not the problem. The force of the sea was taking a toll. This was no placid pool where she could skim along. She was being shoved from all angles, catching waves up the nose and swallowing salt water.

What if she didn't survive? What if she didn't make the photo shoot tomorrow? What if she didn't win any prize money and her mother had to let her disease run its course?

What if she drowned and never saw her mother again?
Don't think of it.
Kick, stroke, breathe. Kick, stroke, breathe.

"Intruder, Your Highness." Prince Felipe's guard brought him a tablet as Felipe was sitting down to a late dinner.
Francois.

His mind always leaped to his twin when something unpredictable and less than desirable happened. Cold hatred threatened to engulf him, but Felipe habitually banked those grim, unhelpful emotions. He focused on exactly what was happening in the moment.

"How many?" He took the tablet.

"Just the one, sir." The guard tapped to show the security footage in both night vision and infrared. A swimmer was approaching the western side of the island.

Situated furthest from the rest of the islands in the Nazarine archipelago, Sentinella had been named hundreds of years ago for the protective armies that had been stationed here. Its lofty cliffs allowed unimpeded surveillance of the surrounding waters and its lack of low, sandy beaches made it difficult to infiltrate.

In fact, any craft attempting to enter that particular lagoon took a beating through a toilet bowl of currents that punched every which way. Once inside, the shallow cove was littered with sharp rocks that lurked below the surface. They shipwrecked vessels and were guaranteed to shred a knee if you didn't know where they were. There was no reward once you reached the beach at the base of the cliffs. It was mostly rocks and coarse sand.

Like its occupant, Sentinella was formidable and inhospitable to strangers.

Felipe tried to expand the image, but it was too grainy to provide many clues as to the swimmer's identity.

"How did they get here? Is there a vessel nearby?"

"The *Queen's Favorite* held a sunset dinner for the pageant contestants this evening. Tenders were buzzing around it, bringing people back and forth from Stella Vista and taking side trips to the smaller islands. That's normal for these things. There was a seven-meter speedboat stalled about a mile out an hour ago. That's the closest any came to us."

The guard's lips were tight. He knew the hostility that existed between the Princes and hated to even mention Francois.

Felipe wasn't ambushed by the news that his brother was nearby. Francois spent most of his life chasing skirt and parties around the globe, but he always came home at this time of year, bringing his sordid little beauty contest to their island kingdom.

He didn't usually send trespassers boldly up to Felipe's front door, though. Not when he had his image and his own personal interests to protect. What was he up to this time?

"Let's greet our visitor." Felipe rose without having tasted the braised duck before him.

"Sir, he might be armed."

He? Felipe looked again at the screen. The swimmer had found a rock to clasp. As their arm came out of the water, the strap of a bikini top was revealed.

"Unless she intends to spit a cyanide capsule at me, I don't think she's carrying a weapon." He strode out the door to the inner grounds of the castle fortress, then across to the gate in the wall.

Two guards followed him, radioing low communications to the rest of the team. Another two fell into place next to Felipe as he stepped beyond the wall of the castle and made for the second gate, the one that blocked access to the stairs down the cliff face.

The narrow steps had been chipped from the stone wall by long-ago soldiers. A weathered rope was mounted through eyelets pounded into the rock, providing a tenuous handhold if a foot happened to slip.

Felipe hadn't been down these steps in years, never at night, but he waved away the guard who tried to illuminate the path with a handheld spotlight. He wanted to approach more stealthily.

The quarter moon made it a treacherous descent. When they came to the bottom of the stairs, cypress trees briefly blocked his view of the water. He could hear the waves fighting one another outside the lagoon, but also heard a feminine cough and some ragged breathing near the shore.

He brushed past the guard who held out an arm, trying to hold Felipe back from advancing the short distance to the water's edge.

In the pale moonlight, a woman—a mermaid? a siren?—was crawling from the glittering, black water. She paused, rearing up so she knelt in the shallows. Water lapped around the tops of her thighs. Her hair was pewter in the moonlight and stuck in vine-like curls against her shoulders and chest. Silver droplets fell off her chin and sat like diamonds against the swells of her breasts before slithering down her abdomen. Her chest heaved and every breath held a sob of effort.

That wasn't a bikini. It was a bra and underwear, a lacy set in an indeterminate color that sat as a charcoal streak against skin that might have been tanned golden or naturally tawny, but in the cool light of the moon, turned her into a timeless black-and-white photo of a castaway survivor. Of Venus, rising from the deep.

She was the most fiercely beautiful thing Felipe had ever

seen. She made his guts twist in a mix of awe and lust, the desire to possess and an instant certainty that she could not be captured or contained.

In a surge of uncharacteristic jealousy, he wanted to physically knock his guards' gazes away from her. She was *his*.

With a fresh moan of effort, she crawled further out of the water and collapsed onto her side, chest heaving, legs still in the lapping surf.

As Felipe strode toward her, he dragged his gaze from her long thighs and trembling abdomen, past the quiver of her breasts to the way her eyes popped open beneath the anguished knot of her brows.

"What are you doing here?" he demanded in the Nazarinian dialect of Italian, crouching beside her.

The noise she made was one of pure suffering. Her arm moved in a sudden arc. A fistful of gravel peppered his face.

How was he *here*?

It didn't make sense, but Claudine didn't think, only reacted, trying to get away from the devil himself. She closed her hand on whatever bits of shells and rocks were on this godforsaken excuse for a beach and threw it at him.

While he swore roundly, she tried to roll away from him and get her arms and legs under her, but her muscles were utterly exhausted. She was shaking and weak, disoriented.

In the same moment, there were shouts and a scuffle of noise. A harsh male voice barked something in Italian. A heavy, rough weight pressed onto the back of her shoulder, squashing her onto her own feeble arms.

She should have let the sea take her because she was going to die tonight regardless of her fight to live. She let her face droop onto the pebbled beach beneath her.

I'm sorry, Mom. You were right. I'm so sorry.

There was a potent moment of silence, one that made her realize she had spoken aloud.

A burst of authoritative Italian came out of the Prince. There was the sound of a dull slap that transmitted a vibration into her shoulder before the punishing weight lifted off her back. It had been a foot, she realized, one with a roughly treaded sole. That's all she could see when she lifted her head. Boots and more boots.

"Don't attack me again," the Prince warned in his accented English. "My guards don't like it."

If only *she* had guards, she thought with brief hysteria. Instead, she had been one woman defending herself against *his* attack.

She tried to push herself into sitting up and facing him, but her arms were overcooked pasta, completely ineffectual. Every part of her hurt. She didn't even have the strength to cry.

"How did you get here?" he asked.

That seemed too obvious to bother answering. She searched for a path of escape, but only saw boots, boots, rocks and more boots. Then feet in what had to be bespoke Italian shoes. Not deck shoes like the Prince had been wearing earlier. Laced leather shoes with fancy detailing.

She could still hear the swish and churn of the water at the mouth of the lagoon. Soft waves were caressing her calves. Dare she try that route again? Swimming had been her only escape the first time, but she hadn't managed to escape him, had she?

With a sob of utter despair, she dropped her head onto her wrist.

"Why are you here?" he prodded.

Seriously?

"I was aiming for Sicily. Is this not it?" she asked in a rasp.

There was a smirk from one of the hovering guards. The aggressive one who'd stood on her earlier nudged her hip with the toe of his boot.

"Don't be smart. You're under arrest. Answer the Prince's questions."

The Prince, whom she heartily consigned to the hottest corner of hell, said something in quiet, lethal Italian that had all of his guards shuffling back a few steps.

"Now," the Prince continued in English, "if you want to lie here waiting for all your cuts to grow septic, we can do that. Or you can come up to the castle for medical attention and give me a full explanation for your presence here. Can you stand?"

He started to take hold of her arm, but a fresh surge of pure adrenaline, the kind with its roots in an atavistic desire to survive, knocked his hand away. She scrabbled for a fresh handful of sand to throw at him.

"No." His knee went into the bed of pebbles in front of her eyes while his firm hand pinned her wrist to the ground. The other immobilized her bent arm against her chest, pressing her onto her back. "We've talked about that."

She was dimly aware of a noise that she had only heard in movies. It was the sound of guns being cocked and readied for firing. She had never been so petrified in her life. Her heart ought to have exploded.

She refused to look at him, though. She stared at the crease that went down the front of his trousers, from his knee to his shoe. Out of her well of pure hatred, she said, "Don't. Touch. Me."

"Open your hand," he commanded.

"Go to hell."

"We're staying here, then?"

She hated him. Really truly hated him.

But when his hold on her wrist didn't relent, she reluctantly allowed her fingers to splay. Her only weapon sifted out of her grasp.

His hold on her lifted away. "Can you stand on your own?"

She could not, but she refused to admit it. "I'm not going anywhere with you ever again," she choked. "I'd rather drown."

There was such a profound silence at that statement she opened her eyes and glanced around, half expecting the guards to have somehow evaporated.

"You were on the *Queen's Favorite*?" the Prince demanded.

"You know I was." She was really at the end of her rope. The salt on her cuts was killing her and her stomach was no longer tolerating all the seawater she'd swallowed.

"You swam the whole way from there? Impossible."

"Well, I didn't have a life ring or anything else to help me, did I? What sort of vile person leaves someone alone in the open water? At *night*?" The force of her emotive outburst put pressure on her stomach. Reaction to all that had happened—and all that she now faced—was starting to hit her with shattering force. She was definitely going to vomit.

"Porta la luce." He snapped his fingers.

One of his guards came forward to blind her with the light of a hideously strong torch. She flinched and tried to duck away from it, but the Prince took hold of her arm again and forced her to stay on her back.

It hurt like hell, but he ruthlessly kept her there and said, "Look." He pointed at the white line on his cheek. "Did I have this scar when you saw me last?"

"No."

Oh no...oh no. She had thought there was nothing worse than being trapped and preyed upon by the Prince of Nazarine.

There was one thing worse, though. One man worse. The *other* Prince.

"I am Felipe. Crown Prince of Nazarine. You will come up to the castle and tell me everything that happened to-night." He rose and offered his hand. "Can you walk? Or shall I carry you?"

She couldn't answer. It took all her strength to roll away so she wasn't violently sick all over his pretty shoes.

CHAPTER TWO

FELIPE SIGNALED HIS men to turn their backs and gently lifted her wet hair until it was behind her shoulders, then he supported her while she returned half the lagoon to its rightful owner.

When she'd finished retching, he drew her to sit braced between the V of his bent legs.

"Lean on me," he insisted while he removed his shirt.

She was trembling, likely in shock. Her long cold marathon of a swim was something even he, with his very athletic habits, would hesitate to attempt. It would also be taking a mental toll.

She was like a cloth doll, boneless as he threaded her arms into his sleeves. He brushed at sand on her shoulder which caused her to flinch, making him realize the skin beneath was scraped raw. Her shins wore similar injuries and there was a dark stain coming through on the elbow of his shirt.

He carefully closed two buttons between her breasts, concentrating on that task rather than letting himself fully take in what she had put herself through to get away from Francois. That reckoning would come later, after he'd had a full account from her.

He gathered her in his arms and stood. She was long and

lean and essentially a dead weight because she was so spent. Barely conscious, he suspected.

His head guard glanced warily over his shoulder, having been warned that one more step out of line—like *stepping on her again*—would cost him his job. His life, if they had lived a short century or two ago.

"A sling is on its way, sir," the guard said, taking a tentative step toward Felipe, arms outstretched.

Felipe shook his head, rejecting the man's attempt to help. He carried her to the bottom of the steps where he met the men who had brought the rescue sling. He gently placed her on it, draped a foil blanket across her and secured her with the straps.

"What is your name?" he asked as he worked. "Is there someone we should call?"

"I want to go home," she said with a pang of longing in her voice.

"I'm sure you do." Pity rose in him. He knew what it was like to be a target of Francois. His brother was cruel enough to enjoy terrorizing someone and dangerous enough to kill them in the process.

Felipe used one bent knuckle to caress her cheek soothingly. "Let's attend to your injuries first. Then we'll talk about what happens next."

She turned her head away from him and closed her eyes in rejection.

That shouldn't have bothered him, but it did. It was proof that Francois continued to leak poisonous lies about him and that people continued to believe them. Usually he didn't care, but he found himself bothered that *she* believed them.

Così è la vita. Such is life.

He took up one of the handholds of the sling himself, helping to carry her up the cliffs, then inside the castle walls to the infirmary.

* * *

Claudine woke in a dimly lit room. She was in a hospital bed with an IV tube stuck into the back of her hand, but the room looked like a five-star hotel. A Tiffany-style lamp stood on a Renaissance-style night table. Judging by the closed drapes, there was an adjoining terrace of some kind. Two wingback chairs faced a big-screen television above the mantel of a fireplace.

Was she back on Stella Vista? Thank God!

She tried to sit up and couldn't help the guttural noise that came out of her. Every muscle protested as though thoroughly bruised. She grabbed at the bed rail, trying to pull herself up, only to watch a specter-like shadow rise from a wingback and come toward her.

Her heart tripped and her throat went dry, making it impossible to swallow.

"Good morning," Felipe said. He was even more imposing in the weak daylight, wearing a crisp white shirt and gray trousers. His dark hair was short and precise. His jaw was shiny with a fresh shave.

That scar on his cheek was both reassuring and terrifying. He wasn't Francois, but what kind of man was he? What did he intend to do with her?

She sank back onto her pillow.

"My medical staff cleaned your injuries and topped up your fluids." Felipe nodded at the IV bag, then pressed the back of his fingers to her forehead and cheek.

A teetering sensation arrived in her midsection. *Don't trust him*, her logical mind cautioned. A more instinctual side of her yearned for someone to look after her.

"No fever. That's good." He reached across her to press a button, filling her senses with the spicy fragrance of aftershave. "Our guest is awake," he said, then released the button and straightened. "Are you hungry?"

"What time is it?" Her voice came out raspy and weak.

He turned his head to look at where a clock hung on the wall. "Six twenty."

Time enough to make the photo shoot? She was supposed to be there by eight.

"Dr. Esposito." The Prince greeted the man who came into the room. "Did you sleep in your clothes?"

"In case I was needed, yes." The doctor looked to be in his seventies. He stifled a yawn as he buttoned his white coat over his creased clothing. "Good morning, Claudine. How are you feeling? Are you in pain?"

"How do you know my name?" She darted her gaze back to Felipe.

"My security team are all highly trained operatives who employ the latest technologies in facial recognition," Felipe told her impassively. "None of which was necessary. I looked up this year's Miss Pangea contestants and there you were, second from the left."

"Your pulse is elevated," the doctor said, holding her wrist while watching the clock. "The Prince has been known to have that effect on a woman. Should I ask him to step out of the room?"

Was that supposed to be a joke? Felipe seemed to think so. His eyelids floated down over his dark brown eyes, heavy with amusement.

She sealed her lips. If she said yes, it would confirm she was reacting to him. If she said no, it would seem as though she wanted him to stay.

It's *fear*, she wanted to spit at him. Contemptuously.

As if he read her mind and was deeply unimpressed, the smug curl at the corner of his mouth deepened.

"I have to use the bathroom," she told the doctor. "Can you take this out of my hand?"

He made a noise of agreement and slid open a panel above her where supplies were kept. He unplugged the IV tube, smoothly removed the cannula and pressed a ball of cotton over the puncture, taping it in place.

He would have lowered the bed rail then, but Felipe swiftly did it on the other side.

"I'll call the nurse to help," Dr. Esposito offered.

"I can manage," Felipe insisted.

"I think he was talking to me," Claudine said, annoyed that one light brush of the Prince's hand was all it took to swing her legs off the bed while his other arm effortlessly slid behind her back, bringing her to sit on the edge facing him.

The abrupt move made her head swim so she wound up bracing a hand against his chest and clinging to his sleeve, waiting for her equilibrium to catch up to the rest of her.

"He was not," Felipe assured her. His firm hand on her waist ensured she didn't topple forward off the bed. "The nurse is also a man, so there's no difference in who helps you except that Dr. Esposito suffered a back injury last year, so he should not."

There was every difference, she wanted to grouse. She didn't want to be near him anymore than his brother.

She slid off the bed and her knees almost gave out.

Felipe caught her.

Dear *Lord*, she hurt. How was it possible to be this wrecked and still be alive?

She clung to his arms, needing his support to stand. She felt a thousand years old as she shuffled to the bathroom, every footstep sending a lightning bolt through her stiff muscles.

His arm stayed firm across her back while his fingers dug into her waist. Heat radiated off his torso through his shirt and the hospital gown she'd been put into. She could have cried at that invasion, being stripped and touched by strangers.

One glance at his indifferent profile and she doubted he had stuck around to watch. His brother might have leered in that circumstance, but Felipe didn't seem to see her as a woman at all.

"Can you manage?" he asked briskly as he lowered her onto a velvet bench beside the toilet.

"Yes."

Even this bathroom, which was clearly still part of the medical wing, was beautifully appointed with gold fixtures, a claw-foot tub, and a huge shower stall tiled in dark blue. On the back wall of the shower tiles, a landscape of a coastal village sat inside a painted frame of golden grape vines.

"Don't even *think* of going through that window." He pointed to the panel of stained glass inserted into a modern casement that allowed it to swing outward. "You'll land on the guard stationed below."

She had absolutely been thinking of doing that. He probably knew it from the belligerent dismay that came into her face at his warning.

"Call if you need me." He left her alone.

She used the toilet since she'd come all this way, then washed her hands before she took inventory of her injuries. Four scrapes had bled enough to need covering, two on her shins, one on her shoulder and one on her forearm. The rest were scuffs that had been painted with something that had stained her skin yellow. There was even a small bruise on her cheekbone.

As she met the appalled disbelief in her reflection, all she could think was, *I can't do the photo shoot. I can't win.*

She had been in the top three in every portion of the contest so far. She was the frontrunner who was expected to win.

Not anymore.

It's over.

Mom...

As long as Claudine could remember, her mother had had good spells and bad spells, but her symptoms had always receded. This time, they were more severe and weren't going away. Ann-Marie was in a lot of pain and having trouble walking. She seemed to be losing vision in one eye.

After two decades of coping with it, Ann-Marie had exhausted all the conventional treatments. She had gone into a secondary progressive phase, her doctor had told her. There were experimental treatments that were showing promise, like stem cell transplants, but they were expensive and held out no guarantees. However, without any sort of treatment, she would definitely suffer more pain, keep losing function, and her life span would be shortened.

Claudine's gamble on winning the prize money hadn't been a sure bet, but it had been a strong one. Even something like being chosen for the calendar would have given her enough money to hire her mother a specialized home care worker.

What would she do now?

With a sob of despair, Claudine sank back onto the bench, hands covering her face only to discover there was still enough sand in her hair to rain onto her knees. Her feet were filthy, her pedicure a disaster.

She didn't think about whether it made sense to shower, only rose to start the water. She dropped the gown and stepped under the spray, reaching for the shampoo. She washed her hair, then rubbed the silky body wash all over her skin, trying to remove salt and dirt and this whole wretched experience.

Maybe the scrapes could be covered with makeup, she thought wildly. As the water soaked through the bandages, she peeled them away, finding long red streaks and skin scraped raw. It would scab even worse before it healed.

The soap stung like living hell, but she scrubbed anyway, trying to erase the scratches and scuffs with the fluffy white cloth only to stain the soft cotton with fresh blood.

Would the pageant even pay to fly her home? Francois would probably accuse her of walking away and disqualify her. He'd been furious when she had fought off his advances.

"Do you want to win or don't you?"

What should she do? Report him? Who would believe a prince had left her to die in the open sea?

She cringed, realizing that even if she could convince anyone she'd been on his speedboat at all, he would only turn it around and claim she had come aboard intent on seducing him to try and win the pageant. That she was a cheater. How had she been so *stupid*?

"Claudine." There was a firm knock.

She ignored him and kept scrubbing.

"Stop that." Felipe entered. "You're making it worse. Stop, Claudine. *Stop.*"

He came right into the shower, ignoring the rain of the spray that soaked his clothes and landed on his gold watch. He snapped off the taps and stole the cloth from her hand, throwing it to the floor with a plop. Then he stepped away and reached for a towel. He shook it out and wrapped it around her trembling body, seeming to take no notice of the fact she was absolutely naked.

As he had done on the beach last night, he easily picked her up and carried her to the bench where he left her soggy and bedraggled and freshly bleeding.

"Give her new bandages," he said irritably as he walked out.

Claudine swallowed a lump in her throat. She was so irrationally bereft at his leaving she almost called out for him to come back.

A man she presumed was the nurse, since he wore scrubs and carried a tray of tape and bandages, used a second towel to dab her shoulders and arms and face and feet. He was efficient and kind, covering each of her injuries again, then offering a comb before saying, "I'll fetch a clean gown."

As she struggled to work the tangles from her hair while keeping her towel in place, he returned with a clean, dry hospital gown and an over-the-counter headache tablet.

"Would you like help dressing?" he asked after she had swallowed the pill.

"She can wear these." Felipe arrived wearing a dry shirt and fresh trousers. He carried a pair of silk pajama bottoms in dark green with a plain, navy blue T-shirt. "It's good you're almost as tall as I am. Leave us. I'll help her."

The nurse closed the door behind him.

Felipe lowered to one knee as he began to thread the pajama bottoms up her calves and thighs. "Stand," he ordered.

With a small catch of her breath, she did, bracing a hand on his shoulder to hold her balance.

He pushed the waistband the rest of the way up, reaching under the towel with that same dispassionate expression. He stood and lifted the drape of the towel to tie the drawstring, then gathered the T-shirt and slipped it over her wet head. He guided one arm and the other through the sleeves then waited for the shirt to fall down and cover her chest before he dragged the towel away.

"My slippers." He set them in front of her bare feet. "Now we'll eat breakfast. I sense you're the type who is grumpy until you've had your coffee."

He wasn't wrong, but that wasn't why she shuffled so resentfully behind him, wincing with every step.

The warm shower and moving around, along with the tablet, were gradually easing some of the ache from her muscles, though.

He took her through an empty ward of a half dozen beds, then past a series of offices where faces glanced up before quickly getting back to whatever they were doing. There was a grand hall of some kind with sunlight streaming in through a dome of colored glass that drew her eyes upward. Stairs curved down from a gallery, but he ignored them. There was a mosaic in the floor beneath their feet, but she didn't get a chance to study it.

They arrived at a pair of open doors where guards stood sentry. He led her through a small foyer that let onto a parlor, then through a huge, formal dining room.

"Are we there yet?" she couldn't help asking.

"Soon." He didn't even glance back at her, but after passing through a small breakfast room, they finally emerged on a shaded terrace where a table was set for two.

Half a dozen staff hovered, eager to pull out chairs and pour coffee and lift silver lids to reveal poached eggs on beds of chopped peppers with herbs and olives atop toasted bruschetta slices.

Claudine was so hungry she barely made herself wait until Felipe waved an invitation for her to tuck in. Flavors of basil and butter and salt exploded on her tongue. Blood oranges appeared with grapes and fresh figs. She gobbled them down, then chased them with a sweet pastry and a second cup of coffee.

When he said, "Bring oatmeal," she realized he had stopped eating long before she had. How embarrassing.

"No. Thank you," she insisted. "I missed dinner." She had missed a lot of meals in the run-up to this pageant, but there was no need to make up for it in one sitting.

She self-consciously sat back only to wince at the various aches and bruises that connected against the quilted seat back.

She finally took a proper look at her surroundings. This terrace was on the ground floor overlooking a courtyard that contained a hedge maze of waist height. A fountain in the center whispered its steady pour of water.

The walls of the courtyard were three stories high and were covered in tangled, verdant vines. She couldn't see the sea or the collection of islands that made up Nazarine, only a thin layer of wispy clouds in an otherwise blue sky.

She looked at the castle behind her, spotting a number of terraces that probably afforded a view to the horizon.

"I don't wish us to be seen by any long-range lenses," Felipe said.

"Why?"

"Because knowledge is power. Right now, I know that you survived your swim, but my brother does not."

The lethal grit in his voice caused her heart to take a swerve.

He looked so much like his brother it was disconcerting. Aside from that stark white line in his swarthy cheek, he was Francois's match in height and build. They both had thick, dark brown hair and equally dark brown eyes beneath stern brows. Their long sloping cheeks were clean-shaven, their jawlines chiseled from granite, their mouths...

Here she saw the difference. The shape was the same with a peaked top lip and a thick, blunt line for a bottom one, but Francois's mouth was softer. He smiled often and quickly and wore a pout when he relaxed.

Felipe's mouth held the tension of discipline and command. He didn't need to charm to get what he wanted, she realized with a roll of uncertainty through her abdomen. He spoke and he received.

"I'd like to go back to Stella Vista," she said.

"You will. In time."

"My mother expects me to check in every day. She'll be worried if she doesn't hear from me soon." That was an exaggeration. "The organizers will be contacted."

"I'm counting on it." His mouth twisted with cruel satisfaction.

Her heart lurched. "Don't do that to her! She has enough to worry about."

Stress was the worst thing for her condition.

"We'll reassure her of your safety through private channels. Is there someone she trusts implicitly? One of these people who drives her to her medical appointments, perhaps?"

"How do you know that about her?" she asked with alarm.

"She thanked her team on social media. The post was set to public," he added when she recoiled. Warning flashed behind his eyes. "I was only trying to get to know my houseguest, not targeting her for anything."

A houseguest? Was that what she was? She hadn't exactly arrived voluntarily, and apparently wasn't allowed to leave. She searched the walls in the courtyard, spotting a door that led where? To a treacherous descent to the water and another life-threatening swim?

She curled her fingers into fists in her lap.

"Tell me about last night. How did you come to be in the water?"

She stubbornly clamped her mouth shut, not wishing to revisit it, especially not with servants and bodyguards standing around listening.

"Take your time. We can walk in the garden if you like. It's very relaxing."

She couldn't resist glancing at him then, wondering if he ever relaxed. He radiated readiness for action.

"I have never spent much time learning about the pageant."
He casually held out his cup for someone to step forward and
refill it. "I expect it's very competitive?"

"I was *not* trying to get an advantage!" she burst out, insulted. Her eyes immediately grew hot and she cast another
annoyed glance at their audience.

"Go." He flicked his hand and they all melted away.

It helped that they were alone now, but would he even believe her? Defensive words bubbled up. She was desperate
to plead her side of it before she had to face all the scrutiny
and disbelief that would be heaped upon her if she reported
it to the pageant, though.

"You started on the *Queen's Favorite*, I presume?" he
prompted.

"For a dinner cruise, yes. The ship is huge. I was part of a
group touring all the decks when the Prince caught up with
us. He invited us onto a smaller yacht. It was inside the bigger one and already had champagne and photographers on
board. I thought it was a surprise announcement that we'd
made the calendar or something. Pageants do that, ambush
us with big news so they can capture our reactions."

She had been so excited at that point, giving absolutely no
thought to being in any sort of danger.

"It was still a really big boat," she continued. "They took
us toward one of the other islands where we could see the sun
setting. Once it was dark, I wandered around and the Prince
found me. He said, 'Look, I have this little boat that won all
these races. Let's pop aboard and zip around to surprise everyone.' It seemed harmless. *He* did. Then he steered it away
from all the other boats and…"

She didn't want to continue.

He didn't move or speak, but she couldn't look at him to
see what he was thinking. She was too embarrassed.

"I feel really stupid for trusting him, but he owns the pageant. He's a *prince*." According to the online accounts, the twins had been competitive when they were young, but Felipe had supposedly been the one with the violent streak. Francois was the forgotten spare who was sensitive and kind and only wished to make his country proud.

"You don't have to tell me what happened, Claudine," Felipe said gravely. "The fact you swam a mile to get away from him tells me all I need to know, but if he…hurt you, Dr. Esposito can do any necessary tests. They're helpful for prosecution."

Her stomach protested the heavy meal she'd put into it. She swallowed and shook her head.

"That's not necessary. He didn't—he was angry that I wouldn't go below with him and grabbed my arm." She rubbed where there was a shadow of a bruise on her wrist. "I managed to pull away and… I jumped overboard. It was a senseless thing to do. I realize that now." She covered her eyes. "I just reacted."

"I'm sorry you felt it was your only option. And I'm glad you survived it," he said in a tone that sounded sincere, but also severe enough to draw her nerve endings taut. "Do you think this is something he's been doing all along? Assaulting his contestants?"

She hadn't even thought of that, but of course this would have been Francois's modus operandi.

She flashed a look upward. Felipe's voice was concerned, but his narrow-eyed visage suggested there was something more calculating behind his interrogation.

"Why do you care? Because you see this as a weapon you can use against him?"

His expression didn't change, but the sweep of his gaze suggested he was reassessing her. He sipped his coffee, giving the impression he was considering how much to tell her.

"His ship is called the *Queen's Favorite* because he is. Our mother adores him." He sat back, lips twisting with weary disdain. "I've always thought the pageant very tawdry. Our mother supports his argument that the pageant showcases Nazarine's beauty, raising our profile and enticing tourists to visit long after the pageant is over. I can't deny there are economic benefits to it, but if this contest is a cover for his sex crimes, then it must be stopped."

She folded her arms across her middle, cupping her elbows.

"Judging by the way certain crew members behaved…" Her stomach turned as she recalled the way the purser's gaze had slid away from hers. "It's hard to describe, but they didn't seem surprised by his taking me out alone. I have a feeling that if I were to go back and say that he had plotted to assault me, the crew would say I seemed happy to go with him. In fact…" She cringed as she saw it in a new light. "The Prince made a point of saying *I* wanted to see how fast his speedboat could go." She covered her face again. "If I accused him of anything, he would say what you implied, that I was just trying to seduce him so I could win the pageant."

"Will anyone have noticed last night that you went missing?"

"Probably not. There were tenders going back and forth to shore all evening. Other people coming and going. Celebrities and entertainers. It was very chaotic. They probably won't notice I'm missing until this morning's photo shoot for the calendar."

Her stomach was churning over that. She had never broken a contract in her life, but here she was missing one of the key requirements of the contest.

It was killing her that she had lost so much so quickly! She should have done as her mother had asked and taken the job at the bank. It was entry level and hadn't paid much. Not enough to support her mother or pay for her treatment. Definitely not both, but she could at least have been *with* her mother.

She'd been so sure she had a shot at that stupid calendar, though! It was easy money. Just *smile*.

"*Please*, can I go home?"

CHAPTER THREE

FELIPE HAD BARELY SLEPT. His mind had been busy running through every scenario and course of action available to him, now that such an odd, and potentially explosive, opportunity had washed up on his doorstep.

He needed more facts, though. And, as much as he had trained himself to be suspicious, he was keenly aware that he had to treat Claudine carefully. Her injuries were not faked. She had been through a terrible ordeal.

She was reassuringly stroppy, despite it. Perhaps because if it. For her sake, he was profoundly relieved she had foiled part of Francois's predatory plan, but he could see what the experience had cost her. She was physically wrecked and emotionally shaken.

Her mental toughness, however, glowed like a simmering star deep within her. It mesmerized him, not that he allowed his attraction to show. It wasn't appropriate under the circumstances. Also, her fear and hatred of his brother didn't mean Felipe could trust her. Any pull he felt toward her had to be ignored while he delved for the information he needed.

"I will make arrangements for you to go home in due course, Claudine. Right now, I want to know how you feel about calling out my brother for what he did. I realize that could be difficult for you on many fronts. That's why I'm asking, not insisting."

"What use would it do?" Her hands came up, palms empty and helpless. "He'll vilify me! I *might* get some modeling work after this, if I keep my mouth shut, but not if I'm seen as the type who makes waves. You're probably right about previous winners. I would tell you to go back and ask them, but I don't know if they can say anything, either. They would have to admit that their win was essentially a consolation prize after he took advantage of them. No, I just want to go home and try to forget any of this happened."

Her eyes were glistening as she stared at the far wall of the courtyard. She bit her lips to stop them from quivering.

"Claudine. I believe you," he said quietly. Firmly.

She sucked in a small breath and snapped her head around to stare at him, seeming to disbelieve *him*.

"That surprises you?" He frowned.

"Men in your position don't see how the world really works."

"We'll argue my comprehension of the world another time, but I assure you I know how my brother works." He paused to consider his words. "Perhaps that's inaccurate. I knew Francois objectified women. Other pageants have evolved to be less sexist, but Miss Pangea is appalling. I didn't ever imagine it was also a cover for Francois to commit sexual assault. Men in our position," he used the phrase ironically, "generally receive enough offers for companionship that we don't have to stoop to taking it by extortion or force."

Her mouth worked unsteadily, as if she was trying to find words and couldn't.

"I take responsibility for not stopping the pageant sooner. My dislike of it was seen as pettiness, so I allowed him to keep his toy. I'll insist this one be our last." It would widen the rift between himself and his mother. Their father would see it as another skirmish between his sons, taking accusations of Francois's crimes with a grain of salt. Ultimately, the King would side with canceling the pageant for the sake of the royal reputation, though.

"Losing the pageant will punish Francois," he continued, "but if you want him held accountable for his actions against you, that will require your testimony."

A tiny sob sounded in her throat. She looked down to pick at her broken fingernail.

"You don't have to decide this moment. I believe he'll be dissuaded from targeting another contestant if he's already stewing in the discomfort of one who has gone missing."

His brother really did think he was untouchable if he was prepared to leave a woman for dead. That news was very sobering and it pinched at Felipe's conscience that he had allowed himself to believe there were lines Francois wouldn't cross. He didn't think of himself as naive, but in this case, he had been.

"I imagine people will be asking for you at this photo shoot. When will your mother make inquiries? I would like my brother to begin fielding awkward questions as soon as possible."

"I text her updates through my day. She sees them when she gets up, but because of the time zones and how busy I am during the day, I usually only talk to her in my evenings. She—" Claudine hesitated, eyeing him as though wondering how much to trust him. "She knows I can get tied up with other things. She won't really worry until it's been a few days."

Felipe touched his phone. One of his security guards poked his head onto the terrace.

"Sir?"

"Use our back channels to offer generous payments for paparazzi shots of Claudine at the swimsuit photoshoot."

"When was the shoot, sir?" He glanced between her and Felipe.

"It's happening now."

"But—" He looked at Claudine, frowning at the obvious fact she was here, not there.

"I want photographers to ask the organizers why she's not among the contestants," Felipe spelled out. "If they see an opportunity for a generous reward, they'll then start looking for her elsewhere, stirring pots of curiosity as to why no one can find her."

"Ah." The guard nodded and retreated.

Claudine sent him a considering look.

"It's a start." He shrugged. "Let's walk in the garden. I think you'll find it soothing."

"I think I'll find it excruciating, but okay."

He bit back a grin of amusement, pleased by that spark of cheekiness in her. Her color was better and, despite a few winces as she rose, she was moving more fluidly, which also reassured him that, physically at least, she would bounce back from all of this.

Four stone steps took them down to the hedges that were trimmed to waist height.

"Do you know the way?" she asked.

"It's a meditative labyrinth. There are no dead ends, only one path. I walk it most days when I'm here. It helps me think." Which was something he needed to do now—contemplate exactly what to do with her.

He mentally scoffed at himself. He knew what he *wanted* to do with her, but he forcibly turned his mind from musing on that.

No, it was the conflict of seeing the means to finally destroy his brother and wanting to seize it, while also seeing a vulnerable woman who needed his protection, that needed untangling.

Testifying had to be her decision. He couldn't push her too

hard on that front or he was no better than Francois, but the stakes were too high to not make an effort to persuade her.

She moved slowly on the graveled path, one hand reaching out to lightly graze the top of the boxwood, as though wading into water and testing the surface temperature as she went.

"The pageant is actually a very sharp tool in Francois's arsenal," Felipe said, wanting her to have a broader picture of his reasons for pressing her. "He makes a disgusting amount of money exploiting things like your image in a bikini."

Claudine frowned and crossed her arms defensively.

"He uses the selection events and the various whistle-stops as opportunities to mingle with diplomats and dignitaries. It looks harmless to the outsider, but he starts whisper campaigns against me. That's why my reputation is as sunny as it is," he said facetiously. "But it's useful for me to be seen as the more dangerous twin, so I don't mind."

Claudine made the first turn and looked back at him, brows pulled together in wary confusion. Her hair had dried and was straight as straw as it fell around her shoulders, casting out glints of gold in single, flyaway strands.

She was genuinely, naturally beautiful. He wasn't so shallow as to embrace classic attributes as an ideal, but he couldn't ignore the fact that her features were symmetrical, her eyes wide and clear, her lashes long and thick, accentuating her femininity. She had elegant bone structure and a mouth that was sensually plump and pursed at rest, as though ready for a kiss while the corners curled up in a secret smile. The rest of her was willowy and graceful, her curves filling out his clothing in a way that belonged on a runway despite the fact they were too big for her slender frame.

All of that appealed to him on a very base level, but beneath that was a quiet resilience that lit a fire in him. He didn't know why it made him want to grab her and hold her, while also revering her, but it did.

It was disturbing and he hid it all from her, keeping an impassive expression on his face because she needed to trust he wouldn't harm her, otherwise she had no reason to help him.

"Francois labeled me the bully from an early age without thinking it through," he continued. "The result is that most people are more afraid of me than they are of him, adding to my influence and power. Which isn't to say I haven't done some terrible things to him. The story that I broke his nose when we were fifteen is true. In my defense, he tried to hit me with his car."

"That part isn't online." She slithered through two short zigzags and looked back at him again.

"My parents have kept his reputation as spotless as possible. He is the spare, after all. There is a small chance—although perhaps not that small given how much he hates me—that I might not survive to take the throne and he will ascend instead."

"I don't doubt that he tried to murder you," she choked. "I can't understand how your parents looked the other way, though."

"Our father encouraged our rivalry. He thought it made both of us stronger. Our mother coddled Francois, feeding into his sense of entitlement and resentment. When he acted out, attacking me, she defended him. Even when he did this—" He pointed at the scar on his face. "Lashing me with a sword before my mask was on. *I* was supposedly at fault for being unprepared."

"That's horrific."

It was. A millimeter deeper and he would have lost his eye.

They were passing each other on either side of a hedge, like people going opposite directions on a street. She stopped to study the scar. Her morbid curiosity caused a teetering sensation in his chest. He never let anyone touch it. It was remarkably sensitive, considering how long ago it had happened, but he had the sudden desire to feel her cool fingertips tracing every centimeter of it.

"I didn't ask for the responsibilities of the crown, but what is my choice? Allow a man with his lack of morals to rule our country? I can't. I'm not a particularly good man, but I know right from wrong. I'm in a constant struggle to hold my own against him without sinking to his level."

"If I did come forward, your parents would interfere to protect him. Isn't that what you're saying?" Dread pulled down the tilted corners of her mouth.

"You'll have my protection," he promised.

"What good will that do?"

They had come to the halfway point in the labyrinth. They stood outside the circle of hedge that surrounded the fountain, but would have to work their way through the second half to reach it.

"You understand those other contestants are my friends?" Her eyes dimmed with entreaty. "They all have hopes and dreams of their own. They're one step closer to those dreams because they participate in something like this. They wouldn't thank me for destroying the pageant when they're counting on whatever fame or attention they're able to get from it. And the past winners? They don't want to be put under microscopes. Helping you means harming others."

That almost sounded as though she had a conscience. He tested it.

"What if I pay you?"

"It's not about money!" Claudine turned in a huff and realized she was trapped. She couldn't go back, not without brushing past him, but the way forward was another point-less retreading of snaking paths.

She started through the next quadrant. He strolled behind her at his own pace, but she still felt pursued.

"There are easier ways to get money," she muttered over her shoulder. "I could have slept with your brother for the pageant prize if that's all I wanted!"

"That's what I keep coming back to. You've made a small career of these things. What is it you want from them? Fame? Adulation? A modeling career? Then pursue modeling."

"Not that it's any of your business, but I'm funding my mother's medical treatment."

"So it is about money."

"Not the way you're suggesting." She stopped to turn and confront him again, supremely annoyed and more than a little distressed by the gravity of her situation. "You probably saw online that my mother has multiple sclerosis. It has begun affecting her ability to work. She's managing some part-time hours from home, but she has to cover her insurance premiums herself. It's not very good insurance regardless. It only pays for the basics. Any kind of stress, especially financial, worsens her symptoms."

She paused to toe a loose rock in the otherwise trampled-flat gravel.

"If all she needed was someone to make meals and do her shopping, I'd move in with her and do that, but she's not responding to her usual medications. She needs a full reassessment and a whole new treatment plan. It'll cost the earth. Miss Pangea was only an eight-week commitment and I've had good luck with these things in the past, so I wanted to try. And yes—" she lifted her head "—I thought that if I could then move into modeling, that would be a better paying career than whatever entry-level job I'm barely qualified for, at least in the short term."

She hadn't been able to find her niche, career-wise. It was frustrating, but she kept trying things on, never quite sure what she hoped to find.

"Do you have other siblings? Does your mother have a partner?"

"No. I mean, she did. My moms were married and living in Sweden when they visited a fertility clinic to conceive me." People always had questions about this part of her life, so she answered before he asked. "The donor was an anonymous student who only gave two samples. Most men donate dozens of times and most prospective parents look for someone who has lots of samples in stock, in case it doesn't work right away. That way they don't have to go through the screening process again and again. My moms liked the rarity of this donor's sample so they each used one. One worked." She waved at herself.

"Theoretically, it's possible he had other children, though."

"Theoretically, yes. And it's a nice thought to imagine I have a half sibling out there and I might meet them through some divine intervention. Or my father."

"You've never tried to find him?"

"Not really." She wasn't bothered by how she had been conceived, but she did wonder sometimes if the piece of herself she didn't understand was the anonymous student. "The one time I looked up the clinic, I learned it was closed and the records destroyed. I've thought about doing one of those DNA tests, but my mother… It's a touchy subject. She did try to conceive another child for our family, but it didn't work. After Mamma died, I've always had the sense that if I went looking for my donor, Mom would take it as a criticism or a rejection. As though she wasn't enough for me."

"She's not the one who carried you?" he asked.

"No. Mamma did. She died when I was eight. Mom brought me to New York after, but we don't have family there, either, so it's really up to me to look after her."

She didn't know why she was bothering to tell him her life story. She didn't care what he thought of her. Did she?

"Those are all expenses I can cover," he said mildly. "I'm a very rich man, Claudine."

He didn't have to sound so smug about it!

He was more than rich, though. He was enigmatic and intimidating, even though he only ambled along behind her, posing no immediate threat.

Which didn't mean she could trust him, she reminded herself. He seemed to be treating her well enough, but it was definitely for his own purposes. She was essentially his hostage. As far as she could tell, he wanted her to explode her own life—and that of every Miss Pangea contestant ever—so he could score a point or two with his brother.

Not that Francois didn't deserve to be knocked down. *He* was the one who was ruining her life. She knew that.

Felipe's talk of a whisper campaign had sounded a little paranoid, but now that she knew Francois was more—or more accurately *less*—than the charming, doting figurehead of the pageant he presented himself as, she had to wonder if she had believed what she had been told to believe about Prince Felipe. Maybe he wasn't as bad as advertised?

He was objectively good-looking, exactly like his brother, but Felipe had an edge. Not the scar. It was more than that. An aura. She was compelled to keep looking at him. Why? Was it the confidence bestowed by the power of his position? Something more intrinsic to him?

She didn't know what it was, but he fascinated her the way a shark or a deadly snake might hold her attention. She wanted to watch him move and listen to him tell her more about himself. She wanted his attention for no sane reason at all and she didn't want him to think badly of her. Why?

She paused, so close to the fountain she ought to be there by now, but she had to go through a final twist and turn, back and forth, to reach the opening to the inner garden.

"I don't know if I can believe anything you've told me," she said wearily as she came through the separation in the hedge. "Not when I'm just a means to an end for you."

Before her, rose bushes bloomed in a multitude of colors around a tiered fountain. Water poured off five concentric layers into larger pools below. The thin curtains of water were nearly silent, only creating a steady shush of sound while the gentle movement of the water wafted the perfume of the roses, heady and sweet, into the air.

Four curved benches were placed to view the fountain. She sat on the nearest one, sighing with relief. The walk had been longer and more taxing than she had expected.

"You would rather believe what Francois has told you?" Felipe idly picked a rose.

"I wouldn't believe him if he told me the earth was round," she muttered.

"Which is why I'm willing to align with you. My enemy's enemy is my friend." Felipe brought her the rose and offered it in the cup of his hand.

The stem was so short, there were no thorns. It was a beautiful blossom on the verge of opening. Each petal held bright yellow in its center that faded to peach and finally an intense pink at the furled edges.

It felt like an agreement of sorts to accept the rose, but it was too beautiful to refuse. She gathered it in her two hands, like scooping water, and found the brush of his palm against her knuckles disturbing. She brought the bloom to her nose where the soft, cool petals caressed her lips and the fragrance of nectarine and tea filled her nostrils.

"Do you really wish to slink back to Stella Vista, collect your things and fly home? And leave your friends to discover for themselves that Francois is a predator while you look after your mother on a shoestring?"

"I can't be paid to tell the truth." She lowered the rose into her lap. "That's wrong. If it came to light, it would completely undermine my claims. People would say you had bought my testimony." She stared at the fountain, feeling responsibility pouring onto her like the weight of that water, layer upon layer until she could hardly breathe. "I have to come forward. I know that. All of this..." She waved at the labyrinth and its singular path into its predetermined, unavoidable destination. "This was me coming to terms with the inevitable."

"It has that effect, doesn't it?" He tucked his hands into his pockets as he sent a contemplative look at the maze.

"I need time to gather my strength, though. I can't do it right now." It was going to be awful. *So* awful. She would stay here forever if she could, inside the peace of a decision made, rather than travel out to execute it.

"Do you want me to help you? Carry you?"

He sounded solicitous, but his objective was to get the result he wanted. For some reason, that put a sting of tears on the edges of her eyelids.

"I can manage." She stood and turned toward the opening in the hedge, but swayed.

Instantly, he was in front of her, cradling her elbow in support.

She set her hand in the crook of his bent arm, tired and overwhelmed and needing to lean on his strength a moment.

His free hand skimmed down her hair, leaving a tingling

path from her scalp over her ear, into the side of her neck and down her shoulder.

She jerked her head back, partly fearful, partly…something else. She was tall, almost six feet. He was taller. Tall enough to look down his nose at her.

"A butterfly was looking for a place to land."

She touched her hair.

"It's on the roses." He nodded.

She looked at the small yellow creature slowly fanning its wings as it sipped nectar.

"Are you afraid of me, Claudine?"

Yes. It was a visceral answer from the depths of her being, but even as she thought it, her gaze clashed back into his and her heart turned over.

She *should* be afraid of him. More afraid than she really was.

Last night, with Francois, her inner alarms had been going off like mad from the time he had suggested the speedboat. She had ignored them, telling herself she was being silly. Francois was only trying to be nice.

Francois was not nice and neither was Felipe.

But Felipe wasn't trying to convince her he was nice. Nor was he being cruel. And even though logic was telling her to be cautious about trusting him, her inner alarms were rattled for other reasons. He had had ample opportunity to hurt her physically, but he hadn't.

No, the sting of danger in her nostrils was emotional wariness. He was slipping very easily past her normal defenses. She wanted to blame what she'd been through for making her feel weak and susceptible to him. It was probably a factor, but there was more at play. She was attracted to him.

Not just *Wow, he's hot.* It went deeper to *Who is he, really?* He was making her long for things she had held at bay most of her life. Like most people, she carried an intrinsic desire to be loved, but she knew it was a double-edged sword. With love came the risk of loss. Loss of autonomy and self and the other person.

"You're safe with me. I hope you believe that." He set a crooked finger under her chin and tilted her face up to his.

He was barely touching her, only cradling her elbow and pressing that light touch under her jawline, but she felt as though he'd conducted an electric current through her, making all of her feel so tinglingly alive that her eyelashes fluttered under the force of it.

He narrowed his eyes and something like satisfaction spread across his watchful expression. His thumb brushed across her lower lip.

"I don't know what to believe," she admitted, trying to prevaricate. Trying to tell herself to pull away, but her hand only rested on his chest.

"Believe in yourself. You have more strength and power than you realize." His light touch trailed into her throat, petting gently, like he was stroking a kitten, coaxing it to purr.

More waves of sensation rippled into her, making her feel prickly and filling her with yearning.

What was he doing to her? She searched his eyes, but her gaze was drawn to his mouth. So stern, but looking as smooth as the rose petals had been. Would they feel the same against her own?

She unconsciously rolled her lips inward, dampening them with the tip of her tongue before she parted them to draw a breath of anticipation.

There was a flash behind his eyes that should have alarmed her, but it only sparked a flame of excitement.

"Do you want me to kiss you?" His voice was a rumble

against the hand still on his chest. Was his heart thumping faster beneath her palm?

"Yes." The word came from the depths of her lungs, without any logic attached. As his head dipped, she closed her eyes.

His mouth settled on hers lightly at first, as though he was giving her time to become accustomed to the wild buzzing that filled her lips. No. His mouth was not the cool softness of the rose. It was hot and damp. He slowly deepened the kiss, releasing a growl of relish, as if she was something he'd been waiting for and he planned to savor every bite of her.

Her heart skipped with thrill. This was a kiss unlike any she'd experienced and she quit trying to analyze it because he was inciting an intoxicating rush that emptied her head. This wasn't sexual attraction, she realized distantly. It was sexual *hunger*.

It was visceral and consuming, driving her hands of their own accord to twine around his neck, hanging on because she grew dizzy while he cupped the back of her head and ravished her mouth with his own.

He wrapped his arm harder around her and her sore muscles protested, but there was comfort in the embrace, too. As if he was sheltering her even as he claimed her. It was the tight hold of a lover as he tipped them off a cliff together.

She pressed closer, savoring the ache. She was in danger of drowning all over again, but this time she had someone to hold on to. She wasn't alone.

They caught their breath and tilted their heads the other way. His teeth lightly scraped her bottom lip before his tongue soothed, then brushed against her own. His wide palm slid down to scald circles of heat across her bottom, sending heat spooling through her abdomen.

She arched closer and felt the thick, implacable shape of his arousal against her mound.

Startled, she drew back.

He kept hold of her, but loosely. His arms were still hard and unbreakable, but he was only steadying her while he looked at her through his thick lashes, expression inscrutable, yet satisfied.

"You're perfectly safe," he assured her. "But you didn't imagine you weren't having an effect on me, did you?" His thumb stroked her upper arm.

She swallowed, utterly disconcerted by that effect.

"I'm not averse to something more personal developing between us, but we'll talk about that after we've dealt with Francois." He slid his hand down her hair again. This time it was a deliberate caress that ended with him pressing her hair into the side of her neck.

Words of protest backed up in her throat, making it hard to breathe.

"Shall we go?" He dropped his hand to catch at hers. He led her back into the labyrinth.

"Is there no shortcut out of this?" she asked plaintively.

"Wouldn't that be nice?" He sounded amused. "But such is life. We're trapped inside the one we're given. It's a pleasant change to have company, though," he added dryly, keeping hold of her hand as he drew her along the twisting paths.

CHAPTER FOUR

As MUCH AS Felipe enjoyed sex, he rarely took lovers. They always seemed to be poisoned by Francois, either working for his brother, or soon turned away by the blood sport between the twins.

Of the relationships he'd had, however, he had never been impaled by such a searing and immediate desire for anyone.

This haze of lust was as dangerous as any haze of rage might be, he cautioned himself. He ought to be taking their kiss as the warning of an uncontrolled burn that it was, but he spent the walk to the guest wing mentally recollecting the melting of her curves against his front, her soft gasp as they barely stopped for air, and the lovely shape of her bottom filling his palm.

That well of sensuality within her was a delightful discovery that teased him to hurry with his machinations against his brother, but now that she had agreed to move against Francois, Felipe wouldn't rush her on any level. Each domino would be placed with precision so they would topple in succession, at exactly the right time. Once it was done, he would have all the time in the world for her. *Them.*

"What—?" She halted as he drew her into a bedroom. She yanked her hand free of his and glared at him with betrayal.

"I brought you here to sleep." He waved at the wide, canopied bed with the royal crest on its silk coverlet.

She continued to look skeptical.

"When you wake, explore the castle, but stay inside. In fact, I'd like you to visit the infirmary to have your injuries looked at. If you want fresh clothes, the maids will bring you something from my closet."

"Why don't I wear something of theirs?" she asked with a confused frown.

"None are tall enough. And you are not part of my house-keeping staff, Claudine. On the contrary, you are extremely valuable to me. I want my staff to know that." He peeled down the blankets on the bed.

She stood unmoving, a mutinous pout on her lips.

Her eyes were so bruised with tiredness he wanted to pick her up and put her in the bed himself, but he had to reinforce this tentative trust between them. What he hadn't expected was that he would have to trust her to look after herself and go to sleep.

His concern for her was a new color for him. As a future ruler, he was invested in the well-being of his subjects, but in a very broad way. On a micro level, he'd always been forced to look after his own interests because no one else had. His inner circle was trustworthy enough that he valued them and would attempt to help any who suffered a health crisis or other tragedy, but they were all replaceable. He didn't *worry* about them.

He was worried about her, though. Mostly because he had a pressing engagement and had to leave her here. That wasn't sitting well with him at all, but it couldn't be helped.

"I'll see you later." He made himself leave and close the door behind himself. "Help her find the infirmary when she rises," he told the guard who had taken a position at the door. "Allow her to go anywhere she likes within the castle walls."

"Yes, sir." He managed to hide the bulk of his surprise,

but Felipe understood they were all baffled as to why he was showing so much deference to one of his brother's contestants.

"Your Highness." His private secretary, Vinicio, rose from a nearby chair, ever-present tablet clasped in his hand. "Your meeting with the King is still on schedule?"

"Yes." Felipe's father had messaged last night. Felipe hated to leave Claudine alone for even an hour, but it would allow him to learn very quickly if she intended to betray him. Also, canceling a meeting with the King would be highly suspicious. Rather than tip his cards, he would continue as if nothing untoward had happened here. "We'll take the helicopter."

There was a boat moored on the lee side of the island, but it sat in a lift next to the wharf to protect it from the constant battering of shifting seas. He often used it on fine days like today, but he was running late.

On his way out, he told his head of security, "I'll be at the palace for an hour. If anything happens to our guest while I'm gone, you are the first one I'll kill." He said it lightly, but he wasn't joking, not really.

The man swallowed. "For anything to happen, I would have to be dead."

Felipe nodded his satisfaction with that answer.

"Send two guards with me. The rest can stay here." He didn't expect trouble, but better safe than sorry.

Fifteen minutes later, he was descending to the palace grounds. Francois's red cabriolet was zipping through the palace gates at the same time. How tiresome. He had hoped this was crown business.

Both Felipe and Francois had apartments here in the royal palace, but the day Felipe had broken Francois's nose was the day Felipe had moved to Sentinella. It was less convenient than living on the main island, but Sentinella did what it was designed to do and held the world—and his brother—at bay.

Francois stayed in his beach villa when he was in Nazarine, but mostly traveled the globe from film festivals to raves to solar eclipse parties, all under his portfolio of "economic development."

They arrived in the upper gallery at the same time from different directions. Felipe acknowledged his twin with a curt nod. Francois curled his lip at him, but said nothing.

Their father's private secretary greeted them and showed them to their parents' parlor.

Family business, then. Otherwise, the King would meet with them in his office.

They entered what might pass for a living room in other people's homes. The furniture made an effort toward comfort over ostentatious style, but there were still plenty of relics that provided as much forgiveness as a church pew.

Queen Paloma wore one of her exquisitely tailored skirt suits, but only minimal jewelry and no hat. She sat on the edge of a sofa cushion, expression somber. She looked up as Felipe came through, nodded politely, then brightened when Francois came in behind him.

"Padre," Felipe acknowledged King Enzo even though his father didn't turn from his contemplation out the window.

"Mamma." Felipe kissed the cheeks his mother offered.

"Cucciolo," she said with affection directed at Francois. "How are your girls this year?"

Girls. Not women. Felipe's conscience gave another twist that he had ignored the pageant for so long, rather than seeing it for what it was.

"Belissima," Francois claimed. "It will be impossible to find the winner."

Felipe bit back a caustic *Oh, I found her.*

"Sit with me." The Queen kept hold of Francois's hand.

"What's wrong, Mamma?" Francois settled beside her, his demeanor one of fawning consolation.

Felipe averted his gaze so he wouldn't vomit with disgust.

The Queen said nothing. The King kept his stiff back turned toward them.

This was bad, Felipe understood. The silence went on long enough to grow a layer of dust before King Enzo finally turned.

"I am unwell. Critically unwell. Pancreatic cancer," he stated. "They've given me a year."

Another silence crashed down on the room.

"How did they not find it sooner?" Felipe asked.

"I felt fine until recently. I will require surgery and other treatments. You'll assume more of my duties, beginning immediately." He sent that order to Felipe with a bracing stare.

"Of course." They were not a sentimental family. Felipe kept a neutral expression on his face as he inquired, "Shall I cancel my meetings in New York?"

"No. For now, this news stays in this room. Everything must appear normal."

"Normal" was being flipped inside out, Felipe thought dourly. He could feel Francois already scheming to turn this to his advantage.

"There will be no more of your faffing about, taking your time in marrying and producing an heir," the King threw at Felipe. "I want to know the throne is secured. Do not make me look at other alternatives."

And there it was, the one twisted pathway Francois had to gaining an upper hand over him. On more than one occasion, Francois had tried to persuade their father to overturn the law of succession. They were twins born within minutes, virtually at the same time. Surely, Francois often argued, he had exactly as much right to the throne as Felipe?

Faced with such a lengthy and complex legal process, King Enzo had never given the request serious attention, but the way he held Felipe's gaze right now was an overt dare.

Felipe wanted to believe his father was bluffing. Given how little time Enzo had left, Felipe doubted he could go through with his threat, but the fact he would level such a stark warning had Felipe's mind cycling through the handful of women he had considered over the years as a potential wife. None had ever appealed strongly enough that he could imagine spending a lifetime with her.

None had sparked a sexual craving in him like the one that had roared to life in him a few hours ago.

"Competition has always worked well to motivate the pair of you," his father continued. "Therefore, I lift my embargo on your marrying before Felipe," he said to Francois. "I want to see the next generation before I die. But those children must be legitimate. Marry first, then make our next ruler." He directed that at both of them.

"Time to break out your short list, Mamma." Francois patted the back of the hand he held. An avid light had come into his eyes. He genuinely saw a chance to leapfrog himself onto the throne.

The Queen started to smile conspiratorially, then straightened her features and looked to her other son.

"You've already seen it," she reminded Felipe in a cool tone. "I'm not sure if you've selected anyone from it, though…?"

"Oh, yes. The firstborn must have first pick." Francois asked with mock deference, "Are there any candidates you consider off-limits to me?"

On principle, all of them, but when it came down to it, one in particular.

Felipe was still highly skeptical his father would go

through with deposing him in favor of Francois, but he couldn't allow Francois to entertain the belief that he had a shot at the crown. Every inch was a mile to Francois.

No, Felipe had to marry promptly and beget his successor.

"Any woman who is willing to have you is yours to court. I have someone else in mind," Felipe said.

"Oh?" Francois narrowed his eyes while their mother blinked in surprise.

"Oh?" their father asked in a tone that demanded more information.

It was an impulsive declaration, one that was also cold and calculated, but Felipe had learned to trust his instincts.

Right now, all his instincts said, *Claudine*.

Claudine woke feeling significantly better.

Her laundered underthings had been delivered along with refreshments and a selection of clothing from—presumably—Felipe's closet.

She rolled up the cuffs of his pin-striped shirt to expose her wrists and tied the tails of it at her waist. His gray trousers needed cinching with a braided leather belt that allowed the tongue to go in anywhere. Once she had tied her hair back with a handkerchief, she felt almost like her old self.

Then she stepped out of her room and remembered she was still a very long way from "normal."

"The Prince asked me to show you to the infirmary," the guard said. "Please follow me."

The Prince. The one who had asked if she wanted him to kiss her, then had swept away every thought in her head. His kiss had broken a spell she hadn't known she was under. She wasn't a particularly passionate person. Or hadn't been. Not before he had awakened her senses and lit fires of bright, physical yearnings inside her.

I'm not averse to something more personal developing between us...

He had cast a spell with that same kiss, making her think that she wanted something intimate with him. That she was capable of matching him in that way.

You have more strength and power than you realize.

She didn't, though! They occupied very different stratospheres and that was only the beginning of their inequalities. He was simply too much in every way. Too masculine, too powerful, too hard. Too hot. She might be pretty, but he radiated the raw beauty of lightning and hurricanes and comets crashing into planets.

He had probably meant she was powerful in terms of the damage she could do to his brother. In that respect, she felt like a pawn, one that Felipe was willing to sacrifice for his own ends.

No, she was susceptible to him because he was an accomplished seducer. Anything "more personal" would be pure self-destruction, so she would steer clear of it.

The doctor pronounced she was "healing nicely," cautioned her to keep her fluids up and gave her another headache tablet for her various aches.

From there, she wandered the gallery, taking in the sculptures and paintings of former rulers—how strange to realize she wasn't in a museum. This was the Prince's family album.

Amused by that thought, she turned down a hallway dedicated to portraits of one bygone queen in particular, shown with her many children at different ages. She looked...defiant?

Claudine found herself studying the one where she sat behind her husband, her hand resting on his shoulder. Claudine looked into the eyes of that hard-faced man, searching for some sign of Felipe or Francois, but they seemed to have inherited their looks from her, not him.

Yes. Felipe might not have anything feminine about him, but he had this Queen's same unflinching stare and enigmatic expression.

"Here you are," Felipe said.

She nearly leaped out of her skin, gasping and clutching at her heart as though she'd been caught with the family jewels in her hands.

"You didn't hear the helicopter return?" he asked with amusement, coming to stand beside her. "Or my voice just now, asking where to find you?"

"No." She rubbed the goose bumps from her arms as she sent a wary look at him.

Felipe studied the image of the woman looking down on them.

"Giulia. My father's grandmother. She was held here on the island. Did you know that?"

"No." Claudine had read a little of the kingdom's history, but had mostly researched its pop culture and trends, finding that was the best way to bring an audience onto her side.

"Sentinella's isolation makes a perfect holding cell. Pirates stored gold here at different times. That booty was claimed by my ancestors when they took possession of the rest of the islands." He quirked his mouth as he glanced at her. "The sailors in our navies were always very loyal while stationed here, since the alternative was a longer swim than yours last night. For a time, it was a monastery. The monks built the labyrinth. Then my great-great-grandfather kicked them out when he ensconced Giulia here." He nodded at the Queen. "She was not warming to their arranged marriage. He kept her here until she had given him two sons. They didn't arrive right away. She bore him four daughters as well." He pointed at the portrait of the Queen with all six of her children. "She was here for twenty years."

"That's awful."

Some unspoken light of knowledge entered his eyes. It was the same one from the portrait. "Let me show you her library."

Her body prickled with awareness of danger as she followed him, but it wasn't fear or dread. It was that other danger that made her nostrils sting while all the cells in her body seemed to swivel and align themselves to an awareness of him. Some involuntary part of her insisted on calling out to him.

She tried to tamp it down as she moved past him through the door he opened and entered the sort of room she'd only seen in movies. It was three stories of shelved books accessed by flights of stairs and narrow, railed galleries, and rolling ladders. There were reading nooks built beneath tall windows and big, comfortable chairs by the fire and a desk with inkpots and candleholders.

"This answers the question, 'How did people survive before streaming services?'" she murmured, trying to imagine how much time one would need to read all of these. "You're saying this castle isn't a dungeon? She had all this? It was still cruel to keep her here, don't you think?"

"It was," he agreed with a nod. "She was not a woman who submitted to confinement without a fight, though. She wrote here." He pointed to the desk. "Subversive, disruptive messages about rights that women still fight for today. She wrote her beliefs in many of these books, so many that her husband couldn't find and destroy all of them unless he burned the entire library to the ground. She smuggled her writings off the island in various ways—often using her children and maids. They were published at different times, humiliating the King. When he finally said she could join him on Stella Vista, she insisted on staying here another three years, purely as a show of resistance. Eventually, she took her place beside him, mostly for the sake of her children. He was well known to have a mistress by then, so they had little to do with one another outside of their royal duties."

"That's so sad."

"Do you think so? I find her inspiring." He moved along a row of books, seeming to look for a particular title. He started to withdraw it, then left it stuck out halfway. A few books along, he pushed three inward an inch. "She found a way to assert herself despite the strictures of her life. She didn't choose to be born a princess, and she didn't choose to be married off to a king, but she found ways to live the life she was given on her own terms."

"Is that how you feel?" She was taken by how the sunlight fell through the window onto him, allowing her to see him perhaps more clearly than she had before. "Are you trapped in a life you didn't ask for?"

"Not trapped, precisely. I have more agency than she did and there's a great deal of privilege that comes with my wealth and title," he said with pithy self-deprecation. "But there are times when I feel cornered into a particular situation or action."

He was working his way back along the shelf, doing the same thing to the row of books above the first, shifting some in, drawing some out so the spine was on the edge of the shelf. It looked like piano keys being played by a ghost.

"Do you do that to remind the staff to dust them?" she asked.

"No, they don't know about this." He reached the end and pressed into the bulk of the shelf. There was an audible ping, like a loud spring. An entire section of shelf next to the ones he'd been rearranging now swung open like a door.

"A secret passage?" she whispered in awe.

"Down to where the monks made their wine. It has an external entrance near the wharf where the supply ships docked. Queen Giulia would lock herself into her library to read, then slip down those stairs to let her lover in below."

"Who was he?" Claudine couldn't help inching closer to peer into the dark well of the stairs, catching a scent of cool, dank air.

"According to her diary, there were many. A captain, a guard, a sailor. Her children were conceived in this room, not her marriage bed. When she thought she might be pregnant, she would write to the King and insist he visit her."

"Did he know?" she asked with hushed astonishment.

"He must have suspected, given the fact that all of his children favored their mother and didn't look much like each other or him, but no one speaks of it. I learned the truth when I chose to make Sentinella my home. I hired a librarian to catalog the books and they found her stash of journals. One explains how she commissioned the shelf to hide the passageway and bribed the journeyman with sexual favors to take that secret to his grave. He would have been executed if he had admitted to touching a queen, so..." He shrugged.

"Why on earth are you telling *me*? This isn't just a family secret. You're saying your family doesn't belong on the throne!"

"The throne was stolen from her family, not his. Giulia was the sacrificial lamb married to her family's conqueror to appease the masses so they wouldn't revolt."

"That still doesn't explain why you would tell *me*." How was she supposed to carry such explosive knowledge?

"I thought you would find it interesting. And I want you to have a sense of who we are as a family and what we'll do for the sake of the throne. What we'll do to keep the right person on the throne." He closed the shelf and moved along, straightening all the books again. "I want you to understand that you have choices, even when it might seem as though you don't. Most of all, I need you to trust me. That means I have to trust you."

"I trust you." A little. Her voice didn't even convince herself. It caused him to send her a disparaging glance.

"When we were fifteen, our father made it clear that he would not recognize an illegitimate child from either of us. Nor would he accept Francois marrying before I have a wife and an heir." He grabbed the edge of the shelf to give it a firm pull, checking it was closed securely. It remained firmly in place.

He brushed his hands together, then looked at her in a way that made her wilt on the inside. Fear? Premonition of some kind. He wasn't a man who told stories and revealed secrets without expecting something in return. Something big. Something of equal weight.

"Are you toying with him? Why haven't you married?" she asked.

"He does everything he can to stop me. It's both spite and strategy. If I have children, he is pushed down the line of succession so he tells women that I'm a brute with a temper, one who encourages our father to hold Nazarine back from the modern world so our people are easier to control. He tells them I have our country's parliament in my pocketbook. Or he keeps *them* in *his* pocketbook. That's what happened with my first fiancée. The second one couldn't take all this animosity and palace intrigue. I didn't blame her for breaking it off. It was better to know early that she didn't have the stomach for it."

"But not *every* woman would be turned off by that!" He was a prince destined to be a king, for heaven's sake.

"True, but I'm cynical when it comes to women and relationships. And I've always felt as though I had plenty of time.

Until today." He became unnervingly somber. "For reasons I can't share with you at this time, our father lifted his embargo on Francois marrying and producing an heir before me."

"Oh?" That strange sting on her arms was her own finger-nails digging into her skin. Her ears were ringing, her breath backing up in her lungs. She didn't know why she had suddenly grown so tense, but she was hanging on his every word.

"Obviously, any child Francois produced would be super-seded by any of mine that came along after, but that would be messy. If Francois were the father of a future ruler, even for a brief period, he would capitalize on all the power that would come with such a position. He would fiercely resist my child taking its rightful place. Rather than put Nazarine through countless, pointless battles of succession, I must marry immediately and do my best to procreate before he does."

He looked straight at her. Into her. She had the sensation that her heart was falling down a flight of stairs and he was watching it happen.

"I don't understand," she said carefully.

"Of course, you do. You know exactly where I'm headed because you're very smart, Claudine. It's one of the things that attracts me to you."

"No. It— I— *No*." Her ears were ringing. "You can't be serious, Felipe. *No*."

"I am very serious, Claudine. I want you to marry me."

CHAPTER FIVE

"You don't even know me." Claudine shook her head, trying to convince herself she'd misheard him. "I don't know you. No. I can't."

"Listen to what I'm offering. I've looked into your mother's condition—"

"Don't you dare threaten my mother!"

"This is not a threat, Claudine. It's bribery. *Listen.* There are a number of excellent clinics, some in the US, some in Europe. She'll have a full assessment and any treatment she feels is right for her."

"*Please* do not talk as if I've already agreed to this mad plan."

"Believe it or not, your reluctance only reassures me that you're not an agent for Francois, or an opportunist. My greatest hurdle to marriage has always been the struggle to find a bride I can trust, one who cannot be influenced by him. That's you."

"Believe it or not—" she barely kept her tone this side of strident "—your demand that I marry you less than twenty-four hours after we met does *not* reassure *me*. Nothing about this does."

She started toward the door, but stopped at the desk, then turned back to him.

"Here is what I'm willing to do." She fought to maintain a

calm voice. "I'll write down every detail I can recollect from the time they told us where we were going last night until I washed up on your beach. I will give you that in exchange for a flight home. You can use my statement however you like. Surely that's enough to slow your brother down?"

"From finding a wife? Not every woman is as discerning as you are. Francois will find someone very quickly," he said pithily. "When you're ready to release a statement, we'll find a way to do it so it impacts you as little as possible. I will protect you to the best of my ability once it's out there, but think about it, Claudine. The best protection for *you* will be as the fiancée of a future king. Look at this fortress around you." He waved his arms.

"These walls don't protect me from public opinion! People will think it's a stunt. Is it? It is! Your family wouldn't allow you to marry *me*. You're trying to use me to make some kind of point."

"When it comes to marriage, you possess the *only* quality that matters to me. You hate my brother as much as I do. You are the one I want to marry and my parents will have to accept you."

"Listen to yourself! You want to base a marriage on hatred? You want to bring children into— I don't even know if I can have children. Do you realize that? I've never tried."

"Is there some reason to believe you can't?"

"No. Not that it's any of your business," she added hotly, then clutched the sides of her head. "I can't believe we're even having this conversation. *Please* send me home."

"Time is of the essence, Claudine. Otherwise, I would woo you."

She strangled on a laugh of disbelief.

"I am very capable of seduction," he said coolly. "Which I will demonstrate at the appropriate time."

That was both terrifying and intriguing. He came to loom beside her, forcing her into taking a faltering step backward.

"For now, yes. It's a good idea for you to record exactly what happened the other night." He opened a drawer in the desk and set out sheets of linen paper with a pen that appeared to be wrought from 24 karat gold. "I'll speak to you after I've checked on a few things."

Felipe was operating on the assumption that Claudine would marry him. He could trust her more than anyone else he'd ever considered tying himself to and he had no other immediate option. Finding a way to convince her was a small detail among many as far as executing his plan went, but he didn't abandon good sense altogether.

He went back to the dossier Vinicio had hurriedly prepared shortly after her arrival, wanting to ensure there wouldn't be any unpleasant surprises in her background.

Claudine's history of entering pageants would be seen as questionable, particularly by his mother. An American beauty contestant was not who she had in mind for either of her sons, especially the one whose wife would usurp her own title.

On the other hand, Claudine wouldn't have consistently won those contests if she had had a history of gambling debts or sexual exploits. Her image was wholesome yet progressive, given she had been born to a pair of women.

Queen Paloma wouldn't have any prejudice against Claudine being the child of a same-sex marriage. Nazarine had been at the forefront of adopting recognition of those unions, but Claudine was solidly middle-class, not even an heiress to a tech billionaire or some other nouveau riche family that the Queen might force herself to accept into the fold.

Her pageants meant she was well-traveled. Her on-camera demeanor was always polished and composed, her responses to questions well-constructed and intelligent, if brief and ide-alistic. She spoke fondly of a childhood dog and developed new talents for each pageant. She could write calligraphy, shoot an arrow into a bull's-eye, recognize birdsongs and perform rhythmic dance.

A wife with valuable connections would be useful, given Felipe would be taking on even more diplomatic and eco-nomic duties as his father's health declined.

Something like regret panged through him. He knew he ought to feel more than that. Vinicio had taken a month off work when he'd lost his father and he'd been a different man when he returned. Not openly morose, but somber. Felipe had accidentally overheard him comforting his mother on a call once and they'd both been crying.

The idea of being emotionally broken by his father's ill-ness was a foreign concept to Felipe. Their relationship had always been defined by their roles. His father had drawn a hard line between his two sons early on, brutally severing Felipe from a connection to his twin. The closest Felipe had ever come to experiencing parental doting was witnessing the Queen showering it upon Francois.

He could see now why his father had given him nothing but a dispassionate visage, though. Felipe's detachment from his father's illness would allow him to continue acting in the best interests of his country while their family dealt with the loss.

Nazarine had small but reliable agricultural and manufac-turing sectors. Their location on a trade route in the Mediter-ranean made Stella Vista's main port an important service and transfer facility for shipping companies. Tourism was also a heavy economic driver, which was why losing the pag-eant could be a blow to hotels and other service industries.

Nazarine had always had an excellent reputation for its boatyards and shipbuilders, too. Felipe had been pressing for

the development of specialized higher education programs—
marine architecture and the newer marine information technologies. That was what his trip to New York was about and
he looked forward to advancing that.

Claudine's citizenship wouldn't hurt him there.

No, the more he thought about it, the more he saw she was
a perfect fit as his queen.

Literally. Did his determination to wed her have anything
to do with this lust he was nursing? Hell, yes, it did. He was
trying to ignore it, but merely coming upon her in the hall
had sparked rampant fantasies. Perhaps it had been seeing her
in his own clothes, as though she'd picked them up from his
floor after he'd ravished her. He'd found himself dreaming
of loosening those clothes and taking her against the wall or
sprawling naked with her beneath the eyes of his ancestors.

He shook off those distracting fantasies and sought out
Vinicio.

"How is the pageant reacting to Claudine's disappearance?" Felipe asked.

"Acute, but well-muffled panic. Some contestants were
told she missed the photo shoot due to food poisoning. Others heard she had a family emergency. The police are quietly
reviewing security footage, trying to determine if and when
she came back from the cruise and whether she returned to
the hotel. One of the Prince's minions has asked a few of the
contestants whether she seemed drunk at the party."

"Setting it up to claim she fell into the water of her own
clumsy accord," Felipe said with disgust.

"Prince Francois was not visible at the photo shoot, either."

"He was at the palace," Felipe reminded Vinicio.

"He then went into unscheduled meetings with the pageant organizers. It seems likely they were discussing Ms.
Bergqvist."

"Perhaps." Francois would be looking for a way to wrap up her disappearance as quickly as possible because he had a new goal. Felipe explained that his brother would quickly become occupied with finding a wife. "He might even shut down future pageants himself, if he's about to become a married man."

Felipe rose to pace off his restlessness.

"May I ask, sir, if you are also—"

"Claudine will be my wife," he stated.

"Very good, sir." Vinicio nodded. "Congratulations."

"Thank you. You have a lot of work ahead of you. Let's hammer out a timeline beginning with my taking her to the palace to introduce her to my parents."

"Claudine."

He startled her again, but not as violently this time. She had been waiting for him, her statement folded in her hand while she stared out the window at the hazy shape of Stella Vista, measuring the distance between agency and responsibility. Between doing what was right for her and what was right for other women, and her mother, and the greater good.

Writing out her statement had forced her to see all the small ways that Francois had manipulated her. He was a truly terrible person who had to be stopped from preying on women, but also from preying on his brother and his country.

Was she really the woman to do it, though? Surely there were other ways Felipe could keep his twin from taking the throne?

She turned and smiled faintly as she brought him the pages.

"Thank you," he said solemnly, but didn't open the document to read what she'd written. Instead, he lifted his gaze to let it travel over her in a way that was both rueful and admiring. "I like seeing you in my clothing."

"Why?"

"Why does any man want to put a ring on a woman? To claim her, of course."

Her heart lurched, but even as she said, "That's very barbaric," there was a primitive part of her that responded to his possessiveness.

Did he know? Was that why that air of ironic amusement came over his expression?

"So…um…now that I've kept my side of the bargain…" She waved at the pages he held.

"Did you think my acceptance of this was an agreement?" He set the pages on the edge of the desk.

"Seriously?" she huffed. "You can't expect me to marry a per—a complete stranger!"

"I've shared some very personal details with you," he said with a hint of indignance. "More than I've ever offered to anyone. What else would you like to know? I prefer cats to dogs. They're more self-sufficient. I don't have a favorite color because I have the type of color blindness that sees red and green as the same shade. I am not close with my family," he finished facetiously.

She wanted to toss back something equally sarcastic, but she was realizing they actually had shared quite a lot of deeply personal things. It wasn't enough to base a marriage on, though. Was it?

"I prefer dogs," she informed him coolly. "For the unconditional love they offer. Which, coincidentally, is what I would look for in a husband."

He gave a small snort of disappointment. "Love is not a requirement for a successful union. It's a detriment to getting what you really want and need from life."

"No, it's not!" She stared at him, astonished. "It *is* what everyone needs from life."

"How?"

"What do you mean, *how*?"

"You can't eat it. You can't breathe it. I have never experienced it yet I am alive, so how can you say it's a necessity of life?"

"Because—" She faltered, startled by the way he had said that so blithely. He had never experienced love. Never? Really?

"No need for pity," he said sardonically. "I don't miss it."

"You must. Have you really never had anyone love you?" she argued. "It's companionship and—and—loyalty, and caring—"

"You really do want a dog."

"Love is offering respect and affection and emotional support to someone you feel great esteem toward," she insisted hotly. "Have you never felt any of that?"

"Have you?" he challenged. "Are you in love with someone right now?"

"No," she admitted sullenly. That was why she couldn't describe it without stammering. She'd been dismissed as a gangly, ugly duckling as a child, then treated as a sex object once she began developing curves. It had been an overnight transformation that she was still trying to reckon with.

"No," he repeated, as if she had confirmed some crime-proving detail in a cross-examination. "Because those feelings you're describing do not magically fuse into something bigger than the sum of their parts. If you want to call loyalty and respect and sexual attraction 'love,' have at it, but it is not an emotion unto itself. It's certainly not a necessity to anyone."

"I've never heard anything so cynical in my life." She could only stare at him, agog. Disappointed. "Did one of your fiancées hurt you? How did you become like this?"

"I grew up," he said flatly.

She physically recoiled from that. "Possessing a heart is immature?"

"Believing that some imaginary manifestation of a heart must be proffered and accepted before a marital relationship can move forward is immature, yes."

"Do you even hear what a cold, empty offer this is that you're making me? You should have left me to die on the beach." She flung out a hand in that vague direction.

"Is this really an obstacle for you?" Impatience edged into his tone. "You're worried that marrying me will keep you from drowning in sentiment over some nameless person you haven't even met yet? If he is out there, why hasn't he come to save you? What will he offer you when he does? Pretty words? Will they complete you in some way that you are deficient in right now? I see you as a whole person exactly as you are. You don't need anyone to prop you up emotionally."

"You don't know that." On the inside she was Swiss cheese, nothing but holes. She suspected it was caused by the loss of her mother at such a young age, but she had suffered this sense of missing pieces of herself for a long time. The pageants hadn't helped. They skewed her self-image into only focusing on the external view of herself. Who was she beneath the superficial surface? Who did she want to be? A nurse? A teacher? Swedish? American?

"If you lack the confidence to recognize your own mental strength, I will build that up along with providing anything else that you lack. Including a dog, if you insist."

"Now you're just mocking me." She folded her arms. "It's not immature for me to want to marry someone who *cares* about me."

"To what degree? I care about you enough not to leave you half-dead on a beach. I care about how this—" he tapped next to the pages she had written "—will play out and affect you. You have to stop thinking of marriage in the terms that were sold to you by greeting cards and ads for diamond rings. I'm hiring you for a position, Claudine. You've devoted yourself to pageants as a career, have you not? Those organizers ask you to uphold a certain image and discourage you from having relationships that could cast you in an unflattering light, no? They tell you what to eat and where to stand and you are compensated accordingly. This is much the same."

"The position you're trying to fill is sex work and surrogacy."

"I plan to do the work, *cara mia*," he shot back. "The sex will be all pleasure on your side. Our kiss earlier was a promise on that front, was it not?" The flare of light behind his eyes dared her to deny it.

Her voice stalled in her throat. She blushed and looked away.

The sheer power he radiated made her quiver deep inside, in a place that was frighteningly vulnerable. At the same time, there was a craving in her, a pull. It was edged with the most primal needs she possessed. She wanted to be closer to that force. To him. She wanted his touch on her, his lips. Him.

"I was under the impression you wanted children," he said gruffly. "Am I wrong?"

"I do," she admitted huskily. It was part of that blank space in her life. Neither of her mothers had family and her surviving mother was facing a life that could be cut short if she didn't receive the help she needed. Claudine's only other family connection was that nascent one to a man who had twice walked into a clinic.

Or she could make a family of her own.

"You're asking me to accept a life sentence in a loveless marriage," she said, torn between her mother's future and her own. "How is that different from the way Queen Giulia was imprisoned here?"

His cheek ticked.

"Five years, then," he said after a moment of thought, teeth gritted. "Give me five years of honest effort at conceiving at least two children. If you wish to divorce and look for your soul mate after that, we can do so. I'll ensure you have a home and everything you need for a good life here."

For some perverse reason, she found his willingness to get divorced very disappointing.

"What about our children? Would I have custody after that?"

"They will have to be raised here in Nazarine, but they will always be our children. Not mine. Not yours. *Ours.* You will have as much influence over their upbringing as I do."

All her objections to this bizarre suggestion of his were being neatly removed.

In casting for another reason to refuse him, her gaze snagged on the pages she'd written. She had offered that to him with supreme dread of the ordeal it promised, but she hadn't seen any other way to get herself home.

"What about...?" She nodded at the papers.

"It remains your decision if and when to come forward. I will absolutely protect you to the best of my ability when you do. In the short term, it's a powerful bargaining chip with my father." He picked up the papers and tapped their folded edge on the table. "To ensure he approves our marriage."

Her heart gave a swoop in her chest. "I—" Was she agreeing to this?

"I'm offering you the care your mother needs and a good life for you and your children. As an added bonus, you will have bested my brother in a way that he could not have foreseen when he thought he could assault you without consequence."

His grim tone made her catch her breath. He really was the darker prince.

He had to be, she realized with a chill in her heart. Otherwise, he would have lost to Francois long ago.

No. Not darker. Harder. He wore a sheen of titanium armor. What he had said about never experiencing love kept echoing in her ears. In her chest. What would that do to a person except force them to form an impermeable shell?

Let me in, she couldn't help thinking.

Foolish. She knew that. There was no changing someone who didn't want to be changed.

Would she want him to change, though? She was enthralled with him exactly as he was.

"There's no one else I can trust the way I can trust you, Claudine," he urged in a low voice. "You're not giving up power by agreeing. You're exercising the power you have in this moment."

Really? Because she felt weak. She felt as though she was capitulating to something inside herself that had nothing to do with personal agency and everything to do with wanting to be near him. To know him.

If she walked away now, she would go back to that blurry version of herself. She would never know who she could have become if he was in her life.

The one thing she did know about herself was that she wasn't a coward. She didn't shy from something simply because it looked difficult.

She bit her lips and nodded. "Yes. I'll marry you."

CHAPTER SIX

IT WASN'T MUCH of an exaggeration to say Claudine's life changed in an instant.

The fact was, it had already changed when she had leaped from the speedboat to swim away from her life as a pageant contestant, but she could have gone back to her old life from there. It would have been altered and she would have faced challenges, but she wouldn't have given her life *to* someone else.

That was how she felt as Felipe whisked her under cover of darkness to the royal palace on Stella Vista.

By then, she had spoken briefly to her mother, who was now ensconced in a private and well-secured clinic for protection against paparazzi and anyone else who might try to reach her. They were planning to visit her after they announced their engagement.

"You'll meet my parents in the morning," Felipe said as he showed her into a private apartment. "Relax, eat. Ask Vinicio for anything you need. Speak to no one but the staff in these rooms."

Did she feel guarded by Vinicio? Yes, but she soon realized this wasn't any apartment. It was Felipe's personal wing. The luxurious space was neat as a pin and included a small, well-stocked kitchen along with a breakfast room, a parlor, an office, a private terrace and a massive bedroom.

She perused the handful of photos on the walls. They showed Felipe in his youth, before he had been scarred, when he was still capable of smiling, and later, when that line on his face seemed to harden the rest of his features into its current hostile expression.

There were no photos of his brother.

She pressed her fist to the knot in her middle and turned on the television. It was set to a news channel and the broadcaster spoke in Italian. Market numbers ran along the bottom.

"I don't think that's a good idea, *signorina*." Vinicio materialized before her.

"Why not?"

"The coverage of your disappearance is unflattering."

"To *me*?" She pointed at herself, astonished.

"*Sì.* Prince Felipe is allowing it for the moment to maintain the illusion you are missing, but you may find it upsetting." He turned off the television. "Perhaps we could run you a bath? Ippolita?" He moved into the bedroom that Claudine had only peered into.

A maid emerged from a dressing room. The pair exchanged some words in Italian.

The young woman smiled and nodded, then went back into the dressing room.

"Ippolita doesn't speak English, but she's been with us for some time and is fully vetted. Prince Felipe asked her to see what she could find for you at the local boutiques."

"Oh?" Claudine leaned to see into the dressing room where the young woman had been hanging gowns and women's clothing alongside shirts and suits.

"You'll be flying to Paris after your engagement announcement," Vinicio continued. "I've arranged for designers from Milan, New York and Tokyo to meet you there. You'll soon have abundant styles to choose from."

Claudine could hardly keep her jaw from dropping to the floor. She often wore designer clothing for the pageants, invariably on loan and always with great trepidation, given their value.

Ippolita reverently drew a peignoir off a hanger and presented it in a drape across her arms, anxiously searching Claudine's face for approval. It was almost too pretty to consider wearing with its lilac-colored satin and oyster gray lace.

"It's beautiful." Claudine blushed slightly, wondering what Ippolita was implying by offering it, but the stunning quality of the piece had her reaching to turn over the small label attached with a loop of satin ribbon. "Local?"

Ippolita nodded.

Claudine had not won as many pageants as she had by not understanding how the game was played.

"You should include this designer with the rest," Claudine suggested to Vinicio. "Most contestants wear the big names because that's what we're offered." It was lucrative for the pageant to promote them and made it more likely for a contestant to be chosen as an ambassador for those products in future. "I find it wins hearts when I wear something made by a designer in the host country, even if it's only a neck scarf."

Vinicio gave a considering nod while Ippolita carried the peignoir into the bathroom and hung it on the back of the door. She stoppered the enormous tub and opened the taps.

The tub was set between marble columns and built into a platform with two steps leading up to it. The fixtures were gold, as were the ones on the nearby sinks. A steam shower took up the entirety of the opposite wall.

Ippolita withdrew a blue bottle from behind the mirror and opened it, offering it to Claudine to smell it.

When Claudine nodded her approval, Ippolita poured a generous amount of liquid into the water, releasing the aroma of lavender, geranium and bergamot as well as starting a froth of bubbles.

Claudine felt rather useless, especially when Ippolita lowered the lights and said, *"Vino, signorina?"*

"Per favore," Claudine mumbled as she followed Ippolita back to the main room. "Can you please tell her she doesn't need to wait on me like this?" she said to Vinicio.

"Are you displeased with her?" Vinicio glanced between them. "We'll begin a hiring process tomorrow for your personal staff—"

"No! I mean, she's lovely." Claudine realized then that Ippolita was auditioning for a job she very much wanted. "I only meant I'm not used to this. I'm feeling very spoiled."

"I'm confident that is how the Prince would want you to feel," Vinicio said with a nod.

He exchanged another few words with Ippolita, who relaxed and smiled shyly, then finished pouring the wine and carried it on a tray into the bathroom.

Claudine was soon cosseted in warm water and a fragrant mass of bubbles that caressed her skin. The lights were dim and the gentle notes from pastoral classical pieces trickled in from hidden speakers. She pinched herself, wondering if this was even real.

It became very real when Felipe let himself in!

She sputtered slightly on the sip of wine she was in the middle of taking and sank deeper into the crackling bubbles. "We need to talk about your habit of barging in on me when I'm in the bath or shower."

"I'm starting as I mean to go on," he said dryly, noting, "It smells good in here." He came to sit on the edge of the tub. His gaze seemed to penetrate past the thick snow of foam. "You're comfortable?"

Naked in front of him like this? Not really.

"Vinicio said the pageant is saying unflattering things about me."

"He told me you seemed upset to learn that. They're trying to cover their own negligence by throwing fault on you. It's driven by my brother. They will all look that much more foolish when it's revealed you were with me all along." He stole her glass and sipped from it. "The King has approved our marriage."

She didn't know what impacted her more, his words or the way his gaze seemed to slam into hers, knocking her deeper into the water.

"I told him our marriage does not buy your silence about what Francois did to you. You'll speak up if and when the time is right for you. I mean that. How much you say, to whom and when, is completely in your control."

"And he accepted that?" She numbly lifted her hand from the water to accept the glass he handed back.

"Not gracefully, but certain things can't be hidden." His penetrating gaze traveled the clouds of bubbles before he touched the edge of the scrape on her arm where she had removed the soaked bandage. "My father has always enjoyed the dogfight between his sons, but this was not an attack on me. You weren't mine yet."

He traced his fingertip from her elbow to her shoulder, where he picked up a damp tendril of hair that had fallen from her clip. He lifted it to curl the tail of it around her topknot.

"Now that you are, I told him that if he expects me to silence you to protect my brother, then he has not been paying attention to the kind of men he has created." His voice was lethal, his absorbed expression mesmerizing.

Her body reacted with shivers of hot and cold. Her muscles were frozen while her bones were melting.

"I still have much to do. Eat something. Sleep." He bent and touched his mouth to hers. "Tomorrow will be a busy day."

Claudine woke with a gasp, aware someone was in the room with her.

"It's me," Felipe said as he slipped into the other side of the bed. "Go back to sleep."

She turned onto her side to face him, only able to see the vague outline of his shape against the darkness. He sighed once and lay still, completely relaxed, as though he had willed himself to sleep and it was done.

This is my life now. This is what I'll do. I'll sleep with this man from now on.

She could hardly fathom it. And sex? For procreation, obviously, but he had stated it would be all pleasure for her.

Her hand unconsciously curled into the sheet. Despite some virginal wariness, she wasn't as apprehensive as she ought to be. In fact, her body heated with a flush of anticipation as she imagined the loom of his wide shoulders over her. How would the weight of his hips feel between her legs? Or the sensation of his strong thighs pushing hers apart? Would it hurt when his flesh thrust into her?

Her inner flesh clenched involuntarily, aching with longing.

"Do you want me to help you sleep?" he asked in a rumble that made her pulse skip.

"What?" she squeaked. "I thought you were asleep."

"How can I sleep when I can feel the pounding of your heart and hear the unevenness in your breath?"

She swallowed, mortified.

"I'm as aroused as you are, thinking of what it might be like when we make love." He shifted to sprawl his arm over his head, staying on his back. "But I came into this bed planning to show you that I won't act on my desires unless it's something you want as badly as I do. The only way this alliance will work is if we trust each other and here, where you're most vulnerable, is the most important place for me to build your trust."

He was aroused? Did he have the same throbbing ache in his pelvis that she did? If she reached out, would she find him as hard as he'd been when he had kissed her? Aside from a few fumbling caresses with fellow college students, she hadn't really explored a man. Even those had been driven more by curiosity than genuine desire.

This fire of yearning in her was a far more carnal want. She needed to know how hard he was. How thick. How hot and weighty against her palm. She wanted to *feel* him.

"I could very easily be persuaded to take the edge off your cravings with my fingers or my mouth. Would you like that?"

The rough texture of his voice might as well have been his tongue between her thighs, her response was such a visceral rush of damp heat into that place.

It wasn't rational! *This* was what made him dangerous to her—his ability to bring her to the brink of climax with his voice.

"No," she choked and rolled away, aware of the thin satin that was riding up her thighs. It would take nothing for him to brush that out of his way and give her the orgasm she craved however he chose to deliver it.

Behind her, he made a noise that was both resigned and amused. "Another time, then. Good night, Claudine."

She lay awake a long time, thinking, *When?*

Felipe's mother was aghast. That was what struck Claudine like a slap as she performed her curtsy to the King and Queen.

Queen Paloma radiated appalled astonishment, clearly blindsided by this impromptu invasion of her morning by her firstborn and the substandard fiancée he'd brought with him. She didn't speak for a full minute, only kept her pink-painted lips in a tight purse. Her stunned yellow-brown eyes pierced like a stiletto into Claudine's lungs as Claudine politely murmured that it was an honor to meet them.

The Queen's voice was thin as parchment paper as she asked something in Italian.

"English, please, Mamma. Yes, you're correct. Claudine is the missing contestant."

Claudine turned one of her pageant smiles onto the Queen. She had a well-practiced arsenal that ran a gamut from a resting expression of poise, worn when waiting in the wings but still likely to be caught on camera, to the full-wattage smile held for long minutes when stuck on stage waiting like a mannequin for the rest of the contestants to be introduced and take their place.

In this instance, she found a midrange smile of polite attention, one she would reserve for a conversation with a judge.

This was not a pageant, though. Rather than the armor of a ball gown and full makeup, she wore an understated three-quarter skirt in navy blue with a matching jacket, ensuring her scrapes were all hidden. Her white blouse had a lace tab collar and she'd had Ippolita pull her hair into a demure chignon. Hopefully, her light coat of face powder hid the bruise on her cheek and the worst of her flush as she faced the Queen's blunt, "No" of rejection.

"I've approved the union," King Enzo stated.

"Why? You're not *that* close to death!" the Queen scoffed.

A silence landed so hard in the room Claudine dropped her wide-eyed gaze to the floor, expecting it to be split wide open. The King was ill? This would be the detail Felipe had not wanted to share with her yesterday.

"Does Francois know?" the Queen asked of Felipe. "Did you take her from his pageant deliberately, to put him in this awkward position? Or has she taken it upon herself to attempt this climb from pageant princess to—? No. Surely you can see that she is the worst sort of opportunist. Enzo?"

"Insults you may speak in Italian," Felipe said coldly. "So my fiancée doesn't have to hear them. But if you must know, Francois sent her to me." Felipe glanced at Claudine, providing her with an opportunity to elaborate if she so chose.

Her throat locked up.

When her reaction was only a subtle recoil at being put on the spot, he smoothly added, "Any embarrassment that Francois suffers around the pageant is very much of his own making. One way or another, this will be the last year his pageant comes to Nazarine."

"Do not try to distract me with that old argument. What do you mean that Francois sent her to you?" his mother demanded.

"Ask him," Felipe invited. "Ah," he said as there was a muted ping from some hidden device. "That will be Vinicio. I had him fetch something from the vault." He opened the door long enough to accept whatever it was.

"You are not giving her any of the crown jewelry," the Queen stated hotly.

"No, Mamma. Just the ring that Great-Aunt Ysabelle bequeathed to me."

"Not—? *No*, Felipe." His mother was truly shaken now, but Felipe seemed to have no pity for his mother.

"This belonged to Queen Giulia," Felipe said to Claudine. "It was given to her daughter, my father's aunt. She never married." Felipe held out his hand in a request for hers. His steady gaze seemed to insist she read every significance into the fact he had chosen to give her this particular ring, because he likened her to that Queen who had been trapped, yet had triumphantly lived by her own rules.

Her hand was shaking as she allowed him to thread the ruby-red stone with its frame of diamonds onto her finger. He brought her cold hand to his mouth and kissed her knuckles.

"I'll have Vinicio release the announcement," Felipe said. "It includes a balcony wave at eleven." He started to draw Claudine from the room.

"No, Felipe." His mother stood, all of her visibly shaking.

Felipe paused, but didn't look at her. He glanced at his father.

King Enzo nodded once.

Felipe's mouth curled into the faintest hint of a smug smile and they left.

While he spoke to Vinicio, Claudine clenched her fist and stared at the blood-red stone on her finger, wondering, *What have I done?*

Felipe did not pander to things like brand and image the way his mother and brother did. He didn't "sell a story" because he didn't have to—even though he knew that eschewing such things was its own brand.

However, he was not blind to the popularity of a good, old-fashioned fairy tale. When a prince chose to marry a commoner, he made anything seem possible. When that commoner was favored to win a contest where half the country had already judged her the most beautiful and deserving, when they were already rooting for her and had grown worried for her because she had disappeared, it became a sensation. The part where she turned up at the side of the Crown

Prince, seemingly no worse for wear, created the sort of fervor a public relations specialist could only dream of.

It amused him that his mother was so appalled by Claudine that she had taken the far end of the balcony away from her. She didn't appreciate how well these pageants had prepared Claudine for this. She was not only flawless, having changed into an ivory coatdress and matching hat, she radiated grace and dignity as she offered a gentle wave.

The crowd had begun to amass outside the gates minutes after their announcement. It was now a throng who cheered so loudly the noise seemed to resound in his chest cavity.

"They're waiting for a kiss," he told Claudine. So was he, but he only watched to see how she reacted.

There was the tiniest crack in her composure, one that caused her smile to falter as she turned to face him.

He knew long-lens cameras would be trained on them. He was deliberate in the way he drew her close with one arm around her waist. He held her left hand so the ring would be visible where he cradled it against his chest.

He hadn't been able to stop thinking of her in his bed last night, when the very air had seemed to be soaked with their mutual desire. Or her in the bathtub, when those snowy drifts of bubbles had hidden all but her shiny shoulders and upper chest from his sight. He wanted her naked beneath him so badly that he was in danger of revealing his lust right here in front of the world.

It was probably evident on his face, given the small shiver that went through her and the way her eyes widened before she dampened her lips with her tongue.

"I don't want to ruin your lipstick." He very much wanted to ruin her lipstick, but he kept his kiss as chaste as possible while also lingering long enough to feel the satisfying cling of her lips to his when he lifted his head. Damn, this need for restraint was erotic. He could have groaned out his suffering, it was so sharp.

The crowd cheered even louder while Claudine dropped her lashes, shy and disconcerted.

"Am I wearing your shade?" he asked, still holding her.

"Only a little." She touched the corner of his mouth, causing yet more wild enthusiasm from their audience.

They shared a rueful smile, then her gaze flicked past him and she stiffened. When she would have drawn away, he kept his arm locked around her, waiting for her gaze to come back to his.

"Your mother isn't pleased." Tension crept in around her eyes. "I think this might have been a horrible mistake."

Felipe expected she would feel that way often. "I gave up trying to earn her approval before I was old enough to ask for it."

It was a throwaway comment, one that was meant to be self-deprecating and to advise her not to take his mother's attitude to heart.

"That makes me sad," she said with earnest sympathy.

He dropped his arm from around her, prickling on the inside. Not angry, but disturbed. He covered it by picking up her hand, offering another orchestrated wave that invited another cheer.

He felt Claudine studying him. "May I ask… What your mother said to your father this morning… Is he—"

"Yes," he confirmed, not allowing his expression to change. It was a fact that his father was terminally ill, not something that caused him to feel anything, one way or another, and that, too, was probably pitiful.

He found himself squeezing her hand. Gently, but doing it all the same. Why? Was he trying to warn her against expressing more sympathy? Or was it driven by something closer to that hollow sensation that seemed to condense around him when he let himself think of his father's impending death?

"That's need-to-know. Please don't discuss it with anyone," he told her, brushing away those pointless emotions.

"I won't," she promised.

Below, the insistent blare of a horn drew their attention. A red cabriolet demanded access as Francois drove it down the narrow path between the cordoned-off crowd. His arrival raised yet another cacophony of reaction.

When he had cut through the gates and parked below them, he stepped out of his car to send a filthy look upward.

"Do I have to see him?" Claudine's hand tightened on his, her nails digging into his skin hard enough to threaten drawing blood.

"I'll have Vinicio escort you to my room, but I need to speak with him."

"What will you say?" she asked warily.

"That if he ever comes near you again, I will kill him."

"Felipe—" She looked shocked as she searched his eyes. "Are you really that violent?"

He could be. He was starting to realize he was exactly that primal and possessive where she was concerned.

"I speak the only language he understands," he said, drawing her inside and directing Vinicio to take her in one direction while he went the other.

Francois must have taken the grand staircase two at a time, trying to catch them on the balcony. He strode down the main gallery in a rush of rage toward Felipe, looking past him, but Claudine was already gone.

"I tried to call you," Queen Paloma said plaintively, coming inside from the balcony.

Francois ignored her.

"In what universe do you think I will let this happen?" The heat of Francois's breath accosted Felipe's nose.

Felipe kept his feet rooted to the floor, giving up not so much as a millimeter as his brother's fury burned like a conflagration in front of his face.

"What bothers you more?" Felipe asked lazily. "That I've found a bride so quickly? Or that she would rather die than spend another minute with you?"

"Is that what she told you?" Francois backed off a hair, trying to convey his contempt for the both of them.

"She told me exactly what happened," Felipe said with icy loathing. "I'll be sure you're sent a copy of her statement before she releases it."

Francois's eye ticked. His brother was nothing if not versatile, though. He quickly switched tacks.

"She's not revolted by you?" Francois asked with a scathing glance at Felipe's scar. It was meant to remind him that his brother had bested him once.

Once.

Felipe had come to appreciate the scar, despite nearly losing his eye. He had also lost his brother that day, realizing once and for all that Francois would never see him as anything but a rival. By then, Felipe had hated his own reflection, seeing only his brother when he looked in a mirror. He had felt haunted by Francois. Watched.

The scar was a gift. It made it clear that the man he faced in the mirror was himself, not Francois. He had no regrets that he wore it.

"You may come to the wedding if Mamma insists. Otherwise, you will stay away from her. Do *not* test me on this. I promise you the consequences will be deadly."

CHAPTER SEVEN

INITIALLY, THE CONSULTATION in Paris was overwhelming, given it was a much higher octave than what Claudine was used to. She often met with a designer, but usually only for a few minutes. She was occasionally invited to a fashion show and had a good sense of what styles made the most of her attributes. She understood the finer points, too. Some pageants wanted a glamorous look while others wanted something sexier.

Despite all of that, she wasn't prepared for two hours of presentations by world-class designers, each offering a portfolio that outlined their particular strengths and forecasts for future trends.

It struck her that she wasn't shopping for a few outfits. She was curating a wardrobe for a princess. That was a tremendous responsibility. She was relieved when Felipe entered the room.

Everyone stood.

Were they supposed to do that? Claudine rose, too, warming with that infernal suffusion of awareness whenever her fiancé was nearby. He came to buss her cheek with his lips, filling her senses with the sharp aroma of his aftershave.

"How goes the battle?" he asked.

"Everyone is enormously talented." She sent a reassuring smile around the room, wanting to convey that she was pleased with everything she'd seen and hoped to include everyone.

"But?"

A small jolt went through her. She flashed a look up to him. How had he sensed this small conflict in her?

"Everyone has presented a strong theme. Elegant, classic, dignified, sophisticated." She nodded at different sketches. "It's a matter of deciding which is the right direction to lean into."

He scanned the images with a more thoughtful expression.

Claudine waited for him to make a pronouncement for her, but he only said, "There's nothing here to quarrel with. All of them are appropriate for the wife of a future king."

"That's my concern." She tapped her lips. "It looks as though I'm trying too hard to prove I belong. If I doubt it, others will, too. I need to convey all of those things, but there needs to be a broader, overarching theme that..." She searched for a way to convey what seemed to be missing.

"An astute observation." Felipe's gaze on her altered, warming with admiration.

Holding his stare caused her to blush. She shyly lowered her lashes.

"Romanzesco," the Nazarinian designer murmured. *"Amore."*

"Mais bien sûr," another agreed in a tone of discovery.

Now the designers were all looking at each other and nodding. "She is his future queen because they are in love."

"Oh. I—" Claudine nearly strangled on her own tongue.

"Shh. You've given them the key. Let them unlock it," he whispered in her ear, trailing his lips into her neck and sending a shiver chasing down her spine.

There was a curl of cynicism at the corner of his mouth when he lifted his head, though. His caress on her jaw was both tender and ironic. He lightly tilted up her chin and dropped a kiss on her lips before nodding and walking out again.

"This is our only free night," Felipe had told her an hour ago, when she had finished her meetings with the designers. "Once we get to New York, we'll have engagements every night. You'll want to see your mother and you'll be busy with hiring your staff. Let's go out for dinner. Have a date."

Technically, it was her second public appearance as his fiancée, but the pressure to make the right impression was enormous. She chose a silver gray sheath with contoured ruching that had the sex appeal of a feminine silhouette without being outright sexy.

Its three-quarter hem covered her healing scrapes without hiding them completely. The one on her arm was visible through the lace on her sleeve if someone cared to look hard enough. She didn't want to advertise her injuries, but she refused to pretend they hadn't happened.

She arranged her hair in a soft twist with a few loose tendrils and kept her makeup subtle. The bruise on her cheek was all but gone.

"You look beautiful," Felipe said when she nervously presented herself. "If naked."

"Wha—? Oh." A flutter of nervousness had her touching her bare throat as he presented a flat, book-sized velvet case.

She opened the case expecting a necklace, but not one so charming and pretty. The extravagant arrangement of pink and white diamonds made a full circle. The pink stones were all approximately the same size, but cut in different shapes of square, round and pear shapes. Each was framed in glittering white diamonds.

"It's beautiful." She didn't insult him by asking if it was real. "Will you?" She turned.

The necklace descended before her eyes and the cool weight of it settled against her collarbone. His fingertips tickled at the top of her spine, then his warm mouth touched her nape, nearly taking out her knees. The man was diabolical!

Catching her breath, she moved to the mirror to admire it.

"I've never worn anything so lovely. Who do I say it came from?"

"Me." His drawled tone said, *Obviously.*

"Wait." She spun and touched it. "This isn't a *gift*. It's just for show. Isn't it?" She thought she might faint.

"It's both." There was that tone again, the one that laughed at her for her naivety.

The necklace perfectly reflected the theme of romance and love, yet she felt neither from him as she traced the cool shapes of the stones. She dropped her hand to her side.

"Felipe... I can't accept this."

He sobered as he studied her. "Given all that I expect of you, Claudine, I suggest you become very brazen about what you will accept as compensation. Shall we go?"

She didn't know what to say to that, so she let him guide her toward the door, but the weight of the necklace sat much more heavily upon her.

A private dining room would have been much simpler, security-wise. Felipe would also have preferred to have Claudine to himself, but he had asked Vinicio to arrange for them to dine at an exclusive restaurant that catered to corporate heirs and Europe's nobility. The decor was a waterfall of dripping chandeliers and mirrored finishes, providing suitable sparkle as he showcased their new partnership.

Everyone turned their heads as they were shown to the best table. Felipe was used to that, but tonight they weren't staring at him. They were mesmerized by the radiant woman he escorted.

He had been aware of the challenges she would face as a red-blooded American and not a blue-blooded aristocrat. After Felipe's threats, Francois might think twice about coming for Claudine, but their mother would pick apart every choice she made. Queen Paloma had her own back channels and social circles who would attack Claudine's ability to call herself worthy of a royal marriage.

When Felipe had checked on her wardrobe selection process, he had been looking for armor. He had wanted her to wear those refined styles in the sketches, the ones that would have allowed her to blend in.

She had taken him aback with her insight and he was still laughing with delight at her brilliance. Of course, they must sell a story of love at first sight. Of course. Besotted people were allowed to be impulsive and would be forgiven for any missteps.

Not that Claudine made a single one. She looked flawless as he held her chair then took his seat across from her.

He was the one who thought he might have miscalculated when her sheer beauty dried his throat. He found himself picking up her hand not to maintain an illusion of infatuation, but because he was unable to resist touching her.

Her gaze swept from the glittering city lights beyond the window to his eyes. Questions shimmered in the depths of her dilated pupils.

Inside him, something shifted as though a single brick scraped an inch out of place from an otherwise thick, weathered, impervious wall. He ignored the sensation and stroked his thumb across her knuckles.

Her lashes quivered and she swallowed.

Their server appeared with the first glass of wine from the menu that Vinicio had arranged for them.

When they were alone, she said, "Will you tell me exactly what you're expecting from me?" Her voice faded as he let his brows go up. She pulled her hand from his. "For instance, is your laughing at me something I should learn to tolerate?"

"I can't help that I find it amusing when you speak to me in a way no one else does. Not outside of my family, at least, and I don't like them, so they don't count."

"You don't like any of them?" She seemed distressed by that, even though she'd met all of them. She had to see it was warranted.

"I liked my aunt." He nodded at her ring. "She died when I was still a child."

She searched his expression, giving him time to expound on that, but he didn't intend to. His affection for the outspoken woman had been as close to a grandmotherly relationship as he'd had. She had lived a long, good life, but the loss of her still stung.

After a moment, Claudine pressed her lips and gave a nod of acceptance.

"I guess I'm wondering what I'll do. We've spoken about children, but I've always assumed I would work in some capacity even after I had a family. Both of my mothers did. I can't imagine being idle."

"What were you planning to do after the pageant?"

"I don't know," she sighed. "I've never known, to be honest. I think that's why I kept entering them, so I wouldn't have to make that decision. I do well enough in science and sports and art, but I'm not particularly gifted with any of them. I enjoy learning new things, but I lose interest very quickly. My looks have always felt like my one asset that was extraordinary. That will fade with age, so I'm exploiting it while I can," she said ruefully.

"You think your looks will fade? I highly doubt it. Nor do I think that's why you win pageants."

"They're *beauty* contests," she pointed out.

"They're contests. And you're competitive as hell."

"No, I'm not." Her brows came together, perplexed.

"You don't see it?"

"No."

He made a noncommittal noise, not interested in arguing the point, but all he could see in his mind's eye was her, kneeling on the beach, proving her superiority to his brother without even needing a witness to it. She hadn't been broken when Felipe had approached her. She had thrown sand in his face and continued to fight.

Damn. Now he was back to wanting to touch her.

"Let's dance." He rose and held out his hand.

Claudine didn't remember what they ate, only the way it felt to be in his arms.

If this was the seduction Felipe had promised her, it was subtle. It wasn't what he did, but what he didn't do that bombarded her with yearning.

His fingertips brushed the bare skin on her shoulder, but only in passing, not lingering. The shape of his mouth in her sightline filled her with curiosity to feel his lips against hers, but he denied her. The press of his hand at her hip was hot and possessive and stayed exactly where it was, no matter how she willed him to cup her breast or fondle her backside.

When the heat of his breath stirred her hair against her ear, and he asked, "Shall we skip dessert?" she was weak with longing for more. Her skin felt electric, her blood molten.

"Yes," she said, feeling drugged.

Paparazzi had gathered outside, blinding them with their flashes as they slid into the Rolls-Royce. They were no sooner inside than they were stuck in traffic.

"An event has just let out, Your Highness. I apologize for the delay," the driver said.

"Do your best." Felipe said and pressed the button to close the privacy screen. "I don't want to wait until the hotel to kiss you. *Come here.*"

The rough command in his voice undid her. The windows were so dark it was nearly impossible to see the lights of the city through them, so she slipped from her seat, which was as deep and luxurious as a recliner, past the wide console between them and into his lap.

With a gruff noise, he gathered her close, enclosing her in the warm cage of his embrace. His mouth settled across hers in a searing brand of heat. His tongue slid past the seam of her lips, the blatant act sending a spear of pure lust straight into the pit of her belly.

While his hands roamed all over her back and breast and hip and thigh, exactly as she had been aching for him to do, she burrowed beneath the edges of his jacket, wanting the man beneath the layers of wool and silk tie and the shirt made of a fabric with such a high thread count it felt as though he was naked beneath luxury sheets.

When she felt the release of her gown's zipper, she drew back slightly.

"No?" He stalled his touch.

She looked to the tinted the windows, but it was so dark back here onlookers probably couldn't even tell she was in his lap.

"No, it's okay."

His mouth came back to hers and the zipper went down to her lower back. She pulled her arm free of one sleeve.

"No bra. I thought not." His head swooped and her nipple was drawn into such a cavern of heat and pull she gasped at the sharp sensation. The damp scorch sent sweet runnels of urgent desire racing to collect in her loins.

"Felipe," she sobbed, wriggling, so acutely aroused she didn't know how to process it.

"Did I not promise to give you pleasure, *cara mia*?" His voice was far from his usual cultured tone and made everything in her twist with need. "Let's put your foot here in the cup holder."

He guided her shoe heel to the console so she had one knee raised against his chest, the other dangling off his thigh. In a small shift, she was cradled deeper in his lap so the thick shape of his arousal pressed to the cheek of her bottom.

As his touch drew patterns along the inside of her thigh, climbing beneath her skirt, she shook. The ache in her core intensified.

"Say you want this," he commanded softly.

"I do. *Yes*."

His features were shadowed and dark, the line of his mouth a cruel tilt. But his tracing touch was barely there as he explored the lace of her underwear.

"Give me your mouth. I want to kiss you again."

She tightened her arms around his neck, sealing her lips to his while his devilish touch continued to draw those maddening lines down her center, the pressure too light. Too teasing.

In a flagrant move, she thrust her tongue into his mouth, trying to tell him how badly she needed *more*.

In an equally deliberate move, he picked up the gusset of her undies and shifted it to the side, baring her damp flesh to the cool air of the back seat.

She looked again at the driver and the guard, both silhouettes facing forward through the dark privacy window, both oblivious to what the Crown Prince was doing to her.

He tipped her another degree off balance and ducked to steal another taste of her nipple. At the same time, he began to explore the wet seam of her sex, parting her folds, deepening his caress, exploring and invading. Claiming.

She released a guttural moan of unrestrained joy, clenching on his finger as he made love to her with his hand. He suckled at her breast and danced her toward an elusive pinnacle.

"Hurry, *cara mia*," he lifted his head to coax. "We're almost there." His touch rolled and pressed, growing insistent. "And so are you."

With another sob of abandonment, she caught his hand and held his touch where she needed it. She crushed her mouth to his and ground her hips and *broke*, flying outward in a thousand pieces. It was so powerful she turned her face into his neck, every breath a cry of ecstasy while he continued to caress her and murmur in Italian, holding her tight with his other arm, keeping her safe while she shook.

Slowly she came back to herself, still trembling and weak. She was dimly aware of him fixing her underwear and lowering her leg and helping her thread her arm back into the sleeve of her dress before he drew her zipper up.

"That is another compensation I want you to be brazen about accepting." His lips pressed to hers with something like tenderness. "I enjoyed that very much."

"Do you…" She was still befuddled, but she was aware of the prod of his arousal against her hip. "Should I…?"

"I'll wait. Go back to your seat. The car has stopped and I can see paparazzi is already gathered here, too."

Felipe didn't want to wait. His body didn't. Pleasuring Claudine and feeling the intensity of her response had nearly put him over the edge behind the sealed fly of his trousers. He longed to lose himself in her for hours. Days.

But therein lay the issue. He would lose himself in the process. He had known this lust between them was powerful. Now he knew exactly how all-consuming it could become, and that simply would not do.

As they entered their royal suite overlooking avenue Montaigne and the Eiffel Tower, Claudine's maid appeared in the door to the bedroom they were sharing.

Felipe had interviewed Ippolita himself before giving her the opportunity to prove herself to Claudine. She had been suitably intimidated by him and very earnest in her admiration for his fiancée. She didn't speak English and he had encouraged her to keep it that way, to help Claudine learn Italian, but also because it was useful in situations like this when he wanted to speak to Claudine without her maid following every word.

"You head to bed," Felipe said to Claudine. "I have calls to make."

"I thought—" Claudine's cheekbones scorched red. Her confused gaze searched his.

"Run a bath," he told Ippolita in Italian, who nodded and hurried away.

"I don't understand." Claudine's brow pleated with hurt. Tension came in around her mouth. There was accusation there, too, and defensiveness in the way she folded her arms so tightly across the breasts he had worshipped. "Did I do something wrong in the car?"

"Not at all. I enjoyed our interlude as much as you did. This is not a rejection, Claudine." It was an exercise in self-discipline.

"What then? A power trip?" Her troubled expression hardened into a glare, one sheened by angry tears. "I thought we were sharing something. Ourselves, maybe, but you were actually proving how helpless you can make me feel?"

She had been delightfully at his mercy, yet sensuously demanding in the way she had pressed his hand to her mound and moaned into his mouth. It had been exquisite.

"I wanted to give you pleasure." He had reveled in it. "It's as simple as that. You asked what you should expect from our marriage and I showed you."

"Yes, I'm beginning to fully grasp what I should expect— to be treated like a toy." A strident note had entered her voice. It annoyed him.

"I do not view you as a toy." He was well aware she was a fully grown, hot-blooded woman. "I'm merely avoiding any slip-ups that could result in a pregnancy that is not seen as wholly legitimate." That wasn't entirely a prevarication.

Behind her shock, a shadow of profound injury moved across her expression.

"You're still worried that I might be carrying Francois's—"

"No," he said firmly. "But a pregnancy test is probably a good idea. The pageants might discourage you from having relationships, but that doesn't mean there haven't been any men in your recent past, does it?"

"I've actually never had a man in my 'past,'" she snapped, putting air quotes around the word. "Recently or otherwise."

For a moment, he was uncharacteristically speechless.

"Am I understanding you correctly?" he asked with genuine astonishment. "Are you saying you've never had intercourse? How old are you?"

"Twenty-three." She glared at him with resentment at his questioning her, but it was so incredibly unusual in this day and age, he genuinely couldn't grasp it.

"But you're a very passionate person. Have you had lovers who *aren't* men?"

"Oh my God! This is why women can't win. If we have

sex, we're sluts. If we don't, we're liars. Thanks for a *lovely* evening." She slammed the bedroom door behind her.

That wasn't what he'd been saying at all. He was tempted to go after her and tell her that, but he'd got what he wanted, hadn't he? Sex was definitely off the table.

Before her bath, Claudine used the translation app on her phone to ask Ippolita to get her a pregnancy test.

She left the negative result on the back of the toilet for Felipe to find when he rose the next morning, still furious with him.

Maybe if she had actually thrown it in his face there would have been some satisfaction in it, but as it was, she only felt falsely accused. Used. She had felt helpless to his caresses last night, which had been okay when she had thought he had merely stopped because the car had, but the way he had touched her so intimately, then seemed completely unaffected by the experience kept striking as a hot iron of shame deep in her belly. She was already in an unequal position with him. That had only driven his superiority home in the worst possible way.

"That wasn't necessary," he said blithely about the test when he joined her for breakfast. "I believed you."

She snorted, not believing *that*.

His phone dinged and he glanced at it. "Vinicio would like to go over some résumés with you, but that can wait until we're in the air."

Her heart lurched. "I like Ippolita." Had she got her maid into trouble, asking for that test?

"You'll need a full staff of your own since a number of royal duties and foundations will fall under your purview. You won't be idle."

"Oh." She pondered that. She liked the idea of learning

about different charities and initiatives, playing ambassador for a good cause, but after last night, she was teetering in and out of thinking she had made a horrible mistake by agreeing to marry him.

On the one hand, she shimmered in echoes of the profound pleasure that had gripped her as she had clung to him, convulsing in his lap. It had been everything he had promised and more, but she couldn't recollect her pleasure without the fires of embarrassment also trying to engulf her. The way he had so easily rebuffed her afterward kept slapping her in the face, forcing her to realize how enormous the power imbalance was between them.

Maybe when they got to New York, she would just break things off and stay there.

The scrape of her spoon into her bowl of yogurt suddenly seemed very loud.

She glanced up to find Felipe watching her shrewdly. Her heart lurched with the sense that he had read her thoughts.

"You're still upset with me," he said.

"Of course not," she lied coolly. "Why would I be?" She rose. "I have to finalize with the designers before we go. Excuse me."

He caught her hand as she tried to brush past him.

She paused to look down on him, not pulling away because—damn her soul—she liked the feel of his thumb sliding over the inside of her wrist, even though he could probably feel her pulse tripping.

"You can't walk away every time a conversation becomes uncomfortable. We'll never speak," he said dryly. "I thought you were being overly sensitive last night, but I've since realized your inexperience made our lovemaking take on more meaning for you."

"I'm not being overly sensitive." How humiliating. She

tried to pull away, but he held on, not rough about it, simply conveying an urge for her to continue listening.

"You're upset because you allowed me more liberties than you've ever allowed any man and I didn't seem to appreciate that. I do now."

She twisted free of his grip.

"I'm upset because I felt manipulated. Go ahead and deny it, but I won't believe you," she threw at him. "I'm pretty, not stupid. You keep talking about how we need to trust each other, but how can we if we're not going to be honest with each other?" A thread of despair entered her tone as she saw endless suspicions and avoided truths unspooling into the future. It wouldn't work. It couldn't. "You wanted to control me and you did. Why the hell would I want to marry that?"

She felt his stare like the concentrated heat of sunlight through a magnifying glass, trying to penetrate her skin.

When she met his gaze, his eye ticked, betraying his inner tension.

"It's not you I was trying to control." He rose so abruptly she gasped and fell back a step. "It was myself. I want you, Claudine. More than is healthy."

His hands descended on her, fingertips gripping her shoulders through the plush velvet of her robe. She threw her arms up between them, but he didn't try to pull her any closer, only held her before him.

"You want honesty? Then stand here and listen to it. The way you fell apart in the car is all I can think about. I want to tear open your robe and clear that table and eat you for breakfast. I want us to break every piece of furniture in here and, after that taste last night, I'm confident we will. When the time is right." He searched her expression with lust in his eyes and concern pulling his brow. "After what you told me—that you're a virgin—I have even more reason to stay this side of rational, otherwise I might unwittingly hurt you."

She couldn't seem to catch a full breath. His strong hands on her upper arms were probably the only thing holding her up.

"The fact that you responded that strongly to my touch, Claudine…" He slid his hands upward to cup her jaw. His thumbs rested at the corners of her mouth. "We're a dangerous combination. Do you understand that?"

He might be right. She had the most indecent urge to turn her head and open her mouth so she could suck on his thumb.

His fingers splayed and he slowly trailed his touch down her throat where he spread the edges of the robe to expose more of her collarbone.

"Are your nipples hard? Shall I feel for myself?"

"Yes," she breathed, eyes fluttering closed.

Her arms fell away as his light touch stole beneath the lapels of the robe, loosening the belt as his hands found her naked breasts and caressed the swells, fingertips grazing the turgid points of her nipples. They stood tall and eager against his light pinch. Dampness gathered between her thighs.

"I bet you could come just from this, if we had time," he murmured, lowering his head so his breath washed across lips that stung as hard as her nipples. "Touch yourself. Let me watch."

It was such a flagrant request she dragged her eyes open, fearful he was taunting her for his own amusement.

If he had been, she didn't know what she would have done because she was willing to do nearly anything he asked, he had that much of a hold over her. It was a disturbing realization. It would have been outright terrifying if there hadn't been a glaze of blind lust in his eyes that mirrored what was going on inside herself. Nothing more sinister, just pure animalistic craving.

Recognizing that sent a drive of compulsion through her, one that wanted to see how far she could push him past his discipline. How far could they push each other?

That was sobering. She checked herself from throwing herself into his arms. He was right. They were a potent combination.

"Now you see." He gently withdrew his touch from inside the robe and doubled it closed again, as though bundling her against an arctic wind.

Then he gathered her close in a hug that would have been purely one of consolation if she hadn't felt the press of his arousal through the layers of robe and trousers.

"Make no mistake about how much I want you, Claudine. I want you more than I've ever wanted anyone in my life. But once we start that fire, it may incinerate us both."

CHAPTER EIGHT

"Mom." Claudine didn't realize how much stress she'd been under until she almost burst into tears at the sight of her mother.

She wanted to crash into her, but she had learned as a child to open her arms and wait for her mother to hug her first so Claudine could take her cue from the strength and length of her mother's hug as to how hard and long she could hug her back. Today, she was wrapped up in a good, strong one that let her soak up some of the reassurance she desperately needed.

She could have stayed there all day, but Ann-Marie drew back. "Introduce me to your fiancé."

Claudine did and watched Felipe gently take the hand her mother offered and simply cover it with his own, being so careful with her it squeezed Claudine's heart to see it.

"How are you feeling?" he asked her. "Are they treating you well here?"

"Better than the celebrities. I feel like a quee— Um…" She sent a perplexed look to Claudine.

"Good." Felipe's mouth twitched and he released her.

"It's okay, Mom." Her mother was down-to-earth and not impressed by fame or wealth, always far more interested in character or heart. "We wanted you here for privacy as much

as medical care, but how are your symptoms? Are they settling down at all?"

They caught up on her mother's condition. Thanks to the
clinic's doting doctors, her pain had already receded to manageable levels. She was eating and sleeping well, which always helped calm her symptoms, but she was still suffering
vision loss and had begun using a walker as a precaution
against stumbling. Aside from worrying about her daughter,
her mental health was positive, though.

"It's very expensive," Ann-Marie whispered to Claudine
when Felipe excused himself to take a call. "How are you
paying for this? Are you really marrying him? Or is this a
publicity stunt for the pageant? Have you read what they say
about him? And what they're saying about you?"

"I know, Mom. Try to ignore all that. And yes, it's real. I
know it's rushed, but…" Her mother would never accept that
her daughter was marrying for her benefit. Or that Claudine
was allowing herself to be used as a pawn, no matter how
terrible Francois was or that a kingdom hung in the balance.
"But this is something I feel is the right thing to do."

A better word might have been *inevitable*. She was still
shaken by the things Felipe had said in Paris. They hadn't so
much as held hands since. They'd been tied up with staff and
travel and other things, but there was a force field of electricity that seemed to contain them inside a shared bubble,
making her prickle with discomfort while he was out of the
room, then softening to a delicious tingle when he returned.

"Forgive me, Ann-Marie. I have a punishing schedule
while we're here, but I wanted Claudine to have this time
with you to reassure you both." His energy rushed in to swirl
like autumn leaves around the room. When he took the empty
armchair, he didn't so much settle as coil with readiness in it.
"Has she explained that I'd like to hire you a private nurse,

to help stave off these flare-ups and manage them when they happen? There are also clinics in Europe that are closer to us in Nazarine, which you might prefer so Claudine can see you more readily. She tells me that rest helps, so I was thinking that, after the wedding, I could make my yacht available to you. Or you could visit any of my residences if you'd like to stay on dry land. Perhaps invite a friend and simply enjoy quiet time to recuperate?"

"Oh my goodness. That's not necessary. I like my life here in New York," her mother said with a polite but firm smile.

"Then I'll arrange security to ensure you're not bothered too badly, but please let me do these things, Ann-Marie. Claudine's agreement to marry me has implications for you that I want to mitigate as much as possible. The paparazzi can be a nuisance, as I'm sure your neighbors are already aware."

"I—" She looked again to Claudine. "When exactly is the wedding?"

"We haven't set—"

"June twenty-second," Felipe said.

"What?" Claudine snapped her head around. It was already the fourth. "When did you decide that?"

"My father's team has just confirmed the twenty-second will work."

Claudine was speechless while her mother's wide-eyed stare asked her if she had parted ways with every single one of her marbles.

"Time is a finite resource in my world, I'm afraid." Felipe rose. "I know you both have a lot to talk about and plan, but Claudine and I have a number of engagements this week. We're already running late. I'll have a car take you back to your home tonight, though. You can meet with Claudine tomorrow to discuss all your options and make a plan for your travel to Nazarine for the wedding."

There was nothing heartening in seeing her mother blink the way Claudine did, breathless at the pace Felipe set. Claudine could feel her mother's concern as they hugged goodbye. She promised a proper chat tomorrow, but her stomach churned with misgivings as she reboarded the helicopter that had brought them from the private airfield after they'd landed in the royal jet.

The helicopter's cabin was small, holding only four luxurious leather armchairs. *Only* four. The other two were occupied by Vinicio and a guard, both of whom offered to serve them from the selection of beverages, chocolate, and nuts that were within Claudine's reach.

She wanted to speak privately to Felipe, but had to wait until they had landed on the rooftop helipad of what seemed to be a residential skyscraper. Staff awaited them as they came out of the elevator into an ultramodern penthouse suite where huge windows showcased the fading sunset.

"Welcome back, Your Highness."

Felipe introduced Claudine to everyone, then Ippolita whisked her away to an opulent bedroom where a stylist had a selection of gowns for Claudine to choose from.

It was her first formal evening with Felipe, a black-tie welcome dinner ahead of an international trade forum that Felipe would attend tomorrow. Then they had a gala on Friday night and an opera on Saturday.

Claudine nervously selected a dramatic, off-the-shoulder gown in midnight blue with a straight cut and a slit that would flash its silver lining when she walked.

The scrape on her shin would be visible, as would the one on her arm, but they were healing quickly, thanks to an ointment that Ippolita had provided. With a bit of spray tan applied atop them, they were fairly inconspicuous.

She removed the gown for some final alterations and had

a quick shower to freshen up after their travel, keeping her hair dry.

She slipped on the silk kimono that Ippolita offered, but was too restless to sit for hair and makeup just yet. June twenty-second? *Really?*

Tightening the belt on her kimono, she left her room and went through the lounge, across to the other closed door.

Vinicio glanced up from his tablet with surprise, but nodded when she pointed at the door, silently asking if Felipe was in there.

She knocked and heard, *"Entrare."*

Felipe's room was a mirror of hers, with a huge bed footed by a comfortable bench, a sitting area in the corner, a walk-through closet to a sumptuous bathroom and French doors to a balcony.

He stood near a side table wearing only a towel and a sheen of dampness on his swarthy skin. His musculature was sheer perfection, accentuated by the pattern of hair across his chest and down his sculpted abs. He held a drink half raised to his lips, seemingly arrested by the fact she wasn't Vinicio.

"Um…" She was disconcerted to find him nearly naked. She pressed the door shut to protect his privacy.

"You should leave," he said hoarsely.

His voice made her skin tighten. The air seemed to crackle with static.

"I…" Her throat was very dry, her own voice husked. "I want to talk to you."

"We'll talk in the car."

"I just want to know why we have to get married so fast."

He let out a choked breath and threw back his shot of alcohol.

"I just spent fifteen minutes in the shower thinking of all the things I want to do with you, trying to tame this lust. I mean this with the utmost respect, Claudine, but get the hell out before I start doing them."

She reflexively backed herself into the door, but couldn't help asking, "What kinds of things?"

"Do you completely lack any sense of self-preservation?" He set aside his glass and stalked toward her. "The kinds of things where you have to set the limits because I don't have any." He guided her hand to the door latch near her hip.

It was the only way he touched her and she felt bereft when his hand fell away from hers. The heat of his body was a spell that wafted out to paralyze her, melting her bones and her ability to think and any sense of resistance. He smelled fresh and spicy and intoxicating. She was mesmerized by the twitch of his nostrils and the tension around his mouth and the way his scar stood out against the flush of color that sat under his skin.

"Are we doing this, then?" He hooked one finger into her belt. The slippery silk disintegrated and the edges fell open.

She didn't move to cover herself, wanting to see his reaction.

His hot gaze scorched her skin as he slid his hands inside the robe. He skimmed her shoulders so the loose robe dropped off her shoulders, leaving her naked. Her breasts were already full and heavy, aching for his touch as he traced his fingertips down her arms before he gathered the swells and gently crushed them.

His mouth came down on hers with equal, tender force.

She moaned at the powerful jolt of need that rang through her. She had been waiting for this, *yearning* for it, but the maelstrom of sensations was so alarming she sought to catch at anything solid. Her hands found the smooth heat of his biceps, his shoulders, the muscles at the base of his neck and the dampness of his hair.

Then he was gone. She opened her eyes to see him sinking to his knees before her.

"This is what I'm going to do," he warned as his heavy hands clasped the tops of her thighs. His thumbs traced the crease on either side of her naked mound. He waited a pulse beat, allowing her to refuse, then he said with foreboding, *"First."*

He was shockingly blatant, sliding his thumbs to part her and leaning in to paint his tongue across her sensitive flesh in a very flagrant claiming.

She gasped at the intensity of it, but she had nowhere to retreat to. She was pressed to the door and had to swallow her cry of pleasure so Vinicio wouldn't hear it.

Felipe showed her no mercy. His clever mouth and touch swept and invaded and caressed until her entire world shrank to this, only this, the place he pleasured so mercilessly. Within moments she was cresting a pinnacle, suffused in a shower of stars.

As she shook and bit back her cries and tried to find something solid to hold onto, she found only the panels in the door and the fine strands of his hair as he stayed on his knees before her.

"You needed this, didn't you?" He rubbed his lips against her skin. "I know, *cara mia*. Me, too." He sounded both sympathetic and amused.

Then he did it *again*.

Her second orgasm was even more powerful.

She was fully sagged against the door in its aftermath, needing the press of his hot chest to hold her up when he rose to kiss her, long and just a little rough. He still wore his towel. Its fluffy texture pressed the tops of her thighs and cushioned the shape of his erection against her as he used his weight to press her to the wood.

She mindlessly ran her hands over the smooth skin of his shoulders and upper arms, trying to sate an appetite that seemed to have only sharpened, rather than been satisfied.

"Now," he said in a guttural voice, nose brushing hers. "I want you to leave before this goes any further."

Now she found her resistance because *no*. She refused to be the only one who was leveled by this acute hunger while he smugly enjoyed how thoroughly he'd taken her apart.

She touched his shoulder so he took a half step back, then caught the towel to keep him from moving any further than that.

A flare of pure, wild hunger flexed across his expression.

It was all the encouragement she needed to tug open the towel and drop to her knees before him.

Oh. She had never had such a close-up look at a fully aroused man. For a moment, she was all curiosity and shyness and fearful of hurting him, touching him very tentatively.

The way his breath hissed in drew her gaze upward.

"Are you trying to kill me?" His abdomen was sucked hollow, his lips thin with strain.

A delightful wave of power rose within her. She clasped him in her fist and did what he had done to her. She offered a thorough, brazen lick that had him slapping his two hands to the door above her, leaning a fraction closer into the heat of her mouth.

Oh, it was satisfying to feel him shake with desire as she learned his shape and textures and taste. His thigh under her exploring hand was rock-hard, his buttock tense—all of him drawn tight with excitement.

He wasn't nearly so uncontrolled as she had been, though. He pulsed his hips a few times and released noises of barely contained restraint, but after a few moments, he caressed her cheek and said, "You can finish me like this if you want to.

It's the most erotic thing I've ever seen or felt, but I want to be inside you, *cara mia*. Would you like that?"

She released him and he helped her rise. He didn't take her to the bed, though. He pressed his body against hers again, trapping her against the cool door again. His hard flesh left its impression against her belly while his hands stole all over her, lighting fresh fires within her as he kissed her again and again.

Her restless hands skated over his taut skin, learning the landscape of his ribs and lower back, his buttocks and flat hips and the pebbled nipples on his chest.

His kiss went into her neck and across her collarbone while his fingers returned to the flesh he had claimed so thoroughly, inciting her all over again, plying and teasing, preparing her to receive a deeper, thicker penetration.

When her inner muscles were clinging to his touch and her hips lifting in invitation, he nuzzled her temple and whispered, "If you want me there, guide me."

"Here?" Against the door?

"It will slow me down." His mouth twisted with self-deprecation. "I won't go too deep or thrust too hard. If you'd rather stop—"

Never.

She felt shameless and overt as she clasped his pulsing flesh and stood on her tiptoes to rub his tip against her slippery, yearning flesh. He bent his knees and here his superior experience came to the fore. Very suddenly, very undeniably, he was penetrating her.

His hand cradled the side of her face. "Look at me. Tell me if it hurts."

"It doesn't. It— *Oh*. A little." The implacable stretch threatened pain, making her bite her lip in apprehension, but she slid her hand to his lower back in a signal for him to continue.

He held still, very still. His eyes glittered behind the screen of his spiky lashes.

"This is the most exquisite hell," he told her with a caress of his thumb against her cheek.

"Please don't stop. I want—" She tilted her hips and brought one knee up to wrap her heel behind his thigh, accepting any pain that might happen because she sensed the pleasure behind it. The fulfillment.

As she pulled him in, there was a fresh sting. Heat. A throb deep inside her and the pressure of his pubic bone against the swollen knot of nerves that sent a gratifying swirl of joy through her pelvis.

With a shaken sigh, he sealed his mouth to hers and dropped his hand from her cheek to cradle her bottom. He used his forearm to hug her leg against his hip. In small, abbreviated thrusts, he ground himself against her, the friction subtle but deliciously effective.

There was something deeply provocative in being trapped this way against an unlocked door, forced to be quiet while such incredible sensuality built inside her. She closed her fist in his hair and sucked on his tongue and reveled in the growing pressure that felt too hot and intense to contain.

Suddenly, he lifted his head and pulled his hips back, only to return in a thrust of couched strength. The flood of pleasure against her sensitized nerve endings was astronomical. She let out a helpless cry, then another as he did it again.

"Now, *cara mia*. Let go. *Now*."

His hips returned to hers. Harder. Faster. He forced all the coiled density of need inside her to collapse and explode. In a rush of exquisite pleasure, she was launched. Flying. Moaning and clinging and arching for more, utterly abandoned in her greed for *all of him*.

He picked her up with both hands beneath her backside and pumped strongly, prolonging her climax so it struck again and again before his whole body crushed her to the door. He strained and shuddered and tipped back his head to release a roar of triumph.

"I'm so embarrassed," Claudine said.

"Why?" Felipe snapped from his doze. Somehow, he had carried her to the bed and scraped back the covers before they'd fallen to the mattress. His attempt to catch his breath had turned into the twilight between reality and dreams.

Actually, that was where he'd been from the moment she had walked through the door.

Virgin, he recalled, and dragged himself into full awareness. He came up on an elbow. He didn't care if she was bleeding on the sheet, but she would feel self-conscious about it.

"Because Vinicio is right outside that door," she whispered with horror, looking toward it. "I didn't even lock it."

"Vinicio would not be my personal secretary if he didn't have the sense to clear the area for a five-kilometer radius when my future wife visits my bedroom wearing nothing more than moisturizer." He fell onto his back again, letting his eyes drift shut, returning to the zen of post-orgasmic high.

"And a robe," she corrected lightly and slithered closer. Her hand came to rest on his chest. "This wasn't why I came in here, you know."

"No? I will maintain an open-door policy in future anyway, hoping for exactly this sort of surprise." He picked up her hand, idly kissing each of her fingertips.

Damn, that had been good. Better than he had imagined

it would be, but he didn't let himself devolve into recollections of her taste or her tongue dancing against his sex or the way her powerful orgasm had seemed to prolong his own. He was already too obsessed with her, thinking about sex when he ought to be—

Hell, he was the keynote speaker at tonight's dinner.

He didn't bother glancing at the clock. Vinicio would have sent a message that he was delayed.

"I wanted to ask you why the wedding is happening so quickly. I thought I would have more time to get used to the idea."

"My father doesn't have much time left. He wants to know the throne is secure."

She picked up her head. "Is that why you did this? Had sex with me?" she asked with a note of suspicion in her voice.

"I didn't drag you in here, Claudine. I told you to leave, remember?"

She held his hard stare, searching for ulterior motives.

A sensation struck inside his chest, one as sharp as the blade that had scored his face. It *hurt* that she didn't trust him. And it was all the more intolerable because it was so unexpected. Since when could she reach so far inside him? Was it the consequence of being inside *her*?

"If you don't trust me, why did you let this happen?" he asked with quiet chill.

"I couldn't help it," she admitted in a small voice. "I needed to know how it would be. How you would feel. How we would make each other feel."

The piercing icicle in his chest melted away.

His hand found its way to her jaw. He cradled her soft cheek, memorizing the way she still wore a heavy-lidded look of sensuality. Her hair was tumbled and her mouth pouted in a way that made him want to—

This was the danger she posed to him!

"We need to dress. We're late for our engagement."

Her brow flinched and her gaze was bruised as she drew her chin out of his palm.

"Such is the life of a royal, my dear. Duty always calls."

He rolled up onto his elbow to press a kiss on her lips, one that he meant to be brisk, but settled and softened into a tender, lingering thing that he hadn't known he was capable of delivering. It hurt, too, deep in his chest, in a way that wasn't as painful. More of a pull, like stretching a stiff muscle.

When he drew back, he was able to breathe easier and words slipped from his lips that he had no idea he was going to say.

"When we return later, I'll be all yours."

CHAPTER NINE

CLAUDINE HAD TOLD her stylist she was unafraid of heights, so her shoes were five-inch silver heels with a bow on the toes. She wore her hair gathered in a sleek topknot and encouraged her stylist to add some drama to her makeup, ensuring her look was well-defined and sophisticated.

When she asked Ippolita for her pink-and-white necklace, Ippolita said something about the Prince having it. Claudine's Italian was progressing at a rapid pace, but she still only caught every third or fourth word.

A bizarre shyness overcame her. She had developed a near unbreakable poise for almost any circumstance when sexuality was abruptly thrust at her—ha ha. But none of those situations had prepared her for a situation where she had actually engaged in sex.

Or for the sense that she now shared something with someone that was bigger than a secret. It was an experience. A profound one.

Did he feel the same? Even a little?

That was the thing she didn't want to face—his potential indifference to something that had left her feeling altered. It wasn't the "I am a woman now" nonsense. It was more the sense that she had shared too much of herself and didn't know how to take it back.

When she was dressed and as flawless as she could possibly feel, she braced herself to walk out to the lounge where she would have to look Felipe in the eye. All sorts of guilty longing were probably flashing neon bright in her face as she entered.

He had put on his tuxedo. Lord, why did he have to be so good-looking? And confident. He wore the addition of his royal sash of green satin with as much casual ease as he wore the shoes that were polished to a mirror finish.

When she appeared, he turned his head and his gaze swept to her toes and came back. Knowledge—so much carnal knowledge—sat as a banked heat behind his narrowed gaze. She was acutely aware they had both run their mouths all over each other's bodies. She had had three orgasms and was tender between her thighs.

There was no mockery in his gaze, though. Only approval. The glow of appreciation in his eyes drew her the way a fire would have beckoned her closer on a cold winter night.

"I, um—" She had to clear a huskiness from her throat. "I asked Ippolita for my necklace. She said you have it?"

Her throat was already dry and grew positively arid when he offered a case covered in silver velvet.

"Not that you need adornment," he said. "You're beautiful without anything at all, as I'm more than aware."

Really? He was going to say something like that in front of Vinicio?

She blushed and flicked a look to his secretary, but Vinicio was doing an excellent impression of a lamppost.

Felipe opened the case to reveal a stunning blue sapphire suspended from a platinum chain. A pair of matching drop earrings nestled beside it.

"I saw these when I bought the other one. I couldn't decide, so I got both."

She was too overwhelmed to speak and wound up standing mutely as he fastened the heavy links around her throat. Her hands shook as she removed her earrings and replaced them with the sapphires.

When she turned back to him, her shoes put her virtually eye to eye with him. A faint smile touched his mouth.

"I like this height." He caressed her jaw and kissed near the corner of her mouth.

"Felipe," she breathed in protest. "I don't want to be bribed."

"We talked about why I like to see you in things that I give you." His fingertip traced the rim of her ear then nudged her earring into swinging.

Why does any man want to put a ring on a woman? To claim her, of course.

Oh, help. He had claimed her. Utterly and thoroughly. She closed her eyes, body paralyzed by the way his fingertips stole into the hollow beneath her ear and caressed her nape, lifting goose bumps on her skin.

"You don't have to leave, Vinicio," Felipe murmured. "We're ready to go."

Oh, Gawd. Felipe's hand fell to catch her own while Claudine tried to pull herself together before she turned to face Vinicio. He smoothly held the door for them, avoiding direct eye contact. They all traveled down the elevator and into a car. Vinicio came in the back with them this time so there was no danger, or opportunity, for back-seat seductions.

The rest of the evening was not unlike Claudine's life as a pageant contestant. She smiled and held her best posture without fidgeting. She shook hands and expressed interest in the people she met and stayed on message when people asked about her engagement to Felipe.

"He whisked me off my feet. It's been a whirlwind."

"And the pageant?" someone asked. "Why did you drop out?"

"I couldn't continue to compete. It would have been a conflict of interest. I miss my friends, obviously, but it's fun to be an observer for once. I can't wait to see who wins." She turned that into asking who that person's favorite was and offered mild inside gossip about this woman's talent or that one's well-publicized struggle to overcome personal adversity.

"And your injuries?" a man asked behind her. "How did those happen?"

Claudine glanced over her shoulder to see a man roughly Felipe's age. He sent Claudine a sly look before turning a more malevolent one onto Felipe.

The blatant implication was that Felipe had inflicted them on her. It was appalling enough to turn Claudine's stomach. She felt Felipe's hand come to the small of her back. His arm was tense, ready to pull her protectively close.

"They happened before I left the pageant," Claudine said, holding the man's gaze without flinching.

"Oh? Is that why you left? You knew you couldn't win all scuffed up like that? Or did you simply find a bigger fish to fry?"

"Have Benedetto removed," Felipe said to Vinicio without otherwise acknowledging the man.

"Your brother is engaged. Have you heard that happy news?" Benedetto said, shaking off the hold of two burly security guards before walking away of his own accord.

Engaged? Already?

Felipe ignored him.

"Shall we dance, Claudine?"

"That sounds nice. Please excuse us," she said to the wide-eyed people they'd been talking with.

Felipe cocked his head very briefly for a whisper from Vinicio before he waved Claudine to precede him.

Claudine pasted an unbothered smile on her lips and let

him steer her toward the floor, but the harm was done. She could feel the sidelong looks.

Despite Felipe's impassive expression and the smooth way he guided her into the steps, she could feel the ire that radiated off him.

"Who is he?" she asked under her breath.

"No one. He raced the speedboat circuit with Francois and worked for the Italian Embassy until he was fired for misappropriation of funds. You'll never see him again. He must have been subbed in as a last-minute plus-one or he wouldn't have been allowed in."

"He's been a thorn in your side before?"

"I couldn't care less what my brother's cohorts say about me, but this salvo tells me Francois is unleashing his hounds on *you*, knowing full well I won't stoop to going after his own fiancée." A muscle pulsed in his jaw.

"Did you know about her? Who is she?"

"Vinicio just received the text. Princess Astrid, the daughter of a Danish prince. She was on Mother's short list." His mouth curled.

"She'll be pleased, then. Unlike how she feels about me." Claudine was starkly aware she fell far short in the Queen's estimation.

"You're not marrying her. You're marrying me." His firm hands pressed her back two steps before he gave her a slow twirl and brought her back into his arms.

It was the smallest gesture, but somehow she was breathless.

The dance ended and they left soon after.

As they entered their suite, he still wore tension across his cheekbones.

"I know what I said earlier, but I need to call the palace," he said.

"That's okay." All the travel and stress were catching up to her, leaving her yawning.

As she started into her room, he said, "Claudine. My bed is your bed."

She paused. "Is that an order or an invitation?"

"I thought it was what we both wanted. It's what *I* want."

Mollified, she said, "I was only going to my room to wash off my makeup and have Ippolita help me change."

His expression relaxed a fraction. "I won't wake you when I come to bed."

"You can," she said over her shoulder. "If you want to."

Some indeterminate time later, the mattress dipped and the covers stirred. She woke and rolled toward him, finding him naked.

"We don't have to. Are you tender from earlier?" He said that, but he was very hard and steely when she found his flesh beneath the covers.

"I want to. Can I try being on top?"

"You absolutely can, my beautiful treasure." He helped her slide the warm silk of her negligee up to her waist.

Claudine's mother had stayed behind in New York to make arrangements with her employer before coming to Nazarine. Felipe hired a nurse to assist her during the day as well as help her choose a specialist and make a plan for her ongoing care.

Claudine already missed her, but it was for the best that Ann-Marie didn't travel with them. Their commitments didn't stop once they left New York. They had engagements in several cities on their way back to Nazarine, attending meetings, dinners and appointments with every type of official including a lawyer who prepared their prenuptial agreement. Claudine also had more fittings and discussions with decorators along with interviews with staff.

Thankfully, their busy schedule meant they didn't see Francois until a few days before their wedding. The Spare had not been so lucky with gaining approval for his own wedding date. Given that his bride, Astrid, was a royal in her own right, she had initially asked for a year to plan their lavish wedding. They had settled on three months from now.

Francois was not hiding his resentment. He was quoted in the papers saying various unpleasant things about Claudine and Felipe and their own rush to the altar.

Claudine wished she could have avoided him indefinitely, but she was forced to attend a gala with the entire royal family where she finally came face-to-face with him for the first time since that horrible night on his boat.

She was standing with the King and Queen when she saw him approaching. She barely looked at his fiancée. Her heart had begun to beat wildly and she unconsciously stepped closer to Felipe.

His arm slid around her, firm hand closing on her waist while the rest of him remained relaxed but ready. His shuttered gaze watched his brother with undisguised contempt.

Felipe's lack of fear, and the calm reassurance he radiated that he would protect her, gave her the courage to stand tall and look Francois in the eye when he turned from greeting his parents.

"Felipe, you've met Princess Astrid. Claudine, I doubt you would have crossed paths with her." Because she was a commoner, his pithy tone implied. "Forgive me, but—"

Never, she thought, keeping her expression impassive.

"All the pageant girls blend together in my mind. Are you the one who never knew your father?"

"She's the one you lost," Felipe said starkly.

"Oh, goodness," Astrid interjected with the dulcet tone of someone well practiced in smoothing over a social conflict.

"*I* know who *you* are. Patriotism had me rooting for our own contestant, but I thought you absolutely deserving of the win if that's how it panned out."

"That's kind of you to say," Claudine said sincerely, aware that Francois's remark had been loud enough to quiet the voices around them. She couldn't ignore it and didn't want to. "I know as much about my father as I need to," Claudine told him clearly. "Sadly, I lost my one mother when I was a child. My other one will arrive tomorrow for the wedding, however. I'm excited to show her around Sentinella. I think she'll find it very interesting."

"Has she never seen Alcatraz? Any Hollywood feature is enough to get the idea," Francois drawled.

"I've always found Sentinella very drafty," the Queen piled on. "Cold and unpleasant."

Claudine couldn't possibly contradict the Queen, not in public like this, but the more she had seen how irrevocably the Queen was on Francois's side, the more she felt it was a betrayal of Felipe, who was equally her son.

"Perhaps my mother would be more comfortable in your apartment at the palace?" Claudine suggested to Felipe, knowing full well the Queen would consider that even more intolerable. "We could stay with her there."

"Perhaps," he agreed, sliding his gaze to Claudine's so she saw the glitter of amusement in the depths of his irises.

His mother sent an icicle-laden stare at them while his father moved the conversation into more stately topics.

When she had an opportunity, Claudine sought the ladies' lounge. It was designed as a small oasis with a sitting area of comfortable chairs in rose-colored velvet. Full-length mirrors were strategically placed to ensure one could scrutinize for flaws at every angle. A door led into a well-appointed powder room, and an attendant hovered, eager to provide any mending, makeup repairs or medical aid.

Two women left as she arrived, so she had the lounge to herself, allowing her to take slow breaths and try to release some of the evening's strain from her nerve endings.

"Oh." Princess Astrid faltered as she entered and saw Claudine at the mirror. "This is a nice surprise. We haven't had a chance to say a proper hello, have we?"

"We haven't." Claudine twisted her lipstick back into its tube and dropped it into her clutch, trying not to feel inferior to her. It was hard, though, after listening to the Queen build up this woman all evening while barely acknowledging Claudine was alive. "Are you enjoying the evening?"

"I'm not sure," Astrid said wryly. "The rivalry between our respective grooms is more overt than I anticipated. I hope you and I will manage to be friends, though." She sounded sincere. Nice. Too nice for Francois.

"I hope so, too," Claudine murmured. "I'll give you your privacy."

As she reached the door, however, she knew she couldn't leave it at that.

"Would you excuse us?" Claudine asked the attendant who looked surprised, but stepped from the room and closed the door behind her.

Astrid looked up from the clutch she had opened.

"I could never call myself your friend unless I told you something you deserve to know," Claudine began.

They flew back to Sentinella for the night.

It was Claudine's first arrival back here since they had left for Paris and New York. As she stepped inside the high walls of the fortress, she felt as though a valve released and she could finally breathe.

She didn't realize it came out as a long sigh until Felipe said, "I feel the same way whenever I return."

Claudine had thought she was the only one to find the royal palace a nonstop pressure cooker of tension. It had been oppressive before she'd told Astrid what Francois had done to her. From that point on, the rest of the evening had been one of sick dread while she waited for the fallout.

She would have to tell Felipe she'd spoken to Astrid, she knew that, but she dreaded that, too.

Ippolita had been on the same helicopter and was following them through the snaking path toward Felipe's bedchamber.

"Thank you, Ippolita," Claudine paused to say in Italian. "I can manage. Have a good night."

"Nothing to eat?" Felipe asked. "You barely touched your plate at dinner."

"No. *Grazie.*"

The maid murmured good-night and turned toward the stairs into the servants' quarters.

"Are you feeling ill?" Felipe asked as they entered the parlor next to his bedchamber.

"A little, but don't get your hopes up." She waited until he closed the door and glanced around to be sure they were alone. "I get this headache and backache every month."

"Ah. I thought you were gone from the ballroom an inordinately long time." He set aside the drink he'd been about to pour. "How bad is it? Shall I get you a pain pill?"

"I took one. You're not disappointed?"

"A little, but it's not something we can control, is it? What are you feeling? You're usually easier to read, but you seem…" He searched her expression. "I don't know. Are you upset?"

"I always get the blues on my first day. And the timing was wrong, so I didn't really expect it to work, but…" She was disappointed. Very. Which didn't make much sense except that she was excited for the idea of having a baby now that it had become a possibility. At the same time, having been subjected to all that coldness at the palace, she had to wonder if it wasn't a blessing that she wasn't pregnant. Did she really want to bring a baby into such a hostile environment?

"I don't know what to feel," she admitted.

"Look. Claudine." Felipe came to warm her upper arms with the light skim of his hands. "I know I've been pushing you where this marriage is concerned, but I am not a medieval monster. Please do not feel pressured to achieve something that is completely out of our hands. Aside from the obvious," he added dryly.

She nodded, appreciating him saying that since she did feel that conceiving a future king or queen was her primary purpose. Would he still want to marry her, though, after she told him what she'd done?

He had drawn her closer and she leaned into him, absorbing his strength, enjoying the warm hand that made soothing circles against her lower back.

"If you don't feel like making love, I completely understand," he said in a rumble. "I will even call Ippolita myself to run you a bath, if you'd like that."

She drew back and admonished him with an eye roll, since they were both perfectly capable of turning a tap, but his lips were twitching. He was teasing her. And cradling her very tenderly. She could have cuddled into him for the rest of the night.

"On the other hand, if you *would* like to make love, I am more than willing," he said with a light trace of his fingertip along her cheek. "No pressure. It's simply information I want you to have."

Why was he being so nice? It made what she had to say

so much harder. She drooped her head against his shoulder, then made herself step out of his arms.

"I told Astrid."

"Told—? Ah." His whole demeanor changed, but she didn't get a chance to read his expression. He went to the bottle of brandy he had started to pour. "How did she react?"

"With suspicion and disbelief." Claudine hugged herself, trying to quell a grim sense of scorn and failure. Possibly the worst part was that she had known this was how it would go, yet she was profoundly stung it had gone that way anyway. "I told her I would never forgive myself if he hurt her in the future and I hadn't warned her, but Francois had already told her I would likely make trouble on your behalf, that I would throw out false accusations against him, so that's what she assumed I was doing."

"Did you tell her we have video evidence that you swam ashore? And Dr. Esposito's report?"

"According to Francois, I got myself banged up on a motor scooter and knew I would lose the pageant. I targeted you and you have helped me to fabricate evidence. Your interest in me is pure spite against him." She shouldn't be surprised by the lengths that man would go, but she had been shocked at Astrid's calm dismissal of all she'd said.

"So she plans to marry him anyway." He finally turned and regarded her over his half-raised glass, still unreadable.

"That's not why I told her. I wasn't trying to stop their marriage. That's her choice. I was only clearing my conscience and telling her something she deserves to know. I told her that if anything comes up in future, I'll believe her and support her any way I can. Are you angry?" She hunched her shoulders defensively, bracing herself for his answer. "Do you think I should have spoken up sooner? Publicly?"

"I'm always angry," he said in a tone that was grim but

weary. "Especially at him." He lifted his gaze from the amber liquid he was swirling, revealing the bitter shadows that lurked behind his eyes. "I understand there is a cost to you whether you speak up or stay silent. I'm angry at *that*, but I try to focus on the things I can change." He threw back his drink. "And I appreciate that you tried, despite knowing that it might have no effect on her."

"Thank you," she said to the floor, kind of touched even though she was also filled with despair. "I didn't know how you would react."

"With pride, Claudine."

His tone of quiet sincerity shook her apart inside, lifting a strange sensation of wonder and yearning behind her breastbone.

"I'll run you a bath." He walked away.

"Rhys," Felipe said as he entered the anteroom of the church. "Thank you for coming on such short notice."

"Felipe." Rhys Charlemaine, Prince of Verina, came forward to shake his hand. "I'm honored you asked. It's also an excellent excuse to sail your beautiful islands and show them to my wife."

"Cassiopeia is well? The rest of your family?" They were a similar age, so they had crossed paths at school and other events through the years. They had many things in common, not least the challenges of royal life and a similar approach to living it. In finding his bride, Rhys had managed to unearth a woman with royal lineage, but she had been raised in Canada in a very down-to-earth manner.

They caught up on the necessary small talk, then Rhys said, "I thought you might ask Francois to be your best man. Things are still less than ideal there?"

"Your diplomacy is as razor-sharp as always," Felipe said dryly.

"Some relationships are more difficult than others. I understand that. It's still unfortunate." Rhys maintained his circumspect tone and expression.

Felipe didn't think less of him for it. Politics could change in an instant. Personal remarks had to be kept as neutral as possible in their circles. Rhys knew that all too well. He had endured his own difficulties in his past, but he had always remained close with his older brother, King Henrik of Verina. The animosity between Felipe and Francois was incomprehensible to him.

"Relationships demand respect," Felipe said, thoughts leaping automatically to Claudine—as if she was ever far from the forefront of his mind. "I lost all of mine for my brother long ago."

In fact, Felipe had thought there was nothing Francois could do to sink lower in his estimation, but he had. The pageant winner had been announced a few days ago, along with the fact this would be the final Miss Pangea. When Francois was interviewed about that, he had fielded questions that were obvious setups to smear Claudine.

"What of the rumor that Miss Sweden was disqualified for ethics violations? Can you confirm that she left of her own volition? Or was she asked to leave?"

"For privacy reasons, I must decline to answer," Francois had said with one of his patented looks of pained regret, making Felipe want to strangle him.

"I'm pleased to fill in," Rhys said magnanimously. "And Sopi asked me to invite you to visit us in Verina as soon as you have time." Sopi was his nickname for his wife. "She knows how overwhelming this can be and wants to be sure your bride knows she has friends."

"I'm sure Claudine would appreciate that. I'll have Vinicio liaise with your people."

Assistants entered with last-minute checks and the news that the bride had arrived. They were instructed to take their positions.

Felipe wouldn't admit to nervousness that Claudine would fail to appear at the altar, but the possibility had been there, especially since she wasn't yet pregnant.

That had hit him harder than he had expected, not that he'd shown it. It wasn't all because of this damned race against Francois, either. In the back of his mind, he'd always had the belief that if worst came to worst, and Felipe sat on the throne while Francois produced the next heir, Felipe would find a way to take custody of the future ruler himself. Because, among the many things that Francois should not be allowed to do, raising children was definitely one.

That was a turmoil best not started unless absolutely necessary, however. Thus, Felipe was marrying Claudine and planning to conceive his own heir with her.

Her innocence kept striking him, though. Her vulnerability. She hadn't said so openly, but he'd seen how upset she'd been that Astrid hadn't believed her. It was exactly what she had feared would happen if she came forward, but she had tried to protect Francois's bride anyway, suffering for the effort. Felipe had no doubt that Claudine's actions were the reason behind his brother taking special steps to muddy Claudine's reputation. It was retaliation.

Rhys had called their world overwhelming and it was, but Felipe's twin made it harrowing for Claudine. If he, Felipe, was a man with any true integrity or conscience, he wouldn't drag her further into it. He would protect her by pushing her as far away as possible from himself.

Maybe he would have, if the music hadn't already started and he hadn't looked up the aisle to catch sight of her.

His breath was punched out of him. She was a vision in ivory silk with a sheen that made her glow. She wore a tiara he'd gifted to her for this ceremony and she held her head high.

He couldn't look away from her. She seemed to hold his gaze the whole way down the aisle, escorted by her mother's slow gait. When she arrived before him, there were questions in her eyes.

He imagined she was wondering if she was doing the right thing. This was the final moment when she could back out, when he should have released her.

They both stayed exactly where they were, held as though by an invisible dome that formed around them, holding them in this moment.

He wanted her, he acknowledged. It had nothing to do with the crown or the future ruler or even the lust that had been simmering in his blood from the first time he clapped eyes on her.

This woman, whose hands settled on his open palms, filled him with more than pride. It was a force. Strength? Possessiveness? Reverence? It was a mix of all of those as well as an intense protectiveness that poured out of him to surround her. No one understood how truly remarkable she was, not the way he did. That was why he had to make her his.

Was it a rationalization to get what he wanted? Perhaps. But nothing in this world could have stopped him from claiming her right now.

So he did.

CHAPTER TEN

CLAUDINE HAD FALLEN into bed on arrival last night, exhausted by their long day. She woke as she often did these days, with the weight of Felipe's arm across her waist and the heat of his body spooned behind hers.

Her own arm was draped across his. Her seeking finger found the gold band she had placed on his hand yesterday. It was done. She was married to him.

Misgivings had chased her throughout the morning of her wedding, when her mother had asked her more than once, "Are you sure?"

The ceremony itself had been beautiful and lavish. She had truly felt like a princess in her gown and tiara. She had been emotional and, for a few moments during the ceremony, had felt bound to him. United. One.

After that, however, it began to feel like a play that was performed for an audience. Felipe had been contained and watchful. Triumphant even, when they had danced and Francois circled past with Astrid. Claudine had been forced to recognize their marriage was not a happily-ever-after. It was an expedient move by a determined man.

With time in such short supply in Felipe's schedule, they were only taking a short week for their honeymoon. They had arrived very late last night in Stockholm after stopping in Switzerland, where Claudine had seen her mother checked into a world-renowned clinic. There, a cutting-edge specialist had met with them and reassured her mother that she would get the help she desperately needed before she went home to New York.

For that, Claudine would marry Felipe a dozen times, but despite waking in a five-star presidential-suite bed, she was worried for her future. She had bound her life to a man she barely knew beyond the fact his family was as broken as they were blue-blooded. Felipe was powerful and driven and had done something invaluable for her mother, but only to achieve his own ends. He didn't love her. He didn't even believe in the emotion.

She did. Worse, she suspected, that was the reason she was here. She was falling for him despite his wall of cynicism. That scared her, because he was not a man who could be moved by anything but logic. Her heart could reach and stretch, but it would never touch his.

What had she done?

"You know I'm awake," he said in his morning-gruff voice, breath stirring her hair against her ear. "Do you want to make love?"

"Do you?" She realized she'd been tracing the bump of his wedding band all this time.

His scoffing noise chided her for having to ask when his erection was pressing the lace hem of her satin nightgown where it had ridden up against her buttocks. He shifted to loom over her and scrape his teeth against her bare shoulder.

She shivered and the yearning in her coiled toward arousal. This was why she had married him, because she only had to lie against him to become saturated with desire. When his body moved with light friction against hers, the flames caught. He opened his mouth against her nape and a delicate thrill ran down her spine, making her hips arch back in flagrant invitation.

With a growl of gratification, he reached up and over her to drag a pillow down, then used his lazy strength to roll her onto her stomach over it.

The covers fell away, sending cool air swirling around her, but she didn't care. She was already burning up.

"Bellissima." His thighs parted hers and his hands scraped up her hips, pushing the edge of the nightgown higher, baring her to his gaze.

She moaned, aware how shameless she was, but it didn't stop her from setting her hands against the headboard and offering herself to the hard flesh that stroked along her slick lips, strumming her flesh into vivid life before he sought entry.

They both released ragged groans as he drove into her. He was on his knees behind her, holding her hips steady for his powerful thrusts. It was raw and animalistic and she gloried in it.

This was why she had married him. This passion coupled with the sense that when they were like this, she gave him exactly what he gave her—utter pleasure. It was a potent aphrodisiac to meet his thrusts and reach to where they were joined and hear his breath change when her fingers brushed his flesh.

She loved most when they reached the pinnacle together. She could tell he was nearly there. So was she. It only took a light touch of her fingers against her most sensitized place and her inner flesh clamped onto his. Orgasm tumbled through her, sending her soaring and floating and...

He slowed his thrusts, moving strong and deep to prolong the convulsive waves that had her in thrall. When she was shaking and weak and still trying to catch her breath, he withdrew and rolled her off the pillow.

"Always so quick," he teased with lusty approval rasping his voice. "I love how greedy you are."

Her heart lurched, led one way by "I love," and yanked in another by the rest of what he'd said.

"I thought you were ready, too." It was disconcerting to realize he hadn't been nearly as aroused as she was.

"I'm greedy for *your* pleasure." He lowered his head to her breast and used his tongue to shift the lace against her nipple.

A fresh jolt of desire shot through her like electricity.

"Poor *cara mia*. Did you think I would do anything on our honeymoon beside make you mine in every possible way?" He slid his hand beneath the lace and exposed her breast, then dipped his head to take her naked nipple into his mouth.

It was a delicious, sensual assault that she couldn't help succumbing to, even as she realized that they might take equal pleasure in sharing their bodies, but he wasn't nearly so helpless to it as she was.

Felipe was a textbook case when it came to being a workaholic, so the annoyance he felt at the end of his honeymoon surprised him. Aside from daily visits to the gym and necessary meals, he worked constantly. Ski trips and other recreation were always combined with work. He had many responsibilities and they'd become heavier since his father's diagnosis.

It wasn't as if he would cease to see his wife, either. They made important appearances on their way home. And, while Claudine might eventually have a heavy calendar that conflicted with his own, it had become their habit to dine and sleep together. When he came out of meetings, she was never far if he wanted to find her.

This irritation with the intrusion of real life pressed guiltily against his conscience. He had been born to the crown, raised to wear it, and, for the sake of Nazarine, it was imperative that he continue to serve the throne. Any distraction from that was a threat to more than his sense of mental peace. It was a danger to the country that depended on him.

He had to remember that Claudine was a means to performing his duty. An extension of it, and nothing more.

His duty had never been such a pleasure, however, as when he escorted her into a charity gala in Portugal and she was introduced as his wife. She was beautiful. That went without saying, but she had the ability to make him catch his breath with a tilt of her smile or the feel of her long silk glove against his wrist.

His enjoyment of her presence beside him went beyond their sexual attraction and the boost to his male ego, too. He'd attended countless events like this with a woman on his arm. None had made him feel so...accompanied. That was it. In nearly every setting, he had always felt apart from the humanity around him, not that it had ever bothered him to be so, but with Claudine he was not alone in this sense of remoteness.

She didn't seem to feel the same removal, though. She shifted between the invisible spaces without effort or even awareness of it. She put people at ease and projected an air of warmth, then looked at him in a way that should have felt invasive, but was a welcome intrusion. Her clear alignment with him undid two decades of Francois's best attempts to label Felipe cold, corrupt and objectionable.

That amused Felipe no end, but he saw it as a liability, too, though. Being known as ruthless had its uses. Their romantic rush to the altar, dazzling as some found it, also made it seem as though he had a soft spot for her.

Seem? he chided himself. He *did* have one. His appearance of loving her offered her certain protections, but that same perception made it clear she was his Achilles' heel.

That concerned him. As much as he adored having her beside him, she created the sense of an unprotected flank. He didn't expect an attack to come from her, but she was not a shield. She was a crack where an attack could come through.

"Vinicio is trying to get your attention," she murmured when there was a break in the conversation they were having with a local dignitary.

"Excuse us," he said to the couple and brought her to where Vinicio offered his phone.

"A message marked *Private*, Your Highness, from Princess Astrid."

Felipe automatically held out his hand, but Vinicio said, "I beg your pardon, sir." He offered it to Claudine.

She took it with a blink of confusion, then her eyes widened as she read. She showed it to Felipe.

I believe you. He wanted to move up our wedding date and did not take it well when I resisted. I'm fine, but the wedding is off. I'm on my way home. I wanted to apologize for not believing you when you warned me about him. I really do hope we can be friends in future.

"Find out what's going on with Francois," Felipe instructed.

Vinicio took back his phone and brought it to his ear as he moved out of the ballroom.

"I guess we didn't need to marry quite so fast," Claudine said with a weak smile.

Her remark had him reaching out to catch at her gloved hand, as if he had to physically restrain her from walking away from him.

"He'll replace her very quickly."

Her brow tugged into a brief frown of agony. He swore under his breath as he heard her thoughts. She would have to rake over her experience again and again, going through the process of being disbelieved again and again, as she continued to warn these other women.

Make a public statement, he wanted to insist, but clamped his lips tight. It had to be her decision.

"I think I expected to feel some kind of satisfaction or sense of vindication if she left him, but there's not," she said glumly.

"Shall we leave?" he asked.

"Only if you want to. I'm fine," she said with another wan smile.

Duty had him scanning the room for people he had yet to greet. It was the last thing he wanted to do or put her through. He was already wondering how Francois would choose to retaliate for this, but Felipe's desire to take her home only underscored how much she was impacting his ability to put his duty to the crown ahead of personal interests.

"Let me introduce you to the prime minister." He nodded at a hovering assistant who hurried to make it happen.

After a whirlwind of appearances, they finally returned to Nazarine and the blissful serenity of Sentinella.

Home, Claudine thought, as Felipe rolled his naked body away from hers.

They had enjoyed a lazy morning of lengthy lovemaking, but now he said, "I have meetings with my father all afternoon. You're welcome to come to the palace with me, but you don't have to."

"Honestly, if I could browse the shops on Stella Vista without creating a scene, I would." She mourned the simple freedoms of her old life sometimes. "Your parents don't expect me, do they?"

"No, this is purely business with my father."

"I'll stay here, then."

"And keep my bed warm?"

"And call my mother." Ann-Marie's most recent messages had been upbeat. The new clinic was trying some advanced therapies that seemed to have halted this latest spiral, and some of her symptoms seemed to be less severe. "Maybe I'll check in with Astrid, too."

Claudine had sent her a brief note, telling her she would also like to be friends and had promised to connect properly as soon as she had a moment.

Felipe kissed her, then rose to shower. He was gone within thirty minutes, swearing that the sooner he left the sooner he'd be back.

He was back a lot sooner than Claudine expected. She had only had time to shower and eat a late breakfast. She was sitting by the fountain inside the maze, contemplating whether to make a public statement about Francois, when she heard the helicopter.

Felipe appeared before she had walked more than halfway out.

"What's wrong?" she asked across the zigzag of boxwood.

"He found your father," Felipe said grimly.

Francois hadn't released the story himself, of course. He had used one of his scandal sheet contacts to blast across the headlines that the new Princess of Nazarine had been conceived by a man who had died of an illicit drug overdose years ago.

Felipe didn't care about such details himself, no matter how sordid the reporters tried to make it sound, but he was livid that Claudine was upset by it—not that she was concerned for herself.

"His poor family. Does he have any? I should call my mother. How is the palace taking this?"

The palace, his own pathetic family, were expressing "concern" and "looking into it." They did absolutely nothing to punish Francois for violating Claudine's privacy. Felipe's meeting with his father had been a short, snarling few words demanding he put his brother in his place.

"You're turning a blind eye to his sullying the royal family like this? Again?"

"She's not family, is she? And she fired her own shots across his bow by badmouthing him to Astrid."

"She told the *truth*," Felipe had roared before climbing straight back into his helicopter to come here and tell Claudine.

She finished up her conversation with her mother. They signed off with their standard, "Love you."

"Love you, too."

That always gave him a strange sensation when he heard that. Envy? He shook it off.

"How is she?" he asked grimly.

"Concerned about how I was taking it," Claudine said, mouth quivering with emotion.

"And? How are you taking it?" Felipe prodded, aware that she had been so upset for others she hadn't expressed her own feelings on the matter.

"Honestly? I'm really sad that he's not still alive. That breaks my heart." Her eyes were bright with unshed tears. "I've always held on to a small hope I might meet him someday. Now that it will never happen, I'm deflated. And I hate that Francois is exploiting him this way when he can't even defend himself."

"It's reprehensible." Felipe drew her into his arms, trying to offer what comfort he could, but his conscience tortured him. "I never should have pulled you into the ring of my fight with my brother."

"He and I fought before you and I had ever met," she reminded him, drawing back enough to look into his eyes. "I'm sorry that you have had a lifetime of fighting with him. Of never knowing what it is to have family who loves and supports you. I can't imagine how hard that's been for you."

Such a wrenching sensation went through his chest that he nearly mistook it for a medical event. He swallowed back the profound ache and held her closer, tucking her face into his shoulder so she wouldn't see how completely she had leveled him with her wish that he had experienced something he had long ago convinced himself he didn't need.

"Don't worry about me," he insisted gruffly. "I want to know how I can help you."

"I don't think there is anything that can help. I presume if he had family, they would have been identified already."

"I asked Vinicio to investigate—" He cut himself off as there was a knock at the door.

Felipe dropped his arms so they both faced his secretary as Vinicio entered with the closest thing to excitement he had ever exhibited.

"Sir. I think this could be positive news."

There was no reason for Felipe to feel a level of threat this intense. It wasn't physical, which was probably why it was so uncomfortable. His team had verified everything, so traveling to Sicily carried virtually no risk to either of them.

Emotionally, however, there was the potential for great jeopardy.

Felipe had trained himself to avoid emotions. The ones he allowed himself to feel were generally the ones surrounding his brother's behavior and even those bouts of fury and bitterness he routinely watered down and ignored.

He didn't allow himself the folly of hope or joy. Never ever the hope *for* joy.

There was Claudine beside him, though, drying her palms on the raw silk trousers she wore, chewing her lip, fairly quivering with anticipation of something that could turn out to be profoundly disappointing.

How was he supposed to protect her from that? He couldn't.

Which churned an unfamiliar helplessness in his gut, but he couldn't deny her this chance, could he? Not when she had told him how much she had clung to the hope that she might one day meet the man who'd made her. This wasn't that, but it was the next best thing.

The helicopter flight was just over an hour. They landed on a private estate where two of Felipe's guards greeted them, having come in this morning to ensure everything was as secure as promised. The pair fell into step with them as they were escorted down a wide, paved path toward a beautiful single-level villa.

As the path brought them into a garden where a freeform swimming pool gleamed in the midday sun, a family waited to greet them.

Freja, Claudine's cousin, was a blonde woman closing in on thirty. She resembled Claudine even more in person than in her photos. It went beyond the physical into the warmth she radiated and the gleam of liveliness in her eyes.

Her husband, Giovanni, looked closer to forty. He gave off a relaxed air, but there was a quiet suggestion of power in his wide shoulders and watchful gaze. Their twin girls were three years old and stood wide-eyed on either side of their father's wheelchair, each clutching a posy of flowers.

As one of the assistants provided introductions, and the men reached to shake hands, the girls hurried forward to thrust their small bouquets at Claudine.

"Thank you. *Grazie*." Claudine crouched to take them, looking deeply moved. "Which one of you is Louisa and—"

"She's Theresa, I'm Louisa," one said hurriedly.

"Where's your crown?" Theresa asked with a worried look at Claudine's hair.

"They don't wear them every day, angel." Freja gave her daughter's fine hair a tender smooth. "I hope you don't mind." Freja bit her lip against helpless laughter. "They wanted to meet a real princess."

"*I* wanted to meet a real cousin and look at you both! I swear I have a photo of myself at your age that looks just like you two." She was blinking back tears of joy.

"I would love to see it," Freja said, then urged the girls, "Off you go with nanny. I'll call you when it's time to say goodbye."

The girls were pulled away and Giovanni invited them to sit in a shaded settee near the pool. Refreshments were served, but Felipe didn't think Claudine noticed anything beyond her newly discovered cousin. She was staring and smiling at Freja and Freja did the same thing back, both seeming nearly speechless with happiness.

"I must apologize for the way this news came out," Felipe said, prepared to offer a more thorough explanation, but Freja held up a hand.

"Please. I'm very used to publicity." Freja's father had been a famous travel writer. She had toured the world with him and developed her own following after writing a book about him. More recently she had released a documentary on her life with him.

Perhaps what she was really most known for, however, was the fact that her husband had been presumed dead some years ago. Yet he was alive and well today, affably pouring wine that appeared to be from their personal vineyard.

"I'm far too thrilled to meet my cousin to let the way I found out tarnish it," Freja continued. "I always knew my father's brother had donated sperm to a clinic. It actually gave my father a lot of comfort, believing that something of his brother possibly lived on, but it seemed impossible that I would ever get the chance to meet any children he helped to make. It wasn't on my radar at all. Not until Giovanni told me this morning that—" She looked to her husband, appearing unsure how much to say.

"Given Freja's high profile, I have robust online alerts set around her name and those of any connections that might crop up," Giovanni said smoothly, as though it hadn't been a needle in a haystack for him to have put this together that fast. "Freja's father wrote about his brother in this book." He reached into the carry-all pocket that hung off his chair. "There are some photos of him, too. I've marked it. Freja thought you'd like to have it."

"Giovanni knows my father's books better than I do," Freja said with a self-deprecating grimace. "But I have other copies, so please keep that one."

"This means the world to me. Thank you." Claudine hugged the book. "What else can you tell me about him?"

"Not much, I'm afraid. I was still very young when my uncle died. I don't have any memories of him at all. You'll be able to tell that my father adored him and missed him all the rest of his life." She nodded at the book. "I remember him talking about Uncle Leif as someone who was endlessly curious, but never stuck with anything for long. He was more interested in the challenge and, once he learned all he needed to, he jumped into something else. He hated to lose any sort of game, whether it was checkers or even solitaire."

"Oh?" Claudine glanced at Felipe, mouth twitching ruefully.

"They were supposed to go traveling together, but my father married my mom and had me. Uncle Leif then planned to go alone, but the night before he left, he went to a rave and took some party drugs that turned out to be toxic. Don't believe what was said online. If he'd been a longtime user of heavy drugs, he wouldn't have been allowed to donate to the clinic. This was a one-time thing that turned out tragically."

"Very tragic," Claudine agreed, mouth tilting downward with sadness.

"The reports around the circumstances of his death will be corrected, I assure you," Felipe promised.

"My team is already on it," Giovanni said. "You and I should discuss messaging. Let the women get to know each other and we'll take this to my office."

Felipe was surprised by that, but after one brief glance at Claudine, who nodded and immediately turned back to Freja, he rose and followed Giovanni into the villa.

An hour quickly passed. Talking to Freja was like talking to an old friend. Or, more specifically, to a close cousin she'd known all her life. It was remarkable.

When it was time to leave, she and Freja promised to keep

in touch and hugged warmly. That signaled the girls to also give Claudine a hug. Claudine fought fresh tears all the way back to Sentinella.

"You haven't said much," Felipe noted when they entered the privacy of his office there. "Are you all right?"

"I'm so happy I feel like I owe Francois a thank-you card."

"Ha!" Felipe barked.

She bit her lip, always pleased when she could get a laugh out of him. If it was at his brother's expense, that was even better.

"I suppose I could say the same," he said dryly. "Here I thought you came without valuable connections. As it turns out, your cousin's husband is a lot more than the domestic family man he portrays himself to be."

"You didn't get that from his billion-dollar mansion and the mystique around his faked death? What did you talk about when you two went inside?" she asked curiously.

"Things I'm not at liberty to repeat, but he is *very* well connected. He's also under no illusions as to Francois's true nature." He narrowed his eyes, staring thoughtfully into the middle distance.

"Freja said her PR team has already begun correcting my father's image. She said I'll soon have an army of her father's 'travel bugs' supporting me." That had made her laugh.

"Giovanni said something along the same lines."

"I liked them."

"Me, too."

Claudine paced a few steps, pensive. "I can't help thinking Francois will look for some other way to attack me now that this route hasn't worked." It was causing her some dread. And a spark of rage. She was so tired of being Francois's chosen victim. "I think it's time."

"Time?"

"To tell my story." As she said it aloud, she felt the rightness of it.

Felipe's mouth pressed into a line, but he nodded once, jerkily. "How would you like to go about it?"

CHAPTER ELEVEN

FELIPE BROUGHT IN his legal team. After a long consultation, Claudine took their advice to lodge a complaint of negligence and harassment against the pageant, since the corporation had yet to be dissolved. Claudine had been a resident of New York when she entered the contest and that was where the pageant headquarters were located, so that was where everything would be filed.

The timing worked with her mother. Ann-Marie would never fully recover the mobility or vision that she had recently lost in one of her eyes, but she was stable and proceeding with a new treatment plan that seemed to be keeping her feeling as well as possible. She was ready to go home to New York where Felipe had a team standing by to help her close up her apartment and move to a new building with better security and a live-in helper.

According to the press release that Felipe arranged, Claudine was assisting her mother with all of that. She was her mother's liaison with all the workers, but she also swore her statements while she was there.

On her return, Felipe met with his father to warn him that charges against Francois were likely.

"Why the hell did you let it get that far?" the King snarled.

"I told you when I chose Claudine that I would let her dictate when and how she told her story."

"And I allowed you to marry her believing you would quash it," Enzo thundered. "You're supposed to be making less work for me, not more. Have her withdraw her accusations."

"No." Felipe wasn't surprised by his father's reaction. He wasn't even angry. He was revolted. "This isn't a scandal. It's harassment and assault that could go much further than Francois. Other people could have been taking advantage of contestants. Do you really want to protect all of those abusers?"

His father muttered a number of overripe curses.

"It will take a few weeks for the charges to be filed. Claudine's statement will be released at that time. Don't bother using your connections to stop it," Felipe warned. "She'll go to the press regardless."

"You couldn't wait until you'd made an heir? Your brother is next in line," his father spelled out as though Felipe was a child without the faculties to understand. "Think about that before you dishonor his name."

"He dishonors this country," Felipe insisted grimly. "How do you not see that?"

"He's all we have until you do your duty." The King smashed his fist onto his desktop. "Tell your mother." Enzo seated himself at his desk in the way he did when he was being as rudely dismissive as possible.

"Francois can tell her himself when he's indicted," Felipe muttered and walked out.

It was a tense time made worse by the fact Claudine discovered—again—that she wasn't pregnant. At least, she had a bit of spotting that ruined her day, making her believe she wasn't, but it disappeared by the next, which was confusing.

"What does that mean?" Felipe asked with a frown of concern.

"I don't know," she muttered truculently. "That I'm putting too much pressure on myself? I think it was the trip to New York. It feels like an ax waiting to fall."

He had told her how things had gone with his father over her statement. Claudine understood the urgency to create an heir, even though she knew that letting the pressure get to her wasn't helpful.

"One day at a time," Felipe murmured, rubbing her back. She knew he didn't blame her for Francois's behavior or their lack of conception, but guilt dogged her like a black cloud.

Her failure to conceive certainly wasn't for lack of trying, she thought dourly. They made love as often as possible despite how busy they were. Over the next weeks, they flew to Berlin and Hong Kong, then came back by way of Cairo, which was fascinating, but hot. She caught a glimpse of the pyramids from the airplane, but otherwise it was nothing but parading in gowns and talking business.

She didn't mind the travel and small talk. She was meeting interesting people, but the only time she seemed to connect with her husband was in bed—where they made love in a pleasured frenzy. Any words they exchanged were sexual, never emotional or personal.

It was frustrating. She wanted…something. Some indication that she meant more to him than the vessel for an heir. Was this all they would ever have between them? Sex and the stratagems of her statement? Because she was feeling very trapped in a prison of her own making.

She was in the library, trying to recall which books he had moved to make the wall open, but it wasn't working. She was frustrated and feeling stymied and blocked. Not imprisoned, but held by an invisible force, one she couldn't name.

She didn't *want* to name it. To name it was to succumb to it in all its vast glory.

And to recognize that she was alone in feeling this way.

"Oh, Claudine," she chided herself exactly as her mother might do if she forgot to study or lost her keys or signed up for a pageant even though her mother had expressly asked her not to.

Because what she'd done was go and fall in love with her husband—fathoms deep in love. Which wasn't a crime. Not by any means. It simply wasn't wise.

What was she supposed to do now?

She heard the helicopter return, signaling he was back from his latest meetings with his father. She stayed in the library, not even turning when the sound of approaching footsteps arrived behind her with a blast of crackling energy.

"You're back early." She didn't turn to face him. Did this one go in? She kept searching for evidence on the shelf, a rail of dust or a fingerprint, but she couldn't find any hints to help her.

"Your lawyer has filed the charges." The door closed. "Francois will be notified shortly, but the statements to the press won't release until after my parents' anniversary party."

"Francois will know, though," she repeated, feeling the invisible clock ticking down. Three more days and the details of her dark night in the water would be known by all. "Will his new fiancée be there?"

"Yes."

Eloise was the daughter of a British duke. So far, Eloise had only met the King and Queen. At least, Claudine wouldn't have to muster up her courage for a heart-to-heart with her. Her accusations would be all over the headlines the following day.

"What are you doing?" Felipe's voice was directly behind her.

"Trying to remember how to open the secret passage.

Queen Giulia could have escaped. She could have seduced a captain and sailed away. Why didn't she?"

"Her children were here. They had entitlements that would have been lost if she took them away from Nazarine. And she knew she had more power inside these walls than out. Why? Are you trying to escape me?" His hand covered hers, moving it down two books and withdrawing one spine.

"Perhaps I'm trying to let my lover in." She was being metaphoric, but also deliberately provocative, wondering if she could get a reaction out of him, even if it was lowly jealousy.

"Your lover is already here, Your Highness."

Her skin tightened with delight, but there was that other, anxious piece that had her stiffening slightly as he closed his hands on her upper arms.

He stilled. "No?"

"I—" She reflexively pushed her bottom back into his groin and instantly felt the thickness of his erection. Mindless passion was no substitute for love, but it fed something in her to know that he wanted her as badly as she wanted him. "H-here?"

"Right here, if that's what you want."

"I do," she whispered.

"Then hold on to this shelf." He guided her hands to the one in front of her eyes.

His touch trailed under her arms and down her rib cage. One hand swept forward to gather her breast through the silk blouse she wore. His body bowed around hers and his other palm slid to press the pleats of her skirt against her mound so she felt the strong flex of his hand there, *claiming*.

She writhed in the trap of his arms, stimulating both of them with the rock of her hips.

His mouth bypassed the hair she had clipped low behind her neck and his teeth scraped against her nape. With the light pinch of his fingers through her bra stinging her nipple, and the relentless pressure of his hand between her legs, she quickly grew aroused.

"Who are you?" she gasped. "A pirate? A smuggler?"

His head abruptly lifted and he slowly turned her. His hand dragged at her hair. "Look at me."

She forced her eyes open to see something atavistic in his gaze. Possessive? Threatened?

"I am your husband. Your future king. The only lover you will ever need."

His command for recognition lit something in her. A fierce compulsion to break past this wall between them and reach him. Without thinking, she clasped his head and brought his mouth down to crush her own against it, then speared her tongue into his mouth.

He gave a grunt of surprise, then tried to take control of their wild kiss, but she refused to allow it. She closed her fingers in his hair and arched against him blatantly, deliberately trying to incite him past his usual restraints. He always took her apart so easily. For once, she wanted to know she could do the same to him.

She loved him and it was eating her alive.

She pushed her hand between them, squeezing his shape through his trousers before delving behind his belt and past the constriction on his boxer briefs to the thick flesh that pulsed as she closed her fist around him.

His breath hissed in and his nostrils twitched.

"Why the hurry, *cara mia*?" He held her bold stare as she caressed him, trying to make him break.

She almost had him. She could see the effort it was costing him to keep his narrowed eyes open. His jaw was clenched, his breaths unsteadily. There was a slippery dampness against her thumb that she rolled around and around his tip, causing him to grow even harder in her grip.

"What is your end game?" he asked in a rasp.

"Why do you think this is a game?"

"Because I can see you are trying to win, *cara mia*. What do you want? To break me? You can try." He opened his belt and fly so her hand easily slipped free when he shifted her backward, causing her to stumble.

He caught her, of course, and pressed her to the narrow, cushioned bench of the reading nook. The high sun splashed down onto her, blinding her, but she didn't need to see when she could feel her skirt being flicked up to her waist and his knee parting her thighs.

And she thought, *Damn you. I will break through to you.*

She blinked against the sharp glare. He was a backlit shadow looming over her, but she halted him from kissing her by catching her fingers between the buttons of his shirt. She wrenched it open so a button pecked her cheek as it flew off. Then she splayed her hands across his naked chest and pressed her thumbs to the sharp points of his nipples.

"Oh?" With one hand, he did the same to her top, yanking it so roughly, the silk tore and hung off her side, baring her bra. He shoved aside the lacy cup, exposing her breast.

Did he think that would disconcert her? She reached down and pulled her underwear to the side, further exposing herself. She caressed herself, parting and preparing herself. Beckoning and teasing and daring him to take her.

His fierce gaze raked down her torso and lower. His expression wasn't so much possessive or aggressive as *exalted*. As though he had discovered something wondrous. His brow flexed and his mouth tightened with strain. It was taking everything in him to hold on to his control.

That was when she saw him. She saw the beast and the

man and the war between them. He didn't trust that beast, so he kept him caged.

The funny thing was, she did trust that animal. She recognized him as her mate and knew he would never hurt her.

That realization caused a strange mix of tenderness and wanton abandon to overtake her. She opened her bra and brought her knee up, inviting him to hook her foot onto his shoulder.

"I am your wife. Your future queen. *Yours.* Take me."

The rush of his breath was the sound a bull might make before it charged. He brushed aside his clothing and braced a hand above her shoulder, pinning her hair as he entered her in one implacable thrust.

Joyous tingles swept up from her loins through her whole body, filling her with gratification as he withdrew and returned, landing even harder and deeper.

"You *are* mine." He hugged her thigh and moved with uncontained power. "Look at me. Say it."

She could hardly make her eyes open, too overwhelmed by the thrill of pushing him right to the edge.

"You are mine," she taunted with a wicked smile.

His back flexed as though he'd been lashed and his teeth bared, but he didn't stop claiming her with those formidable thrusts of his hips. Each impact of his pelvis to hers caused every nerve in her body to sing, but he moved his hand between them, caressing to increase her pleasure even more.

She knew what he was doing, though. He was trying to push her past her limit, trying to make her break first.

Rather than try to best him, she took the advice he had given her the first time he had touched her so intimately. She cupped her own breasts and threw back her head and moaned to the high ceiling as she reveled in the powerful orgasm that soared upward, throwing her into the clouds.

He swore sharply and lost his rhythm. His hips crashed once more into hers and they were both convulsing in the pulses and throbs of a powerful climax.

When he swore again, it was with defeat. His weight sagged onto her and she cradled his head, finally understanding.

He kept that wounded, angry part of himself walled off to preserve his own sanity. To love him was to climb into that cage with that beast and he would never allow it.

She sifted his hair through her fingers, looking to the ceiling with equal parts yearning and despair.

Three days ago, Felipe had gone back to Sentinella with a sense of urgency snapping at his heels. Or rather, with a sense that something was slipping through his grasp.

Through the course of his life, he had carefully constructed his world in a way that was not unlike the meditation maze. Anyone who wished to get close to him had to work through layers of backtracking to even come close. It was the defense mechanism that allowed him to cope with his father's indifference to him as a human being, with his mother's cold rejection of him in favor of his brother, and with his brother's open aggression.

He trusted no one absolutely and cared only a superficial amount for those who were allowed close to him.

Then Claudine had fought her way onto his island. He had carried her himself into his stronghold. Into his bed.

Was it the sex? Was that why he was so infatuated and obsessed? If so, he was no better than an adolescent getting his first taste of passion.

It went so much further than that, though. She was constantly on his mind. He weighed every decision he made against how it would affect her and, when he had picked up the message that the charges had been filed, a sense of dread had accosted him. The train had left the station. There was no stopping it now.

His father was already furious and his mother's appalled resentment was a given. He had no feelings whatsoever for Francois's reaction, except perhaps satisfaction that he was being forced to face the consequences of his actions.

No, the cloying angst within him was solely for Claudine. What would this mean for *her*? And would all this fallout cause her to pull away from him? He deliberately held her at arm's length, but that was as far as he would let her go. He needed her within reach.

He needed *her*.

That was terrifying, but it had driven him back to Sentinella to find her playing with the wall, talking of leaving and taking other lovers. Her teasing had clawed into a raw place inside him, stripping him of his usual patience and finesse.

Their lovemaking was often intense and primal, but that day in the library had been different. She had provoked him, yes, but a type of desperation had been driving him. A need to be inside her that had nothing to do with making the baby they were mandated to conceive and everything to do with binding her to him.

He stood on a knife's edge of wanting to be an absolute barbarian who chained his wife to his bed to ensure she was always with him and the civilized man who knew that was utterly mad.

They were married. That ought to be enough, but it wasn't. He couldn't help thinking that, at some point, she would come to her senses and leave him. And there was not one damned thing he'd be able to do about it.

"More bribery?" she admonished as she came out of their bedroom here at the palace. It was the King and Queen's anniversary celebration tonight. Possibly his father's last public appearance. "I didn't think I needed more sparkle, but I guess I was wrong."

She wore a shimmering gown covered in iridescent sequins. A mesh ruffle at the neckline glinted with crystals, but the diamonds from her ears dripped like icicles in the sunlight. The tennis bracelet on her arm was six rows wide.

"Thank you." She blinked the sooty lashes that fanned below the silver shadow on her eyelids and pursed her glossy lips.

"You look stunning," he told her, feeling a pinch behind his heart as he touched his mouth to the corner of hers.

Mine, he thought yet again, and wanted to put his hands on her, as if that was all it would take to ensure she was always his.

"You look nice, too." She slid her fingertip along his satin lapel, then searched his gaze. "Is everything all right?"

"My mother has been informed." Or so Vinicio had told him a moment ago.

"Ah. Are we worried?"

"No. The news won't break into headlines until tomorrow. We'll get through one last, civilized evening." That felt like a lie, but he was only trying to keep her from fretting.

"I'm sorry that this makes your relationship with them that much more difficult," she said anxiously.

"Don't," he commanded gruffly. "*They* make it difficult." She made it bearable.

He took a moment to appreciate that. To bask in the light that was the pureness of her soul. It hurt the way bright sunlight hit the backs of his eyes, making them ache.

"Felipe?" She searched his expression, but he wasn't ready to pick apart what was happening to him.

He offered his arm and escorted her to the top of the grand

staircase where they were announced right before the King and Queen followed them down.

The evening progressed as these things usually did. They mingled for an hour before the formal call to the dining hall. They were seated apart from one another, but Claudine was across from him at the table.

Two hundred guests were attending. An army of servants began to fill glasses and set the first of twelve courses. The din of conversation was near deafening, but settled each time someone gave a speech. Felipe stood to offer one. Francois gave another.

Claudine rose after the fish course, sending Felipe a look that was both apologetic and fretful before she walked away. He watched for her return, growing concerned when a quarter hour passed and she was still absent.

Francois's fiancée was still here at the table. Claudine wasn't tied up speaking to her.

Felipe looked to his brother and discovered Francois was staring at him. His brother wore a smug curl at the corner of his mouth.

Felipe's heart lurched.

Even as he started to rise, Vinicio was leaning to say in his ear, "Ippolita has called an ambulance. Her Highness is very ill."

CHAPTER TWELVE

DESPITE BEING SO violently ill that she was certain she would die, Claudine woke in the royal wing of the Stella Vista hospital.

Felipe stood over her, unshaven, eyes sunken into dark pools of brooding anger. He wore his tuxedo shirt open at the throat, his bow tie and jacket abandoned somewhere.

"How do you feel?" he asked in a voice that rasped across her dulled nerves. He gently brushed his fingertips along her jaw.

"What happened?" Her voice floated across the dry creek bed of her throat.

"You were poisoned. Francois is the culprit, not that I have proof. Now you're awake, I'll go to the palace to oversee the interrogations myself." He took out his phone and glanced at it. "Your mother has landed. She'll be here shortly."

He was avoiding her gaze, mouth tense. She had no doubt he was upset on her behalf, but all his emotions seemed to be directed at the palace and his brother. She couldn't discern how he felt beyond that. How he felt about *her*.

If he had told her in these moments that he loved her and was frightened for her and was grateful she had pulled through, she might have had a different reaction besides despair. As it was, all she could think was that even if he found the servant who had tainted her food, Francois would still be protected.

"For now, the pregnancy is unaffected."

As she gasped, his gaze slammed into hers. Inside those dark depths, she read shame and fierce protectiveness, helplessness and agonized yearning. That was why he was avoiding looking at her. She had nearly lost a baby she hadn't even known she carried!

"They did a blood test." His hand squeezed hers, perhaps reminding her to breathe because she suddenly realized she had no oxygen in her lungs.

She made herself shakily hiss air through her nostrils.

"I'm sorry, Claudine. I'm sorry it's come to this." His brows flexed in torture. "It never will again. I swear that to you."

All she could think was that if Francois had the means to slip her poison, he could dose her with a medication to end a pregnancy. She would never be safe! Neither would any child she had. Felipe would have to stay on guard forever, never allowing himself to love her or their child because he would be too afraid of losing both of them.

"I wouldn't leave you right now if I didn't have to," Felipe continued gently. "You understand that, don't you?" He rested his hand atop her head, looking so anguished it hurt to see it. "I have to go to the palace and finish this."

He did care for her, in his way, which meant she would hurt him when she did what she had to do, but it was the only way. She couldn't stay here and be the instrument his brother used to persecute him.

"I know," she murmured. "Can I have my phone?"

"Of course." His hand squeezed her limp fingers once more before he pressed her phone into it. "Your guards are right outside the door. You're completely safe." He leaned down to touch his mouth to her forehead. "Text me if you need anything at all."

She nodded and watched him leave before she texted Freja.

Claudine was a fighter.

Felipe had spent a long, dark night clinging to that knowledge while accepting that he could not ask her to be part of his fight any longer. Not if it might cost her her life.

A sense of déjà vu had gripped him as he stood over her, except that three months ago, he had seen her as a very useful pawn. Now he was ashamed to have pushed her into such a dangerous position, especially when she had come to mean so much to him. More than anyone else in the world. That was what he had acknowledged as he finally watched her blink her eyes open, only for fear and confusion to come into her pallid face.

And a baby? He couldn't even process that. Not yet. Not when Francois's actions could have taken both of them in the blink of an eye.

Leaving her had physically hurt, especially when paparazzi surrounded the hospital, clamoring at the news that had broken overnight about her accusations against Francois. It was an absolute nightmare, but once Felipe knew she was conscious, and would have her mother on hand, he *had* to come to the palace to deal with this once and for all.

Predictably, his father was uninclined to do what needed to be done.

"The culprit has been identified and is in custody," King Enzo said dismissively. "He claims to have acted out of spite toward America."

The King was gray beneath his normally swarthy complexion. It wasn't only the toll of a difficult night. His illness was beginning to run him down.

Felipe steeled himself against pitying him. He had never been shown such a thing by this man. "You really believe that? For God's sake, think of the damage he could do if he took the throne. Do you want that?"

"It doesn't matter what I want, Felipe. Francois is the spare." He whirled away in frustration. "I cannot believe I'm still having this conversation with you. Work it out! You're not children."

"You dare say that to me?" Felipe barely kept his grip on his temper. "When you have pitted us against one another our entire lives? No, we are not children. This is not a case of my brother stealing my favorite toy. *He tried to kill my wife. She's pregnant.* That is an attempted assassination of a future ruler."

"Is she?" King Enzo took a moment to absorb that, then, "Once she delivers—"

"No," Felipe roared. "Now. We take action *now*."

There was an urgent knock, then Vinicio entered with a wild look in his eyes.

"I am deeply sorry, Your Majesty. Your Highness…" He dipped his head as he hurried toward Felipe. "A helicopter has just landed on the hospital's pad. It's from Sicily. The Princess appears to be boarding it with her mother."

If the blades had sliced and diced him into pieces, Felipe could not be more torn apart. For a few seconds, his entire being was incinerated by this news. By rejection. Loss. Scalding urgency rose in his chest with commands for her to be stopped, but he steeled himself against the searing pain and cleared his throat.

"Let her go." They were the hardest words he'd ever said, but a blinding truth arrived with them. She did not want to be married to the man he would have to become.

Vinicio hurried out to relay the message.

"You're allowing her to leave you?" his father scoffed. He blinked once, then turned his face away as though too filled with contempt to look at his son.

"You want me to keep her here where Francois can continue attempting to kill her? He has to be stopped," Felipe demanded. "If you don't have the stomach to deal with him, then give me the power to do so."

"Step down? No," Enzo said flatly.

"Then I'll do it my way." A sensation had arrived in Felipe, one he didn't know how to name. It wasn't vengeance or scorn or anything like the ugly bitterness he'd carried all his life. It was a clear, chilly calmness. Resolve.

He wasn't being honorable in releasing Claudine. He was setting aside his selfish desire to meld her to his side like an extension of himself. Instead, he would do what was necessary to ensure she lived a long, safe, happy life—even if it cost him his own.

Opening the door to his father's outer office, where a handful of assistants were going about their duties, he called, "Vinicio. Tell Francois to put his affairs in order and meet me in the courtyard at dawn."

Like in most Western countries, dueling with swords had fallen out of popularity in the kingdom once pistols were invented. Nazarine had very strict gun laws, some dating back to those early days of muskets and the like, in an effort to curb the practice, but dueling with swords had never been criminalized.

Thus, when Felipe threw down his gauntlet very publicly, promising the winner would take the throne, there was nothing to stop Francois from accepting except cowardice.

First, he tried labeling Felipe an unstable sociopath, but Felipe had only one response.

"Does that mean you forfeit?"

Francois did not. He showed up in the palace courtyard at dawn the following morning. Vinicio spoke to Francois's assistant long enough to explain that they could settle this without a fight if Francois gave up his right to the throne and left Nazarine forever.

"I would rather die," Francois called across the courtyard when his second relayed the terms.

"I can make that happen," Felipe assured him.

"You forget who wears the scar from our last duel. Have you held a sword since?"

Had Francois? To the best of Felipe's knowledge, neither of them had. Even back when they had learned to fence, the training foils had been blunt enough that a strike to an un-protected face would result in a bruise, not a cut.

Their instructor, however, had buckled to Francois's pleas and allowed the pair of *schiavonas*, antique cut-and-thrust swords, to be taken off the wall for their inspection.

A pair of guardsmen brought those same swords now, each in its leather scabbard, with the scrolled, polished steel of their basket-style hilts visible. A bright jewel glinted in each pommel.

"Stop this," the Queen ordered as she came outside in plain breakfast dress and a knitted cardigan. "You're making a mockery of the entire family. *Felipe.*" His name was a command to bend to her will.

"Look on the bright side, Mother. He might win. You'll fi-nally see your favorite on the throne." He nodded at his head of security to examine both swords before Francois's guard was given first choice of the weapons.

Queen Paloma stood taller, her hands curled into fists, but she didn't contradict him. She didn't say she *didn't* want Fran-cois to take the throne. She didn't tell Francois not to fight.

Still standing on opposite sides of the courtyard from his twin, Felipe accepted the sword that was brought to him. Its double-edged blade had been freshly sharpened and polished. He gripped the handle that was wrapped in soft leather, then drew a figure-eight with his wrist, testing the sword's weight and balance.

"What's this? You're not even dressed yet," King Enzo grumbled as he came out to the courtyard. "I was going to keep score myself. Best of five should do it."

"This is not a game, Padre. There will be no protective gear." Felipe moved toward the middle of the courtyard that would serve as their *piste*. "We fight until surrender. Or death, in my case, because I will not surrender."

"We'll see," Francois drawled as he approached. "You seem to have surrendered your wife without much struggle."

Felipe had no doubt that was how it looked to outsiders, but Felipe had Claudine within him. She filled him with strength. With power. With *will*. With a force greater than all of those things combined.

"Are you saying there are no rules at *all*?" the Queen cried.

"Even if there were, my dear brother would never play by them," Felipe said. No, he would have to be on guard against every type of underhanded cheating. "Prepare to lose one of your sons today, Mamma."

"You want everyone to believe you are better than me," Francois complained. "The fact is, you won't do what it takes to get the better of me. You're *weak*. That's why I deserve to be king and you do not."

"That's where you're wrong," Felipe assured him. "Exercising scruples isn't the same as being bound by them. But continue to underestimate me. That works to my advantage."

They each held out their swords and took up the *en garde* position, creeping forward until their swords began to engage.

For a few moments, they tested each other, barely moving beyond the flick of their blades in a very subtle parry and riposte, each trying to duck around the other's weapon. Each trying to make the other think he would attack from one side, only to quickly move to the other.

Felipe watched Francois as closely as he watched the movement of his sword, judging his reaction time, his level of arrogance. Felipe's contempt for Francois did not mean he failed to see him as dangerous. Quite the opposite. Despite a profligate lifestyle, Francois's reflexes were sharp. He wanted this. He relished the chance to finally take Felipe down. Felipe had no doubt his brother would run him through, given a split second of lost focus.

What Francois didn't believe was that Felipe would do the same, if he had to.

Felipe tapped a little harder on Francois's blade. His twin reacted in a feint that Felipe countered, but he was equally ready for Francois to turn it into a genuine attack from another angle—which he did.

Felipe swung his blade in a swift arc to parry Francois. The clash of steel rang across the courtyard, making the Queen's gasp nearly inaudible.

They were closer now, moving like waltzing partners, holding the distance between them, each with one arm protectively tucked behind his back while they shifted their weight backward and forward in their lunge.

The clip and scrape of their *schiavonas'* steel became a steady, uneven clatter.

This was a warm-up as they both moved with increasing speed, each attempting to surprise the other with a thrust and throwing up a defense, then swooping into a fresh attack.

"You realize, don't you…" Francois was trying to sound lazy and unbothered, but they were both beginning to sweat from the exertion. "That *you* called *me* out. If I kill you, it's self-defense."

"You still won't have the throne, though. Claudine is pregnant." His declaration did what Felipe had hoped it would.

Francois faltered just enough for Felipe to catch him off guard. He thrust, slicing through Francois's trousers and into his thigh.

It would have gone deeper, but Francois swung his blade down to deflect the worst of it and quickly parried Felipe's follow-up thrust.

For a few moments, they clacked and clattered their swords, using more force now. They advanced and retreated, circling, each rattling his blade against the other's once again as they searched for an opening, keeping their movements small to conserve energy.

"After you're dead, I'll marry her and raise your—"

Felipe had been waiting for that threat. He feinted a lunge as though reacting with emotion. He allowed Francois to block it, then used the force of the parry to swing up his blade and swipe the tip of his blade across Francois's chin.

Francois jerked his head back, then lunged in the next second, aiming for Felipe's shoulder. He grazed Felipe's upper arm, but Felipe pivoted a quarter turn, sidestepping the worst of it, then used this new angle to take advantage of Francois's position. His sliced a line across Francois's waist even as his brother took another jab at him.

There was a shout of anguish from the Queen.

Blood was dripping from his brother's thigh and chin. Felipe was distantly aware of various burns and stings on his own body, particularly his upper arm. He didn't pause or show any mercy, however. He was utterly focused on the fear edging into his brother's eyes.

Francois began to hack with more panic than skill. The

noise of their blades clanged unrelentingly in Felipe's ear as he grimly fought Francois off. He took no comfort in his brother's desperation. It made Francois all the more unpredictable and dangerous.

There were no rules. This was a fight to the death.

They were close enough, and the blades sharp enough, that they were both picking up nicks and cuts. And they were both moving fast enough, with enough force, that they were equally winded.

"Surrender," Felipe commanded.

"Nev—" Francois roared a curse as Felipe scored another line against his brother's arm.

Felipe had him on the defensive. He kept advancing, pushing him backward.

Francois's arm had to be aching as much as his own. Felipe's grip was slippery with sweat and he was breathing as though he'd been running for miles, but he drew on the well of endurance that had brought Claudine to his island. *Her* life and the life of their baby depended on this.

He continued to push Francois with inexorable purpose, until his brother turned his ankle and fell onto his back.

Francois thrust his sword up to defend himself, slashing pain across Felipe's hip, but Felipe parried and lunged forward, standing on his brother's arm until the sword clattered to the cobblestones.

He held Francois on his back with the point of his blade against Francois's throat.

"Felipe!" his mother screamed.

"Renounce your claim to the throne," Felipe demanded.

Francois slid his gaze past Felipe.

In his periphery, Felipe saw his mother's blue-gray skirt and his father's pin-striped trousers.

"Enzo, *please*," their mother begged.

"You are not fit to wear the crown." Felipe didn't step off his brother. He gave him another pinprick under his jaw. "Admit it. Renounce your claim. Say it loudly enough for everyone in this courtyard to hear it. Swear it to our king and queen."

"Padre," Francois beseeched, begging for mercy.

"I have no reason to spare his life," Felipe said heavily to their father. "He will only keep challenging me for the throne, we all know that. It ends here. You decide how."

"Don't kill him." Enzo touched his arm and sighed heavily. "I will abdicate the throne to you."

"As King, I will see that he faces the charges leveled against him," Felipe said clearly.

"As King, you may do as you see fit." Their father sounded infinitely weary, but relieved. "You may acknowledge Francois after this," he said to the Queen, "but I never will. Francois is no longer welcome in the palace," he called out to the palace guards. "He is no longer my son. Remove him and never grant him entry again."

It was a pronouncement as brutally harsh as their father had always been. Felipe's only pity was for the children who had once looked to that man as a guiding light only to find he was ruled by power and duty and not one iota of heart.

"Take his sword," Felipe said to Vinicio, not trusting Francois for even one second.

Vinicio quickly picked it up from the cobblestones.

Felipe remained armed even while Francois was escorted to his car.

The Queen followed her favorite son, crying, "I'll talk to him. Don't worry."

Felipe watched his mother ignore that he was equally exhausted and covered in cuts that bled freely, staining his clothes. She didn't once look back at him.

He sheathed his sword, keeping it as he went to his helicopter.

He flew back to Sentinella alone.

"You should have watched with me," Ann-Marie said.

"Watched what?" Claudine looked up from sweeping flower petals off the path down to the helicopter pad where they had landed shortly after Freja's husband, Giovanni, had arranged to take her to a secure location.

This remote villa in the Italian Alps was secure all right. Claudine supposed someone could hike in, if they knew it was here, but it would take days. All the supplies were flown in and it ran on solar, but it was not the least bit rustic. It was incredibly luxurious and built to accommodate a wheelchair, suggesting it was Giovanni's secret lair. It even had caretakers who kept urging her to relax and enjoy the nearby walking trails, but Claudine preferred to keep busy.

"The coronation ceremony," her mother said with a lilt of exasperation.

"Oh. That."

"That? Your husband is a king, Claudine. Enzo was there. He looks quite ill."

"He is," she murmured and went back to what she was doing.

"Honestly, Claudine, this can't go on. You're pining yourself into a decline."

She wasn't pining, exactly. She was doing the equivalent of walking the meditative maze, sweeping a long, winding path that she knew would be littered with petals in an hour, accepting that her actions were irrelevant and her fate inevitable.

She would have to go back to Felipe, even though he hadn't tried to stop her leaving him. Even though he hadn't reached out to so much as ask if she was still alive. When she had tried to talk to Giovanni about money, he had said that Felipe had already told him he would cover all costs.

Was her husband *glad* to have her out of sight and out of mind?

"I spoke to Giovanni," her mother continued. "He said that Francois has been cut off and cast out. The buyer for the pageant backed out. Francois has sold his yacht to pay legal fees, so he's stuck in Montenegro. If he goes anywhere else, he'll be extradited. The charges against him have grown, by the way. Five more women have come forward."

"Good." She supposed. Claudine didn't know how to feel about it. Validated? She'd rather no one else had suffered at Francois's hands, but at least her coming forward had provided an avenue that seemed safe enough for other women to tell their stories and hopefully find some sort of justice or closure.

"Giovanni said it would be safe for us to return to New York if that's what you want. We don't have to keep hiding here," her mother prodded.

Claudine sighed. She *was* hiding, mostly from herself. From the weakness in her that yearned for Felipe no matter how fraught her life was when she lived inside his world. She could bear the restrictions and the weight of his responsibilities and even his mother's dislike.

What she couldn't bear was the isolation within their marriage, the one that left her feeling alone in it.

She couldn't avoid him forever, though. Not when she was carrying the next heir to Nazarine. Tears of joy pressed behind her eyes every time she thought of her baby, but what kind of life would their child have if their father didn't love them? She had seen what that had done to Felipe.

Turning the ruby ring on her finger, she asked herself, *What would Queen Giulia do?*

She wouldn't run away, Claudine realized. No, despite all her trials, Queen Giulia had found a way to live a very difficult life on her own terms.

With a nod, Claudine started back to the house.

Felipe had achieved what was necessary for the health of his country, but there was no satisfaction in it. His mother was barely speaking to him and his father was not likely to last the year.

Enzo had mentioned more than once that Felipe should reconcile with Claudine and Felipe couldn't argue with him, but he couldn't ask Claudine to come back to him, either. Given what he'd put her through, it had to be her decision.

He missed her, though. He missed her and he wanted to know that their baby was well.

He moved through the duties of his station because it helped him push through the hours of the day, but he was so hollow and empty of purpose he wondered what the point was in living at all. He felt as though he lacked something vital to his survival. He had air and water and food and sunlight, but he didn't care about any of it.

A murmur went through the crowd around him, forcing him to recall he was in Rome at a charity gala. Why? He couldn't recall what organization it benefited or why he'd agreed to speak or even what he was supposed to say. He would rather not be here at all.

He glanced around and realized people were staring at him and then turning their heads to look at—

He caught his breath. Life flowed back into him the way water soaked into a desiccated sponge. The music no longer blended into the din of conversation. It suddenly sounded beautiful and alluring. The stale air developed notes of seafood and puff pastry, perfumes and aftershaves. The icy crystals in the chandelier refracted to project streaks of bright yellow and deep blue.

Every step she took toward him filled him with oxygen and ferocity and gladness. With something glowing and meaningful. Something necessary to his very existence.

Claudine was a vision in a dark blue gown that fell down her figure like a coat of paint. A swirl of white hung off one shoulder, adding laconic elegance to the look. Her hair was up, exposing her long, bare neck.

There was no hesitation in her steps as she approached him. She looked straight at him, reminding him of how she'd come down the aisle toward him, so confident on their wedding day and so weak the last time he'd seen her.

When she was close enough to speak, she said only, "Felipe."

"Claudine." Her name was a vibration inside his breastbone. A call. Every cell in his body was trying to sync with hers. God, he had missed her. "What are you doing here?"

"Showing my support for the preservation of the Mediterranean ecosystem. You?"

Waiting for you.

That was what he wanted to say, even though it was whimsical and wistful and far more sentimental than he knew how to be.

"Your Majesty," Vinicio greeted her with a deferential nod. He was no doubt having a subtle conniption that he hadn't known Claudine would be here.

"Majesty?" She looked up at Felipe. "But your mother—"

"Has a new title. *You* are Queen of Nazarine. Shall we dance?" He ached to touch her.

She mutely let him take her hand and lead her onto the floor.

He could have crushed her, he wanted so badly to absorb

her into his skin, but he made himself lock his arms in a civilized embrace.

"We need to talk about some things," she said.

"If you're here to ask for a divorce, I've instructed my lawyers to negotiate in good faith."

Her step faltered.

He steadied her and noted the way her face had paled. Was she well? The baby? His blood congealed with fear in his veins.

"There are things they're not in a position to give me," she said cryptically.

"Such as?"

Her brow furrowed with frustration. "I want your heart, Felipe."

"On a silver platter?" he said on a husk of a laugh, tempted to say, *You have it.*

Everything in him went very still. He stopped moving as realization poured through him. *That* was why he had been feeling so empty. She had taken his heart when she left. He loved her.

He stood there with his eyes closed, absorbing that stunning realization, utterly speechless as understanding of that emotion finally exploded through him. It was esteem and loyalty and admiration and so many more things than she had described. It was beauty and affection and faith and joyous laughter.

"Please don't make jokes." Her mouth quivered and she looked down at the ruffles on his shirt.

He could only blink in bemusement at her, utterly thrown by what was happening to him. But a remarkable tenderness was rising in him like a king tide.

"I shouldn't have done this here," she continued under her breath. "I thought I could be bold and brave. I thought I could be in control for a change."

"Do you really think I've ever been in control where you're concerned?" he scoffed.

Cupid's arrow had pierced him the moment he saw her. He remembered it clearly, yet it was such a foreign concept that he had dismissed it as lust and fascination. Those things didn't leave you feeling as though you were bleeding out when you were apart, though. Only love could have made him suffer this intensely.

"People are staring," she said, aggrieved. "I have a room upstairs. Can we talk there?"

"We'll go to mine." He cradled her elbow and the crowd parted as they made their way to the elevators.

He was pleased to see she had a bodyguard shadowing her—one who had previously worked for him. Vinicio and his own guard for the evening joined them as they waited for the elevator and the three men nodded a friendly greeting at each other.

The doors opened and the startled occupants slipped past them, allowing them to enter the empty car.

Felipe took her hand and drew her to the back, unable to stop staring at her. She was magnificent. She was *here*.

She looked up at him and a soft noise that was anguish and helplessness and relief left her as she pressed herself into him, sliding her arms around his waist as though she had every right. Which she did. He was hers in every way that mattered.

Her yearning gaze matched the longing that stretched out inside him. Her mouth lifted in invitation and her hand went to the back of his head, urging him to kiss her.

Catching her close with one arm, he cradled the back of her skull with his free hand, covered her mouth with his own. Then he stole back every kiss he had missed while she'd been gone. No matter how hard he tried, he would never be able to kiss her thoroughly enough, or hold her closely enough, or fill her deeply enough, to quell this need in him for her.

The elevator pinged and the doors opened. Vinicio stepped out and the two guards shifted to stand in the opening, forming a wall of privacy while freezing the elevator in place.

Felipe could have made love to her right here. He wanted to. Badly. But she was already drawing away, blinking and glancing self-consciously at the backs of their guards. She touched her mouth where her lipstick was smudged, looking contrite.

That had nearly got out of hand! Claudine was mortified.

Felipe offered his pocket square and cleared his throat. The guards shifted and Vinicio led them down the hall to the sort of presidential suite Felipe always occupied when he was in Rome. The guard who was stationed at the door brightened when he saw her and gave her a nod of greeting.

"Will you be need—" Vinicio began.

"No," Felipe interjected. "Good night."

He closed them into his suite so abruptly it bordered on rude.

He reached for Claudine, but she held up a hand and took a couple of steps backward. She was still running his white pocket square around her mouth. She found a mirror and glanced to see she had erased as much as she could.

"It's only the two of us here," Felipe assured her. "I couldn't care less how you look."

"I know, but…" She shook that off and came closer to offer the stained silk back to him. "How, um, how are your parents?"

"Sick." He discarded the square onto a side table. "One physically, the other emotionally. I can't do anything about either."

She took that to mean his mother was still favoring Francois and still blaming Felipe for the trouble his twin was in.

"Are you angry?" she asked.

"I can't remember a time when I wasn't," he said flatly. He moved to pour himself a brandy.

"At me, I mean."

"No." He paused in pouring. His profile grew reflective. "Yes," he amended. "I don't want to be, but I am."

"Because I left? You think I'm a coward?"

"No." His laugh was a rasp of dark humor as he picked up his glass. "No, I think you are the bravest, toughest, most exceptional person I know."

"Even though I ran away?"

"You didn't, though. You did what any mother would do. You took our unborn baby to safety. Didn't you?" He turned and pinned her with his stare, the force of it so piercing she caught a shaken breath.

Her hand went reflexively to her abdomen. "I had to. It wasn't about not trusting you. I didn't trust him. Or your parents. I couldn't take the risk that they would side with him again."

"I know. I know that you would have fought him alongside me if it was only yourself you were worried about. You weren't even protecting our future ruler, were you? You were simply protecting a helpless baby. *Our* baby." He seemed to need a drink to chase that acknowledgement. He gulped. "Is everything well? How are you feeling?"

"Fine." She clasped her elbows. She had seen a doctor here in Rome when she landed, to be sure everything was as it should be, and it was.

"You look apprehensive. Why? Francois has been neutralized. Any staff who ever showed a hint of fealty toward him has been culled from the payroll. The palace is completely safe. You don't even need to see my parents if you come back. My father is accepting hospice care on Sentinella. Mother is having the *vedova* villa on Stella Vista redecorated so it will be ready for her after he's gone."

"I'm so sorry, Felipe." She searched his hard features. "Are you upset at all? Beginning to grieve or…anything?"

"Grief comes from losing someone you love."

"And you told me a long time ago that you didn't believe in love." *That* was why she was apprehensive.

"I didn't," he agreed solemnly. "Until I grieved the fact that you were absent from my life."

Her heart swerved. A small soar of hope rose in her, but she fought it back.

"Please don't say anything you don't mean. I'm prepared to come back. I know I have to. Our baby deserves to know his or her father."

"Our baby is entitled to the throne," he pointed out.

"Our baby is entitled to be loved." Her insides shook as she said it, but she rooted her feet as she added, "As am I."

"What do you think I have just said to you, *cara mia*?" He took a step toward her.

"I think you are saying what you think needs to be said to bring your child into the palace." She held up a hand to stave him off. "I need your honesty more than ever, Felipe. I'm only asking that you promise me you will *try* to open your heart to us. I can't trust you if you lie to me now."

"Tell me first why you left. You didn't trust me to keep you both safe, did you? I failed you. I did. I will never forgive myself for that and I will never make that mistake again. But I don't think that's why you left. Is it?"

She shook her head. "I knew we were a liability for you. That as long as he could attack you through me, he would."

"I don't think that was it, either." He nodded thoughtfully

as he ambled closer. "I think you were forcing me to make a choice."

"Not between the crown and me," she cried. "I know that's not fair."

"Between bitterness and love." He drained his glass and set it aside. "Between the life I was told I had to accept and the future I could have with you, if I was prepared to fight for it."

"I didn't expect you to duel him, Felipe." She searched across his frame, looking for injuries. "The reports said you both had several cuts."

"Cuts, yes. Nothing compared to the way you carved out my heart then left with it."

"That's not f—"

"No. Listen." He captured her hands. "Try to imagine never being loved, Claudine. Not for one moment in your whole life. There was a little affection when I was very young—a kind nanny. An aunt who gave me sweets and told me stories, but my mother preferred my brother and my brother hated my guts. My father never had a thought in his life that was not wrapped up in duty to the crown and I was told to emulate that. Now imagine you have found a sort of comfort in that vacuum of true caring. You understand how it works the way people learn to exist in the arctic. Then along comes someone who radiates love. Who pours it over you. I didn't even know what it *was*, Claudine. Sex? Charisma? A needy child finally tasting what it is to be noticed? Nothing made sense."

She tilted her head, so anguished for that child he'd been. For the man who'd had to learn to live in isolation and like it.

"I accept your pity. I accept your mistrust of the man who saw you as someone who was useful, rather than the person who would save him, not from his cold family, but from his own cynicism. I was determined to remain autonomous. It was comfortable. Loving you *hurts*, Claudine. Every part of me is unprotected because you are walking in this cruel world, susceptible to harm. Whether it's my vindictive brother or a mosquito, I don't want anything to touch you because that will hurt *me*. It terrifies me to be this vulnerable."

He was crushing her hands, but she didn't protest. She only clung right back, letting him know he wasn't alone anymore. He never would be again.

"But I can't go back to that life of emptiness. You can have my heart because I have yours. I know I have it because I feel it inside me. It's soft and endlessly warm and fills me with light. I am keeping it, Claudine. It's *mine*."

She had to bite her lips because they were quivering so hard.

"Will you take mine in return?" he asked humbly. "Please? It's small and hard and will need a lot of tending to make it grow, but I know you can make it happen. I know I will be a better man for it."

"Oh, Felipe." She was blinking her wet eyes as she thrust herself into his arms. "I love you so much."

"God knows why you do, but I will take all that you'll give me." He scooped her up and carried her into the bedroom.

"Not the sofa?" she teased as she looped her arms around his neck. "Even the floor has served us well in the past."

"You're pregnant." He frowned in a small scold, then his mouth kicked to the side. "Also, I'd have to carry you to bed after so it's better to get it out of the way while I still have my strength." He came down onto the wide mattress with her and carried her ring hand to his lips. "I do love you, Claudine." His face flexed with emotion. "I don't know why I feared saying it. It fills me with power to tell you. With a certainty that I can and will do anything for *us*." His hand slid to her abdomen. "All of us."

They kissed as though sealing the promise. Hot tears spilled from her eyes, it was such a fiercely sweet benediction.

Passion mingled with this new, profound tenderness, slowing them down. As they kissed and undressed each other, their caresses were unhurried and sure, imbued with caring. With need and admiration and love.

When they were naked and he shifted to settle between her legs, she cradled him with her thighs and welcomed his intrusion with a blissful sigh of utter contentment. With supreme rightness.

They stayed like that a long time, barely moving, enjoying the sensation of being joined while still pouring affection on each other. A trailing touch here, a chain of kisses there.

"I've never felt so free as when I'm with you like this," she murmured.

"I've never felt so alive. You *are* my life, Claudine. Never believe otherwise," Felipe told her.

He began to move with more purpose. When climax arrived, it was a startlingly new pinnacle, one intensified by the naked emotion between them, melding them together as they tumbled through the cosmos. Joined. Forever.

EPILOGUE

Four years later

"How are you, my love?" Felipe's voice still had the power to make her skin tighten and her pulse ripple when he caught her unawares like this.

She covered the hand that came to rest on her shoulder and tilted her head back for his kiss, but didn't rise from her comfortable position on the lounger.

"You're finished early."

"We have places to be, don't we?" He leaned down to kiss her and gave her swollen belly a caress of greeting. "Unless you have your own work to finish?"

"Not right this minute." She set aside the tablet she'd been holding.

For the last three years, she'd been working on finding, transcribing, editing and translating Queen Giulia's many notes, essays, letters and other writings. The first volume was finally at a copy edit stage and would be published next year—if she managed to finish her corrections before this baby was born. She still had two months to go, though.

"Papà!" Romeo cried, noticing him. "Rico!" he called to his brother as he started to run. "Papà is here." He paused to wait while Rico leaped up from the sandbox to hurry after him.

They were three and a half and near impossible for anyone

but their parents to tell apart. Aside from her and Felipe, only the late Dr. Esposito knew which boy had been born first.

Rico fell and his small cry of surprise had Romeo stopping in his tracks. He ran back.

"Are you hurt?" He dropped to kneel beside his brother.

Rico sat up and clutched his knee, blowing on it.

"I've got it." Felipe squeezed her shoulder, urging her to stay on the lounger as he strode toward the boys.

It never ceased to swell her heart when she saw him dote on their children this way.

"Let me see." He crouched and gathered Rico up to examine the tear in his pants. "No blood. I think you'll survive." He kissed the boy's hair.

"You have to kiss his knee, Papà," Romeo explained. "To make it better."

"Of course." He playfully swung Rico upside down to do it, dispelling the last of Rico's upset into a gale of laughter.

Now Romeo wanted to be part of the silliness and fell on them. Felipe tipped onto the grass as though bowled over by the small boy. He wrestled with them like an alpha wolf with a pair of cubs.

When he had worn them out sufficiently, he sat up, both boys secured in his strong arms. "Are we going to Sentinella or not?"

"Sì!" they cried and tried to get away, but he kept hold of them, causing more giggling and cries for "Mamma. Help!"

"Are you not coming?" she called as she rose. "I don't want to go all by myself."

"No. Mamma, wait! Papà, let *go*."

They all loved their time at Sentinella where they were alone, but together.

Felipe released them and they ran toward the helipad, glancing back to ensure their parents were following.

Felipe waited for her, hand outstretched. When she came alongside him, he slid his hand beneath her hair to cradle the back of her neck, gaze still on their boys as they paused at the fence, as they had been taught to do. They once again examined the tear in Rico's pants, but now it was something that made them giggle.

"I do love you, you know," he said, gaze troubled, as though he was searching for stronger words to impress that truth into her. "I could not have taught them to love each other that much if you had not taught me to feel it. I love you more than I know how to express."

"It's okay. I believe you," she assured him, snuggling herself into his side. "I love you, too."

* * * * *

COMING SOON!

We really hope you enjoyed reading this
book. If you're looking for more romance
be sure to head to the shops when
new books are available on

Thursday 31st
August

To see which titles are coming soon, please visit
millsandboon.co.uk/nextmonth

MILLS & BOON®

Coming next month

INNOCENT'S WEDDING DAY WITH THE ITALIAN
Michelle Smart

"Do you, Enzo Alessandro Beresi, take Rebecca Emily Foley to be your wife?"

He looked her in the eye adoringly and without any hesitation said, "I do."

And now it was her turn.

"Do you, Rebecca Emily Foley, take Enzo Alessandro Beresi…"

She breathed in, looked Enzo straight in the eye and, in the strongest voice she could muster, loud enough for the entire congregation to clearly hear, said, "No. I. Do. Not."

Enzo's head jerked back as if she'd slapped him. A half smile froze on his tanned face, which was now drained of colour. His mouth opened but nothing came out.

The only thing that had kept Rebecca together since she'd opened the package that morning was imagining this moment and inflicting an iota of the pain and humiliation racking her on him. There was none of the satisfaction she'd longed for. The speech she'd prepared in her head died in her choked throat.

Unable to look at him a second longer, she wrenched her hands from his and walked back down the aisle, leaving a stunned silence in her wake.

Continue reading
INNOCENT'S WEDDING DAY WITH THE ITALIAN
Michelle Smart

Available next month
www.millsandboon.co.uk

OUT NOW!

MILLS & BOON

THE HEART OF ROMANCE

A ROMANCE FOR EVERY READER

MODERN
Prepare to be swept off your feet by sophisticated, sexy and seductive heroes, in some of the world's most glamourous and romantic locations, where power and passion collide.

HISTORICAL
Escape with historical heroes from time gone by. Whether your passion is for wicked Regency Rakes, muscled Vikings or rugged Highlanders, awaken the romance of the past.

MEDICAL
Set your pulse racing with dedicated, delectable doctors in the high-pressure world of medicine, where emotions run high and passion, comfort and love are the best medicine.

True Love
Celebrate true love with tender stories of heartfelt romance, from the rush of falling in love to the joy a new baby can bring, and a focus on the emotional heart of a relationship.

Desire
Indulge in secrets and scandal, intense drama and sizzling hot action with heroes who have it all: wealth, status, good looks…everything but the right woman.

HEROES
The excitement of a gripping thriller, with intense romance at its heart. Resourceful, true-to-life women and strong, fearless men face danger and desire - a killer combination!

To see which titles are coming soon, please visit

millsandboon.co.uk/nextmonth